THE EYE OF RA

Jeanne D'Août

First Edition, February 2015

Edited by Charlotte Yonge, Ms Baiden and Jeanne D'Août

This book has been printed on eco-friendly paper.

ISBN-978-2-9539396-6-8

jeannedaout.com
barincapublishing.com

"Take the two Eyes of Horus,
the black and the white.
Take them to your forehead,
(so) that they may illuminate your face."

From the Pyramid Text
[Sethe, 1908/1960, § 33a]

Côte Vermeille, France, October 12th 2011

At the top of the cliff, high above the azure Mediterranean sea, a tall, handsome man in a beige Gucci suit was leaning casually on his bright red Maserati GranCabrio Sport, while gazing through his binoculars at a sleek clipper with voluminous black sails, approaching the harbour of Collioure. He smiled and chewed on a Cuban cigar while he zoomed in to check the name on the ship, just to be completely sure. The 'Laurin' lowered her black sails and gently made her way through the harbour entrance to drop anchor. The clipper was much too large to dock at the berth in the port below.

"Come on, let me see you..."

Four men appeared and boarded a small sloop. He recognised two of them, lowered his binoculars and smirked with long-awaited pleasure.

"Gotcha!"

Tossing the binoculars into the front seat of the Cabrio, he jumped behind the wheel and sped dangerously through the steep, hairpin turns into the village. After boldly parking the car on the sidewalk, he raced out - grabbing his mobile phone as he dashed from the car.

As soon as the sloop had been gently eased into its place at the dock, the four men split up into two pairs and headed in separate directions. The picturesque town of Collioure, famous for its historic church tower and idyllic natural port, had long been a favourite stop for travellers. Indeed, many artists in the early 20th century had come here to create their now-famous paintings of the village, attracted by the welcoming colours of the houses, the vibrant blue sea and the ever-changing, somewhat mystical light.

Two of the sailors strolled to the nearest café and ordered some coffee, seating themselves where they could enjoy the view, right at the water's edge.

They admired the castle of Collioure, which in the late 12th century had been the seat of the Grandmaster of the Knights Templar. The impressive, medieval fortress was strategically built atop the rocks overlooking the harbour, making excellent use of its vantage point for those who needed to keep a close eye on both sea and land. In the 17th century, architect Sébastien Le Prestre de Vauban had added massive defence walls to the castle and the town. The tall, medieval tower, where the Templar Grandmaster once welcomed the knights who had returned from the Holy Land, had not yet lost its grandeur, in spite of the 800 years that had gone by.

The coffee was served and its spicy aroma and complex flavour refreshed the weary seafarers. Otto Adler - a man in his mid-thirties with dark hair, grey-blue eyes and a rather playful yet probing regard, revealing his undying curiosity - pointed toward the bridge that led to the entrance of the castle.
"Look, beneath that bridge at water level was the entrance to hidden tunnels underneath the castle. Who knows what treasures were taken into the castle through those tunnels - shiploads of relics and scrolls from the Holy Land, I'm sure!" Otto smiled knowingly, thinking about his past adventures and the history of the area. In fact, he was still amazed that he was actually living in the 21st century. Formerly known as Otto Rahn, a Nazi relic hunter, he had officially died before World War II, but had been brought to the present time just seven months ago, thanks to the invention of a time travel device by a clever professor.
Otto pushed back his chair so he could see his handsome young companion more clearly.
"You know Art, I believe we are sitting in the Holy Land right now. Occitania is as sacred as it is mysterious. Much has been hidden here. If only we had a car!"
Arthur, a twenty year old with bright blue eyes and dark, curly hair, turned to him calmly, though he was more than a bit irritated about Otto's remark.

"We would have had a car, Otto, if you hadn't blown all your money on that bloody boat!"

BAAAOOOOOOMMMMMM…

Behind them, the Laurin had blown up with a resounding roar. Otto and Arthur couldn't move; they were frozen in disbelief. Fragments of the demolished boat were cascading down on the harbour beach as well as on the boulevard and it was clear to Otto that it was indeed his ship. Stark white from shock, he simply couldn't turn himself around to look at what had been his pride and joy and their cherished transportation over the past week.

However, the tragedy was far worse than just losing the clipper. Arthur, who also couldn't look at the scene, cautiously stood up; his legs were shaking.

"Otto, you know Hadi was still on the ship. Oh no, poor Hadi!"

Their Egyptian guide had stayed behind to guard the ship.

Suddenly, Otto gasped as he realised another alarming fact.

"The Eye! We've lost the Eye! There's no way we will be able to find a small stone at the bottom of the harbour - it will be deeply embedded in the sand by the time we can dive for it. It would be easier to find a needle in a haystack!"

Otto felt his pockets in search for his mobile phone, all the while carefully resisting the urge to look at the remains of the clipper, most of which had already disappeared beneath the surface. They could hear police sirens in the distance and decided to slowly walk away. Otto speed-dialled a number and spoke cautiously, fighting to keep his voice steady.

"Fred, the Laurin just exploded! Yes, the Eye of Ra was on board, but also Hadi, all our research, your secret files and just about everything we possess."

Alfred Zinkler, Otto's chief and friend, the head of an organisation called SBS-Sion, was speechless. Poor Hadi! And the Eye of Ra, lost! All the work they had done in these past weeks had now been wasted. The organisation, created to unearth the true history of Biblical events, had put Otto in charge of finding a rare relic, purported to have belonged to the Zadok Priest Aaron, Moses's Biblical brother. Aaron had possessed several items that are now lost to the world; firstly, a rod or staff; secondly a breastplate with the 12 gemstones representing the 12 tribes of Israel called the 'hosen' and last but not least, the Urim and Thummim divination device. These two stones were used by kings, priests and judges to determine who was the 'sinner' and who was the 'saint'. Alfred, a collector of relics and historical objects, was himself a clairvoyant. He had discovered that the stones, when used as a pair, would give the owner great power, insight and clarity of mind. For obvious reasons, he was very keen on finding these ancient artefacts, not just to keep them safe in his collection, but also to make use of them.

As they were walking uphill, all the while staying close to the buildings to avoid running into the curious people who were on their way down, they realised that they could now no longer see the spot where the clipper had exploded. Still trembling, Otto leaned against the wall of a café and rubbed his eyes. On the other side of the line he could hear Alfred sigh. "How could this have happened, Otto? Could anyone have boarded the Laurin without you knowing it? Or... perhaps we have a leak?"
Otto laughed out loud, a raw laugh of discomfort with a sarcastic undertone.
"A leak? A leak? The whole damn boat is kissing the harbour floor!"
Arthur touched Otto's arm. "We have to go, look..."
Otto turned and saw how the harbour was filling up with marine dinghies. Several police officers on the boulevard were now interrogating people who had witnessed the explosion.
"Gotta go, Fred."
Otto hung up on Alfred and joined Arthur, who had already started to walk away from the harbour, uphill into the village. Wanting to appear nonchalant and above suspicion, they took a slow but deliberate pace.

The loss of the ship and all their belongings was catastrophic. They had lost their laptops; their research; the recovered sacred artefact and, last but not least, a trusted friend. All they possessed right now were the things they were carrying: two mobile phones; their IDs; some money; a credit card and the clothes they were wearing. While making their way uphill, they passed a gentleman in a beige Gucci suit wearing dark sunglasses, who now started to follow them surreptitiously.

Meanwhile, the once peaceful harbour area was now buzzing with the lively observations of curious people, shouts from overwhelmed policemen and the frantic efforts of the local marines, all seeking to regain some semblance of order. Two helicopters had arrived in record time to evaluate the situation from the air, but what they saw below wasn't what they had expected.

As if the sea had overindulged and then ungraciously regurgitated, an imposing form had appeared mysteriously on the very spot where the clipper had exploded. The abrupt and entirely unexpected emergence of this gargantuan object had caused a towering wave, not unlike a mini tsunami. Seawater, pushed into the harbour, rose to a threatening height. Everyone raced away as fast as they could to find shelter behind the buildings, but for some it was too late. One forceful wave wiped people, chairs and tables from the boulevard like a one-armed titan. Oddly enough, the water withdrew as quickly as it had come, so the people who were in the water were able to reach the harbour beach safely.

The commotion persuaded Otto and Arthur to turn around and look at the harbour.

Then they saw it.

On the spot where the clipper had blown into a thousand pieces, a monumental statue had appeared, standing at an alarming angle on the uneven, sandy seabed, but tall enough to appear above the waves. It was the Colossus of Memphis, the giant statue of Pharaoh Ramses II.

2

Sion, Switzerland, ten days earlier
The conference room was impressive, commanding a prime space in the stately manor house. The room, which had a medieval atmosphere, was in fact a modern, high tech office. The penetrating scent of the fresh wax that protected the artisanal woodwork on the walls permeated the air. It was a quiet, Sunday afternoon and despite some early October sunlight that was streaming through the leaded glass windows, it was chilly. A fire blazed in the hearth, but it only heated the immediate area effectively. The rest of the room had a pervasive chill. Three men were standing in the room, but silence hovered about them, as if all words had been temporarily banished. A tall, blonde man in his mid-fifties was planted firmly behind a massive, oak desk, studying a report. The other two waited silently while their report was read.

Twenty-year-old Arthur Griffin stared at his new friend, Otto Adler. He had been attracted to Otto because of his complicated and mysterious personality. Their relationship was young and still rather innocent. Arthur, who had never had any romantic feelings for another person before, was more confused than excited. He had given up his life, his education in London and the draining relationship with his disapproving parents to be with him. Otto was his hero, his friend and his lover. The German stood next to him, motionless, staring blankly at the floor. Otto was not only much older than Arthur, he was literarily from a different time. Behind Otto's blue eyes were the terrible memories of a Nazi victim who had once worked for Heinrich Himmler, the head of the SS, until he discovered the horrors behind the scene. He owed his life to the man now on the other side of the oak desk. If it hadn't been for him, Otto would have died a lonely death on a mountain slope in Tirol, Austria.

When the giant Swiss had appeared from nowhere, it had admittedly scared the wits out of him. However, a minute later he had found himself safely inside an underground laboratory in Switzerland, more than 70 years into the future. Being an experienced relic hunter and therefore of great value to his abductor, he was asked to assist a team of researchers on a secret mission in southern France. Arthur had been part of the team, so perhaps it was fate that had brought Otto and Arthur together that summer.

Otto was very fond of the young man and wondered if what he felt for him could be love. His experiences in Nazi Germany had changed him from a warm-hearted lore-loving author and poet to a person who had, out of self-preservation, become as detached as possible from his feelings. Arthur had brought some of these repressed feelings back to life. In a way, Arthur had become his drug, his elixir of life.

Otto suddenly felt that Arthur was staring at him. He turned and their eyes met. Otto smiled and blinked an eye at his friend, who immediately felt the chemistry; the well-known, tender pain in the stomach followed by a sweet sting. Unwilling to stop his stare, Otto noticed how Arthur's face started to flush. It amused him.

Suddenly, the report was thrown on the desk and the slap startled them. Before them stood the man they both worked for - a man that everyone called 'sir', except for Otto, who boldly called him 'Fred'. Alfred Zinkler had succeeded his late father as head of SBS-Sion, a secret order created to investigate and protect human history heritage.

Wormhole time travel was the amazing new technique they were using to study historical events. This would not have been possible without the brilliance of Professor William Fairfax, who had been taken on at SBS-Sion a year earlier specifically to create a means of travelling through time. In the spring and summer of 2011, this 'time machine', that they had named the ERFAB, had already been successfully used.*

*Read 'White Lie' by Jeanne D'Août

This time however, Otto and Arthur had just come back from a mission in present-day France. Otto had requested to go back to the Languedoc-Roussillon to check out the mysterious enigma of Opoul-Perillos. On his previous mission in France, Arthur had proven to be very useful, thanks to his extensive knowledge of the history of that particular part of France. In fact, when Otto had asked Alfred if he could bring him along, Alfred had immediately agreed. However, apart from a few interesting links that might shed new light on the origins of the Parsifal story, they hadn't been able to find anything solid and had returned to Sion empty handed. Alfred was, nevertheless, intrigued by Otto's report and regretted having to ask Arthur to leave the room, but there was something he had to talk to Otto about in private. As soon as Arthur had closed the door behind him, they sat down in two comfortable brown leather Chesterfield armchairs. Alfred observed Otto with a broad smile. He noticed his shiny leather shoes and well-cut suit; his expensive cologne and carefully trimmed 2-day beard. Alfred was pleased to see that Otto's eyes were bright and shining and that the dark shadows around his eyes had almost disappeared. He approved of the tan and the smart haircut. Yes, Otto was acclimatising well to his new life. When Alfred had teleported himself back to March 16th, 1939 to save Otto from his untimely death in the Austrian snow, the German had been just skin and bones; weak and traumatised by his experiences. On top of that, his extensive smoking habit had almost destroyed him. It had taken Alfred months to help him restore his health and with great willpower and iron discipline, Otto had even given up smoking.

Alfred was extremely pleased. "I am glad to see you in such good shape, my dear friend!"

Otto smiled and felt he wanted to repay his compliments, but Alfred didn't look well at all. Instead he asked about the report. "So, what did you think of my findings? I didn't find anything special and I didn't have time to do a lot of archaeology there either, but still, Parsifal! It is where it all began, isn't it?"

Alfred smiled. Otto's first and biggest passion had always been the Parsifal story of the Holy Grail. His life's mission to find it had brought him to southern France, to Cathar country, in the early 1930s. He had written his first book about the heretics and history of Occitania and a second book about Nordic lore and forgotten European myths and legends. Still, it had all started with Parsifal and the Grail. First he thought that the Cathar castle of Montségur might be Mont Salvaesch from the Parsifal story, but when Arthur had pointed out that there was another Mont Salvaesch near Perpignan, he felt he had to investigate the place and so, in the summer of 2011, Otto had requested permission to travel to France, to Opoul-Perillos. The expedition, however, hadn't been what he had expected. He couldn't help comparing this new expedition in southern France to those happy days back in the early 1930s, when Otto had joined forces with the French Polaires research group on an archaeological dig at the French castles of Lordat and Montségur. He had fallen in love with the Ariège district and had very much enjoyed the research and diggings there. He had half-expected a similar experience in the Roussillon, but had found the area around Opoul to be of a very different energy. He could feel the cold draft of ghosts of long ago and not so long ago, when they were exploring the castle of Opoul in September. The once grand edifice had crumbled into ruins many centuries before and the remains had appeared forlorn and abandoned on top of the table mountain that dominates the Terre Salvaesch. Perhaps the foggy weather had heightened the intensity of the atmosphere. After all, he was a sensitive man and couldn't help picking up the presence of lost souls - not all of them from the distant past and there were vultures in the air. He had counted at least 30 of them. It had given him the shivers.

However, Otto hadn't written everything down in his report. One incident was still very vivid in Arthur's memory.

While he was waiting in the ante-room, wondering why he was asked to leave the conversation, Arthur remembered an awkward situation which Otto might want to keep from Alfred; when they had left the castle of Opoul and were driving back toward the main road, they passed the barracks of what was once a German concentration camp. Back in 1944, many people had been held there until they were taken to the death camps in Germany. Arthur had discovered this piece of history while researching the history of Rivesaltes and naturally, when they were passing the deserted barracks, he wanted to share this with Otto. For a few minutes, Otto had been quiet, without giving any response to the story, but then, all of a sudden and without any warning, he had broken into tears. It had startled Arthur. He knew his friend had been inside a concentration camp twice; the first time in Dachau to help build a herb garden and the second time in Buchenwald as an SS officer doing paperwork. He thought that Otto had told him everything about his life, but he was very much mistaken.

At the other side of the thick, wooden door, the conversation between Otto and Alfred had fallen silent. Otto stared at Alfred, who didn't look fit at all. His face was pale, his eyes betrayed fatigue and the look on his face reflected melancholy. Obviously, something was very wrong. Otto braced himself, knowing he was probably in for some bad news.

Alfred stared out the window, his eyes fixed on the fortified rock church of Valère, which dominated the Swiss town of Sion. Deep inside that mountain was his laboratory and a time travel device, hidden from the world, where only four months ago their very first adventure had started.

The situation had been quite complex. Alfred had sent two carefully chosen women with knowledge of ancient languages and several sciences to ancient Judea to research the historic backgrounds of the Gospels. One of them had come back pregnant.

Danielle Parker was carrying the child of one of the most important people in history; a son of an uncrowned Hasmonean king, heir to the throne of Judea and high priest of the Zadok line. His name was Oshu Amanil bar Zahari.

Two people outside the team already knew of this fact. The first person was Cardinal Antonio Sardis, a 67-year-old devoted Catholic with ambitions to become Pope. He had interfered with Alfred's expeditions that summer, but had eventually become an ally inside the Vatican. Cardinal Sardis wholeheartedly supported Alfred's dream of creating a Universal Temple that stood above religion, hoping to end religious conflicts around the globe. The Cardinal had shared that dream with another Prince of Rome, Cardinal Bergoglio, who applauded the idea and had become interested in Alfred's ideas of changing some of the doctrines and dogmas of the Catholic Church ever since.

The second person who knew about Danielle's condition was Izz al Din, a powerful oil magnate who had started out as Sardis' partner. Unfortunately, it had turned out that he had been following his own agenda all along. While using Sardis to infiltrate the facilities at Sion, he had not only become obsessed with the infinite possibilities of the ERFAB time travel device, he had also fallen passionately in love with Danielle and had his eyes fixed on her and her unborn child. Al Din, however, had been shot on their last encounter. Being in a coma, he was now being held at the medical ward of a Swiss airport prison.

With too many outside people knowing too much, Alfred had to come up with a plan to keep Danielle and her unborn baby safe, so on that very same day, his new agent David Camford and his adopted daughter Danielle were brought to a safe house at a secret location. However, though the situation was troublesome in many ways, these were not the problems that had caused Alfred's fatigue.

"Otto, I want you to listen carefully. What I am going to share with you I share in complete confidence, do you understand?"

Otto nodded. His smile had gone.

Alfred looked hard at Otto with eyes that betrayed his fear.

"I have stomach cancer. I have been suffering from chronic abdominal pain for some time, so last week I had a thorough check-up at the clinic."

Alfred turned and looked at the floor. "It doesn't look good. Needless to say I am worried about the order, about Danielle, about all of you, now that I know I may not be around for much longer."

Otto reached out and grabbed his arm.

"Do you mean to say, it can't be treated?"

"I will be having a high-risk operation next week and several tests over the following days. While I am in the clinic, my assistant Georg Hauser will take over, but first I have a mission for you that cannot wait."

Otto was surprised. He thought that Alfred's new agent, David Camford - a retired film maker from England who had proven himself invaluable over the summer - would be the person to take over. They shared the same ideals and had quickly become good friends. After he had moved to Sion to look after Danielle, David had quickly taken over many tasks and was always at Alfred's side.

"Why Georg and not David?" he queried.

Alfred stared out of the window. "David is looking after Danielle in a safe house. He cannot leave her side for a minute. Georg is my personal agent who knows all the ins and outs and therefore the logical person to replace me when everyone else is away. I have also suspended all other projects until either I'm back or my successor takes over."

An awkward silence followed. Then, with a soft voice, Otto asked the unavoidable question.

"May I know whom you have appointed as your successor?"

"Danielle. As you know, I have adopted her, so she is now legally my daughter. Therefore she is not only the official heir to all my possessions and assets, she is also the one who will succeed me as Grandmaster of SBS-Sion. David has committed himself to assist her as Vice-President of the board of directors. So if something happens to me, they will lead the order."

Otto was relieved. He didn't like Georg and would have disliked having to work for him. Then, Alfred asked him a question he hadn't expected.

"Would you be willing to accept a seat on the Board of Directors?"

Otto cleared his throat and touched his face in serious thought. "Who else is on that Board?"

"Me, David, Danielle and of course, Georg."

Otto paused and studied his thumbs. He had worked with David during their mission and had found both him and Danielle to be amicable people, but Georg was a different story. This man clearly mistrusted Otto and he had kept a close eye on him and all of his moves from the moment he had been brought to Sion. Otto compared Georg to a shepherd dog who always needs to bring bones to his master. It had irritated Otto enormously. He was certain to run into all sorts of problems with Georg.

He shook his head. "I don't approve of Georg."

Alfred stood up; his pale face turned red. "What? You don't approve of Georg? Have you forgotten that he has saved Bill's life? I have known him longer than you and he is the most trustworthy person I have ever met. I have placed my life and that of others in his hands and have never felt I was at risk. He has merited my friendship, my trust and my loyalty. You should look upon him as an example!"

Otto hated it when he was made to feel subservient to others. He needed to be trusted so he could also trust himself. He needed to be respected, so he could also respect himself. The feeling of honour he had enjoyed upon being asked to be on the Board of Directors of the Order of SBS-Sion had now been replaced by a feeling of being degraded. He felt misunderstood and mishandled.

"Then, I must regretfully turn down the job, Alfred. You have made your choice. It's Georg or me. Please, give me assignments, send me on expeditions! I'm a field man! I would much rather go on adventures and bring back reports than be locked up in a dusty office having to endure Georg's untrusting eyes burning in my neck all the time."

Otto could only repress the urge to get up and leave, because he allowed his empathy for Alfred's medical condition to soften his anger. Alfred, however, understood Otto's emotional response. He knew him better than anyone.

Alfred relaxed, returned to his seat and smiled. He had in fact been quite sure that Otto would turn down the job, but he wanted him to know he had been asked. He had also hoped that Otto would prefer to go on missions instead, for he had a new assignment for him and Arthur, which would send them on an exciting, but dangerous new adventure.

"Understood. However, Georg will still be your temporary superior when I am at the clinic. Maybe this will give you both the opportunity to get better acquainted."

Alfred put his hand on Otto's knee and looked deep into his eyes. "Otto, you and I, our destinies are entangled. Without your help this summer I would have been struggling in the dark. I know you. I trust you. I need you. Please, do not let me down. I will have a word with Georg. If I tell him to trust you, he will. If I tell him to assist you, he will. If you give him a chance to get to know you like I have, you will gain a new friend."

Otto could see the deep-seated strength behind Alfred's current weakness; the light that was within him, guiding him in making important decisions. Otto had found Alfred to be a man of great wisdom, knowledge and honour. Within him there was great love. Who was he, to let him down in his hour of need?

"You have my word, my friend. I will not let you down."

The two men got up and Alfred embraced Otto like a father would embrace a son on an important occasion.

The silence that followed was suddenly broken by a soft knocking on the door. Alfred stepped back and took a deep breath to cover his emotions.

"Yes?"

The door opened and a woman came in, carrying tea and sandwiches on a serving platter. Behind her was a very inquisitive Arthur, who took advantage of the opportunity to try and see what was going on.

"Your tea, sir."

"Thank you, Melissa, what perfect timing! Arthur my boy, come in and join us!"

Otto's eyes met Art's and betrayed mixed emotions; his sadness about Alfred's illness, but also his excitement about the prospect of a new mission. He knew he couldn't talk to Arthur about anything, because he had promised Alfred to keep the information he had just shared with him confidential. However, it wasn't very difficult for Otto to keep information to himself. He was an introverted person with hidden agendas that he never shared, not even with Alfred or Arthur. Still, he had the sensitive heart of a poet and couldn't help feeling sorry for Alfred, who was now facing a risky surgical intervention. Otto was worried. In only a few days' time, his newfound world within Alfred's comfortable realm could change forever.

Meanwhile, almost 300 miles away in the medical ward at the airport prison in Zurich, a confused patient was slowly waking up from his coma.

3

Sion, Switzerland, October 2nd 2011

The cucumber and peanut butter sandwiches had disappeared from the plate and Alfred felt it was time to explain the new mission to Otto and Arthur. He had called for Georg to join them. All were seated around the table when Alfred produced a ring in which was set a round, black stone.

"This is a very rare object. Not the ring, but the stone it holds. It's very strange how objects I have been looking for have their own mysterious ways of finding me. This ring was sent to me by my former professor of Egyptology at Oxford, whose father used to work for Sir Flinders Petrie, the famous archaeologist. My professor was still a boy at the time, but when boys are introduced to the exciting world of archaeology in exotic places, they can become quite captivated by ancient artefacts that come out of the earth. Petrie was an archaeologist who had been searching ancient sites to investigate its history and to look for important objects. Sometimes he gave small objects away, thinking they were unimportant because they had no inscriptions or markings. One day, during excavations at Tell el-Far'ah near Gaza in Palestine in the late 1920s, Petrie had found - among other things - a small stone, that didn't seem to have any particular value, so he decided to give it to the curious but shy boy who had come to visit his father. That is how the stone came into my professor's possession. He had no idea what it was, but it intrigued him so much, that he had it set in a ring that he has worn ever since. He has just turned 93 years old and for some reason he decided to send it to me, along with several notes he had made while searching for the identity of the stone."

Alfred took out the notes and displayed them on the table, next to the ring. Everyone bent over to take a closer look. The notes were written by hand and the legibility of the handwriting left much to be desired, but the drawings and the Hebrew letters had drawn Otto's attention.

Otto had a trained eye for identifying the authenticity of ancient relics. In his younger years he had enjoyed exploring the intriguing mysteries of European, Middle Eastern and Asian folklore by reading extensively about it. Having had direct access to these specialised books, he could read to his heart's content and used his broad knowledge to recognise similarities. Studying these similarities had always helped him understand many aspects of past cultures. If they only had the stone, he'd have thought it was nothing but an onyx or some other type of gemstone that was completely black, polished and round, but having seen the notes, it wasn't difficult to realise that what they saw in front of them on the wooden table was of Biblical proportions.

However, it wasn't complete.

Alfred noticed the twinkle in Otto's eyes and smiled.

"Anyone?" he looked around the table. Everyone shook their heads except for Otto, who confidently folded his arms. Then he picked up the ring and studied the stone, which looked like a tektite; a piece of black meteorite that had turned into glass. Speaking as if he were before a group of scholars, Otto decided to share his theory.

"I have seen fragments like this before in the Sabarthès, in France. The area around Tarascon and Ornolac is littered with such scattered fragments of black and green tektites and impactites. Some of these stones consist of 95% extraterrestrial iron and are called 'blood stones'. Others are chunks and pieces of green or black glass."

Meteorites had always intrigued Otto because of their possible connection to the Lapis Excellis, a stone that Wolfram von Eschenbach's had described in his version of the 'Holy Grail'. This was a subject he had researched thoroughly. He had always found it to be particularly poignant that the holiest stones and rocks of many of the world's great religions were, in fact, meteorites.

Seeing that he had captured the full attention of his listeners, Otto continued, "When a meteorite hits the Earth's atmosphere, it becomes so hot that it turns into a fireball."

"When it hits the earth, it leaves an impact hole or a crater. The bigger the meteorite, the bigger the crater. However, sometimes a cluster of space rubble hits the atmosphere and instead of hitting the Earth's surface as a whole, it burns up and turns into a huge fire bolt, scorching the Earth with temperatures as high as 1800 degrees Celsius, but without leaving a crater. Apart from scattering fragments over a large area of the Earth's surface, its heat transforms the sand on the ground into glass. These glass fragments are known as impactites. Over a long period of time - sometimes many millions of years - the glass cracks up into many pieces. After the last ice age, some fragments were washed away by the currents of new-born rivers. In the Sabarthès region in southern France, many fragments of these impactites and tektites were flushed into the caves by the Tarascon River and were left behind when the river retreated to its present-day, lower water level."

Otto looked out through the window and sighed. It was in one of these caves that Otto had found the meteorite fragments called 'bloodstones' that he cherished so much, for at that time he believed that it was this particular stone that the Pyrenean Grail was originally made of. The stone in Alfred's ring was, however, not a bloodstone, but he was almost certain that it was a tektite and a very fine sample indeed. It was flawless. To the ancient priests, its value must have been huge.

He looked again at the Hebrew notes and put the ring back on the table. "Fred, I don't know Hebrew very well but I think what you have here is the Thummim."

Alfred laughed with immense pleasure and slapped his hand on the table surface, making the others jump. "Oh my, am I glad that I have you working for me, my dear man! Yes, yes! It is the Thummim! Of course it is! But it has a missing twin brother: the Urim. An almost white, crystal-like stone that was not only the black stone's counterpart, it was also used as a lens. When placed on a stick or rod to catch the sun's rays, it could create fire. In those days this was regarded as 'stealing from the sun' and it was used only by high priests. The stone was obviously a powerful tool to possess. The two stones together were used for divination. Black means 'yes', while white means 'no' or 'maybe'."

Alfred paused and gazed at the ring. "No one truly understands their power. That is why they were separated from each other over 2500 years ago. In 597 BCE, King Nebuchadnezzar II of Babylon started his siege of Jerusalem. To save them from their enemies' hands, many Jewish relics were smuggled out of the city and among these were the Urim and Thummim. The Thummim was taken to Egypt, or at least that was the plan. The brave courier was probably robbed in the city of Shur; a fortified town on an important crossing of ancient trade routes; roads that not only connected Egypt with Syria and Mesopotamia, but also the Mediterranean with the Red Sea. The thief must have kept the stolen valuables while throwing away the black stone, thinking it had no value. Deeply embedded in the sand, the Thummim would rest there until it was found again. Shur, you see, is present day Tell el-Far'ah, the town that Flinders Petrie excavated in 1928 and 1929."

Alfred picked up the ring and looked at his audience, "As you know, the stone was not recognised without the presence of its twin brother; the Urim, which had been taken to another destination. I will be direct with you. I want the Urim... and you are going to help me find it!"

Everyone looked at Alfred, his enthusiasm, his glistering eyes, his broad smile and his obvious faith in their being able to retrieve a tiny, white stone from some ancient site in Egypt; Jordan; Judea; Babylon or where ever it may have been brought to, or whatever sand pit it had fallen into.

Otto thought he'd gone mad.

"Fred, do you realise that the expression 'needle in a haystack' is an incredible understatement relative to what you are asking us to fetch for you? You must have some idea of where to look for it?"

Alfred smiled and sat down. He folded his hands, looked at his audience and beamed an impish smile.

"Dear friends and colleagues, yes. I think I know where to look. I really wanted to go myself, but alas I have other priorities that cannot wait."

He paused a moment and looked at Georg. His eyes now expressed tiredness and worry. Only Georg and Otto knew about his illness, but he didn't find it necessary to worry anybody else right now.

He looked at Otto. "While Georg holds the fort here at Sion, you and Arthur will be going to Egypt. There you will join your guide and translator, Hadi. Together you will travel back to 1337 BCE. Destination: Amarna, Egypt."

Arthur covered his mouth with his hand. He was completely in shock that he would be going on a mission; a quest for another relic, not just anywhere, but in *ancient Egypt*.

He knew what had taken place in Amarna around 1337 BC. This was the golden year of Pharaoh Akhenaten, the heretic pharaoh who worshipped the god Aten, the sun disc. He had abandoned all the other gods of Egypt - all but the sun god Ra - who he saw as the soul of the Aten. Arthur recalled from his studies that Akhenaten had also momentarily accepted the bull-deity Apis - represented by the Mnevis bull - but that he had prohibited the public rituals for this deity by the time he had arrived in his new capital. At the time, the Mnevis bull deity wasn't only worshipped in the form of a bull, but also in the form of a cow or a calf, as long as it was red and flawless. This may have been the origin of the Hebrew Red Heifer from the book of Numbers and the worship of the golden calf in the book of Exodus.

Alfred continued, pleased to see that he had everyone's attention. "I'm sure you are all familiar with this pharaoh, but allow me to refresh your memory. In the 4th year of his reign, Akhenaten convinced his people to leave the capital of Thebes and move into the desert, where he founded a new capital; Akhetaten - present-day Amarna - where he reigned for 13 more years."

"He was married to Queen Nefertiti, whose famous bust is exhibited in the Neues Museum in Berlin. This extraordinary work of art might have given her the reputation of being the most beautiful queen of Egypt of all time, but she was certainly a queen of mysteries."

Arthur knew that by agreeing to stay with Otto as his personal assistant he had the chance to experience remarkable adventures, but he had never expected this.

"Wow, wicked! We're going to see Nefertiti in real life!"

Everyone stared at Arthur as they took in his unusual choice of words. The silence made him feel ridiculous. Then, Alfred's slight frown was replaced by a mild-mannered smile, as he remembered when he was that age.

Alfred opened a brown leather briefcase and took out a file, which he promptly opened. He produced a large photograph of the bust of Nefertiti and another photo of one of the statues of Pharaoh Akhenaten. With his broad hips and elongated face, this very different and seemingly abstract art form has been the subject of speculation for decades. Was he indeed deformed due to an illness, or did Akhenaten want his statues to look 'androgynous' - mixing male and female into his divine images - portraying himself as the living Aten?

Alfred noticed the perplexed faces in his audience and felt he needed to explain why he had thought of the Amarna period in his search for the Urim.

"I believe that the Urim and Thummim were originally Egyptian relics, known as the Eyes of Horus or Thoth. One was white, representing Isis or Ra, while the other was black, representing Horus. According to ancient texts, the white stone was sometimes put into the headpiece of the staff of Ra. Therefore, the goddess Isis was also called; the 'Eye of Ra'. It's interesting to see that the staff of Ra was briefly mentioned in the first Indiana Jones movie, when it caught the rays of the sun to point out the exact location of the Ark of the Covenant on a model of the city of Tanis in Egypt. It was also mentioned in the Hobbit movies based on the famous book of Tolkien. This time the stone is called the

'Arkenstone'. The Eye itself has found its way into the All-seeing Eye we know from Christian and Masonic symbolism. Although many secret orders know of the stone's existence, no one knows where it is now. It is obvious that this stone has always been considered to be of great value and was kept in the most sacred place of all; the inner sanctum of a Temple. So, why am I looking for the stone in Akhetaten? Well, I believe there's a very likely possibility that Pharaoh Akhenaten was none other than the Biblical Moses. My reasons are well documented. First, Akhenaten warned the people of Egypt that great terrors would befall them if they didn't abandon their gods to worship the Aten and journey with him to a new promised land. Secondly, he literally left Thebes, the capital of Egypt, to travel north into the desert. The entire army and many of his people travelled with him to live in the desert. This, I believe, was the Exodus. The Exodus to Akhetaten."

Everyone was wide-eyed, but as the words sank in, some began to nod with an understanding of the revolutionary ideas Alfred had just shared with them.

Arthur raised his hand. "Then what about the 40 years in the desert? They didn't stay in Akhetaten that long?"

"You are right, but remember that 40 is a popular symbolic number in the Bible. It could mean that they went through a period of trials, challenges and temptations, or a period of judgment. It could also just mean 'a generation'. I believe that Akhenaten's original name was Thutmose, which means 'born of Thoth' or 'son of Thoth'. He changed his name to Amenhotep IV when he succeeded his father, Amenhotep III. Then he changed his name to Akhenaten when he was already in his new capital, the holy city of Akhetaten. In the 17th year of his reign, he no longer had the power or the resources to withstand the priesthood of Thebes and Memphis, who had insisted on going back to the more profitable worship of Amun and the other deities. Egypt had been suffering economically during Akhenaten's reign and finally, after the disappearance of Akhenaten, the Aten was again replaced by Amun. While Akhenaten's children had no choice but to accept the reinstallation of the old deities, he, his high priest Meryra and his remaining followers vanished from Egypt. Perhaps they even had to flee the country. It is possible that, by that time, Akhenaten had taken back his old name; Thutmose, while leaving out the reference to the god Thoth."

Arthur raised his hand, "So, Meryra was Aaron?"

Alfred nodded, appreciating the boy's enthusiasm. "I believe so. He may have been the *S-d-ch* or *Zadok* priest in charge of all rituals and relics and responsible for the mobile shrine for the Aten on their journey to the north. It was common in Egypt to have mobile shrines for their gods. These shrines rested on two long, wooden poles, so they could be carried by priests during ceremonies. Even Amun had his own mobile shrine. One particular mobile shrine - in this case dedicated to the Aten - that was carried through the desert is now known as the Ark of the Covenant. There is an interesting coincidence, that could perhaps explain the name Aaron: In the 18th Dynasty, during the reign of Amenhotep III, the name of the second prophet of Amun was 'Aanen'. He was the uncle of Akhenaten and an important person in his day. Of course we know Aaron as the keeper of the Ark of the Covenant during the Exodus. Interestingly, the Hebrew name for Ark is 'Aron'. So I have come to think that throughout the years, these two names may have been mixed up in Jewish history to become 'Aaron'."

Everyone nodded in agreement to Alfred's theory. That was certainly an interesting explanation.

Alfred continued, carefully watching Arthur to be sure he was still following. "It is possible that Akhenaten, now called Mose, took his people to Petra, in southern Jordan, where he and Meryra were buried. Although their bodies have never been found, Aaron's empty tomb in Petra is still considered to be genuine. Perhaps at a later date, their mortal remains were taken back to Egypt and reburied somewhere in the Valley of the Kings, which wasn't at all uncommon."

Arthur chuckled, "Maybe Akhenaten really *is* the mysterious mummy in tomb 55."

Everyone stared at the boy. It all made perfect sense and because Aaron had possessed the two stones, also Otto began to realise that it was only logical to start looking for the Urim - aka the 'Stone of Isis' or the 'Eye of Ra' - in Akhetaten.

Alfred smacked his lips and produced a white crystal-like stone of the same size and shape as the black stone in the ring. He stared at his audience with a strange glitter in his eyes. "All you need to do is find it, replace it with this fake stone and bring back the real thing."

Otto grinned. He knew that the Knights Templar had done the same thing in Ethiopia in the late 12th century, when they took the real Ark of the Covenant and replaced it with a fake the night they journeyed back to the north. So yes, why not? Nobody would notice the difference. It was worth a try.

Otto looked at Alfred and nodded, showing him that he was willing to take on the mission. Alfred smiled contently; he had hoped that Otto would accept.

Alfred now continued his lecture in a more relaxed manner, "The ancient Egyptians already knew the deep symbolism of black and white. I believe it was one of the teachings of Akhenaten's Mystery School."

Otto looked quizzically at Alfred. "Do you mean that the Egyptian Mystery School - the one that most Greek philosophers visited - already existed at that time?"

"Yes, I do. That particular school was founded in Thebes by Akhenaten's father, Amenhotep III. The teachings were based on the knowledge of Thoth or Tehuti; the god with the head of an ibis. The Greek philosophers called him Hermes Trismegistus and they introduced the teachings to their own followers back in Greece. This is how the teachings travelled to the west and are now known as the Hermetic Philosophy. These teachings include the study of the Physical and Metaphysical world and sun worship. Akhenaten's father, Amenhotep III, had already introduced sun worship and had even ordered the construction of several Aten temples."

"The Colossi of Memnon, the seated stone giants near Luxor, that still greet the rising sun today, are gigantic statues of none other than Amenhotep III himself."

For Otto and Arthur, everything became very clear now, but they could see it wouldn't be an easy mission. They'd have to find a way to get inside a sacred site that most probably will be very well guarded, but Alfred made it sound so simple.

"Don't worry, it's easy! You become initiates! You will be allowed inside the temple and once you're inside, you can look for the stone, replace it and return to the present."

Otto leaned over to Alfred, smiling cynically,

"Sure! Piece of cake..."

Georg gently tapped his watch while looking pointedly at Alfred. It was getting late. Alfred got up from his chair, after which the others did the same.

He turned to Otto on their way to the door. "You haven't met our new professor yet, have you? His name is Wong Chi-kit and he is from Hong Kong. He is replacing Bill and I must say I am very pleased with his work so far. I have asked him to develop small, portable time-travel devices, which can be carried like a mobile phone, making it possible to come and go from any place and any time."

Otto became a little nervous. "These have been tried out, haven't they? They're safe, right?"

"Yes, of course, don't worry! We will go to the lab and meet with him. There isn't much time. Your flight is leaving tonight."

Georg and Alfred exchanged guarded smiles. They understood the risks involved in supporting a potentially dangerous expedition right before Alfred's high-risk operation. Yet Alfred was confident that the two stones, when united, would give him the clairvoyance to predict his own future; to find out whether his operation would be a success or a failure and to see what would become of Danielle and her precious baby; the child and heir of an ancient Judean priest king.

For Alfred, understanding important events yet to come figured utmost in the greater scheme of things. For only then could he act appropriately in the present. He was determined to know what lay ahead. The ERFAB could send people into the past, but it was impossible to travel from this modern present into the future. There were too many possible 'futures', making it virtually impossible to travel back to the same present. He believed that there were multiple dimensions and that time travelling was a dangerous thing. After all; one alteration in the past could change their present forever.

Georg brought the black Lexus SUV to the front of the manor house and everyone got in quickly. The weather was cold but beautiful and the air was sweet with the fragrances of autumn. It was only a short drive to the base, but when they got to the lab, Professor Wong was nowhere to be found.

4

Sion, Switzerland, October 2nd 2011

Wong Chi-kit was sitting cross-legged on a tiny rug on the grass at the top of a mountain slope. He appeared to be in meditation. With his eyes closed he could almost imagine himself surrounded by the giant, lush forests that start just outside the city of Hong Kong, his hometown. He missed the temples; the ever-changing skies; the flowers; the indigenous birds and the forests, but he did not, however, miss the city itself, his home or his friends and most certainly not his old job.

Having benefited from some of the best educations available at the most elite schools in Hong Kong, at 28 years old he was already very familiar with the most up-to-date aspects of quantum technology. However, he was disgusted by his first employer in Central Hong Kong, as his objectives were certainly not in the interests of furthering the welfare of mankind. In search of a truly benevolent employer with an ethical philosophy, pursuing much worthier goals, he had sent his CV to a carefully-chosen, small selection of companies in Europe. Finally, his personal interest and accomplishments in wormhole theories had led him to a new employer, a mysterious man with an even more mysterious laboratory, hidden underneath a jagged mountain in Sion, Switzerland. He was asked to sign a confidentiality agreement before his interview.

Both the company and his interviewer had intrigued him.

Intense questioning was followed by an admission that this unusual job could be unpredictable, to say the least. He relished the idea of adventure in his life, perhaps even some danger, so he could feel alive.

It was as if the job had found him, rather than the other way around.

Immediately upon arrival, Wong had been introduced to the person he would succeed: Professor William Fairfax. He found Bill to be a pleasant man and easy to work with, so after a short trial period he had familiarised himself with everything he needed to know about time travel.

Wong had come to Europe with almost no luggage, but there was one thing he would always take with him everywhere he went; a small bonsai tree, which he had meticulously tended for over 15 years. He had even brought it today on his hike to the ruins of the castle of Tourbillon, in the hills just outside the city of Sion.

The tiny tree gave him peace.

The understanding and care of bonsai trees has been passed along to him by skilled masters of the art through many centuries. Growing and caring for bonsai trees requires experience, perseverance and close attention to detail to keep the tree from growing too large without killing it in the process. The size of the bonsai tree might be small, but the willpower of it to grow within the restricted area of its shallow terracotta pot - to live and even thrive, in spite of this restriction - reminded Wong of his own willpower. No matter how small the house is that you live in, or the body you are incarnated in, the spirit knows no size and can thrive nevertheless. Like a bonsai spirit, Wong's Universe was much bigger than his modest stature, so he most certainly did not need much luggage. His body was his house and his life and he had no need for trinkets or souvenirs from his childhood or from his travels. He was content with just being. Wong was confident that he would find everything he needed right here in Sion and what he needed most right now was some peace.

The sound of a gong woke him from his thoughts. He grabbed his mobile phone from his pocket and when he saw who was calling him, he answered nervously,

"Sir, yes sir?"

"Wong, where the hell are you?"

Alfred was annoyed. It hadn't been easy for him to accept professor Bill Fairfax's resignation. For almost a year, the professor had worked for Alfred on a device that could create an artificial wormhole, through which people could not only travel through time, but also within the same time span to different places. His creation, the ERFAB (named after the Einstein-Rosen-Fairfax Bridge), had been a fantastic means of researching unconfirmed historical events. However, something had gone terribly wrong at the end of their last mission. Fairfax had been shot by accident and had nearly died. Because the professor had never expected to be in such danger on the job, he had made the decision not to extend his contract with SBS-Sion. As a consequence, Alfred needed to find a replacement, but he had never imagined he'd find someone so soon.

Initially, Alfred had found Wong to be a Godsend. In the past month, Bill had explained to him every detail of how to work the ERFAB. It was clear that Wong knew at least as much as the professor did, so within a short time he had learned all he needed to know to take Bill's place, but somehow, Bill's absence had made Alfred feel uncomfortable. Alfred needed to be able to trust Wong, but so far, his new employee had spent every minute of his free time outside the complex. Where did he go? Did he speak to anyone? Should he have him followed?

"Wong, I want you to get back to the base immediately," Alfred snapped.

"Yes sir, of course, I will come immediately, sir!"

Wong quickly grabbed his beloved bonsai, almost dropping it in his haste. Despite his efforts to hurry, it took him half an hour to get back to the base and when he arrived, he took just a moment to marvel at the clever setting. The carefully concealed base could only be reached through a house, which was nestled at the foot of the hill upon which the imposing fortified rock church of Valère had stood for generations. After typing in a complicated code above the doorbell, the door automatically swung open. Behind the door was a corridor leading to another massive, steel door. Beyond it was the entrance to yet another corridor leading deep into the mountain toward an underground complex, complete with rooms; corridors; elevators; restrooms; showers; private apartments; a meeting room; a restaurant and finally, the amazing laboratory. Inside the lab - on an elevated level - a wall of one-way, tinted glass assured total privacy to the occupant of the office, while in his turn, the occupant could overlook the entire lab. This was Alfred's office.

Wong almost ran up the stairs. Alfred had been pacing up and down the office while waiting for Wong. He was not the kind of man anyone would want to keep waiting and when Wong finally entered the glass office, Alfred couldn't help raising his voice. "Where the hell have you been!"
"On a hike, chief! It's my afternoon off!"
Deeply dissatisfied, Alfred scrutinised Wong and asked him a question Wong didn't expect. "Who told you that you could go outside the building during your free hours?"
Silence. Wong lowered his head. He might have missed that particular detail at the briefing and realised he might not have been listening very carefully at the time. He had been much too excited.
"Sorry, sir."
Arthur found Wong's lisp amusing, but after feeling Otto's elbow in his ribs, he quickly regained his serious expression. Georg remained silent, as usual. He was present at every meeting, but always in the background, observing everything. Once in a while he exchanged looks with Alfred, as if they shared some kind of wordless code. It had irritated Otto immensely.
While studying the scene, it became clear to Otto that Alfred was willing to forgive Wong for his unauthorised hike and without any further delay, Alfred moved forward. "I think it is time to explain to these gentlemen how to operate the mini ERFAB. Have you programmed them with the right data?"
"Yes sir, I will get the devices for you and the manual. Right away, sir!"
Wong ran down the stairs, opened a safe, slowly took out a box and carefully walked back to the office.

All eyes were now on the mysterious box. He took out one of three devices, which looked very much like a mobile phone in a dark plastic, hard cover. The green signal light indicated that it had been fully charged.

"It is easy to use, but the button is very sensitive. You must always keep it in its hard case when you are not using it. Always keep it on your body, in a pocket or on your belt. It only needs sunlight or bright light to charge itself. You must keep it fully charged. When the battery is low, it might not work properly. You'll know when the battery is low; it will vibrate. All the necessary data for your trip has been uploaded and checked. There is also a 'home button'. If you press it, you will automatically bring yourselves to this laboratory in the present."

Wong smiled broadly. He was proud of himself for having perfected this small manual device. His predecessor, Bill Fairfax, had invented the device on paper, but he hadn't stayed around long enough to build it. Wong had tried it out several times. First with items, then with small animals and everything seemed to work perfectly. Then he had not only sent Alfred to a specified co-ordinate, but had also succeeded in bringing him back safely. Wong was impressed with Alfred's courage. Had it been up to him, Wong would have had someone else try it out first, but Wong was still getting to know Alfred. He didn't yet understand that Alfred would never risk anyone else's life before his own.

"Thank you, Wong. No one will use the device unless it is absolutely necessary. That is why Otto and Arthur here will travel to Amarna the conventional way; by plane and car."

He looked at the two men. "The moment you use the device, you will only travel through time without having to travel to another co-ordinate. Choose a safe place outside the ruins of the old city. You will then appear on that very same spot in the year 1337 BCE. When you succeed, you must press the home button. If you do not succeed, you can still travel back to the present by selecting '1' and then you must contact me immediately for further orders."

Otto furrowed his brow, "I assume that means that there is a plan B?"

"Yes, if the stone isn't there or if you should fail to replace it, I have an alternative plan. It is all in the files, but let's hope the alternative won't be necessary. Now gentlemen, if you would follow me?"

Alfred escorted Otto and Arthur into an apartment where they could prepare for their journey. The selection of clothes they found in the bedroom included their Egyptian clothes for their visit to Akhetaten. There was a shower room, a fridge with some refreshments and next to a desk stood a locked briefcase. Alfred pointed at it. "I will give you the key code the moment you are inside the plane, but before that, no one can see its contents."

"Sure, I understand. How much time do we have?" queried Otto.

"You should still have a few hours to familiarise yourself with the layout of the city of Akhetaten. This television has a DVD player. It will play several documentaries about Akhenaten and the archaeological site of Amarna, so I suggest you watch them with full attention and memorise what you see. I will see you later."

Alfred left the two men to prepare for their adventures. They agreed to make themselves comfortable and play the DVD. While Otto embraced the adventure, Arthur was more than a bit nervous. In fact, he had a bad feeling about their journey and a painful ache in his stomach, reminding him of his uncertainties and low self-esteem. However, it also saddened him that he couldn't share his adventures with his family, from whom he had cut off all communication a few months ago over his relationship with Otto.

Arthur's parents had always prided themselves on setting high standards and had been incredibly strict about every facet of discipline. Both he and his two sisters had been raised the 'old-fashioned way', with serious, often harsh punishments, intended to make sure whatever had happened, absolutely didn't happen again.

It was nothing short of a miracle that he had been allowed to go on his French holiday with his friends that summer. He had convinced his sceptical mother and father that it would be a once-in-a-lifetime educational experience and a first-hand study of history that he simply couldn't pass up and it had been, though not for the reasons he had expected.

He and Otto had met quite by chance. Their relationship was innocent at first, but quickly developed into something much more. By the end of the summer, Arthur had decided to stay with Otto. He had found happiness in meeting his soul mate and was finally coming to terms with his struggle over the sense of duty he felt to his family and his innermost feelings, but then there was that horrid phone call; the call in which he had to tell his family that he wouldn't be coming home at the end of the summer. His coming out of the closet was a traumatic announcement that had shocked his family, but when he had added that he had made the life-changing decision to also leave school and become the assistant to an explorer, it was more than his parents could abide. His father had told him he would never be welcome under his roof ever again and while his mother cried softly, she finally hung up on him. He hadn't called his parents since. His sisters still hadn't called him on his mobile phone, probably because they weren't allowed to contact him. He didn't want to get them into trouble, so he didn't make any effort to contact them either.

He browsed through some of the photos that were stored on his phone and became melancholy. There they were; his mother and his two sisters in Blackpool licking their rapidly melting ice cream; their dog Sheltie dashing about on the beach and his father standing next to their car. He was terribly homesick and the sharp pangs in the pit of his stomach were unrelenting. Despite the tough upbringing, he loved his family and he couldn't help missing them.

Otto, who was trying to make sense of the remote control of the TV-DVD combination, suddenly noticed how his friend had become very silent.

"Hey buddy, what's up?"

"Oh nothing, I guess I miss my family a bit. I can't really call them after what's happened, but what if things go wrong and we're stuck in ancient Egypt forever? I'd never see them again."

"Stuck in ancient Egypt? No way! We have a home button on our devices. It'll be okay. Don't worry so much. Besides, if you can't call them, why not send them a text message, saying that you love them, instead?"

That made sense to Arthur - it felt safe.

"Just don't tell them anything about our mission. Remember what Fred said. Our business is our own. The outside world; friends; family; they can't know where we are or what we do. Just tell them you love them and then turn it off again. When we get back from Egypt, you turn it back on and see if you've had a reply. Okay?"

Arthur nodded. Immediately he started to type a short message and decided to send it to his mother and his two sisters, Carolyn and Cassandra.

'Hope you are ok. I am ok. Love you all. Just wanted you to know. Bye.'

Within a minute, Alfred was back at the door. Both jumped up from the bed. Alfred raced toward Arthur, who was still holding his phone.

"Give me your mobile phone. Now!"

Immediately he gave Alfred what he was asking for. The giant Swiss had always frightened him, ever since their first encounter that summer, but right now he just wanted to shrink down to the size of a mouse.

"What did I tell you? No messages!!! I am going to keep your phone until you have come back. Do you understand?"

Otto, who cared deeply about Arthur, got upset.

"Hey cool down, Fred! He didn't say anything about where he was, or where he was going. He just sent his parents and sisters a message, saying he's ok. What's wrong with that?"

"What is wrong with that? Don't you see that anyone can trace his call now? Please think! Suppose his parents have reported him missing? Then the police will now have a signal to trace his mobile phone to this address!"

Otto looked at Alfred with big eyes.

"Is that possible? Wow!"

Alfred calmed down as he evaluated the situation silently to himself. Of course Otto didn't know. Being from 1939, he didn't know that it is possible to track a mobile phone, even when it's just on, let alone when you send a message or call someone. However, Arthur should have known better. Perhaps the boy didn't realise the seriousness of their secret mission. He would though, soon enough.

By now, Arthur felt really bad. Alfred noticed it and felt sorry that he had upset him. "It's okay son, but this means that we need to go to the airport a.s.a.p., so start packing your things."

As soon as Alfred had left the room, Otto reached out to Arthur and hugged him tight.

"It'll be okay. I am with you, no worries."

Arthur wept silently. They stood there for a minute in a tight embrace, sharing the warmth and deep affection that was the basis and heart of their relationship. Otto kissed his tears away and looked at him with a tender smile.

"Well, you've sent your message and we're soon going on an amazing adventure. Come now, clean your face. We have to go."

Arthur managed to pick himself up and smiled back at him. He was grateful to be with the person he loved; the person he looked up to; the one who believed in him; the friend who gave him so much love and friendship in return. He wondered if this new adventure would try their relationship. Otto seemed to be so stable and strong; so much in control; so sure of himself, but Arthur didn't know that Otto's outward confidence was all show.

5

Airport prison, Zürich, Switzerland, several days earlier
It took a while before Izz al Din could see everything properly - the white walls; the barred door; the end of his bed and next to him; a small table with a clipboard. He noticed the steady bleep of a machine and turned his head to see where it was coming from. His head pounded even more when he tried to sit upright. He tried to breath in and out deeply to clear his mind and to sharpen his blurry eyesight. Then he spotted the IV in his left arm and the tubes going into his nose and elsewhere.

Slowly it all came back to him; someone had shot him. He even remembered feeling the blow to his head, so he touched the spot, but could only feel a simple adhesive plaster. How long had he been there? Weeks? Months? There was no guard, no nurse in sight. Maybe they thought he would never pull out of this mysterious haze.

He nodded off again. When he next woke up, he was less groggy, more aware of his surroundings and, sadly, also of his wretched aches and pains. Slapping his face a few times in an effort to rouse himself, he noticed not only how much weight he'd lost, but also how intolerably dry his mouth felt. Weak, hungry and thirsty, he knew that he would never be able to get far in this condition, so he decided he had better not let on that he had even woken up.

In the days that followed he trained his muscles and clocked every visit from a nurse or a doctor, planning the right time to escape. It was always quiet at night. Every day he remembered more of his life: his name; his ideals; his profession as an oil magnate; his expensive tastes; his bank accounts; his women…

Danielle!
The adrenaline rush strengthened him, but it also raised his heartbeat to such an extent that it made the beeper emit its irritating tone even faster. Immediately he tried to calm down. The one thing he didn't want was to draw attention.

Where would Danielle be? There was only one place he could think of: the site of the underground base at Sion, Switzerland. The place where he had nearly died.

Izz al Din decided he would try to escape in the quietest of moments; the earliest hours of Sunday morning. His hunger and thirst had almost become unbearable and he could wait no longer. After painstakingly removing the maze of tubes and the catheter, Al Din tried to get up. He moved his legs and his feet, hoping they would be able to carry his weight. Carefully he stood upright and immediately felt the dreaded weakness in his legs. He stood as if rooted to the floor for a moment, then gingerly tried to walk a few cautious steps. The incessant beeping had at last stopped when he had detached the sphygmomanometer from his finger and he knew that he'd soon get unwelcome company. He had to get out of there quickly and steal a mobile phone, or even better; a car. He remembered the phone number of his assistant and hoped he and his partner would still be in the area - as had been instructed - waiting for him to get in touch, but it had been a long time. Would they still be there, or had they given up on him by now?

Al Din walked toward the door, steadying himself by holding first onto the bed and then onto the closet. Then he heard footsteps approaching. The adrenaline rush made him shake uncontrollably and he quickly drank some water at the sink in the corner. The footsteps became louder; someone was definitely approaching his room.

When the male nurse entered the room, he saw the empty bed and instinctively wanted to call for help, but Al Din was fast. He knocked the man down before he could make a sound; undressed him; laid him in his bed and attached the sphygmomanometer to his finger. Fighting grogginess and pain, Al Din pulled on the nurse's trousers and lab coat, searched the pockets and found his car keys, a mobile phone and key card. Allah was with him. Excitedly he checked his stolen watch. It was 03:06 am, time to leave.

Sion, Switzerland, October 2nd 2011

Alfred had a strange feeling about the entire mission. Why were there so many obstacles? Why did a tumour suddenly enter his body and his life? He had wanted Otto and Arthur to study the history and mysteries of ancient Amarna that evening, while waiting to go to the airport, but now that Arthur had sent that text message, the entire mission had suddenly been compromised. Arthur hadn't been in touch with his family for a month. What if his parents had gone to the police? His outgoing signal might have attracted unwanted attention to the Sion base.

They'd have to leave for the airport immediately.

Alfred's assistant, Georg Hauser, was walking next to him through the long corridors. Georg had a million questions reeling around his head, but he rarely spoke. He was a man of few words. Georg had noticed how stressed Alfred had become over the past few days and couldn't help feeling sorry for his chief, whom he considered his friend.

Georg had been Alfred's bodyguard ever since Alfred's father died. That had been a very trying time for everyone at Sion, not just for Alfred. Alfred's father had been a man of great power and dignity. He had earned the respect of practically every Freemason lodge and Templar organisation worldwide. When Alfred inherited everything from his father, he also inherited his responsibilities and his staff and Georg had been part of that staff. He remembered well how Alfred's father, Joannis Hugh Zinkler, had gripped his arm and made him swear he would look after Alfred, his only son. Georg had sworn he would, to the death. He had taken this oath very seriously and it was true.

He would give his life for Alfred.

In this past year, Georg and Alfred had grown close. Maybe this was the reason why Georg couldn't understand why Alfred had adopted Danielle; a *woman,* who had now become his heir. He had been even more disturbed when he learnt that Alfred wanted *David* to guard Danielle with his life and be at her side as his successor. He felt ignored.

Maybe Alfred really only saw him as his personal assistant and bodyguard, nothing more. The entire situation had upset him, but he would never show it. He had promised his father to protect him with his life and he would. Always.

Perhaps he just expected too much from his chief.

When Alfred had told Georg about his tumour and the need for an operation within two weeks' time, they had immediately made all the necessary preparations. Today, Danielle and David were on their way to a safe house at a secret location; Otto and Arthur were about to be sent on a mission that could not wait and Georg had been asked to replace Alfred temporarily while he was in hospital for the operation. Finally he felt that he was getting the respect and the trust he deserved. Taking over SBS-Sion - even temporarily - was a huge responsibility. The base alone had 28 employees - among them, the only recently commissioned Professor Wong, whom he hardly knew. It wasn't easy for Georg to trust anyone. He had certainly never trusted Otto, despite Alfred's confidence in him.

The two men arrived at the lab. All the collected luggage was now taken to two vehicles parked outside. Within a few minutes, the first car had been filled with luggage and had taken off in the direction of the airport. In the meantime, the last details were checked and re-checked by Alfred and Wong and the ERFAB devices were carefully put into their hard cases. At the last minute, Otto and Arthur arrived at the entrance with their personal luggage. Alfred noticed Arthur's red eyes; signs that he had been crying and he realised how much the boy must be suffering. Otto saw Alfred looking at his friend and empathically pursed his lips, as if he wanted to say; 'go easy on him.' In only a few months' time, Arthur had not only discovered he was gay, he had also dropped out of school and lost all contact with his family. He was in a very fragile, new relationship with a man from a different time, who was also fifteen years older than him. On top of it all, he was going on a scary, high risk mission.

Many things could go wrong and there was a possibility they would not be able to make it back, or survive the time travelling. Alfred's shouting a few minutes earlier had simply burst the bubble. However, there was no time to lose and Alfred needed both Arthur and Otto to focus.

"Alright listen up! We are now leaving for Sion Airport. Everything you need for your mission is inside your luggage. Study the files with your full attention; familiarise yourself with every detail. Learn from memory how to use the ERFAB devices without having to refer back to the manual. Upon your arrival in Cairo, you will meet your guide, Hadi. He has been briefed and knows everything he needs to know. Do not share anything else with him. Do not trust anybody and follow the instructions in the files to the letter. Do you have any questions?"

Otto shook his head. "Not yet, but I'm sure I will have a few questions before departure."

Arthur avoided eye contact with everyone. Normally he would have jumped on the chance to go on a mission like this, but right now he wished he could just go home. For some reason his courage had left him completely, but then he felt Otto's hand in his, squeezing gently. He looked at him and saw the gentle smile on his friend's face and the spark in his eyes.

"People would kill for an adventure like this you know?" he whispered to Arthur. "I'd never want a boring desk job, no matter how safe that could be. We're off to experience the ancient sand of Egypt, one of the world's most mysterious places. Of course, I am a little nervous too, but sometimes you have to trust the larger picture. Have a little faith, hmm?" Arthur managed to produce a mild smile. Otto was right; if things are no longer in your control, then let go and simply enjoy the ride. Within minutes, the black Lexus SUV headed off to Sion Airport. The base had now been sealed off from the outside. None of the employees - including Wong - was allowed to leave the base and no one was allowed to enter, except for Georg and Alfred.

It was only a short drive to the airport parking area. Georg left the car and closed the door, but when Otto tried to open his door, he found that it was locked.

"Fred, aren't we getting out here?"

Alfred shook his head. "Georg is arranging your helicopter flight to Zürich. You will be on a separate, private flight from Zürich to Cairo later tonight."

Arthur was suddenly excited again. He had never been in a helicopter or a private jet before, but knew that Otto had travelled in Alfred's jet a few months ago. When he looked through the rear window, he noticed they were parked in front of the other Lexus, which was now pulling out to continue ahead of them. He realised that this was indeed a major operation and he felt small and insignificant in contrast to the power Alfred seemed to possess. Nevertheless, he was apparently important enough to be brought along on this mission, which seemed to be of great importance to Alfred.

He just hoped he wouldn't jeopardise it.

It didn't take long for Georg to reappear and both cars now reunited at the helipad. A white AS 350B3 helicopter - hired from a local company called Eagle Helicopters - slowly started rotating its blades. Three employees ran toward the helicopter and the luggage was quickly taken on board. Alfred was on his mobile phone almost constantly, making one call after another. Otto watched him and smiled. "Around the world, thoughts shall fly in the twinkling of an eye!"

Arthur looked at him with wide eyes, "but that's Mother Shipton! One of her late 15th century prophesies!"

Otto beamed and boxed Arthur's shoulder with his fist. He was proud of Arthur, who, like him, had amazing general knowledge. "Yep. You gotta know your Mother Shipton, Art!"

Both laughed while they climbed into the helicopter. To their surprise, Alfred, too, stepped into the helicopter and secured his seatbelt. He noticed Otto's frown.

"I need to get you through customs in Zürich. I may have cart blanche myself, but there wasn't enough time to arrange that for you. Now, fasten your seatbelt, we can't afford to lose any time!"

Alfred looked down at Georg - who was staying behind - and nodded sourly. He hated travelling without his special agent. Then the helicopter rose and swept smoothly across the sky. Otto and Arthur admired the Alps, with their snow-covered tops reflecting the last rays of orange light that lingered after the sunset. They flew over the impressive Sanetschpass and the cities of Interlaken and Luzern. Above them was the darkening evening sky. They could now make out several stars and Arthur recognised Orion's belt - three stars in a row with one slightly off angle. He explained how the pyramids were supposedly constructed as a mirror image of that particular star constellation. Otto smiled. Somehow it felt as if these stars were luring them into Egypt. He had read somewhere that in Spain, Portugal and South America the Orion belt was also known as the Three Marys.

Which Marys, nobody knew.

After a flight of 50 minutes they landed safely at Zürich Airport and Alfred took out his mobile to inform Georg.

In the meantime, Georg had decided to get a coffee at the restaurant inside the airport building, knowing that it would take several hours for Alfred to return to Sion. He was getting hungry and tired; these past few days had been hectic. It had taken a lot of time and effort to prepare Danielle and David's transfer to the safe house, not to mention all the work that had gone into organising the mission to Egypt. Alfred had relied on him to do most of the legwork.

His own team of agents was now far away, guarding Danielle and David and he hadn't been able to bring more agents to the airport. The entire mission was too secret to involve too many people and, as far as he knew, everything was kept under the radar. Spending a few hours alone at a quiet airport at nightfall made him regret that he hadn't been able to bring at least one agent. At the very last minute, plans had changed and now they were out of time. He had no choice but to wait it out. He looked at the menu of the brasserie and saw some mouth-watering dishes. Would he order an 'Ardoise Valaisanne' or would he risk waiting twenty minutes for the 'Rack d'Agneau?' He decided to order the Tournedos and wished that he wasn't on the job. He would have loved to have sampled one of the red wines to go with it.

After an hour he decided to get some fresh air and stretch his legs. He left the terminal building and started to walk toward the parking area. Then he noticed something strange. One of their SUVs was parked in the middle of the street with the headlights on. He was certain that the other driver had gone back to Alfred's manor in the hills, while he himself had parked his own vehicle in the parking space not far from the restaurant. Something in his lower belly told him this was bad. He decided to take out his Glock and approached the car carefully. As he came closer, he could hear that the engine was revving up, but he couldn't see anyone sitting inside.
Suddenly the car roared directly toward him at top speed. One of the back doors swung open and two arms pulled Georg into the car, which now drove off toward the city.
No one had noticed that Georg's Glock had fallen onto the ground in the parking lot.

Meanwhile, at the airport in Zürich, everything seemed to be going very smoothly. Within half an hour the luggage had been transported to Alfred's Learjet and Otto and Arthur had successfully gone through customs. They were now on board, enjoying the luxury of the supple leather interior and the comfortable reclining seats.
Alfred was on his way back to the helicopter when he placed another call to Georg to tell him he was now on his way back to Sion, but much to his surprise, his call was switched to Georg's answering machine. A minute later he tried again, but Georg still didn't answer his phone.

"Georg, call me the moment you get this message?"

A feeling deep in his gut told him that something was terribly wrong and experience had taught him that his gut feelings were nearly always right.

The next moment he received an incoming call from the airport prison, which was also located in Zurich.

"Mr Zinkler? I am so sorry to call you at this hour, but the man you brought to us in July has escaped. I don't know h..."

"What!!!"

Alfred hung up. Suddenly the earth beneath his feet seemed to turn into quicksand. He ran toward the helicopter and ordered the pilot to fly back to Sion as quickly as possible. The next fifty minutes seemed to last a lifetime. If Al Din had indeed taken Georg, as his gut told him he had, then who knows what he would do to the man who had shot him.

A shot that had been aimed to kill.

Alfred remembered the moment all too well. Al Din had taken the professor hostage and had used him as his shield to protect himself. Georg could only aim for Al Din's head. No one had expected him to live and even when he did, no one had expected him to wake up from his coma. Obviously, the wound had healed beyond expectations and had left no serious brain damage. A violent sting struck his system like lightening when another thought entered his mind: With Izz al Din on the loose, Danielle and David will be in danger. Alfred was certain that Al Din - for whom time had stood still - would want only one thing: To get to Danielle.

The moment Alfred arrived at Sion airport, he raced out of the helicopter to find Georg, but there was no trace of him. The waitress at the brasserie remembered he had bought a meal there, but after his dinner he had gone for a walk. She had seen him leave in the direction of the parking lot.

Alfred ran outside.

It didn't take long before he saw something on the tarmac.

It was Georg's Glock.

6

The Bailiwick of Guernsey, Channel Islands

The romantic 16th century cottage could have come straight out of a story book. It was located just outside St. Andrew, discretely situated far from the main road and hidden away from spying eyes. Writers often rented the house as a retreat, especially for its solitude. The only sound to be heard was coming from a multitude of birds in the garden, the wind rustling the trees, the babbling brook that bypassed the garden and the cries of the seagulls. Rose Cottage was a private home owned by a British couple by the name of Bertram, of Lincolnshire. The Bertrams rented out the cottage at holidays, but with the arrival of their first grandchild, they had decided to rent it out for longer periods of time; Mrs Bertram didn't want to miss a minute with her new granddaughter and the extra income from the cottage would come in handy.

Then, on September 30th, when the last of the summer tourists had gone, a gentleman from Switzerland had called to ask if Rose Cottage was free and if it was available for an extended rental. He had also offered a large sum of money for taking the website offline. Of course, Mrs Bertram had immediately agreed. Normally, people would move in directly after picking up the keys from Mrs Peel, who lived nearby. However, in this case, two men dressed in black, who spoke with a foreign accent, had requested to inspect it first. The widow Mrs Peel - who was not only the key holder, but also the caretaker of Rose Cottage - was finding it all very suspicious. As the men meticulously inspected the property, the garden and the surrounding area, Mrs Peel nervously trotted behind them to see what they were doing. She was, after all, responsible for the cottage.

When all requirements were met, the contract was signed and Mrs Peel was told that the new renters would arrive late that afternoon. After a polite goodbye, the two men in black drove off in their car.

On Sunday, October 2nd, a helicopter landed in the fields just outside the cottage garden. The ever watchful Mrs Peel was afraid that the violent gusts of wind, caused by the helicopter blades, would destroy the roses, which were still in bloom and indeed, hundreds of rose petals in red, pink, yellow and peach were now swirling through the garden. She held her hands over her eyes in despair. 'Those poor rose bushes and all that noise! And on a Sunday, too!' She thought. Previously, all arrivals at Rose Cottage had been on a Saturday, which she found much more civilised.

"Four men and a woman!" she told Mrs Bertram, the owner, on the phone that night. "There were four men and a woman coming out of that helicopter I say! I'm telling you Mildred, there is something fishy going on in your cottage, there is!"

"Now, now, Hazel, calm down. They're probably rich and famous, you know. Are they Americans?"

"The men I gave the keys to said they were from Switzerland, but they could be famous, yes. They are rich, for sure! The amount of luggage they brought could hold enough to stock Harrods. Fancy going on a holiday and travelling by helicopter! And the men, all dressed in black, you know. It was eerie. Maybe they were bodyguards!"

"Well, keep an eye on them, will you Hazel?"

"Aye, dear, I will. I will keep a close eye on them."

Mrs Peel hung up and took a deep breath. She was very excited. If only her Donny was still alive. How he would have loved having the rich and famous next door. She walked to the kitchen and put the kettle on. While staring through the kitchen window, she could just make out the light from the window at Rose Cottage, half a mile across the field, on the other side of the brook.

Danielle smiled and looked at David with gratitude. "For a safe house, this is actually rather lovely, don't you think?"

"Yes, it is. Alfred did a good job to find us a place that is not only comfortable, but also really nice, but I still can't get used to having those agents around us 24-7. I understand, it's for our own safety. In case our location does leak out, we will need them to protect us and, if necessary, to take us somewhere else."

David Camford ran his hand through his long brown hair. The handsome ex-filmmaker from England - who had just finished a short training program at Sion and was now in charge of Danielle's safety - had to admit that he felt at home here on Guernsey. He understood that the island, being a bailiwick, might not technically be a part of England, but it was still part of the British Crown. Its olde-worlde British atmosphere gave them both a sense of peace and seclusion.

An old atlas tucked away on a shelf in one of the floral-curtained bedrooms helped them identify on a map exactly where they were. David read aloud to Danielle, as if he were reciting a lesson in a classroom.

"Guernsey is the second largest of the Channel Islands after Jersey. These idyllic islands are located south of the British Isles and west of the French coast of Normandy, where the North Sea meets the Atlantic Ocean. It has a mild climate thanks to the warm Gulf Stream and together with Jersey, Herm, Sark and Alderney, Guernsey has become a popular tourist destination."

They both chuckled softly, at the same time comforted by the fact that the location of the cottage had been chosen with extreme care. Danielle was a little over five months pregnant and it was Alfred's intention to keep them there if necessary until after the child was born. In case she needed urgent medical care, the Princess Elizabeth Hospital in St. Andrew was only a short drive from the cottage. No one knew their location but the two of them, the four men they came with and of course, Alfred and Georg. They felt safe and comfortable.

"Look, there is a hearth! Can you make a fire in it tomorrow, David? Please say you will!"

David pursed his lips, but agreed when she threw a cushion at him. In the Corbières region in France, he had lived in a renovated cottage that had a huge, stone fireplace.

"Now, it's time for you to have a rest. It is getting late. If you need anything, you will let me know, won't you?"

Danielle smiled and slowly got up from the seat. So far, her pregnancy hadn't been the easiest one. She had been under a lot of stress and her annoying morning sickness had only disappeared a few weeks before, but recent examinations had given everyone some good news. It was a healthy young girl and as far as they could see, everything was going well. All she had to do was to get plenty of rest and avoid any heavy physical labour. So she obeyed willingly and withdrew to her room. However, as she sat on her bed and had a good look around, a sense of loneliness came over her and she felt somewhat uneasy, so she decided to close the shutters and have a bath with some lavender oil before lying down. The tiny bathroom looked even smaller than it actually was, thanks to its bright, magnolia-coloured carpet and evocative, flowered wallpaper. The free standing, white-enamelled bath with its decorative claw feet made her smile as she pondered on how they had ever got the tub into such a tiny room.

She turned on the tap and started to gather her necessities from her suitcase. When she opened her bijou case, she discovered a small piece of paper rolled up like a piece of parchment and held together with a green ribbon. She carefully untied the knot and unrolled the letter. A tiny dried lily flower fell onto the bed. Immediately she knew where the letter had come from.

Dearest Danielle,
Knowing that you are now in a safe house somewhere in a secret location, smuggling a letter to you will be impossible for me. So when I helped you pack, I took the liberty of putting this into your luggage.
Oh, how I would like to be with you now, my dearest friend.
Know that Bill and I are thinking of you always and that you are in our prayers.
Wherever you are, be well, stay safe, don't do anything I wouldn't do and know that I am with you in spirit always.

*Good luck with the baby! I'm sure everything will go just
fine!*
Many hugs and kisses,
Gabby

Gabby had been her colleague on their last mission* and had
quickly become her best friend. Danielle missed her already
and finding this note with a recent photo of them together in
Sion, meant the world to her. The photo was taken at one of
the musical get-togethers at Alfred's house and they were
both dressed in their long white robes; precious souvenirs
from the time they had spent with the Essenes in ancient
Palestine. She placed the photo against the lamp on the night
table next to her bed.

As Danielle stepped gingerly into the hot bath, she could
smell the aroma of the lavender oil and winced at the sudden
change of temperature. She took a towel, wrapped it around
her long blonde hair to protect it from getting wet and placed
another one under her head to use as a pillow. She sank
deeper into the tub and closed her eyes. Memories of the
summer came back to her out of order. She wondered if
memory was stored in the brain in chronological order, or in
order of the strength of impact of a given experience.
Insignificant events - even recent ones - are always quickly
forgotten, while an important memory from childhood can be
as fresh in one's memory as if it had happened the day
before.
Time is a strange thing.
If events are not registered in chronological order in the
brain, would time itself need to appear in any logical order at
all, anywhere?
Travelling through time had confused her sense of order and
had made her ponder on things she had never given any
attention to before.

*Read 'White Lie' by Jeanne D'Août

Studying with the Essenes and reading about the Hermetic Teachings in books such as the Kybalion had given her insight into larger concepts. She was now much more open to the fact that what she saw is just one of a variety of perceptions. There are many other ways of perceiving an event, or even a tangible object; ways that would surely go beyond Danielle's comprehension. For one, she had to come to terms with the fact that she was carrying the child of a man who had died two thousand years ago. Still, the baby in her womb was very much alive and literally kicking. She looked at her belly. Danielle knew that by now the baby could hear her voice, so she started humming a lullaby, though she had forgotten most of the words. Still, the sweet tune was one she remembered well from her own childhood.

David heard her humming in the bathroom and looked up from his book. Next to him was an unlit pipe and a glass of some fine Irish whiskey he had brought from Sion.

It was a gift from Alfred.

"This bottle of whiskey is 80 years old. It's genuine uisge beatha, 'water of life'. Drink it with respect." Alfred had said earnestly, with a strange glitter in his eyes. David grinned broadly at the memory and wondered how much that bottle had cost, or where on earth Alfred had got it from.

Suddenly, he heard an odd beeping sound, which seemed to come from his jacket. Looking over his shoulder at his olive green, all-weather jacket, he got up from the over-stuffed, worn leather sofa to check the battery of his mobile phone, which was still inside his jacket, but it wasn't the battery. It was the red alert button on a beeper Alfred had given him, to warn him when they would be in danger. David yelled at Danielle to get dressed as quickly as she could. His heart was racing. Their location had already been compromised.

7

Cairo, Egypt, October 3rd 2011

When Otto and Arthur arrived at Cairo International Airport they had no idea what kind of adventure they were heading into. So far it had been a smooth flight in Alfred's private jet. The Learjet had provided them sufficient peace and comfort to sleep for several hours. Otto had noticed the mini bar. He had opened it in search of a cold soda and had noticed the tiny liquor bottles, which were very tempting on this new, exciting adventure into the unknown, but he had resisted opening one. He knew that he needed to keep his head clear. Drinking had brought him nothing but trouble in the past. Being able to find the strength to resist, also made him more self-confident. He had actually found it more difficult to resist the offer of a cigarette from the friendly, but very introverted pilot. After all, he had only stopped smoking a few months ago. However, seeing Arthur's approving smile the moment he had turned down the cigarette had felt like a reward. He loved it when Arthur smiled at him. Getting a display of approval from people he was fond of, helped him through his moments of self-loathing.

Knowing what he knew now about the horrors of World War II had resulted in moments of deep depression. It had taken some time before Alfred trusted him and he was certain that his assistant Georg still didn't. He needed to feel that he was trusted, so he could trust himself. Also, he felt a certain responsibility for young Arthur. This sense of responsibility helped him put on a strong and stable façade, though deep inside, the memories of the Buchenwald concentration camp still haunted him at night in frequent nightmares. He could still hear the screams and other sounds that had turned his entrails to ice. It was as if the sounds had been implanted permanently into his head. He couldn't shut them off and dreaded going to sleep. Alfred knew that deep inside, Otto was still traumatised, so to ensure that Otto would get the rest he needed to successfully complete this job, Alfred had given him a few tablets of Zolpidem, but not many. Otto had tried to kill himself with an overdose of sleeping pills before, while he was in the Austrian Alps in 1939. It would be unwise to tempt fate. Both he and Arthur had slept like a log.

The sign to fasten seatbelts was switched on and the *ping* sound woke them up. There was a breath-taking, orange sunrise and with awe they gazed upon the land of Egypt below them. The adrenaline rushed through their bodies the moment the plane touched down.

They did not have to wait long for their luggage, because they had landed in-between the other airlines. Appearing confident, their 37 year old Egyptian guide Hadi was waiting to help them through customs. Dressed in a loose-fitting, brown and white galabya and white turban, Hadi was short with a round belly and a non-stop smile. In his line of work; guiding foreign businessmen, he had to be assertive, somewhat directive - yet congenial, or he would not keep his clients long. Many other guides and taxi drivers were constantly browsing the airport lobby for possible clients. Like birds of prey, they observed every new arrival closely, ready to solicit the first unsuspecting tourists coming through the door. The moment Otto, Arthur and Hadi stepped into the lobby, two unknown men approached them as though they were old friends. Enthusiastically, they offered them every service a visitor could ever desire. They offered to be their bodyguards and private guides; with the promise to take them to places 'no tourist ever sees', including hard-to-find, inexpensive papyrus shops and cheap rides near the Pyramids. Hadi raised his voice authoritatively, saying something in Arabic which made them retreat instantly. As if he was in a hurry, Hadi immediately took Otto and Arthur to a small restaurant and after an early breakfast of rice with meat, accompanied by vegetables and fruit, they drove off into the chaos that was normal Cairo traffic. Like a frantic computer game player, Hadi manoeuvred his white Mercedes from one lane to another, ignoring all traffic lights. Everyone else did, too. Otto paled and clutched the back of Hadi's seat when they turned a corner without slowing down. Arthur soon realised that having a big breakfast before the road trip may not have been such a good idea after all. Otto stared hard at Hadi; he couldn't believe the way he was driving; leaning over the wheel with his steering hand placed strategically over the horn, which he beeped almost constantly. His left elbow was out of the open window, his hand waving at people who were crossing the street, to get them out of the way. Sometimes he shouted something in Arabic that sounded like an insult. While taking it all in, Otto decided to try something that had been on his wish list for a long time.

"I was hoping there would be a chance to take a small detour and see the Pyramids. How far are they from here?"

Hadi shook his head wildly in utter dismay, fighting back words he knew would not be well received.

"That is a big detour, Mr Adler, they are on the other side of the city. We need to get to Tel-el-Amarna as soon as possible. Mr Zinkler's orders!"

Otto was disappointed. He had dreamed of seeing the Pyramids ever since he had read about the seven wonders of the ancient world in one of his cherished books.

So close and yet...

Hadi didn't really want to talk, so he turned on the radio. When he heard 'Aïcha' by Khaled, he increased the volume and sang along in sounds that mimicked the French, but didn't come close to the song's lyrics. It amused Otto, who spoke French rather well. He even eased his grip on the edge of the seat.

It took them quite a while to get out of the busy traffic and onto the Cairo-Aswan road. Hadi had carefully calculated how far and how fast they needed to go and wanted to reach the car ferry at El-Menia within 4 hours' time, so he speeded up the moment they turned south toward Malawi.

Arthur was totally mesmerised by the passing countryside. How strange, this exotic, parched world, dotted with clumps and groves of huge palm trees. The road traffic seemed to function well, in spite of the utter chaos. He was a bit feverish, probably due to the last minute vaccination back in Sion. This 'cocktail' was a mix of unknown composition that was meant to prevent any exotic illness they might be susceptible to while in Egypt. However, the shot didn't seem to affect Otto as much as it did him. Slowly, his face turned white, then grey and suddenly he shouted, "Stop!"

Hadi hit the brakes and stopped the car at the side of the road. Art pushed open the door, raced out of the car and spent several long minutes retching up his breakfast on the side of the road. Otto looked away; his fingers in his ears so he wouldn't hear it. He could feel his stomach turn.

Always prepared, Hadi gave Arthur a strong mint-flavoured chewing gum and a bottle of water on his return to the car. Arthur felt weak and decided to lie down on the backseat.

About twenty minutes later, Otto too became sick and took his turn emptying his stomach on the road side.

By now, Hadi was getting irritated and mumbled,

"هتافاشـــــــمنزاز،والأجانب"*!

When their stomachs had settled a bit, Arthur and Otto, who now shared the backseat, opened the briefcase that Alfred wanted them to guard with their lives. Inside they found several files. The cover of one file case was made of soft, brown leather and seemed to be the most important one. When they opened it, they saw a file containing print-outs, neatly bound and protected with a white cardboard cover. When they moved it a little, they could make out a title, which was printed in shining silvery letters: 'Lux et Veritas'. In smaller print below it were the words 'A Study of Egyptian Magic'.

Otto and Arthur looked at each other incredulously. "Egyptian Magic? Quick, let's see what's inside!"

*Ugh, foreigners!

58

Impatiently, Otto leafed through the file from back to front and they began to realise that they'd have to read fast to even begin to understand their mission before it started. They now had about 3 hours left to study 50 pages.

Arthur smirked, "We would have been better off with a book called 'Egyptian Magic for Dummies!'

Otto looked at him and frowned. "You think we are dumb?"

"No. No, that's not what I mean. There is actually a series of self-help books called 'For Dummies' which includes 'English for Dummies', 'Math for Dummies' and many more. You haven't seen any of them, have you?

Otto just stared at him blankly.

"Oh never mind."

While the two men were studying the contents of the file, Hadi was keeping an eye on his rear mirror, getting increasingly nervous. He didn't want to say anything until he was completely sure, but after taking two detours which made no sense at all, there was no longer any doubt in his mind. They were being followed.

8

Sion, Switzerland, October 3rd 2011

Alfred felt completely abandoned by the gods. He was staring into the early morning light, still holding Georg's Glock in his hand. Last night he had sent the signal to David on Guernsey, warning them that their location had been compromised. Then he had taken a taxi home, but he couldn't sleep. All through the night he had been tossing and turning in his bed. Was there a curse on this mission? Was this a sign that his desire to possess the Urim and Thummim stones was going a step too far? However, Otto and Arthur were already in Egypt and well on their way to Amarna by now. It was too late to call it off. Still, was it all worth it? He was so afraid for Georg. What would Al Din do to him? Would he recognise Georg as the man who had shot him? Alfred's stomach was churning and he suddenly realised that he would have to face going through surgery alone, with his best friend in danger or worse and everyone else out of reach. He allowed himself to cry.

It was all simply too much for him.

At the same time, on the concrete steps just outside the Eglise du Sacré-Coeur in Sion, a body was found. He seemed to have been placed there gently, lying on his back with his hands on his chest, like a knight. The woman who had found him was aghast. Immediately she had called 112 and within 5 minutes a police car drove onto the sidewalk just off the yellow-striped crosswalk on the Avenue des Mayennets. The moment she saw the two police officers step out of the car, she waved with both arms to attract their attention.

"I always cross the square on my way to work and there he was. First I thought he was a tramp, but then I noticed his fine, black suit. So I thought maybe he had come from a party and was too drunk to go home, but he doesn't want to wake up! I think he's dead!"

One of the police officers checked the man's vital signs. He couldn't feel a heartbeat, but his colleague produced a little mirror and held it close to his nose.

"He's still breathing!"

A few minutes later, an ambulance arrived and one of the emergency care assistants checked the body for bruises and possible wounds, but none were found. He still had his wallet, his mobile phone and his driver's license on him. The police officers looked at the items carefully, hoping to find a home address. Then, one of them found some information on a strange ID. "His name is Georg Hauser. No address though. Check his phone; who's under his speed dial?"

"It just says X. Shall I call the number?"

While the officer tried to reach Mr X, Georg was waking up. From his angle, he saw a red structure that reminded him of a pyramid and a large white building with big windows. He could vaguely distinguish a spooky face - or was it a dove - in the windows. Though he could hear people talking in the distance, the blurry image producing the sound was standing right next to him. "He's waking up! Look!"

"Are you Georg Hauser? Sir? Are you alright?"

Then everything went dark.

Alfred was driving like a madman toward the *Hôpital Regional de Sion*. His mind, too, was racing. He blamed himself for everything that had happened and his emotions jumped from sadness to anger; something he always tried so hard to avoid. By the time he arrived at the room where Georg was undergoing examination, he had a throbbing headache. The doctor carrying out the examining turned to Alfred when he entered the room and immediately noticed that Alfred wasn't well at all, but he decided not to say anything just yet. One patient at a time.

"So, you are Mr X?"

Alfred nodded and returned the doctor's smile. He was amused to learn that Georg had named him Mr X in his mobile phone contact list. "Is he going to be okay?"

The doctor spoke calmly, indicating that any emergency had been averted. "Yes, the drug needs some time to leave his body, so it will take a few more hours before you can take him home. Of course we do have a few questions, if you don't mind."

"I do. I will take him home as soon as he can walk and do not worry about the bill, I will pay it right away, but no questions."

"But, the police will..."

Alfred showed him an ID that made the doctor take a step back.

"Understood, sir! No questions."

Now it was Alfred's turn to take the offensive. "However, I do have a few questions for you, doctor."

The doctor pulled up a chair for Alfred and sat down on another one.

"Doctor, has he been hurt? In any way?"

"Not really. Apart from several needle marks, which indicate that he has been injected several times, we only found a few minor bruises on his arms. This would suggest that he had been taken somewhere against his will and he put up a fight, but he hasn't been hurt in any other way. I also checked the whites of his eyes, but there were no signs that he had suffered a lot of pain; just the effects of a drug that slowed down his heartbeat considerably. The drug would have put him to sleep for at least 8 hours. He has already woken up once, just before he was placed in the ambulance, so we expect him to wake up properly in the next hour or so. He's a little dehydrated though, so we're giving him an intravenous infusion with saline; a water and salt solution. He should feel a lot better soon."

"So they found him on the square of the Eglise du Sacré-Coeur?"

"Yes. He was lying on his back with his hands over his chest. They thought he was dead at first. Do you have any idea who could have done this?"

Alfred got up from his chair. "I'm sorry, I can't answer that."

The doctor, who understood Alfred's unique status from his ID card, also got up from the chair.

"I am sorry, sir, I'm sure you know what is best, but may I perhaps ask if there is any way that I can help you?"

Alfred was taken aback. Was it so obvious that he was ill?

"It's that visible, is it? Well, you are right. I am having surgery for a stomach tumour later this week at the clinic, but I need to look after Georg first. I'm sure you don't mind if I stay here and wait until he wakes up?"

"I'm sure that won't be a problem."

On his way out, the doctor put his hand on Alfred's shoulder. "Good bye sir and eh, good luck!"

"Thank you doctor and thank you for taking care of my number one."

Georg, who had been waking up slowly, had overheard the conversation and was moved by Alfred's last remark; 'his number one'. Georg opened his eyes and turned his head to look at him, but he was alarmed to see Alfred looking so pale. The man was clearly exhausted. When their eyes met, Alfred quickly approached the bed. "How do you feel? What happened? Was it Al Din? Did he hurt you? How much does he know?"

"Wohoho, hang on, give me a minute..." Georg tried to sit up and asked for a glass of water. He drank it down and started to massage his temples, trying to remember what had happened the night before. Most of it he remembered vividly, so he decided to start at the beginning.

"It happened right after I had finished my meal at the airport. I was expecting your call, so I went outside to get more privacy and to stretch my legs. When I was walking toward the parking lot, I noticed that the Lexus was standing in the middle of the road, with its headlights on. I was sure that I had parked it properly, so I was alarmed. I took out my Glock, but before I knew it, the car drove toward me in great speed and I was pulled inside the back of the car. When I looked at my attacker, I recognised him immediately"

"Al Din?"

"Yes, but he was very skinny. Gaunt face, empty, dark eyes - it was as if I was seeing a ghost. It was eerie. He smiled at me and apologised for our rather rough meeting, but he had a few questions for me. If I answered all his questions to his satisfaction, he would let me go. In the meantime we were driving very fast. I saw a tall man with dark hair behind the wheel, but I never saw his face. There was someone sitting in the front seat who was wearing a cap and dark sunglasses. I don't think I would recognise them if I saw them again. It was very dark."

"What did he want?" Alfred persisted.

"What do you think? Of course, I had no intention of telling him anything, so I remembered our emergency plan, giving him answers that would lure him away from Danielle."

Alfred smiled. He and Georg had created an emergency plan in case Danielle's location was ever compromised. If either of them were separately interrogated to betray her location, they would both confess to the same, false one.

"Did he buy it?"

"It wasn't easy. I didn't want to give in too soon, or he would think I was lying. So I played dumb for a while."

Georg fell silent and looked at his folded hands. Never in his life had he been so afraid as he was the moment he recognised Al Din.

He remembered how the car had stopped not far from the train station, realising that this area was quiet and abandoned. He knew that it would be a bad idea to try and flee, so he suppressed the urge to open the car door and run. They would simply shoot him down. He had no choice but to play along and hope for the best.

Al Din, who saw Georg as a loyal soldier, simply doing what he was told, had noticed his heavy breathing and wet brow. Though he hadn't taken it personally that Georg had shot him, Georg didn't know this and Al Din decided to use Georg's fear to his advantage. "Were you happy or sad when you received the news that I didn't die by your cunning shot?"

Al Din looked deep into Georg's eyes. He could see the fear, the abandonment of all hope.

"I don't know where Danielle is, so if you want to kill me, then do it now!"

"Aha, straight to the point! But we will get to that later. You mustn't worry; you didn't kill me, so why would I kill you?" Al Din showed his empty hands. "See? No gun."

Georg looked at the two men in the front seats. On Al Din's command, they also showed their empty hands. Georg noticed the ring on the hand of the driver; It had a big flat, blue stone. He had seen it before, but couldn't quite place it.

"Now, I have asked you a question..." Al Din snared.

"Of course I didn't want to kill you," Georg snapped, "but you were holding Bill hostage and your head was the only thing sticking out from behind the professor, so I had no choice. When we heard the news that you hadn't died, of course we were relieved. What do you think we are, assassins?"

Al Din smiled. "That is good to hear, my friend. Now, about Danielle. Of course you know where she is. You are your master's right hand. You do everything for him."

"That is not true! He does many things in secret and doesn't share everything with me! I tell you, I don't know where Danielle is!"

Al Din grabbed Georg's chin; his face was now only an inch away from Georg.

"I know you know! No more games! Where is she?"

Georg could feel a shower of spit on his face. He wasn't going to give in so soon, but was worried about what Al Din would do next. He closed his eyes and remained silent.

"You are not making this easy for us, or for yourself. If you do not speak, you will leave me no choice."

Al Din opened a small suitcase and took out a syringe. He pushed the needle into a small bottle and drew the clear liquid up into the syringe. Georg panicked and tried to open the car door, but it was locked.

"Ha, you thought you could escape? Come now, let's not be foolish. The contents of this syringe is lethal. Oops, I guess I lied about not killing you. So, dear man, if you could be so kind as to tell me where Danielle is, then I will put the syringe away. If you do not tell me, you will give me no choice but to inject you with liquid death. It won't hurt, it's just a mild sting and then, sleep. Eternal sleep."

Al Din grabbed Georg's arm and pulled up his sleeve. Georg tried to free himself, but Al Din was stronger than he thought.

"Alright, alright, I will tell you!"

The needle had already pricked his skin, but Al Din pulled it out quickly.

"A wise decision, my friend. Now, where can I find the pretty Danielle?"

"You mean, when! She is not here in this time. She is in another time and you will never find her!"

"And I should believe that? Mr Zinkler would never risk Danielle's baby by sending her through a wormhole again! I know she is in the present. Now, tell me where!"

Again Al Din pricked his skin and threatened to inject the lethal fluid into his vein. Georg was struggling and panting and noticed the drops of blood on his arm. Struggling with Al Din had already given him multiple wounds from the needle, so he decided to sit still and activate plan B.

"Norway. She is in Norway! In a large, yellow house in Filtvet in southern Buskerud. Now let me go!"

Al Din was pleased. That sounded very genuine indeed. He could also see that Georg was very upset about the 'betrayal'. The man was close to tears.

"Alright, I believe you, but remember, if she is not there, I will come back and next time I will not be such a gentleman."

The car drove off toward the city centre. Georg was relieved. Al Din had bought it, but to make him believe he was genuinely upset about betraying Danielle's location, he had to keep up the show.

He put his hands in front of his face and started to moan. When they drove into a small, quiet street, Georg thought he was being released. The driver got out of the car and opened the door for him. When Georg wanted to step out of the car, Al Din jumped at him with the syringe and injected him in the side of his neck. Georg collapsed almost immediately. The next thing he remembered was waking up in the square in front of the Church of the Sacred Heart.

Alfred took a deep breath. "My God, Georg, you are stronger than you thought! If that syringe was meant to kill you and you are still alive, they must have overestimated the dose."
"Yes, I know, I was lucky! He doesn't know anything, so I guess you can contact David and let him know that it's safe to stay at the cottage."
Alfred nodded and took his mobile. "David? Your location is still secure, so there's no immediate need to relocate, but stay alert. Al Din is out there looking for Danielle. He thinks you're in Norway though... Oh don't ask! Yes, well, you know how to reach me or Georg if something comes up. Back to Plan A. Keep your heads down!"
Alfred nodded resolutely and then hung up. One situation solved - hopefully the rest would go more smoothly. However, Alfred didn't know that he was very much mistaken.

On the other side of town, Al Din and his two accomplices checked the laptop that was in front of them.
"Cloning his mobile phone is one thing, but tracking a number in his mobile phone is incredibly clever. Well done! Now, where's my baby? *Where is my baby?"*
Al Din licked his lips and grinned broadly when a tiny light finally lit up on the map on the screen.
"Gotcha! I've always wanted to visit the Channel Islands! Yalla! Let's go! A gentleman never keeps his lady waiting."

9

Guernsey, Channel Islands, October 3rd 2011
David and Danielle enjoyed their breakfast outside on the terrace. It had been a stressful night. They had been on high alert ever since the alarm had gone off the evening before, but after Alfred's phone call to David earlier that morning, they could now finally relax. As long as Al Din didn't know where they were, Rose Cottage was still a safe place to hide. Two of Alfred's agents were keeping an eye on the surroundings and some high-tech equipment had been installed, that was part of an intricate alarm system. If anyone weighing over 80 pounds were to come within a 200 meter radius of the house, the alarm would go off. There was also a heat sensor - picking up suspicious movement - and a smoke sensor. Cameras were placed to monitor almost all corners of the house and the gardens. No one could come close to them without being noticed.

It was a lovely, sunny autumn day and the blackbirds were still singing their beautiful, unique songs. Especially at this time of year, the mild climate of the Channel Islands attracted many tourists from England, who would spend a midweek break or a long weekend on one of the islands. Danielle planned on taking care of the rose garden after breakfast. The poor roses had taken quite a beating from the strong gusts of wind created by the helicopter blades, but the scent that was coming from the roses and the rose petals was divine. The heavenly scent was perceptible even in the house. "You can't keep me indoors all the time, I'll go bonkers," she said to David, who shook his head in calm but definite disagreement.
"Danielle, until I know we are completely safe here, I would rather have you close to the house. The rose garden is in front of the cottage and too exposed. Here, at the terrace behind the cottage, it's more private."

Danielle sighed. He was right, of course. Al Din was out there and although he and his men were probably on their way to Norway by now, no one could guarantee that they were really safe, but Danielle loved the roses, especially the old ones with their exquisite perfumes.

"I'm sure it's safe. Please, David, indulge in me?"

Danielle pursed her lips like a little girl asking for an ice-cream.

"Okay, but I am coming with you. Besides, I wouldn't want you to do any heavy physical work. You know what the doctor said; take it easy."

"Don't worry, I'll do the cutting while you do the sweeping. Oh and you can carry my basket."

David smiled. She loved his smile and right now she felt as if she could drown in his light-brown eyes. However, the intensity of the spark ignited between them at that moment, took them both by surprise. She was the first to look away.

Half an hour later, both were out in the rose garden and Danielle was in seventh heaven. She admired and examined every rose bush, made some necessary cuttings and checked the name tags to see if she recognised any of them. As a hopeless romantic she had always loved red roses, but some of the pinks and yellows in this garden were absolutely sublime. She was first attracted to a dark yellow rose called *Amber Queen* and the stunning red *Invincible*, which was still in flower. Another one that was still in flower was *Abraham Darby,* trained against the wall not far from the scented pink tea rose called *Catherine Mermet.* On the other side she recognised *Crimson Shower,* doing exactly what the name suggested.

"May I borrow your pruner for a minute?" David had a mysterious smile on his face as he asked and half a minute later he came back with a bunch of beautiful pink roses that had no thorns. Danielle blushed as he handed them to her.

"Oh I know these! They're *Zephirine Drouhin*. My mother had them in her garden because they were safe for children. No thorns. Thank you darling!"

She went into the house and put them in a vase. David was right behind her. Once she had put the vase on the kitchen table, he embraced her and pressed his lips gently on her neck to plant a subtle kiss. In her ear he whispered sweetly, "You are beautiful like a rose."

David could feel how her heart was racing. He took a few steps backwards to give her some space and said, "You don't have to love me back. Just let me love you."

Danielle stared into his eyes and tried to think of something to say, but couldn't think of anything that would make sense. She felt the spark and was aroused by his kiss, but she was still not sure whether she was in love, or whether it was perhaps just a crush. She knew only too well that David was an alluring, yet quite enigmatic man.

David Camford had always been unusually handsome, even as a boy. Bright and well-educated, he had followed his dreams and became involved in creating films. Success followed and his work was internationally acclaimed. He had married the 'love of his life' and they had a son, Michael, but as a filmmaker in constant demand, he had always been too busy and too involved with his career to devote enough time to his marriage and family. It had put a lot of pressure on the relationship and when his wife discovered that he had had an affair with another woman, she ended the marriage and their relationship. Within several months they were divorced. That time in their lives was extremely painful, especially for David, because he no longer lived with his 18-year-old son, whom he missed terribly. Michael was studying in England and could only see his father on holidays.

The divorce had affected David deeply, making him think about starting over. He wanted to start a new life in another country, but not too far from his son. After months of searching, he had found a business to run; a charming Bed & Breakfast - complete with holiday cottage and small campsite - in southern France. He had bought it on a whim, but had never looked back.

David had felt something there that he simply couldn't find in England; an inner peace and a particular energy that was present in that area. Living in such an historical part of southern France had even inspired him to take up a new hobby: researching the enigma of the Knights Templar.

Thankfully, Michael too loved it there and together they had explored many mysterious caves and historic sites to their heart's content. Their worlds had once again become a joyful place. However, their worlds were about to follow a whole new course that last summer, when David and Michael became involved in a fantastic adventure with SBS-Sion and its secret mission to find certain lost relics in southern France.*

During this adventure, David had turned out to be of great help to Alfred, who had offered him a position at SBS-Sion in July. The downside had been that he had to sell the house in France and move to Sion, Switzerland. Once in Sion, David had followed a training course to become an agent and had worked closely with Danielle. He vividly remembered the day they had met in Rome, which was also the moment he had fallen head over heels in love with her.

Falling in love with Danielle wasn't difficult. The blonde beauty was not only one of the brightest, but also one of the sweetest women he had ever met. However, Danielle held a very precious secret that only a few people shared. Her secret was linked to her pregnancy and he could see that this was the reason she had initially kept her distance from him. Though he was curious to know, David never asked.

His acceptance of her mysterious circumstances, however, seemed to make her feel more at ease with him. He also could see that this new environment was having a relaxing effect on her. Perhaps one day she would let him into her secret world. His brave first move certainly seemed to have some affect. Danielle knew that there was only one way to find out if she really loved him:

*Read: 'White Lie' by Jeanne D'Août

She had to give him a 'kiss of life'. Her belly would reveal the truth. Slowly she put her arms around his neck. She let her cheek touch his cheek and her nose touch his nose, until finally their lips met. A soft, tender kiss was repeated until she allowed him to kiss her more passionately. This kiss of life changed Danielle's feelings toward David from a mild crush to erotic desire and complete surrender.

Then suddenly, David stopped. "We mustn't go too far."

Danielle nodded; her face was as red as David's and while turning around she said shyly, "Thanks again for the roses."

She walked back to the rose garden, knowing David would follow. He would follow her until the end of time.

Michael Camford, David's son, was in his final year at college. He felt fortunate that his father had supported his choice to study geography, history, languages and philosophy at the UCL (University College of London), but he wasn't too sure about the kind of job he would find once graduated. He figured things would all fall into place once he had his diploma. Right now, he was taking advantage of a school break and was trying to get his head around some rather complicated details in several subjects for upcoming tests, though he realised that his passion for his chosen field made studying for it almost effortless. He created works of art when he was only asked to write a thesis and most of his teachers were proud of the work he had produced so far.

Michael was highly intelligent and like many intelligent people, he bored quickly with repetitive work. At times, those people could fall into deep depressions. Also, Michael tended to be short on patience when working with people who didn't grasp ideas or concepts as quickly as he did. Being the only child of divorced parents didn't make things any easier either. He had long held it against his father for having an affair with another woman than his mother and it had taken him two years before he could get back to speaking terms with his father again. Once back on speaking terms, the relationship between Michael and his father slowly began to build again and in the following years he had enjoyed spending his summer vacations with David in southern France. So when Michael got the news that David had sold the place and had moved to Sion, he was astounded and somehow construed it as another form of betrayal. It had led to another falling-out with his father.

The previous weekend, David - in an effort to reach out to his son again - had called, but had only reached his voice mail. He had hoped that Michael would pick up the phone, for he also needed to tell Michael that from October 2nd onward he'd be away on a classified mission and that he might be unreachable for several months, but Michael hadn't answered the phone. He still felt too betrayed to take his father's calls. How could he have sold their father-son paradise in the Corbières? He was broken hearted over it. However, Michael often replayed the message his father had left on his phone,

"I know you are still mad at me, Michael, but this was a job opportunity I couldn't refuse. I too loved it in France and yes, I too felt sad having to sell the place. All I ask is that you try to understand that sometimes, life presents once in a lifetime opportunities that require a sacrifice. I had to make that sacrifice. I had to choose that path. My heart dictated it and I had to listen. I..., I am going away for a while and I want you to know that you won't be able to reach me for a while, possibly 4 or 5 months. I wanted to hear your voice, hear you say that it's okay, that you forgive me. I am leaving in a few hours, so please, would you call me a.s.a.p.? You know I love you son."

Michael hadn't returned the call and it was now Monday. He knew, that if he were to call his father now, he probably wouldn't be able to pick up the phone. He didn't even know where he was, what mission he was on or whether that mission was even safe. He knew the SBS-Sion from his own experience, several months ago. He too had been part of the relic hunting adventure in France with his friends.

They had all had such an amazing time and he so missed it. Then suddenly it struck him; he missed his father. His love proved to be stronger than his anger, so Michael grabbed his mobile and dialled his father's number, only to find out that his presentiment was right; it was too late. All he heard was the irritating sound of a number that has been disconnected. Michael couldn't believe that he wasn't able to reach his own father and dialled again, only to hear the same sound again. Was he supposed to just sit and wait until his father reappeared? The situation was insane; intolerable. It was as if his father had disappeared from the face of the earth.

10

Sion, Switzerland, October 3rd 2011

Professor Wong Chi-kit was not in his apartment. All night long he had been in the laboratory, checking recalculations. Why was he being pursued by a tiny whisper of doubt in his mind? Everything had been calculated, recalculated and tested. Why would he find a flaw in his calculations now? The mission had already started and his mobile ERFAB devices were now in Egypt with Hadi, Otto and Arthur, but the nagging whisper in his mind wouldn't rest until he was absolutely sure that his calculations were, after all, correct.

Then, suddenly, from the corner of his eye, he saw it and for a nanosecond, he froze. Then his body jerked as a nerve sting went straight through it. One digit on the far end of a calculation - many digits behind the last comma - didn't match the return data. He had looked for it all night on a sickening gut feeling, but now that he had found it, he felt even worse. Why hadn't he looked there first? Why did this tiny discrepancy have to be the source of such cruel truth? This seemingly minuscule difference in data could result in Hadi, Otto and Arthur disappearing into a completely different dimension altogether, but then why had Alfred re-appeared without any problem when the devices were first tested? Perhaps the flaw was not something inter-dimensional, but connected to the geographical coordinates? Perhaps it was just an inch. If that were the case, then it would not be such a problem.

Wong left the lab and returned to his private apartment, where he let himself fall backwards onto his bed like a felled tree. He rubbed his eyes and groaned. Maybe it was better to just keep this to himself for now.

Later that day, Alfred and Georg left the hospital together to return to the manor house in the hills just outside Sion. Georg was still feeling a little lightheaded, but tried to hide it as he felt that Alfred had enough problems of his own to deal with right now. However, Alfred wasn't blind. Nevertheless, Alfred had his mind set on going back to the base as soon as possible, in case Otto and Arthur succeeded in retrieving the Urim. If they were successful, they would press the 'home' button on their devices and arrive at the base in Sion that same night at 19.00 hours, even if a week had passed in ancient Egypt. If they were not successful, they would simply get back to present day Amarna and contact the Sion base that same evening - as soon as they'd have the chance - for further instructions. In either case, he wanted to be at the base that night.

Alfred turned to Georg and put his hand on his shoulder. "Georg, I am going to the base, but I want you to stay here and rest. I will ask Melissa to cook you a proper lunch. When you feel up to it, please join me."

Georg nodded. He knew he probably only needed a few hours of rest and some good food to get his strength back, but he felt ashamed to see Alfred leave without him. Georg had come to realise how important he had become to Alfred, when he had overheard him calling him his 'number one' back at the hospital.

As soon as he was alone, Georg walked further into the room and allowed himself to stretch out on the soft, brown leather of the 3-seater Chesterfield sofa, while pushing a soft pillow under his head. He didn't have much time to rest. In the distance he could already hear Melissa's footsteps approaching the living room. Alfred's housekeeper was also an amazing cook. "Ah, there you are." she said, "Alfred said you'd be here. Shall I make you an omelette with cheese and mushrooms? That would help put some colour back into your cheeks!"

Melissa smiled and walked right back out, without waiting for Georg's response and singing loudly. He wanted to shout after her that he'd rather have some soup and bread, but she had already gone. Her perpetual good mood amused him. How nice it must be to always be in a good mood.

Georg was very thirsty after his ordeal and looked around to see if he could spot a decanter of water somewhere, but all he saw was a closed liquor cabinet. Maybe there was a decanter of water in the cabinet? Georg got up from the sofa, but was suddenly struck by dizziness. He sat down again and held his head between his knees to avoid fainting. This wasn't good. He realised he'd better lie down again and try to get some sleep, but as soon as he was comfortable, he became inordinately cold. He had goose bumps all over and his feet and hands were as cold as ice. Didn't Alfred have a plaid somewhere? He looked around for it, until his eye fell on a painting on the wall that he hadn't noticed before. It was a striking painting of a large format, but it didn't seem to be an original. The bigger part of the scene was a blue sky with a few clouds. The landscape was dry and desert like, with small villages in the distance. On the left, a man appeared to be looking for something. The man was painted in an unusual way that suggested one of Dalí's works, but this was certainly not one of his famous works, or at least nothing Georg had ever seen.

Now completely absorbed by the painting, Georg tried to get up to get a closer look. Aha! He was right! A small card next to the painting revealed the title and the artist.

It was indeed a Salvador Dalí and the painting was called, *'The Chemist of Ampurdan in Search of Absolutely Nothing [1936]'*. What on earth would be Alfred's fascination with this print? The idea intrigued him. It could mean that whatever we are searching for in our lives is merely a means to create a goal to keep us going, giving us a reason to continue the struggle of life. Humans need a purpose - something to create or something to look forward to. Everyone needs something that gives meaning to our lives. As soon as we die, that goal is gone. The goals we create only exist in our minds and only serve for the duration of our lifetime. Some people, who have no idea what to do or what to look for, feel lost. Their lives are meaningless to them, so we keep searching, not always having a clear idea of what to look for, but finding the search itself sufficiently fulfilling. Georg smiled. Alfred could perhaps be called a searcher; his search for the truth and for special historically significant items - among which, relics of incredible value - was his *raison d'être,* but he could never share his findings with the world. His search for the truth may be important to him, but what good would it do if he could never share it? Because whatever significant knowledge that Alfred had gained access to in his life would die with him, and Alfred was very ill indeed. Would Alfred see himself as the chemist in the painting? A man in an ardent search of absolutely nothing? Maybe that was the reason why he had adopted the pregnant Danielle as his heir, being without a child himself. Now, his legacy would be kept in the family and SBS-Sion would continue, even after his death.

Georg was jolted from his thoughts when the door opened. Still humming the same song, Melissa came in, carrying a large tray. On it, Georg could see a plate covered with a silver bowl, a teapot and a cup.
"Here you are, Mr Hauser. A nice omelette with some Emmental cheese and mushrooms and your favourite tea as well. I have already put the sugar in the pot."
"Thank you Melissa, but please, call me Georg. How long have we known each other now? Five years?"
"Five years it is, Mr Hauser, but it's probably wiser to stick to the protocol. You know how dear Mr Zinkler Senior felt about protocol."
Georg knew all too well how strict Alfred's father had been when it came to company policy, house rules and protocol and he certainly found Alfred much easier to work with, but Melissa, who had been with Alfred's father for 8 years, had found it hard to accept his passing on. Not much had changed since Alfred had taken over, but the distance between Georg and Mr Zinkler Senior had been much greater than the distance between Georg and Alfred. Perhaps because they were of the same generation.

Although the adventures they'd shared had brought them closer, there was still a lot about Alfred that Georg did not know. Alfred always had a certain air of mystery about him. His family background, leading back to the first Grandmaster of the Knights Templar; Hugues de Payens, could be seen in Alfred's coat of arms. The holdings, the vast amount of family capital, his carte blanche ways when travelling and the obvious respect he commanded from certain institutions and organisations, while remaining in all aspects so humble and discreet, made Alfred look like an interesting person indeed. All operations were secret. Even Georg sometimes felt as if he was some kind of a 00 agent, who didn't exist in the outside world. His entire life had been absorbed by Alfred and the SBS-Sion. Georg smiled; it certainly beats the boring office job.

The omelette was delicious, as was the Darjeeling tea which had exactly the right amount of sugar added to it, just as Georg liked it. After the meal, he no longer felt cold or dizzy. He pushed a chair toward the window and decided to sit there for a while, just until he felt strong enough to drive to the base to join Alfred. He had always enjoyed that view. He could gaze at that gorgeous valley amid the high mountains, the city of Sion with its ruined castle of Tourbillon and the old fortified rock church of Valère all day. This corner of the world had become his home. His life was now rooted in it. As the light outside faded into a deep orange sunset, Georg slowly but surely nodded off and sank in a deep sleep.

Meanwhile at the base, Alfred couldn't believe that Wong had been fast asleep in his apartment and not on guard in the lab, keeping an eye on the ERFAB and staying close to the communication centre, as he had been instructed to do. Little did he know that Wong had worked all night. The professor wasn't at all ready to share his alarming discovery of the tiny flaw in his calculations with anyone just yet, so without speaking a word and still dizzy from his short nap, Wong quietly followed the irritated Alfred into the lab, where he returned to his post behind the communication centre. Now he was alone with Alfred. The silence was deafening and he could hear his own tummy rumble. He had missed breakfast as well as lunch and wasn't sure when or if he would get dinner. The loss of sleep on top of the lack of food and drink enhanced the panic he had been feeling ever since he had discovered the flaw and if Alfred hadn't been so angry with him, he would have asked permission to order a sandwich and something to drink. How on earth could he last another few hours in this condition? However, Wong didn't have to wait long to get the answer to that question. Alfred was just about to call Georg to see how he was doing when it happened. In one smooth move, Wong slipped from his chair and hit the floor.

11

A few miles south of Memphis, Egypt, October 3rd 2011
Otto had stopped speaking mid-sentence. The car was now driving far too fast to his liking and the bumps in the road made it impossible for them to read the files.
"My God man, slow down!"
However, Hadi didn't react. If anything, he drove even faster. Arthur and Otto quickly put their seat belts on, just in case.
"What's the matter with you!" Otto barked at Hadi.
"We are being followed, Mr Adler. Not good!"
Otto and Arthur both turned and looked through the rear window. They could see a military land rover approaching them at top speed. It was undoubtedly going to catch up with them in just a matter of minutes.
Arthur faced forward again and stared blankly at the back of Hadi's seat. "It's an Army land rover. What would those guys want with us?"
Hadi was now transpiring terribly, as he knew he couldn't outrun them. He decreased his speed and put his arm through the open window, signalling them to overtake, but as he had feared, they didn't want to overtake. Instead, they signalled to him to stop the car. When both cars drove side by side, one of the soldiers shouted something in Arabic. Although Otto and Arthur couldn't understand the words, it was clear that it was an order. Hadi had no choice but to pull over. The disgruntled soldier who was sitting behind the wheel began with broad gesticulations, "Idiot! Why were you driving so fast? We couldn't keep up with you!"
Hadi rubbed his face. "Damn, Ashraf, I couldn't see it was you. You should wash your windshield!"
"Urgh! On these roads it wouldn't make any difference! Who is in your car?"
"Just two tourists. They want to see the town of the heretic pharaoh at Tel el-Amarna. We are already late!"
The two soldiers peered inside and studied the pale faces of Arthur and Otto, who had no idea what was going on.

Neither of them spoke Arabic, so they were visibly nervous. They looked at Hadi for reassurance, but Hadi still wore a worried look. Satisfied that the tourists were not a threat, the over-zealous soldier waved his hand. "Okay, you can go, but we will be following you for your own protection. You know Amarna isn't safe! Yalla, on your way!"

The two soldiers returned to their dust-covered car, regretting they hadn't thought of asking them money.

Otto and Arthur watched them go with a sigh of relief, but when Hadi tried to start the engine, it wouldn't respond. He tried again and again, but the engine only made a hoarse coughing sound. The two soldiers stepped out of their vehicle and approached cautiously, as if fearing a cleverly planned trap. Tension was rising, along with the sun. It was getting hot. With the engine off, the air-conditioning was also off. Otto reached for his water and immediately the soldiers grabbed their rifles and aimed at him. Otto, unable to resist a violent flashback from his pre-war years in Germany, reacted with anger. "It's only water! Look, du Missgeburt!"

Arthur, who understood German, couldn't suppress a smile when he heard him swear, though calling the guy a 'bastard' seemed a bit risky. Hopefully they wouldn't understand. However, now the soldiers were now looking at him. "What's so funny huh? Do share it with us! Out of the car! Now!"

Everybody stepped out of the car and, as if they were used to it, raised their arms into the air, showing the soldiers that no one was armed. While one soldier, a man with mirroring sunglasses and a cigarette in his mouth, held Otto and Arthur at gunpoint, the man called Ashraf decided to talk to Hadi alone and took him aside. Hadi couldn't suppress his anger.

"What the fuck, Ashraf!"

"I don't trust you, Hadi. I never have. You are up to something, I can feel it in my little toe. Tourists are dressed in colourful clothes, carry cameras and listen to their iPods. These people here seem to me to be businessmen. Look, an expensive leather briefcase, very fine quality indeed; no photo cameras; no video cameras; no iPhones... We have been following you for the past half hour and we know you saw us from the very beginning. We know because it was at that point you suddenly started to drive like a madman on the main road. So tell me, why did you try to get rid of us? You are up to something."

"No, I am not, believe me. I picked them up from the airport. They want to see Tel el-Amarna. You are right, they are businessmen, but businessmen go on road trips too you know!"

Ashraf looked at Hadi, staring deep into his eyes until Hadi looked away. "What do you want, man?" said Hadi, while staring at the horizon.

"I want to be your clients' bodyguard. It's 100 dollars, per day, per person. You know the drill."

"And what do I get in return for that?"

Ashraf spat on the sandy desert ground and then declared, as if signing up for a military mission, "We will make sure that nobody comes close to you or your clients. We will guard you and watch out for you like hawks. You don't have to worry about anyone at the site who would want to try to steal from you; try to sell you something; beg you for money or bar your entry. Really, you know how annoying these things can be. Your guests can visit the site without being bothered and we can personally guarantee your safety. Come to think of it, I might even ask you a little more for all this. It's quite a service we are offering you!"

Hadi knew there was no getting around this deal. "No, no, 100 dollars per person, per day. You got it, but don't come too close, give them some air, okay?"

Ashraf smiled broadly, showing his plaque covered, cigarette-stained teeth. He knew Hadi would get it at some point. The men surreptitiously exchanged some banknotes and Hadi slid back into his car. Carefully, he turned the key in the ignition and this time it started immediately. Ashraf nodded and Arthur and Otto quickly climbed back into the car.

The moment the doors were closed, Ashraf slapped on the car roof as a sign that they could take off. Hadi drove slowly, allowing the soldiers to catch up.

Otto and Arthur, who had both noticed the exchange of money, were very nervous about what kind of negotiations Hadi had been carrying out with the soldiers.

"Why did you pay them, Hadi?"

"Let me do my work, Mr Adler. I will take you to Amarna, don't worry."

Hadi turned the music back on as a sign that the conversation was over.

Arthur looked at the files again. That was some amazing stuff. Never before had he thought of Egypt the way he did now. The descriptions of some of the culture, magic, rituals and way of life of the ancient Egyptians had been a real eye opener for him. Some of the text was almost poetic. The author must have been completely taken by the sheer beauty of ancient Egyptian life, but then a thought struck him; the author was probably Alfred himself.

It all started with that one sentence that had seized their attention immediately:

The ancient Egyptians didn't have a word for religion.

That alone had made them think about how the world had changed in these past few thousand years. To be able to understand what the ancient Egyptians believed in, you would have to unlearn everything you had learned so far and re-emerge with an open mind in the north-African desert, where one large river was the source of life and the sun was a constant during the day in its path from east to west. The stars and planets were clearly visible in the night sky for all to see and study. Nature was their school, their life, the mirror image of the gods. It was only normal that the spirits of the natural world were one with the spirits of their gods. As below, so above.

In Egyptian mysticism and magic, All is One and One is All. Everything around us is part of a whole. Therefore, all the deities they worshipped were also part of the One and they discovered that the earth and the heavens act one upon the other. They knew that everything - whether it is a sound or a solid rock - is energy, vibrating at a frequency. Therefore, speaking The Word held power beyond imagination, as it is a means to create.

In mysticism, The Forgotten Word is related to the secret name of the supreme god of ancient Egypt. Only Isis knew his secret name and drew immense power from this knowledge. To know the Forgotten Word or The Lost Word, one had to be initiated into the mysteries of Isis and Thoth. Thoth, patron of all magicians, was the Master of the Divine Words, he who acts as an interpreter to all the gods. His eyes - drawn on the forehead or worn on a headband - would make the wearer able to communicate with the gods. It would make him or her a visionary prophet.

Otto enthusiastically pointed to a part of the text and explained, "Look, it says here: 'Thoth, guardian of wisdom, inventor of the sacred language, astronomer and mathematician, was also the healer of the Eye of Horus. The black, left eye of Horus, also known as the *wadjet,* represents the moon, while the white, right eye of Ra represents the sun. The phases of the moon have given the eye of Horus the reputation of being un-whole until it was healed [full moon] by Thoth. The healed eye is called *wedjat.'"*

Musing as he remembered the myriad of myths he had studied, Otto added, "It reminds me of a Nordic myth, in which Odin sacrificed one eye for a single drink of the enchanted water from Mimir's well, located under the roots of the tree of life called Yggdrasil. The knowledge of the cycles of the sun, the moon, the stars and the earth as they move through the Universe is often hidden in myth and legend."

Arthur, who knew that Otto was an expert on Nordic myth and legend, was aware of the tale, but he hadn't made that connection himself. He felt privileged to be with him and to be on this unique mission, which had proven to be extremely educational so far. He hadn't thought that he'd ever be driving through Egypt, studying Egyptian magic. He looked out of the window into the dusty, desert landscape, but within seconds his curiosity drew him to back to the files.

Reading slowly - relishing every word - Arthur mouthed the words on the page,

"Magic is the essential energy of all of God's secret names and magic is in everything. Spirit and matter are woven from the same substance."

It made them both think that perhaps the ancient Egyptians called the vibrating frequency of energy; 'magic'?

According to the teachings that were written down for the 10th dynasty pharaoh Merikare, mankind was given the knowledge of magic to repel the thunderbolt of what is to come, to see the future and act upon that knowledge. In short, mankind was given the gift of divination. The quality of the 'divinator' is, however, directly linked to the quality of his heart. It is therefore important to develop intuition and a devout lifestyle. Magic, therefore, was above all a sacred science.

The sacred square or sacred cube that is sometimes attached to magic, consists of 64 squares; a perfect number which can still be divided by the sacred number 7. The 64 squares represent the mosaic of possible destinies, but in ancient Egypt, the sum was 63/64.

For one part was always left to magic.

The ancient Egyptians believed in the power of the *Peret Kherou:* 'that which comes forth at the voice'. They believed that words were even capable of giving life to matter, because a word cuts through the emptiness like a sword and opens up the path to the forces of life.

Otto and Arthur noticed a hieroglyph, that looked like a long, wavy line with a hand attached to its end. It was the hieroglyph for magic.

"The wavy line must represent the vibrating frequency of energy, while the hand represents the act; the deed. I have seen this before, but I cannot remember where." Otto leafed through the files until he found the image of one of the steles of Akhenaten and Nefertiti. They were both sitting down, playing with their daughters. Above them was the Aten disc and coming from the Aten disc were wavy lines with either an ankh or a hand attached to its end.

"Here it is, Arthur! Right here. Do you see it? The sun, Aten-Ra, gives off life and thus, magic. Vibrations coming off the sun, giving warmth, light and life. This magic is as old as the Universe itself. They must have understood the qualities of the sun's rays in a much deeper sense than most people do today."

They returned to the page they were studying before.

'Magic is the fluid that awakens bodies and animates everything on earth and in heaven. Understanding how nature works is the key to understanding magic. Magic demands attention, discipline, sensitivity and courage. Magic is one of the three arrows of illumination, together with alchemy and astronomy. Thoth, equipped with magical powers, knows how to open the sealed magical papyri, which have been written by his hand.

Isis, the daughter and consort of Ra; the Eye of Ra; the one who knows his secret name, is the queen of magic. She relates in many ways to Sophia, who is honoured as the goddess of wisdom by Gnostic Christians. The original Egyptian name for Isis - which is in fact her Greek name - is Auset [throne]. The throne is also the hieroglyph for Isis, symbolising the power she can exert upon the earth. In Jewish mysticism, the Throne became the Chariot, known as the Merkabah.

Seeking knowledge and wisdom to aid our understanding of that what is above [the metaphysical] and that what is below [the physical] is an on-going attempt of mankind to marry religion, spirituality and science into a whole new concept of study. For now, however, the magic of Isis is still beyond the comprehension of mankind. As is written in ancient texts:

I am all that is and ever will be
and no mortal has ever lifted my veil'.

Otto stared out without looking. In a soft voice, he slowly repeated what he had just read.
"I am all that is and ever will be and no mortal has ever lifted my veil. I wonder, Art, if science will ever be able to fathom her..."

12

Guernsey, Channel Islands, October 3rd 2011

All was well in David's world. Danielle had finally returned his love, but he knew it would take time for her to open up to him completely. However, apart from Danielle, there was another loved one tugging his heart; his son Michael had not returned his call. The thought that he might not be able to talk to him for months was simply too much for him to bear. Since he had had no choice but to change his mobile phone and number for this safe house mission, he felt helplessly out of touch with his son, who would not be able to reach him, even if Michael would be in trouble. Maybe he already was. Those thoughts kept re-emerging, though he repeatedly fought them back, reminding himself that Michael wouldn't easily get mixed up in anything. Still, London was a city of many temptations, especially for young adults like Michael. They hadn't spoken for weeks.

Of course, his ex-wife didn't want to interfere either. David could still remember their phone conversation word for word: "This is your own problem, David, I will have nothing to do with it." she had said defensively, over-articulating each word. "You seem to forget that you cannot always place your own priorities above those you love, without hurting them."

Though it was painful to hear, she was undoubtedly right. He understood perfectly that from another perspective, his decision might appear selfish, but this opportunity had been presented to him as a once in a lifetime chance. Working alongside the heir of Hughues de Payens was a dream come true. Alfred had also been a most generous person to work for. His wages were considerably greater than what he could have hoped for, compared to running a B&B for the rest of his life. With this salary he could pay for whatever university anywhere in the world that his son might wish to attend, making Michael's educational dreams come true. This wasn't only about him; it was also about Michael's wellbeing. Though desperately wanting to reach out to his son, David was aware that using his mobile phone to call any number other than Alfred's was strictly prohibited and for good reason. It would give away their position and make it immediately possible for Al Din to find them. David knew he could go into town and use a public phone, but then he'd have to leave Danielle alone for a while. He was torn between his loyalty to his highly secure mission and the gnawing urge to call his son. Then suddenly, an opportunity arose.

Mrs Peel was a curious woman who was dying to find out more about the mysterious guests in the cottage next door. Besides, she had promised Mrs Bertram, the owner of Rose Cottage, that she would keep a close eye on them. At half past one in the afternoon she decided to walk over and ask how they were doing, knowing for sure she'd be back home by teatime.

Danielle spotted her approaching in the distance.

"David, we have company."

With a jolt of slight panic, David looked up, but calmed down the moment he saw that it was only the widow Mrs Peel. He momentarily punished himself mentally for having been lost in thought and not noticing the approaching visitor, but immediately considered the opportunity at hand.

He could use her mobile phone, if she had one.

"Mrs Peel, how lovely to see you!"

Danielle waved and walked toward the gate. She could hear Mrs Peel chatting away, but couldn't understand a word she was saying. Then she realised why. Mrs Peel was just talking to herself - perhaps a habit she had picked up after the death of her husband. She was mumbling non-stop and by the time she was at the gate she had become quite breathless. Danielle couldn't help smiling at her with compassion.

While David went inside to wash his hands, Danielle showed Mrs Peel how they had tidied up the rose garden. Satisfied that the young woman knew what she was doing, Mrs Peel was not only relieved, but quite pleased to see the garden looking so lovely again after yesterday's damage.

"You know, dear, Mildred Bertram; the lady who owns this cottage, has planted this rose garden almost twenty years ago with just a shovel and some horse manure from the farm opposite the fields. It has always been her greatest passion and it almost broke my heart when I saw the damage yesterday, but I can see now that the garden is in good hands."

Mrs Peel smiled at her and then glanced down at her softly rounded belly. "Expecting, are you? How many months?"

"Just over five months. It's beginning to show now, isn't it? Last week I felt her kick for the first time!"

"A Girl? Well, you're simply glowing. Call me Hazel, dear."

"Thank you, Hazel! I'm Danielle. Pleased to meet you! Won't you come in for a cup of tea or coffee?"

"Oh, that would be lovely! I prefer Earl Grey with lemon. Do you have Earl Grey tea and lemons, dear?"

Danielle laughed. She liked Mrs Peel. It was good to have a friend close by, she thought.

While they were inside, Mrs Peel began looking at everything - the books; the documents; the equipment; the laptops; the monitors - there was so much to see. She could even see herself on one of the monitors and tried to find the camera, which was cleverly hidden inside the bookcase, in between *The Ingenious Gentleman Don Quixote of La Mancha* by Miguel de Cervantes Saavedra and *The Adventures of Huckleberry Finn* by Mark Twain. Her heart was racing. What on earth was going on here? She decided to confront Danielle with the question right away, just to get it out of her system. "Are you a famous American actress on the run from the paparazzi?"

Danielle chuckled and almost dropped the teapot. She turned around and put her finger to her lips.

"Shhhh, I need the peace for my baby. Don't tell a soul!"

"Mum's the word, my love. You have picked the right spot. Hardly anyone ever comes over to this end of St. Andrew. This road is a dead end and the other lane over there goes to a farm, you know, the one who gives us the horse manure for the roses."

"So, you think this is a good hide out for us?" Danielle asked in her most sincere manner.

"Absolutely, dear, I won't tell a soul. That handsome young man, is he your husband?"

Danielle bent over to get a little closer to Mrs Peel and whispered in her ear, "My boyfriend."

"Oh my! Is it his child you are carrying?"

Danielle definitely didn't want to go there, so as she searched her mind for a way to change the conversation, David - who had been in the downstairs bathroom and had overheard the conversation - decided it was the right moment to join them. He also had a burning question for her. "Mrs Peel, how lovely to meet you! I'm David. May I ask you a favour? Do you have a mobile phone by any chance?"

Mrs Peel, who could immediately hear that he was an Englishman, took one of the most modern iPhones available out of her handbag and brandished it happily.

"My son has given this to me. I still don't know how to take pictures with it, but I can call him and he can call me."

"May I use it to call my son, Mrs Peel? Of course I will pay for the cost of the call and the privilege of using it."

David took out a ten pound note from his wallet and gave it to her. She took it without hesitation and handed over her iPhone, pleased she could be of help.

"Thank you so much, Mrs Peel, I will give it back as soon as I have reached my son."

David left the room, so no one could overhear their conversation and called his son's number. His hands were sweaty and his heart was beating fast. Would he be at school? It was Monday afternoon after all. Oh wait, no, it was supposed to be his week off.

Suddenly, a weary voice answered, "Hello? Who is this?"

"Michael? Michael! It's your father. Listen, don't hang up, please!"

"Dad? Where are you? Why can't I call you back? What's going on?"

"Michael, I can explain only so much. I am on a mission and cannot use my own mobile phone. In fact, I'm in a safe house."

"So, how come you can call me now? Are you in trouble?"

"No, no, I am fine, listen... I just wanted to say I am sorry and that I love you. I just couldn't bear not talking with you for such a long time! How have you been? Are you okay?"

"Yes, dad, I'm fine. You sound emotional. Are *you* okay?"

David sighed quietly and suppressed his surging emotions.

Thank God Michael hadn't hung up.

"Dad, where are you? I need to know where you are!"

David looked around to make sure he was still alone and that no one could overhear him. His tone was now very soft and close to whispering.

"I'm on Guernsey. I'm calling on someone else's phone right now so I need to hang up soon. Promise me you won't come to me? I may be in danger at any time and I don't want you to be in danger too. You hear me, Michael?"

"Yes, I hear you, but that doesn't mean I like it. You take off just like that and now you tell me you might be in danger. How do you suppose I feel?"

"I know, son, I'm so sorry. It's too much to explain right now, but please, forgive me? You know you mean everything to me. I will come and see you as soon as this mission is over. I promise."

"Whatever you say, dad. Listen, I gotta go. Don't get yourself into trouble, okay? Don't... don't get hurt."

The line was silent for a few seconds. David suddenly realised the consequences of his decision to work for SBS-Sion. However, he reminded himself that this wasn't just about him. If only he could split himself into two. How he wanted to fly out to London and spend time with his son, but he couldn't. He had taken it upon himself to protect Danielle and her unborn child in any way he could, knowing that he himself could be in danger too. It was a choice he had had to make. Something he couldn't explain to his son.

"Dad? Are you still there?"

"Yes, sorry. I know this is a difficult time right now, but I am protecting someone who is in a safe house and you have to believe me that it's of the utmost importance that I keep her safe here."

"She? Dad!"

"No, Michael, listen..."

Michael had hung up. He couldn't forgive his father for cheating on his mother, for letting him down by selling the B&B in France and now his father was with yet another woman and Michael didn't care whether it was for his work or not. Nevertheless, hanging up on his father wasn't easy and he regretted it the moment he had pressed the red button. He didn't hate his father, he just missed him more than he had ever imagined he would. He had re-lived every intriguing minute of the time they had spent together in France, their adventures, their mutual interest in history and mystery and the fun they'd had in Rome.

Then he recalled that David had said that he was on Guernsey.

Michael quickly stored the number David had called him from in his mobile phone, booked an airline ticket and threw it on his bed. Then he packed some clothes into a backpack with his wallet, ID and mobile phone and walked out, closing the door resolutely behind him. No way did he want to leave his father alone now. They had been a great team this summer and they would be a great team now. He only hoped that he could find him.

13

Cairo-Aswan road, Egypt, October 3rd 2011

The car was coated heavily with the penetrating, invasive desert dust the wind had whipped into every crevice. At times, visibility was dangerously impaired, but Hadi was moving through it all like an archer's arrow, intent on reaching its mark. They drove straight through the town of Malawi without stopping and Otto was wondering if they would ever get lunch. He looked behind him and noticed that the Egyptian army rover was still behind them. The two soldiers saw Otto look back at them. Ashraf's partner, Beni, pulled a funny face and waved at him. Hadi had given them half of the money already and they knew that they would get the rest afterward, but only on the condition that Hadi's clients were satisfied with their protective services. Otto waved back, but didn't smile. The whole scenario didn't feel right. Still, Alfred trusted Hadi, so Otto decided to give him the benefit of the doubt. At least for now.

They had almost finished reading through the files now and were thrilled with what they had learned so far. They now understood how the Hermetic knowledge of the energies that connect all things, which is sometimes referred to as the Word, Nous or the Holy Spirit, strongly relates to the sacred Egyptian perception of magic. This knowledge goes beyond understanding the material world alone. It refers to the heart that is within the heart, in which the heavenly origin beats. In ancient Egypt, knowledge was written down in sacred papyri and kept behind locked doors in the sacred library of the House of Life. The House of Life was the place to visit when you were seeking answers and assistance with life's vicissitudes - to consult a priest about a toothache or to buy a love potion, a formula to cure an illness, or a protective amulet. The priests even knew a spell to ward off the evil eye, which amused Otto. Especially poignant was the sentence: 'You cannot harm me, nor my shadow'. It made him smile - he could have used a spell like that.

The House of Life was also the place where the royal archives were kept, carefully guarded by a special priest-magician. According to Alfred, this could be one of the places where they might find the elusive Urim, or Eye of Ra. The precious stone might be kept in what was called the 'holiest of holies' at the temple. The temple was the most sacred place of all and seen as the manifestation of the physical world and its position in the Universe. Inside this holiest of holy places in the temple was a special shrine to the deity, called 'Heaven'. The doors to the shrine were called the 'Doors of Heaven'. Painted on the doors were two eyes that enabled these doors to 'come to life'. For the ancient Egyptians, these were the living doors to the otherworld and no deed would go unnoticed, for the eyes that were painted on the doors could see everything. Each morning, just before the first light, the high priest would open these doors and say: 'The doors of the sky are open, the doors of the temple are unlocked. The house is open to its master. Let him go out when he wishes to go out, let him enter when he wishes to enter.' It was at this morning ritual that the god became 'one' with the priest.

It was clear to Otto and Arthur that the rituals in ancient Egypt were an enactment of the powers of nature and of the continuous path of the sun, the moon, the earth and the stars. According to the texts, every evening, the sun god would become Osiris the moment he entered the Nun; the primeval ocean surrounding the earth, where the sun regenerates itself. At night, the sun would travel in a barge, under the protection of the Eye of Horus and the chants of the priests, ensuring safe passage. This chant was one of the greatest secrets of the House of Life. It was a secret that was well-guarded by the priests, who made absolutely sure that this knowledge would not to fall into the hands of common men.

While the sun god Ra, who they named Osiris in the evening, sets in the nether realm in the west, the priests would sing: 'Let not the one in the water raise his head before Osiris has passed'. Then, the sun would travel through the Duat - the realm between the earth and the sky - to be refreshed. In the morning, the sun emerged as Horus in his barge, coming from the east, renewed and purified. The priests would chant 'Oh Ra, oh old man who becomes young again in his own time, old man who becomes a child again.' Then, the priests would purify themselves in the sacred lakes of Egypt, which contain the primordial waters of the Nun, the primeval ocean. "Do you think these sacred lakes were filled with rain water?" said Otto.

Arthur hummed. "The water that fell from the sky? I don't know. Perhaps they thought that there was some kind of ocean up there, or they saw the Milky Way as the Cosmic Nile River. Still, what was the weather like, 3300 years ago? If it were as dry as today, rain would be rare. It only rains something like a few days a year now. Their sacred lakes would dry up in no time. Maybe they used well water. I read that Akhenaten taught the people of Akhetaten how to dig wells in their own courtyard, so they could have a private water source. This reminded me of the story of Moses hitting the rock to find water for his thirsty people. If the ancient Egyptians saw the sun go down, vanishing into what looked like a vibrating horizon, maybe they thought it vanished into a big pool of water. I think that the sacred lakes were filled with source water, not rainwater."

Otto read on quickly and surmised, "Well, it could also be river water from the Nile. Look, it says here: 'The sacred lakes were filled with primordial water, the water that comes from Elephantine, from Nun itself.' Elephantine island is much further south, near Aswan, many miles upstream. I think the Nile itself was seen as Nun on earth."

Arthur nodded. "You may be right. Okay, river water it is. Did you see the chapter about the incredible irrigation system they had at Akhetaten? It made it possible to grow enough crops to feed at least 10.000 mouths. I can't wait to see the place!"

Otto nodded. He too was getting more and more excited about seeing it as it really was, 3348 years ago.

Hadi, on the other hand, was getting increasingly nervous as he sped along. He hadn't counted on having Ashraf and his sinister friend Beni on his back and knew he had to get rid of them somehow, because they had to hide their car with all their modern equipment inside before they could time travel to the year 1337 BCE. The only modern thing they could keep on their bodies - close to a very private place - was their personal ERFAB device. Hadi knew that Alfred was counting on him and he had given his word to him, but now, his word was in jeopardy with these unexpected intruders, who had forced themselves into his mission. He felt the pressure of his commitment weighing on him. The last thing he wanted is to come back to the present and find the car and all their things stolen. Then how would they get back to Cairo?

Hadi immediately hit the brakes and jerked the steering wheel to abruptly turn the car around. The Army rover stopped and blocked the road, but Hadi didn't mean to flee from them. Jumping out of the car and gesticulating boldly, he went over to have a brief conversation with Ashraf.

Otto and Arthur looked on intently, as Hadi's sudden move had taken them quite by surprise. When Ashraf nodded his head, they understood that their 'protectors' seemed to agree with whatever Hadi was saying. Then, Hadi got back into the car and the 2 soldiers let him pass when they headed back to Malawi. Otto tapped Hadi's shoulder.

"What's going on, Hadi?"

"No worries, Mr Adler, I forgot to do something in Malawi, my mistake. It won't take long!"

"Can't we have lunch there? I'm starving!"

Hadi sighed.

Westerners! Always thinking of food and comfort.

"I can try to find a food stall, or better still, I'll buy some bananas on the market, if we must cater to your tender stomach's requests!"

Otto heard Hadi's sarcastic undertone and it bothered him. Why did he have an ominous feeling about their guide? He knew that trusting people had become an issue for him. Otto may have been naïve before, but that had suddenly changed with his horrific experience with the Nazis. The feeling he had right now was not a question of trust in someone that Alfred had obviously invested trust in. This was more of a gut feeling. He wanted to tail Hadi on his errand in Malawi, but Hadi insisted that they stayed inside the car. Hadi made sure all the windows were closed and even put the child safety lock on, so they wouldn't be able to get out. As soon as Hadi got out of the car, he disappeared behind a block of buildings, wearing a broad grin.

Being locked inside, Otto and Arthur - who felt trapped like dogs - were getting very hot indeed. The fifteen minutes in which Hadi was gone seemed like an hour and their clothes were completely soaked with sweat by the time he returned, still wearing that big grin on his face.

"All is well, we can continue our journey. Look, I even got you some bananas and more water!"

He cavalierly tossed the bananas to them, but was more gentle with the water. The bananas were small and full of brown spots, but the taste was intensely sweet.

While Hadi chewed on sweet dates, he turned the car and speeded back to where they had parted with the two soldiers. Hadi was content. He was glad to have thought of it before it was too late. In case they did come back to the present to find their car and all their possessions stolen, he would now have a cash reserve carefully hidden in Malawi. This money would not just buy them a train ticket back to Cairo, but also a new mobile phone, clothes, meals and a hotel room. If it turned out that their possessions weren't stolen, then all he would have to do is pick up the money as soon as the opportunity arose.

Humming along to the music on the radio, Hadi drove on until they came to a junction. Here, he turned left and took a side road to a car ferry.

"We're nearly there. Mr Adler!" he said to the rear view mirror. Otto, who could feel adrenaline coursing through his veins, loved the exotic atmosphere and the thrill of the adventure. Still very fresh in his memory was the discovery of Tutankhamen's tomb in the Valley of the Kings in 1923. It had been all over the newspapers. Otto was 19 years old at the time and the discovery had made a deep impression on him. He chuckled, enjoying the memory of jumping through time like that and was grateful for the experience. Leapfrogging 72 years into the future in one lifetime had been quite a shock to him, but his jump in time had taken place within Europe; it had been a mind slamming experience to discover the advanced technology and considerable change in landscaping. However, here in Egypt, time seemed to have stood still.

While Otto was staring from his vantage point out onto the beautiful landscape of Egypt, with the delightful water of the majestic Nile river, exotic palm trees, colourful people and the tops of the golden sand dunes on the opposite riverbank, Arthur was still reading the last few pages of the files.

"It says here that the Coptic language is very similar to the ancient Egyptian language and that Hadi is a Coptic Christian. That is why he is coming along! He is our interpreter!"

Hadi - who had overheard - smirked, knowing they would now arrive at the most interesting part of their instructions.

The blue ferryboat was small and looked very old. Arthur closed his eyes when Hadi drove the heavy car onto the boat, but it all went well and they enjoyed the short trip across the Nile river. However, they weren't alone on the boat. Several tourists from Cairo, who were on a mini-bus day-excursion; a Belgian family with a rental car and a German foot passenger were also coming along for the ride.

The German was a tall man in his sixties with dark hair and a carefully-trimmed moustache. He had picked up Otto's German accent and so attempted to start a conversation. He walked toward them, praising the splendid view in German. He talked about the food and complained about the constant begging as he leaned casually on the iron railing, staring at the opposite riverbank. Otto studied him assiduously.

"From Freiburg, are you?" he said.

The German looked at Otto with wide eyes. "Yes, I am, actually! How do you know?"

"Your accent of course. Where do you think I'm from?"

"Hessen, I'm sure!" said the German resolutely.

Otto laughed out loud. "Ja, correct! So, what brings you here, Mr.?"

"Max Müller! Freut mich! I'm in Cairo for business, but my client didn't show up. He will now be arriving on Wednesday, so today and tomorrow I am visiting as many sites as possible. And you are?"

Otto didn't think it would be wise to give him his name, but he didn't want to be rude, so he avoided the subject and said, "I love the desert. Isn't it beautiful?"

Although Otto looked away, he could see from the corner of his eye that the German was staring at him with sudden distrust at his answer. Going along with Otto, he replied, "Yes, it is. Very beautiful."

Getting the message, Max walked away and passed two Egyptian soldiers, who had been staring hard at him ever since he had started chatting with Otto. Behind the soldiers he noticed a young man and an Egyptian, also staring hard at him. Feeling a bit awkward, he turned around to join the Belgian family on the other side of the boat. While walking leisurely across the deck, he smiled a victorious smile.

Otto gave a sideway glance to Arthur and Hadi, who nodded approvingly. Alfred had advised them not to make any unnecessary contact with anyone. Though Otto would have loved to explain everything to Max, that would have been a big mistake.

When the ferry docked, they were the first to drive off and onto the dusty, worn, tarmacked road that led to the ruins of ancient Akhetaten. They were tailed by the mini-bus carrying the tourists from Cairo and the Egyptian army rover, who seemed to have given Max Müller a lift. As soon as they were out of the town of Tall Bani Umran, they drove into a dream-like landscape. Even Arthur couldn't concentrate sufficiently to read the last page of their files and looked out. It was all so dry, so empty, so hot. It was hard to believe that three and a half thousand years ago there were 10.000 people living here and that there had been much more green. Even more striking was the vastness of the archaeological terrain.

Hadi drove toward one of the small, modern buildings, not far from the location of the Aten Temples and stopped the car. "Have you finished reading the files?"

Otto and Arthur quickly bent over the last page of their instructions. They had to change their clothes, put on the belt with the device underneath their galabyas and memorise the contents of the instructions manual: only in case of an emergency, or if they succeeded in replacing the stone with the original Eye of Ra, would they be allowed to use the 'home' button. If they didn't succeed, they had to select '1'. In either case, they would only lose four hours in the present. Also, they needed to recharge the battery in sunlight or a bright light for at least 5 minutes before use. They had to let Hadi do all the talking and they were never to interfere in any way, touch anything that wasn't absolutely necessary and never to show anyone the devices they carried, nor the counterfeit stone. Otto realised that Alfred must trust Hadi 100%, something he wasn't all too happy with.

Meanwhile, Hadi was busy keeping the two soldiers at a distance. They roared with laughter when they saw Otto and Arthur come out in their Egyptian clothing and continued to snicker even after Hadi came up with a clever cover story of a souvenir photo shoot.

When they were all ready, Hadi locked the car. Their modern clothes; their luggage; files; mobile phones; money; ID cards and laptop had all been stowed inside the locked car, that was parked in a public parking area, next to a graffiti-smeared, small building on the edge of the archaeological field. They all understood the risk, so Hadi made a deal with Ashraf. If they'd stay with the car and make sure it wasn't touched by anyone, they would be paid double. Ashraf agreed with a big smile and a firm handshake. "Always nice to do business with you, Hadi. Beni and I will guard your car like a lioness guards her cubs."

The adrenaline was rushing through their veins the moment they set off for the ruins. All they had to do now was to make an intelligent choice for an 'arrival' spot.

14

Sion, Switzerland, October 3rd 2011

Wong dreamt that someone was slapping his face. At first he thought that he was dreaming about another fight with his father, but then the dream-face of his father slowly morphed into the face of his new chief, Alfred. A face with a gravely concerned expression.

The sound of a voice, which seemed distant at first, suddenly became very loud indeed.

"Wong! Wake up, Wong! What the hell is the matter with you?"

His vision became a little sharper, but then he noticed the black spots, dancing in front of his eyes.

"Sugar. Cookie. Anything with sugar. Please..." he sighed. Immediately Alfred sent for a coffee with 4 sugar lumps and a pretzel, which was brought in a minute later. It didn't take long before Wong's condition was more or less back to normal. Alfred waved his index finger. "Next time you need something to keep you going, you just ask for it, okay?"

Alfred had panicked when Wong fainted. He knew that if Wong wasn't able to do his job properly, he'd have to try and talk Bill into temporarily coming back, just for this specific mission. However, he knew very well that Wong's predecessor, professor Bill Fairfax, had resigned for a reason and that getting Bill back to work at the lab was probably just wishful thinking. He understood it though; the risk of getting shot on the job had not been part of the job description. No, he simply had to talk to Wong and make him understand the importance of this mission. If only he could get through to the man; Alfred felt such a distance between them. He found Wong to be nervous and introvert, as if he was hiding something. On top of it all he had left the base - without permission - to go on hikes, which was explicitly prohibited and clearly stated in the house regulations. Then he had found him asleep in his apartment, when he was supposed to be at his post in the laboratory.

To add to that, the man apparently had a problem with his sugar levels, adding another reason for concern. Clearly, it was time for a talk and while Wong finished his coffee, Alfred sat down and closed his eyes for a few minutes to clear his mind. First of all, he had to overcome his growing anxiety and worry and remembered the *Art of Polarisation;* turning negative feelings into positive feelings. He had to turn this anxiety and worry into faith and trust. Secondly, he had to overcome the growing pain in his stomach, caused by the tumour. The pain was a constant reminder of his upcoming surgery and the limited time in which he needed Otto and Arthur to succeed. He tried a breathing technique, relaxing his muscles and letting his emotions wash through his belly like a waterfall washing over a rock. He felt calmer and re-ran the current situation through his mind; Otto and Arthur weren't expected to arrive back into the present before 19.00 hours. Furthermore, they were only to report back to Sion base before their departure if there was a problem, so no news was indeed good news. He knew that Georg was most probably fast asleep at the manor house, Al Din was on his way to Norway and David and Danielle were safe on Guernsey. So all he had to deal with right now, was Wong. When Alfred opened his eyes again, he saw Wong, staring at him with open mouth. Alfred smiled at him. "I find meditating helpful. Do you meditate?"

"Yes, I do, sir! That is why I was in the mountains yesterday. To find peace."

The two men stared at each other.

Finally, they had something in common.

The Swiss smiled. "Talking about peace, I have noticed that you are very uptight when you are in my presence. Do I frighten you?"

Alfred had grown accustomed to seeing fear in people around him. He was a big man with broad shoulders, wealthy and powerful and above all, he had piercing, blue eyes - the eyes of a clairvoyant - that seemed to look straight through you. His clairvoyance enabled him to look beyond the visible world, which gave him an advantage at meetings, in negotiations and when he had to make an important decision. However, for some reason, the tumour had taken most of this gift from him. If he did have a 'flash-forward', it was unclear. Feverishly, he hoped that the Urim; the Eye of Ra, when reunited with the Thummim, would be able to help him see what he needed to know.

Wong, on the other hand, was a short man and he had a lisp. His youth had been filled with intimidation. He had suffered mockery not only from his cruel classmates, but also from his father. He was constantly being told what a disappointment he was to him. More than once, his father - a military man - had slapped him because he wasn't brave enough to stand up to his opponents. His father didn't understand or want to know about the hierarchical bullying system that schoolboys typically imprison schoolmates into. Reprisals, surprise attacks and free beatings in private were daily fodder for the unfortunate boys born with more gentle dispositions or lack of confidence. By the age of 16, Wong had all the makings of an introvert, keeping a safe distance from school social life, shutting himself up in his room and focusing on his schoolwork and his passion subject; wormholes. Into adulthood, he remained afraid of the outside world, where most men were bigger, stronger and could express themselves better than him. Alfred was no less intimidating.

So, in answer to Alfred's question, Wong nodded, hesitant to admit his true feelings to Alfred. "A little bit, sir."

Alfred smiled. He could see beyond Wong's eyes where his fear might have come from.

"Wong, I need your help on this mission. I need your expertise, your honesty, your complete focus and all your knowledge to pull this mission off, but above all, I need your loyalty. Share everything with me. Your thoughts, your feelings and your opinions. Never be afraid to talk to me about anything. If there is something on your mind, always tell me about it. Okay?"

Wong nodded again, but this time he looked away, unable to look Alfred in the eye, for he did have something on his mind; something he tried very hard *not* to share with Alfred. He couldn't solve the problem anyway, not anymore. Any minute now, Otto and Arthur would use the mobile ERFAB devices. If anything should go wrong, they would find out soon enough, but then, something incredible happened.

Alfred opened up to *him*.

"My father was a very strict man and a person I looked up to. He was my role model; a noble, lionhearted man with only one flaw: he didn't understand children's need to be children. Unfortunately, I was an only child, groomed to take my father's place, so I had several teachers; one for languages, history and topography, another for calculus, math, geometry and science and a third for social studies, management and law. He himself taught me myths and legends, philosophy, mysticism and forbidden history. When I was at the age of eight, he insisted that I attended his secret meetings with the Lodge and though I could hardly understand anything they said or did, I loved to watch the rituals and listen to the men. When I was twelve years old, they gave me my own apron and I had to make the vows. When I was sixteen, my father gave me this ring with the compass and the square. By then I knew that most of the secrets were connected with knowledge of measure, weight, size and vibration. It was the secret knowledge of the Masons, passed on orally, but most of it had come from the Knights Templar's great discoveries in the Middle East. I realised that my father was their grandmaster and I've always had great respect for him. He gave me everything; everything but my childhood. I was always either studying or riding my horse, Lancelot, through the woodlands behind the manor house. My mother passed away when I was young, so all the while I was growing up trying to please my father, missing out on what most other kids had; game time and the comforting arms of a mother when life became a little rough."

Alfred sighed and studied his Masonic ring. "Beauséant! Be fair! Walk straight! Be just! Preserve the knowledge!"

Wong had been listening to him with open mouth. He could see that Alfred was tired, even a bit melancholic, but he understood all too well how it felt to try to live up to the expectations of someone you loved and looked up to. Treading lightly as he spoke, Wong inquired softly, "So, where is your father now?"

"He died last year, just before Christmas. Naturally, I inherited all his duties and I can only hope that I will run SBS-Sion as well as he did for many decades before me. I'm just sorry I could never give him a grandchild. I know that that had been his biggest disappointment in me."

Wong smiled. "I haven't met the right woman either. Women don't find men like me attractive."

Alfred smirked. In truth, he felt no attraction to women at all, but he thought it was best not to share that with anybody right now. "I have an adopted daughter, Danielle, who is expecting. So, technically, my father *will* get his grandchild. It may not carry on his bloodline, but interestingly, it will restore the family bloodline to an even purer origin. However, the safety of my adopted daughter and her unborn child depend largely on the success of this mission. So you see, I need your co-operation and complete loyalty to pull off this mission. So, Wong, can I count on you?"

Wong looked away, torn between whether or not he should reveal his secret: the flaw in his calculations. He hesitated for a moment, but then suddenly - in spite of his fear for the inevitable consequences - he decided to come clean.

"Sir, there is something you need to know."

Tel el-Amarna, Egypt, October 3rd 2011

The two rumpled soldiers with their rifles were dutifully standing guard next to a dust covered white Mercedes, that was parked just outside a small building on the edge of the modern town. The sun was low in the sky and it was no longer hot.

One of the men opened a small flasket and drank from it before he passed it on to the other. Beni looked at his watch.
"They take their time! When did they say they'd be back?"
"They didn't. I guess we have no choice but to wait. It's worth the money!" chuckled Ashraf.
"Yes, it certainly is. Well, the area is bigger than most people think. Maybe they went to the tombs in the hills."
Ashraf handed the flasket back to Beni and nodded. They decided to walk toward the archaeological site to see if they could spot them. Meanwhile, in the trunk of the white Mercedes, a mobile phone was vibrating nervously.

15

Akhetaten, ancient Egypt, 1337 BCE
Morning had broken at Akhetaten. The glorious, red sun disc slowly became visible above the horizon, displaying for all his venerated majesty, reborn and rejuvenated after his nocturnal journey through the Underworld and the Land of the Dead. The opposite skyline behind the river Nile gallantly withdrew the dark, black night and allowed itself to be slowly filled with soft pink, yellow and orange pastel shades. Neferkheperura-Waenra Akhenaten was lying on his belly on the floor of the temple of Aten. He was completely naked; his arms stretched sideways and his eyes fixed on a window in the east wall, through which the first rays of the morning sun penetrated the Holy of Holies. He let the rays of the sun enter his pupils, which narrowed as the rays became stronger, but he did not blink and feasted on the 'food' that was generously given by his father; the god Aten, through his life-giving rays. Not only did he worship the sun disk, he also felt worshipped by it and believed he knew its secrets.
In a soft whisper, Akhenaten recited the hymn he had written for Aten, in which he expressed his gratitude for the knowledge and understanding of the Great Mysteries of the sun. The last lines of the hymn were recited quickly as he felt how the sunrays were becoming too bright - even for his trained eyes - to bear.

Every leg is on the move since you founded the earth.
You rouse them for your son who came from your body.
The King who lives by Ma'at, the Lord of the Two Lands,
Neferkheperura, Sole-one-of-Ra, The Son of Ra who lives by
Ma'at.
The Lord of crowns, Akhenaten, great in his lifetime and the
great Queen whom he loves, the Lady of the Two Lands,
Nefer-nefru-Aten Nefertiti, living forever.

Tears were rolling down his cheeks, but his smile was that of a happy man. Was he not fortunate to have a loving and wise wife at his right hand to help him rule and six daughters who were his pride and joy? Meritaten was 11 years old. Being first in line as a princess royal she needed to grow up fast. She envied her younger sisters, who had much more free time. Meketaten and Ankhesenpaaten were a few years younger than her. They were equally well-educated and wise, but also happy and very beautiful. Their braided hair was washed with henna and twisted artfully to one side. The two sisters, who were always together, were wearing heavy make up around the eyes. Like living dolls they loved to run through the large rooms and hallways of the palace. Meketaten, however, was not as strong as her sister and their games usually ended with Meketaten having to rest in the nursery, where Ankhesenpaaten would then create drawings on the wall for her sister's pleasure. Their mother and father adored the three eldest girls, who had been born in Thebes.

After their arrival in the new city of Akhetaten, three more girls were born. Neferneferuaten, Neferneferura and Setepenra. Although the whole family loved them all, Akhenaten had expected to have at least one son by his beloved great wife Neferneferuaten Nefertiti, but she had given him only girls so far.

At the death of Amenhotep III, Akhenaten, who had originally been called Thutmose, became Pharaoh and changed his name to Amenhotep IV in honour of his father. On his coronation day, he had taken over his father's harem, which included the Mitanni princess Tadukhipa, whom he lovingly called Kiya. No longer expecting Nefertiti to father him any sons, it was with Kiya that Akhenaten now hoped to produce a male heir. He knew she had given birth to a son before. When still in his father's harem, Kiya had given Amenhotep III a son, Ankhkheperura. So, if Akhenaten was unable to father a son himself, his half-brother Ankhkheperura would become his heir. If Akhenaten wished to continue his own bloodline, he would need to have sons.

He even considered marrying his eldest daughter, Meretaten, at her coming of age. However, to Akhenaten's great joy, Kiya had given him two children consecutively, a boy and a girl. The boy was now three years old, but his name and that of his baby sister had not yet been added to the royal steles. As many children died before the age of five, it was customary to wait five years before any names were added to the steles or decorations that adorned the temples, tombs and palaces. At the moment, both children were healthy and strong.

As wonderful as life seemed to be in this great new capital of Egypt, there was always trouble lurking in the corners of paradise. Especially after the birth of his first son, Akhenaten's love for Kiya had become so great, that the jealous Nefertiti couldn't bare it any longer, so she had demanded that Kiya and her two children would live in a separate palace. Akhenaten had found his queen and co-regent to be rather dominating, much like his mother; the Dowager Queen Tiye, who had also always been stronger than his father. The only difference between Nefertiti and his mother Tiye was, that his mother was always on *his* side. Therefore, the presence of his mother became more and more desirable to him. Queen Tiye, however, did not live in Akhetaten, but in Thebes, so he needed an excuse to persuade her to move to Akhetaten.
The idea had struck him like lightening on a clear day; all he had to do was dedicate a Sunshade temple to his mother and invite her over to the ceremony. She would not refuse such an honour.

His mother was a very strong-willed, proud woman. As First Queen of Pharaoh Amenhotep III she had been a devoted wife, who had ruled the royal household with order and discipline for many years. She was proud of the fact that her most beloved son Thutmose had courageously taken over after the death of her husband.

Like his father, Amenhotep III, he too had his mind set on changing the religious system that had been the source of so much corruption. He had chosen his father's favourite deity, Aten-Ra, to lead the people and the priesthood into a monotheist religion. Immediately after his coronation, Amenhotep IV had started to change the system, having all representations of Amun smashed or painted over and he had warned the people of Egypt and the priests of Amun that great misfortune and disaster would befall them and sickness and death would strike all who didn't respect the new, albeit unprofitable system. Plague and death would seize the land if they did not abandon the business of multiple deities and worship instead Aten-Ra and only Aten-Ra.

It was in the fifth year of Amenhotep IV's reign that he had decided to change his name to Akhenaten. The new Pharaoh had now himself become the embodiment of the Great Aten. He himself had become the Great Word, through which he could give life, just like Aten, for the Great Word alone was capable of giving life to matter; to create.

Akhenaten was determined to free the people of Egypt from the bondage of the powerful and power-hungry priests of Amun and to lead them to a new promised land: the Birthplace of Aten-Ra. He had risked everything to destroy the corruption of mysticism and to bring the people and the priesthood to the one and true god: Aten-Ra.

If only Aten-Ra would grant him more sons.

The need for a strong royal household demanded the birth of many royal princes to produce at least one strong heir who would be capable of taking over the administration and throne of Egypt when Akhenaten's time came to pass on to the next world and so far he only had one three-year-old son. It was for this reason that Akhenaten had asked his mother to bring his sister, Beketaten with her. Beketaten was as strong a woman as his mother was and might be able to give him strong sons. Akhenaten could hardly wait for them to arrive.

On the other side of Akhetaten lived a young family with two children; the hard working Mudada, his gracious wife Sitre-Meraten and their two sons Ishaq and Chenzira, who were seven and four years old. They had been part of the exodus of people who had followed the Pharaoh to the new city, several years earlier. Here, at Akhetaten, they had built a house and dug their very own well, not far from the river and close to the main Aten Temple. Mudada had found himself a job at the Temple and within a few months' time, the family had been thriving.

In the meantime, Akhetaten had become a jewel on the Nile, with its many gardens, temples, suburbs and busy port, where cargo boats were docked, bringing grain, wine and cattle from the western oases and carrying amphorae filled to the top with incense from Syria. There were many fishing boats on the river that brought fresh fish to the markets every day. Akhetaten was buzzing with life, so there were markets, shops, workshops, kilns, warehouses, livestock holding stables and storehouses for grains. There was a clever irrigation system, making it possible to grow food further away from the river. The main market square was always busy and the city was growing every day with new arrivals. New houses were being added to every free plot available, creating suburb after suburb.

The Great Palace, the port, the fields, the Great Aten Temple and several government buildings were constructed on specifically chosen plots. Even the location of Akhetaten itself had been carefully chosen by the Great Pharaoh Akhenaten and he himself had chosen the name: 'The Horizon of Aten', a landmark visible from the hills east of the city. Akhenaten was certain that this was the place where Aten-Ra was born. This would become a city devoid of corruption, situated in the purest of nature where no one had ever lived before. It was the Chosen Place; the Promised Land and soon, the Great Pharaoh had changed the entire worshiping system, replacing Amun-Ra with Aten-Ra and demanding abandonment of almost all the other deities.

The people who had listened to Akhenaten's sermon had been moved by his message; a warning so powerful, that even the entire army had followed their pharaoh to the new Promised Land. Most of the common people seemed to accept the new system of Aten worship and accepted the lack of commerce that came with it, but some were still afraid that by forsaking the other gods and goddesses, including the Neteru* - whom people believed had been in power from the very moment the Mound of Creation had emerged from the Sea of Chaos during the First Sunrise of the First Day (Zep Tepi) - would lead to the destruction of the known world. Superstition ran deep for the common people.

Among others, Mudada couldn't let go of the old gods and this difference of opinion had caused considerable friction between him and his wife, although they both knew that transition and acceptance were difficult at the best of times. So much had changed. Mudada had given it a lot of thought, although he understood that he should not openly question the new beliefs, nor share his views with just anyone, so he only voiced his worries to his wife. "I am certain that the priests of Amun in Thebes still practice their magic in secret. Who else would do the magic every day to make the sun rise again, make the waters safe to fish from and the land fertile for food to grow and women fertile for babies to be born? Who but Amun could give the pharaoh good health and a safe passage in the afterlife? How can Aten-Ra enter the Temple if there is no statue for Him to live in? The Temple here only has an altar to Aten-Ra! Yesterday I heard that the pharaoh has even suspended the Opet Festival!** He had all references to Amun destroyed, as if Amun doesn't exist and did you hear the Queen the other day? She has announced that she is now the embodiment of Isis and Hathor, while her husband is the embodiment of Osiris and Thoth!"

*Divine powers
**The Egyptian Festival of rebirth and re-coronation, centred around Amun and Mut.

"Shhh, you fool of a man, you may not talk like this!" His wife admonished him. "Don't you see that we have two healthy sons, that food grows here and that the river still flows every day, bringing us our fresh fish? That even here, in Akhetaten, the air we breathe is renewed again on the first day of each new year? Pharaoh does his work and he does it well."

That silenced him, but it did not silence his mind. He was afraid that Sitre-Meraten would find the little figurine of the goddess Bastet that he was hiding in a box in a corner of their house. He could not part with it, but did not have the courage to tell anyone. The goddess Bastet had always brought them protection. He also believed that it had been Bastet who had saved their baby on their journey to Akhetaten. The journey had been long and tiring, so the baby was born early. Nevertheless, all had gone well, because he had kept Bastet close to Sitre-Meraten, both during the delivery and for the rest of their journey. He tried to let go of the other gods, but couldn't possibly let go of Bastet. However, that day, the inevitable would happen.

After the argument, Sitre-Meraten had gone back to work in the garden, but Mudada - who was still sulking - couldn't help the way he felt, so when he thought he was all alone, he cautiously opened up the box in which the figurine of Bastet was hidden. Carefully he took it out of its box, stared at it with gratitude and then kissed it. He didn't know, however, that he had a witness. His oldest son Ishaq, who adored his father, had seen everything. Curious to find out what his father had just kissed, Ishaq waited for him to leave the house to go to the temple, where he worked. Making sure he was completely alone, he carefully took the image out of its box. Ishaq stared at it and vaguely remembered having seen it before. The statuette was small and black, with painted golden ornaments and strange inscriptions. Why was his father hiding this? He was too young to understand that before he was born, an older religion had been common among the people; a religion that had been full of magic and multiple deities. Therefore, Ishaq didn't know that the worship of any god except Aten-Ra was now strictly forbidden and that the possession of an object such as the figurine of Bastet could get his parents into a lot of trouble. Ishaq, however, was completely taken by the little cat figurine, so when his mother shouted from the courtyard that she needed him to look after his little brother, it was difficult for him to put it back. When she called for him a second time, he hid it quickly and ran outside to pick up his brother, who had been playing in the mud and was now filthy and crying.

When Sitre-Meraten went back inside the house, the half open box immediately caught her eye, so she opened it. The moment she saw the image of Bastet, the shock struck her body like lightening and she could only just suppress a scream. Merciful Aten, what was he thinking! The very existence of this image could get them all killed! She grabbed a scarf and wrapped the figurine into a tidy bundle.

"Ishaq!" she called, "Stay with Chenzira. I am going out on an errand and will be back in a short time!"

Ishaq, who was still busy cleaning his little brother, watched his mother run out of the house. Just that moment, his friend from the family next door came in to play with him.

Ishaq told him everything.

Little did he know that this innocent chat between two friends would change their lives completely.

16

Akhetaten, ancient Egypt, 1337 BCE

The moment that Otto, Arthur and Hadi arrived in ancient Akhetaten, they realised that something was terribly wrong. The light was different; not like normal sunlight, but an unnatural glow that seemed to emanate from an invisible source. There was an inexplicable energy in the air, as if the entire landscape, including the houses and the people, was a fata morgana. Although they could feel the substance underneath their feet, their footsteps left not even the faintest footprints. They could barely feel anything, let alone pick anything up. When they took a few steps, it felt as though the world was moving separately from them, out of sync, as if they were not entirely there, but inside some miraculously invisible bubble that moved along with them, keeping them separated from the outside world. Otto asked Hadi what was going on, but when he heard his voice, it sounded distorted, as if he were talking inside a tiny bathroom. The short, hollow echo that followed made it even more eerie.

Suddenly, a woman appeared. She was walking toward them, which alarmed them at first, but as she came closer, it became obvious that she couldn't see them. She walked straight through Arthur, who squealed from the shock of it. He felt tingling throughout his entire body from front to back as the woman advanced through him. With open mouths they witnessed how she hastily rewrapped a cat figurine into a scarf and after digging a deep hole in the earth, buried it in an unused, dry corner of the garden they were standing in. As she laboured, she repeatedly looked nervously over her shoulder, reassuring herself that she hadn't been seen. Of course that doubly reassured Otto, Arthur & Hadi that they truly were invisible.

Otto rubbed his eyes with his thumb and index finger. "Gentlemen, I don't know about you, but I definitely do not feel at ease with this situation. Let's press '1' and find out if we can still get back to the present."

"No!" said Hadi resolutely. "Mr Zinkler wanted us to locate the stone. If we cannot replace it, then at least we will know where to look for it when we come back. Don't you see? People cannot see us. We can go everywhere, even inside the Temple of Aten-Ra, without being seen. We must take advantage of this situation before we go back to the present."

"If we *can* get back to the present. Jesus, Hadi, are you not just a *tiny* bit worried about our return ticket right now?"

"Of course I am, Mr Adler, but it's too late now to worry about it. Let's make the most of our invisibility, it's a wonderful advantage!"

Hadi started to stride determinedly toward the Aten temple, so Otto and Arthur had no choice but to follow him. It was a disconcerting experience to walk through the streets, trying to dodge the passers-by who would have run smack into any of them if they'd had any substance to them. The most disturbing of all was seeing that their bodies cast no shadows, though shadows were clearly visible from everything else under the sun in their vicinity. It made Arthur think of a scene from the 'Lord of the Rings' trilogy, where the moment the hero puts the ring on his finger, he finds himself physically in another dimension. Then, suddenly, something unnerving happened.

A stray cat looked right at him.

The penetrating feline stare was so alarming that Arthur immediately squeezed his own arm, which felt quite solid. He could also feel the pressure of his squeeze and when he checked his pulse, he was relieved to feel his heartbeat. Also, he was able to breathe, so they weren't dead, but Arthur couldn't help feeling as if somehow they had become ghosts, haunting the streets of ancient Egypt, visible only to cats.

Arthur stayed close to Otto, fighting to supress his urge to hold his friend's comforting hand, but he relished seeing how Otto seemed immersed in the very essence of the city - taking in all the exotic sights, unafraid and eager to explore. This was Akhetaten; a hastily built city of white washed mud brick buildings, with its narrow streets bustling with exotic people from a variety of cultures, not just Egyptian. They came to the bridge that connected the Grand Palace and the King's House and then saw the high walls and pylons that made up the great temple of Aten. Suddenly, a smile curled around Arthur's lips and his anxiety was replaced by an excitement only the sudden understanding of a great truth can inspire. "I actually think it's kind of cool. We really can go everywhere, even into the most sacred part of the Aten temple. You know, if people could see us, I think I'd be a little bit more nervous!"

Otto smirked. "You're right. Have you seen how many guards there are around? We'd probably never get in. Although we won't be able to replace the stone, we can at least see if it's here and if that's the case, we must compare it to Fred's fake stone, just to see if it looks exactly the same."

They walked directly to the entrance of the temple and gazed upon the high pylons made of talatat blocks.*

Otto touched his forehead. "Wow, it's much larger than I thought! Look at this place, it's immense!"

Hadi was walking very fast now and they could hardly keep up with him. Although they couldn't technically bump into anything, or stumble over a rock, they still automatically walked with care while observing life at Akhetaten. Hadi was almost out of sight now and they had to run to catch up, but then something strange happened. Immediately after they had started running, they noticed how everything around them suddenly went into slow-motion, but also the sound was morphing; the barks of dogs sounded like the repeated growls of a bear. They felt as if they were running vertical circles inside an hourglass-treadmill. Taken totally by surprise and shocked at such an unexpected reaction, Otto grabbed Arthur's arm and they both stopped at the same time, which seemed to restore the normal speed.

"Hadi, wait up!"

*Stone blocks of a standardised size (ca. 27 by 27 by 54 cm, which corresponds to ½ by ½ by 1 ancient Egyptian cubits)

Hadi, who had expected them to be right behind him, turned and saw the panic on their faces. "Stay close to me, you fools! This is not a school outing!" he exclaimed.

The three men now walked through the huge pylon gate and into the courtyard of the great Aten temple, where they passed several people. Judging from what they were wearing, they could make out whether they were priests or normal citizens of Akhetaten. Priests were wearing half long kilts of beautifully pleated, white linen, while others were simply dressed in a galabya, which didn't look much different from what some of the locals were still wearing in the present.

They walked on, crossing the first courtyard. On the other side, they faced another pair of pylons flanking the doorway and noticed the flapping crimson pennants, topping the flag posts. Upon entering the *Per-Hai,* the House of Rejoicing, they could feel no difference in temperature between the areas baking in the hot sun and the shaded areas along the walls, pillars and high pylons, that should offer a much cooler temperature in a 'normal' dimension. Their eyes, however, were still blinded by the glare of the sunlight. Accustomed to wearing sunglasses to protect their eyes from bright sunlight, it took a while before they could make out everything properly. In front of them were shady colonnades with altars; each and every one beautifully carved and painted with images of Akhenaten and Nefertiti, making their daily offerings of food, flowers and perfumes to Aten. Hearing ethereal harp music and delicate, faraway singing, they strained to see where it was coming from, but to no avail. It was an unfortunate side effect of the dimension they were in.

Struggling to identify the source of these pure and alluring tones, Hadi, who had been searching earnestly, suddenly pointed toward the northern wall. "Look, it's coming from over there. They're the blind singers of Aten."

Arthur was alarmed. "Why are they blind?"

"All I know is, that the singers of Aten, as well as the harpist who accompanied them, were all blind. People without eyesight naturally have more highly developed other senses; they often become singers and musicians, because their talents are so great. It is a rewarding way for them to make a living."

When they came out of the Per-Hai, they saw another pair of pylons, flanking the entrance to the *Gem-pa-Aten* (He Who Found the Aten). This was a series of six courtyards, all separated by even more pylons, strategically placed and architecturally magnificent. Each courtyard was vast, impressive and almost completely uncovered, so that the rays of the sun could fully penetrate the temple. There were, however, hundreds of small, whitewashed stone tables, neatly placed in rows. On these tables, bread and other food was laid out to be 'impregnated' by the life-giving rays of the Aten as an offering, before it was consumed. In the background, the hollow sound of cattle mooing created a forlorn, somewhat creepy atmosphere. Hadi tried to explain why there were so many cows just outside the temple enclosure. "One of the things they did at Akhetaten on a regular basis was to sacrifice the life of a cow to Aten-Ra. The cows probably feel that one of them will be taken soon."
They gazed upon the magnificent and vibrant images on the walls, depicting Akhenaten offering bread and other food to the Aten. There were also statues of Akhenaten, but they hadn't expected to come across a sphinx, protecting the temple. It had the body of a lion and the head of Akhenaten. Seeing a sphinx inside the temple just blew their minds. They knew that the sphinx was seen as a likeness of Kheper-Ra, whom Akhenaten saw as the soul of Aten. One of Akhenaten's titles, Neferkheperura-waenra, even contains the god's name: 'Beautiful are the Forms of Ra, the Unique one of Ra'.
The first courtyard had a high altar and on either side of the courtyard there were chambers and chapels for public use. In the other courtyards there were also 'magazines' in which food was stored. The food would be used as an offering at

first, but was then eaten by the priests, the royal family and some of the citizens of Akhetaten. When they walked into the fourth courtyard, they saw furnished, shady rooms, where people were talking and eating. In the final courtyard stood the royal high altar for Akhenaten and Nefertiti. This high altar was surrounded by 365 small altars, one altar for each day of the year. It was separated into two groups, one for Lower Egypt and one for Upper Egypt. The temple was vast, but the men hadn't arrived at the end of it yet. The temple seemed to never end. They continued their stroll in an easterly direction, hoping to find the Sanctuary called the 'Holy of Holies' and eventually came upon a large, square building, where people were chopping up meat from the slaughtered animals and preparing it with spices for consumption before offering it to Aten. Our team was grateful that they were unable to smell it.

A stele, placed to the side of the chopping table, attracted Otto's attention. "Look, this reminds me of that image we always see of the stone tablets of Moses, the ones with the ten commandments. It has the same shape with the rounded top. Hadi, do you know if Akhenaten had also written down 'commandments'? You know, rules and regulations?"

Hadi scratched his head in thought. "Well, much has been lost, as the city of Akhetaten was damaged beyond repair after the pharaoh Akhenaten had disappeared and the city was abandoned. He certainly made his own laws, as we can see by the radical changes in Egyptian culture and the religious system, which is recorded in the ancient writings. So yes, I believe he did have 'commandments' on stone tablets just like this. Besides, Akhenaten strictly forbade the making of any carved images of the god Aten as well as the worship of any other gods, just like Moses wrote in his commandments."

It was becoming increasingly evident to Otto and Arthur that there were a remarkable number of similarities between Moses and Akhenaten. No scholar could simply push these facts aside.

Going through another pair of pylons, they finally found themselves in the sanctuary situated at the very easternmost end of the temple. Again they walked into an open courtyard where they saw what looked like huts or small houses; three, small living accommodations for the priests, built against the southern wall of the courtyard, but then, behind the second pair of pylons, they witnessed an area of such architectural beauty, that it went beyond their wildest imagination. Two large colonnades with towering statues of Akhenaten, wearing the red and white crown of Upper and Lower Egypt, led them into the last of the courtyards, which was again filled with offering tables and a private high altar for the royal family. Arthur couldn't believe the beauty of the colourfully painted carvings of images of the royal couple, sometimes holding flowers, but always with the rays of the sun touching everything, offering life giving magic. He could see the hieroglyph that depicted the word magic; the wavy lines radiating from the sun, ending in the form of a disembodied hand, next to other lines radiating from the sun, that ended in the form of an ankh; the hieroglyph that depicts the word for life.

The high altar itself contained 5 perfectly round, hollowed out recesses, that were used for offerings of flowers, oils, incense or other liquids.

It was now getting busy around them. Clearly, something was about to happen. One of the priests - who was dressed more elaborately than the others - walked toward them and crossed his arms, his hands resting on his shoulders as a greeting. Then suddenly, a deep, clear voice came out of nowhere: "May the face of the Lord Aten shine upon you today and bring you peace!"

Hadi froze. How could this man see them? The priest then walked forward - passing right through him - and kneeled on the floor behind them. They turned and while the priest bowed deeply with outstretched arms, they discovered where the voice had come from.

For behind them stood Akhenaten, dressed in a ceremonial kilt of the finest white pleated linen and wearing a ureus 'sporran' placed in the centre of his kilt. The ureus snake was a symbol, indicating that the bearer benefitted from protection by Ra. It was normally worn on the crown of the pharaoh. Akhenaten, however, chose to wear it also on his kilt, connecting Ra's protection to his own fertility. His face, although somewhat long, did not look like the famous statues with the elongated faces. His body looked normally proportioned, unlike the carvings, which made him look slightly deformed. His upper body was naked and his already dark skin showed signs of overexposure to the sun's rays. His brown eyes were dramatically lined with thick, black kohl, giving him a rather powerful expression. He was wearing a tall, blue, rounded cone shaped crown, topped with another ureus snake - the tail of which was curled artistically around the edges of the crown. Underneath his chin and attached to his long, multi-layered wig, was the pharaoh's false beard, neatly braided with blue ribbon.

Next to him stood Nefertiti in a pleated white linen gown. She was wearing a multi-layered wig with beaded hair and a tall, flat-topped, cone shaped blue crown with a ureus snake. She wore a necklace of colourfully painted, clay beads that lay in a semi-circle on her chest. Her stern facial expression reflected the intensity and seriousness of the situation. When she raised her kohl rimmed eyes and looked unblinkingly at the priest, he respectfully dropped his gaze. When Akhenaten asked the priest to stand up, they understood that this had to be Meryra, whom Alfred believed to be the Biblical Aaron. Immediately, Hadi started to translate as much as he could into English, which was more difficult than he had anticipated, since there were words in the exchange that were unknown to modern research.

"Great One, Lord of the Sedge and the Bee, your servants the Lord Ay and the Lord Mahu are ready. We can leave immediately."

Akhenaten and Nefertiti both nodded, slowly and only once, in the most gracious way.

"Are the two men at court to be given an audience?"

"Yes, my Lord, they are awaiting your judgment."

From a distance they heard a somewhat distorted sound of approaching chariots being driven through the courtyards as well as the hollow crackling sound of approaching foot soldiers, marching in rhythm. The Amarna police escort, led by the chief of police, Mahu and Akhenaten's uncle, the General Ay, waited respectfully until the majesties had climbed into the two wheeled chariot. A magnificent horse, adorned in a stunningly elaborate head ornament, festooned with large feathers, drew the chariot. The moment they rode out, Akhenaten, who had taken the reins himself, persuaded the horse to go into a trot with a short flick of his whip. The soldiers, who were carrying sticks, had to run to keep up with them. Immediately behind the king and queen - riding in three similar chariots - were some of the women from the royal court, including the princesses.

Otto, Arthur and Hadi quickly followed them to observe the scene that was unfolding before them. The people of Akhetaten - who had come to witness the parade - were kneeling on the sandy floor, bowing low and keeping their heads down as the royal family passed. These people had previously been accustomed to witnessing a parade of the statues of deities such as Amun, Osiris, Isis, Hathor, Horus or one of the other important gods of Egypt, but the living bodies of the pharaoh and his wife - who was also Akhenaten's co-regent - had now replaced these statues. Akhenaten and Nefertiti had made it clear to their people that they and they alone had become the embodiment of all gods, who together composed the different faces and voices of the Aten and that whatever they had previously conceived their gods to be, actually made up the one god, Aten. Therefore, Aten alone was to be worshipped instead. Some of the people in the crowd wore a sour expression and it was clear that not all the people of Akhetaten were happy with this concept.

Behind the chariots, a group of priests - led by Meryra, whom they had already 'met' in the temple - followed on foot. Hadi, who had been observing their surroundings carefully, suddenly got excited. "Look! The door with the all-seeing eyes that leads to the Holiest of Holies is open!"

Not having totally accepted the idea that they could have walked straight through a wall if they wanted to, they walked back to the sanctuary. Once there, it struck them that the Holiest of Holies was just a small, wooden shrine; a cabinet with open front and back doors facing East. When they looked through it, they recognised the Horizon of Aten in the hills, but no matter where they looked, they could not see any place where the priests could have hidden the precious black and white stones they were seeking. They were also annoyed that they couldn't touch anything. It meant they wouldn't be able to open anything, or push anything aside, if necessary.

"It has to be somewhere else. Maybe it is kept in the small Aten temple or in Akhenaten's private quarters." said Hadi.

At that idea, the three men ran excitedly out of the building, which was an easy mistake to make on impulse. Hadi now also experienced the side effects of running in this strange dimension. Quickly, the three men slowed to a normal pace and followed the dusty trail of the chariots toward the small Aten temple. They were now on the so-called 'Royal Road'. The chariots had already gone under the bridge that connects the King's House to the Great Palace and had now come to a full stop in the open courtyard in front of the small Aten temple, which was attached to the royal family's private apartments. As the clouds of dust were settling, they could see Akhenaten and Nefertiti climbing out of their chariot, surrounded by their guards. Graciously, the royal couple - now walking separately from their children and courtiers - walked through the second pair of pylons and up the steps leading to an elevated floor. It wasn't clear at that moment why the princesses were taken elsewhere.

The temple looked like a miniature version of the large Aten temple, although part of the foundation was laid out in the form of a cross. The temple was obviously used for a different purpose. Otto, Arthur and Hadi, now much more confident in their invisibility, followed the royal couple into the Sanctuary. Arthur, who had a healthy sense of humour, mimicked a 'selfy' with Akhenaten, but did not get the response he had expected from either Otto or Hadi, as they were too busy watching two men bound in chains, lying on the floor, bathing in sweat. These men, probably prisoners, were clearly terrified. Being the second priest after Akhenaten - who had given himself the title of High Priest - Meryra wore an official white pleated, long linen robe and a cap, which covered most of his head. Raising his hands high above his head he asked for complete silence, after which he took out a small purse.

Then, it happened.

17

London, England, October 3rd 2011

Michael Camford had raced out of his student flat in Gower Street, London, to get to Gatwick airport in time to catch the four o'clock flight to the island of Jersey. Though it was too late to book a direct flight to Guernsey, he had managed to book a one-way ticket online to Jersey, using his bankcard. The ticket had only cost him thirty Pounds. As he was flying with British Airways, he was even able to check in online from his mobile phone. Once on Jersey, he'd be able to get to the Condor ferry terminal in St. Hellier on time to catch the six o'clock ferry to Guernsey.

The moment he stepped into the almost brand new BA City Flyer, an Embraer 170, he got excited. He didn't care if his mother got mad at him, or his father for that matter, because he felt in his heart that he had to do this. He had finally listened to his heart and knew that this decision was profoundly right. Finding his father on Guernsey was the right thing to do.

He was thrilled to see that he had a window seat that didn't look out onto the wing. He hadn't flown for several years now and it brought back some happy memories. Many years ago, when his father, David Camford, was still in the movie making business, Michael and his mother used to travel with him to film locations in Europe and Asia, accompanied by a private tutor. These had been major events in Michael's life. Sometimes an entire airplane was chartered to fly the whole crew including the actors and all the film equipment to their destinations. He had enjoyed those years a lot. Michael remembered such a happy childhood, until his parents suddenly divorced. He still remembered the moment his mother had found out about David's affair with another woman, a moment he would never forget.

It was on a rainy Wednesday afternoon when a woman had called. His mother, who had come home early, seeing the name 'Angelica' on the screen of her husband's vibrating mobile phone, picked it up before David could get to it. The caller, not waiting to hear David's voice, blurted out, *'Darling? David, I'm waiting. Have you left yet? Are you on your way?'* His mother had a meltdown right there in front of him. Having put up with his lack of communication, his lack of participation in their relationship for so long, she cracked. She shrieked at David to get out of the house, adding that she didn't want to hear his excuses or explanations. She never wanted to see him again.

His father had stood there, his arms by his sides, saying nothing in his defence. He had no excuses, no explanations to give. Not this time. David silently turned and walked upstairs to pack his bags. Michael still remembers the last words his father had said to him before he walked out of the door: 'I'm sorry son. This is between your mother and I. This is grownups business, it has nothing to do with you. You are my son, I love you and that will never change.'

At that crucial moment in both their lives, David had been unable to find the courage to look back at his son as he left the house. The moment the door had closed behind his father, his happy childhood had come to an abrupt and painful end. At that very moment, it seemed to him that the entire earth had ceased to exist, both for him and for his mother. Life as they had known it; life as a family, was over.

The Christmas that had followed that terrible day was a sad and lonely affair. His mother hadn't even tried to create any kind of Christmas spirit. The family was incomplete, so she had refused to buy the traditional Christmas tree; she just couldn't face the emptiness of having a family Christmas tree without being a family. While his mother became openly sad, lonely and depressed, she didn't realise that she was also making her son's life miserable, until Michael confronted her. That Christmas morning, knowing that all his friends were opening Christmas presents and enjoying a Christmas Day lunch with their families, he had walked into an empty living room devoid of even one ornament, not one Christmas present and nothing special planned for lunch.

He had been so focused on the innocent hope that his father might try to come back, that he shouted and cried at the same time. "What if dad decides to come back and we don't have a Christmas tree, mum? What if he's sorry and wants to be a family again and wants to come back? It's Christmas! He's never missed a Christmas, ever!"

That very moment, Shannon realised that she alone was in charge of her own happiness and she knew that things had to change. If not for her, then certainly for her son.

The day after Boxing Day she had put the inevitable wheels into motion and after the divorce papers were signed, Michael understood that his parents would never live together again. His last shred of childhood hope for the reunited family he'd lost - which had so far enabled him to put one foot in front of the other – had disappeared into thin air. The void that remained, however, was quickly refilled by other emotions; frustration and anger.

He thought he'd never be able to forgive his father.

Not long after the divorce, Michael and his mother had moved to another town, where he knew nobody. Leaving the house he had grown up in was another painful moment in Michael's life. He had so many happy memories in that house. Consequently, moving from a large manor house in the country to a small apartment in an unfamiliar, new town had proved to be even harder than he had expected.

However, moving house wasn't the only thing that would turn Michael's world upside down again. Michael had decided to attend University College in London after the summer, where he'd also have a student flat close to the UCL campus. It was just before that very summer, that something unexpected had happened.

His father had reached out to him again.

Deep inside, he still loved his father; he still needed him, he needed some kind of relationship with him and he had missed him terribly, especially at holidays. His favourite photo of him and his father was when they were in Japan together. He had torn up the photo, but couldn't throw it away.

In a sudden haste, he had taped the photo together and had carefully placed it inside his wallet, for his anger had been dulled by his pervasive feelings of love, sorrow and emptiness, so when David had reached out to him, Michael could only embrace it.

While settling into his seat, he smiled when he remembered the first time he had met his father again. It was on his 16th Birthday and David had hugged him so tightly. Naturally, Michael had felt a mix of regret and happiness, but then David had invited Michael to stay at his house in France for the summer holidays. He would never forget that summer. However, getting to know each other all over again hadn't been easy. Michael had confronted his father with the big 'why' and wanted him to know just how much he had suffered since David had left. He had also let his father know how much his mother had suffered. That discussion had led to multiple arguments and David tried very hard to make Michael understand the ins and outs of married life. He himself had found peace in southern France, running a B&B, complete with *gîte* and mini-camping, which was something completely different from the world of movie making. It had changed him. He had even found a new interest; studying the enigma of the Knights Templar and David had decided to introduce the mysterious history of his beloved *Corbières* to Michael. One day he surprised his son with a very special gift: a black and white spotted appaloosa horse. They named him 'Beauséant', after the Knights Templar black and white flag. Michael had been overjoyed and couldn't wait to learn how to ride and take his horse into the woods.

Not long afterward, an unexpected event had brought father and son even closer. While on an overenthusiastic ride, Michael had fallen off his horse and had ended up in a hospital in Carcassonne with a broken arm. In the weeks that followed, Michael had been handicapped with his arm in plaster, unable to ride and unable to be as active as he had been.

David never left his side; giving his son all his time, attention and love. The summer of 2009 had been summer of healing, in more ways than one and when Michael had returned to England, the father-son bond had become stronger than ever and two more delightful summers had followed. The B&B in the Corbières had become their special place. Naturally, the moment Michael had discovered that his father had sold his French B&B, he had been terribly upset, but never in a million years would he abandon his father while he was potentially in danger. The strange telephone call from David had alarmed him. He could hear something in his father's voice that he never heard before; genuine fear and worry.

Why wouldn't he be able to contact his father for such a long time? What was he up to and why hadn't he called from his own mobile phone? Michael checked his Blackberry and searched the phone log. Knowing that this was the only chance to find his father on Guernsey, he was relieved to see that the number that David had called from was safely registered in his phone.

The seatbelt sign came on and he was asked by a very pretty flight attendant to turn off his mobile. The noise of the engines grew to a roar and when the plane began its slow drive toward the runway, Michael could feel the sweet sensation of adrenaline rushing through his body. It was a treasured feeling that he recognised from his former adventures. He remembered his first trip to Asia with the plane full of actors and crew members, the first time he'd sat on his horse and the very first time that Beauséant had gone from a canter to a gallop. He enjoyed the exhilarating speed just before lift-off and the pleasant sigh in his stomach when the plane suddenly dipped. Within minutes he saw the suburbs of London, the ring roads around the capitol and the centuries old checkered green, beige and brown hedge bordered fields that made up the countryside of southern England, with its many small towns and winding, glistering rivers. Good old 'Blighty'. It was indeed a beautiful sight.

It didn't take long before they were flying over the coastline and toward the southeast, heading for the Channel Islands. Michael realised that he didn't know much about the islands and decided to leaf through the tourist brochure in the seat pocket in front of him. His eye immediately fell on the gorgeous photos of Guernsey, his final destination and a website link he needed to remember: visitguernsey.com.

'Guernsey may geographically be closer to France, but it remains loyal to the British crown and has done since Norman times. With evidence dating from the Neolithic period, the island has been pivotal in battles between the UK and France as well as being an important port for international imports into the UK. Today the island is independent and self-governing.'

How funny it was that he had always been under the impression that the Channel Islands were part of England. He was interested to see the island culture, as they were so close to France. The islands probably had a little bit of both worlds.

When they arrived at Jersey Airport, he looked for a taxi to drive him to the harbour of St. Hellier, to ensure he would reach the ferry on time and he was in luck. Travelling light, he didn't have to wait for any luggage and quickly found the taxi stand. While driving toward St. Hellier with the window down, he enjoyed feeling the unusual warm air on his skin, breathing in the invigorating, spicy scent of autumn. It reminded him of those rare, late summers on the southern coast of England. Nature seemed to enjoy these relatively high temperatures, as everywhere he looked he could see roses and freesias in bloom. He felt as if he were somewhere on a Mediterranean coast, gazing at an unreal, fairy-tale like landscape, while in reality he was on a rather serious quest to find his father.

It didn't take long to get to the harbour, so he had plenty of time to buy a ticket at the Condor Ferries ticket office.

At the ferry terminal he discovered more leaflets providing lots of information on the islands, including the smaller islands of Alderney, Sark and Herm. It made him feel sad that he wasn't here to explore, but to find his father. Reluctantly he put the leaflets back and decided to keep only the one about Guernsey.

The main town on Guernsey is St. Peter Port, but he had a feeling that he wouldn't find his father there. David had told him on the phone that he was on a mission and that he was in a safe house somewhere on Guernsey, which probably meant that he was hiding somewhere well out of sight and in some inconspicuous lodging. So where else was there to stay on Guernsey if one wanted to stay off the beaten track? Would David hide somewhere along the very dramatic looking south coast with its high cliffs, or on the spacious bays of the west coast? Would he hide somewhere in the rural countryside with its countless greenhouses and green pastures - on which the *Golden Guernsey's,* the world famous red-brown cows, grazed - or on the coastline, in one of the Martello or Loophole Towers? These famous towers had been built to defend the island from attacks from France during the reign of Napoleon and were now popular tourist attractions.
No, perhaps not the Martello towers. Too many tourists.
The adventure he had embarked on seemed less and less realistic each minute, but he was glad he still had that phone number his father had called him from.

It was almost time to board the catamaran that would take him straight into the harbour of St. Peter Port on Guernsey. He looked around him and noticed that there weren't very many people getting on board. Scanning the group, he noticed a family with young children, a group of students, a few men in suits, a group of young girls with shopping bags who were obviously coming back from a day out on Jersey and a man with Arabic features who appeared to be ill. The poor man even needed assistance from his two friends to help him walk. He noticed that one of them, a huge, frightening man, was staring at everyone with fiery eyes, observing his surroundings like a hawk. It made Michael feel very uncomfortable and he felt it would be safer to not sit close to them. When he passed them to get to the other side of the ferry, he noticed that the one with the fiery eyes was wearing an interesting ring; a ring with flat, blue stone inlay.

18

Sion, Switzerland, October 3rd 2011

Georg was fast asleep. The world around him had gently faded away a few hours ago, only moments after he had eased himself in a comfortable chair, positioned to look out over the stunningly beautiful valley of Sion. His sleep, however, was troubled and restless. The traumatic experience and the effects of the almost lethal injection had taken their toll. As an agent and personal bodyguard to Alfred Zinkler, he was toned, trained and strong, yet for some peculiar reason, he hadn't handled yesterday's situation very well. He recalled how it had played out in the airport parking lot. Al Din had suddenly pulled him into his car and the shock of seeing the man he had shot the prior summer had all but paralysed him. Sitting on the back seat of the car, he had done nothing to fight back or escape. Why hadn't he done anything? He could have at least tried to fight him.

The psyche of a hostage is a mystery.

Georg Hauser was above all a man of firm principle. He believed it to have been an honour to have served Alfred's father and he considered it an even greater honour that Alfred trusted him as much as his father had. He knew Alfred was not holding what had happened the day before against him and that instead, Alfred was proud of the fact that Georg had not betrayed Danielle's location. Not even under the threat of imminent death had he faltered. Still, his thoughts of personal responsibility persisted in punishing himself, as he believed that he shouldn't have let himself get caught in the first place. While enjoying his savoury mushroom omelette, Georg's overly analytical brain had worked non-stop. How on earth had they got into his car anyway? He was sure that he had parked it in the airport parking lot, locked it and he had even double checked that he had locked it. As he was still wearing the same clothes, he had immediately checked his pockets, but couldn't find his car keys.

So, somehow, somewhere, they must have taken his car keys. Perhaps when he was having his meal at the airport restaurant. He admitted to himself that he hadn't been observant enough, being just on his own. Once Alfred was safely on his way to Zurich in the chopper, Georg had let down his guard and hadn't really checked his surroundings carefully enough before and while having dinner. Most of all, he couldn't stand the fact that someone had actually got close enough to him in the restaurant to steal his car keys. Why hadn't he noticed it? Then, like a flash of a photo being taken, he had remembered the ring. The ring, worn by the man who had been sitting at the bar with his back toward Georg, drinking a beer. Georg had passed him when he had entered the restaurant. He suddenly realised that it had been the same ring that was worn by one of Al Din's accomplices - the one who had been driving the car - but whose face he hadn't been able to see properly in the dark. What had taken him so long to see this connection? Had he let his guard down that much? With a shock, Georg had realised that he had been watched, followed and in danger all along, from the very moment Alfred had left him alone at the airport.

Although Georg was now in a deep sleep, his grey-blue eyes were rolling wildly. He was having a strange dream that took him to the far corners of the Universe. He had no idea how he'd got there, but when he looked over his shoulder, the earth was only a tiny little blue dot in the distance, surrounded by many other planets and stars. In front of him was an exquisitely beautiful mix of blue and orange colours, making up the Orion Belt. It was so beautiful he almost cried. He felt weightless, swimming in slow motion toward the colourful belt. He suppressed the urge to find something solid to land on, knowing he wouldn't be able to find anything solid anyway. In the distance he could hear the sound of iron scraping on iron, but when he came closer, he could see that the sound came from a Tibetan singing bowl, played by a bald monk in orange robes.

The monk - a being of light without a face - was sitting cross-legged on a blue and orange cloud. "What do you seek?" said the monk, while he continued to play the bowl. Georg thought about it, but didn't know how to answer. He wanted many things, but then he thought about Alfred and how much he wanted him to be able to fulfil his mission. He thought about Alfred's illness and slowly he understood that what he really wanted, wasn't something for himself. He wanted Alfred to get better and wished with all his heart for Alfred's mission to be successful. However, when Georg tried to explain to the monk what he really wanted, the man turned into a golden Buddha and everything around him burst into a bright, golden landscape, beaming with auras of liquid golden fireworks. The light that emanated from the golden rays was so bright that it was blinding and Georg covered his eyes with both hands. A moment later, when he opened his eyes again, he could see Alfred walking through what looked like a desert, while dressed in an old fashioned, pinstriped suit. Georg called out to him, but Alfred didn't hear him.

He was busy looking for something in the sand.

Then Georg understood.

Alfred had turned into the 'Chemist of Ampurdan in Search of Absolutely Nothing' by Salvador Dalí.

Suddenly, Alfred seemed to have found something in the sand and he bent over to pick it up. It was a hat. After he put it on, he saw something else, glistering in the sand; it was a strange piece of milky glass, almost pure white with a slight yellow-green gloss, but perfectly round. Alfred looked at it while holding it up into the light of the painted sun, which was shining in the blue, painted sky. As Alfred held the stone up above his head, the sun - shining its light through the stone - produced a laser beam that started to burn a hole in Alfred's hat. Within seconds the whole hat was on fire. Immediately, Georg wanted to run toward Alfred to help him get rid of the burning hat, but his legs couldn't move fast enough. No matter how hard he tried, he couldn't get closer to Alfred, who didn't even realise that his hat was on fire until his whole body was on fire. Georg screamed and yelled and tried to help him, but he couldn't get to him.

Upon hearing his own scream, Georg abruptly woke up. What a crazy dream! Strange; he remembered every detail, but couldn't comprehend how his mind could have come up with such a scenario. How could he be so certain that what he saw was the Orion belt, not another constellation and where had the bald Tibetan monk come from? Georg rubbed his face with his hands and looked at his watch. Almost half past six. What?! he almost shouted. He raced out of the room toward the front door. He had to get to the base before seven. Still a bit dizzy, he welcomed the cold breeze when he stepped outside and drove all the way to the base with the window down. In his hurry he had forgotten his mobile phone, but didn't want to go back to get it. He had a very good reason for wanting to be at the base before seven. He thought about Otto and how he had tried to convince Alfred that Otto couldn't be trusted. He couldn't fathom why Alfred insisted on working with that man, someone from the past whom he didn't really know, someone who had been in the SS in the 1930s and who had worked for Himmler. Why would Alfred want to work so closely with an ex-Nazi? However, Alfred refused to listen to Georg's protests and even defended Otto, telling him that the Nazis themselves had tricked Otto and that he wasn't a criminal, but a victim of the Nazi propaganda. Obviously, as Alfred's bodyguard, Georg felt it was his responsibility to ask Alfred what proof he had of this, but Alfred had never responded to that question. Georg was afraid that Alfred was making a big mistake, trusting someone who'd been involved in one of the darkest periods in recent history. How could he protect his employer from someone who was already so close to him? How could he protect him from a man who's history was an enigma?

To be able to trust people and to actually show people he trusted them, Alfred always gave people the benefit of the doubt. Alfred assumed people's good intentions and noble spirit and in his employees their loyalty. In doing so, Alfred made himself vulnerable. Georg had sworn to himself he'd keep a close eye on Otto, but now, Alfred had sent this man on an important mission. Not only was Otto far away from Sion and therefore not under Georg's watchful eye, but on top of it, Otto had even been sent to another time and they all knew that Alfred had taken great risk in doing that.

What if Otto bolted with the top-secret devices?

Though trying to stay calm, thoughts were racing through Georg's head while he was driving. Alfred was a powerful and wealthy man with a big, generous heart. Being responsible for Alfred's safety, Georg had tried to confront Alfred with the danger of placing too much trust in others. He had warned him about human nature and how to recognise beggars and greedy people, who appear to be very loyal and friendly at first, but then suddenly start to turn people against each other, twist the facts and deceive others to obtain what they want. People can be very cunning and can go to great lengths when they have hidden agendas, causing destruction and suffering where ever they go. It was his task to protect Alfred from such people. Georg had found Otto insolent, calling his employer 'Fred' from the beginning. Even he, Georg, his loyal employee, despite his years of service to the family, always called Alfred 'sir', as was the tradition at SBS-Sion when addressing a superior, but perhaps he was too suspicious, too untrusting. Perhaps Alfred was right and Otto didn't have a hidden agenda, but how could he be sure? Georg recalled how Otto had immediately bolted the moment Alfred had given him his new identity, a new passport and a generous bank account. Then, when Otto had contacted SBS-Sion again to meet up in Rome in July, Alfred had immediately welcomed him back, no questions asked, as if nothing had happened. So, if Alfred, being the seer and mystic that he was, felt he could trust Otto so completely, then why couldn't he?

What exactly was he basing his suspicion on? That Otto had been in the SS working with Himmler, a man who had been responsible for the deaths of millions? He knew very well that Otto hadn't been a soldier, but a writer and a researcher, hired to do the field work he was specialised in; searching for lost relics, researching genealogical backgrounds for all sorts of people and finding historical references of hidden, omitted or forgotten history. Georg knew that Otto had a Jewish mother and that he was gay, two things a true Nazi could never get away with. Georg knew it would be wrong to judge Otto, without taking into account the particular circumstances when weighing up his participation in the pre-war Nazi regime. Still, Georg was not at ease with the man and his intuition had never been wrong before.

Georg searched his inner self and thought that his antipathy for Otto was perhaps just based on something personal. He had realised from day one that Otto would never respect him and apart from that, both men had always felt uncomfortable with one another, as if there was some kind of competition. He knew that Alfred and Otto had spent a lot of time alone together, which always made him nervous. What if Otto saw Georg as some kind of competition for Alfred's time and attention? What if Otto was really trying to push Georg out of SBS-Sion? Was Otto after Georg's job?

Damn!

Pressing the gas pedal to the floor, he accelerated rapidly to sixty and proceeded to drive through a red light on a busy crossing, nearly crashing into a large truck. In an effort to avoid an accident, Georg frantically turned the wheel, but his hand slipped and the car hit the sidewalk. He pulled hard on the wheel and only just missed a lamppost. He got back onto the road just in front of a zebra crossing. If he hadn't hit the brakes with all his might, he would have run over several pedestrians. The blare of car horns filled the air as irate drivers made their feelings known. Georg closed his eyes, took a deep breath and drove on, hoping he hadn't caught the attention of the police with his wild driving.

His heart was pounding, so he slowed down a bit, but the very moment he saw an opportunity to, he accelerated again, overtaking cars one after another. He desperately needed to be at the base before seven.

19

Akhetaten, ancient Egypt, 1337 BCE
Meryra took out the small, linen sac and there was dead silence. Only a few people attended what looked like a ceremony and most of them appeared to be priests. The small Aten Temple, the elevated sanctuary of which appeared to be built in the form of a cross, was filled with the most beautiful roses. The building, which had three pairs of pylons, each leading to three different sections, was different from its larger brother on the other side of the royal road. This temple looked as if it was a little older. Like the Great Aten Temple, this temple was devoid of a roof, open to the sky, but among the usual themes, the inner walls were now mainly covered in painted depictions of stellar themes and a strange zodiac.

The priests were standing next to each other, their arms hanging on their sides and their heads bowed with respect. The two men lying face down and bound on the floor, made no sound. They knew that their lives were in the hands of the king and queen. If they were found guilty, they might well be executed on the spot. Showing respect, fear and humility was part of the trial, carefully playing the mood of the judges. One of them, however, was convinced that he would not be harmed, for he had come to seek knowledge and had committed no crime. Her-Uben had travelled far to become a student at the renowned mystery school of Egypt, for the word was out that in the new city of Akhetaten, such a school existed. Knowledge such as the measure of weight, size, shape, depth, geometry, the study of the movements of the stars and planets the forces of the heavens and the forces of the earth were all taught to the chosen adepts at the mystery school. The principles of energy and harmonics and the interaction of it with life - which encompasses the concept that everything is in motion, everything is energy, vibrating at a unique frequency and that nothing is wasted - was taught at the mystery school. The differences between the various manifestations of matter, energy, mind and spirit can be measured according to the frequency of the vibration. The higher the frequency, the higher the position on the universal scale. Some things vibrate to such a high frequency that they appear to stand still, like the spokes of a fast spinning wheel. Other things vibrate to such a slow frequency that they seem to be motionless. In between these two extremes are many millions of varying degrees of vibration. Even thoughts vibrate and thoughts are powerful. To master one's thoughts and to make creative use of the knowledge of energies is the true power of the mystic. This knowledge is very ancient and it enables the student to understand life itself and how to properly navigate through life's vicissitudes.

Her-Uben had arrived at the city of Akhetaten the night before, all excited and ready to learn and the last thing he had expected was to get himself arrested. He hoped that the stories told by Akhenaten's enemies were not true. If they were, he would be in great danger. However, the knowledge of his innocence and his faith in the Aten; the one true god, kept him positive and his breathing was relaxed and normal. At the same time, the other man - who was lying next to Her-Uben - was breathing heavily. Mudada had feared that his son would one day find his figurine of Bastet, but he had no idea that Ishaq would actually reveal its existence to his best friend Khu, who had immediately told his father. Mudada knew very well what this meant for him and his family. How could he have been so careless! He had always kept his belief secret and the figurine so well hidden! When the soldiers had come to arrest him, it was as if the earth had sunk from underneath his feet. The shock had made him dizzy and he had collapsed on the spot. However, to his great surprise he had not been thrown in prison, but brought to the small Aten Temple instead, where another man was already laying bound on the floor. The instant the pharaoh and his queen had entered the temple, he had been thrown on the floor next to the other. His half naked body, shaking in fear, had broken out in a cold sweat as he saw the sanctuary of the temple being transformed into a court room. He did not dare to look up. Instead, he kept his eyes firmly closed and tried to wish himself away. In his terror he could only think about his son. Poor Ishaq. The boy will feel terrible once he finds out that what he had shared with his friend was the reason for his father's execution. Even now, facing certain death, he was thinking of his son. While trying to think of a way to keep his family from harm, he knew that he had no chance of saving himself, as the pharaoh had been ruthlessly suppressing all recognition of the old gods. However, instead of thinking of his death, he decided to think about his life. In his mind he searched for all his happy memories; meeting his wife and falling in love; the birth of his children; the journey to Akhenaten; completing his house and finding a job at the temple. Seeing the pharaoh and his beautiful and powerful queen for the first time when he was first shown his duties at the temple, had not, however, erased the doubts he still had in his mind about forsaking the old gods and forsaking Amun. Perhaps this was the real reason he was being punished.

Meryra came forward and emptied the little purse on the floor in front of the other prisoner, Her-uben. Two stones rolled out, coming to rest not far from the two prisoners. One stone was black and the other white. Otto raced toward the stones to take a closer look. "It's the Urim and Thummim! Look!" Hadi and Arthur approached the stones and saw how the white stone had parked itself next to Her-uben's nose, while the black stone had rolled away in a different direction, coming to a halt in a neutral position. In a hollow voice, Akhenaten addressed Her-uben and Hadi raised his index finger; he had to concentrate on what the pharaoh was saying, so he could translate it for Otto and Arthur.
"Stranger, get up. Your soul is pure and you may go free."
One of the priests stepped into the centre, cut Her-Uben loose and helped him up. Her-Uben was overjoyed, but still worried for the fate of the other man, who was now alone on the floor, waiting to be judged.

Meryra walked over to Mudada, collected the stones, put them back inside the purse and took a few steps back, all in one, straight line. He uttered a few words in various intonations and then threw the stones to the ground again. This time, the black stone had touched Mudada's head, while the white stone landed close to his hand. Meryra was puzzled. This was a complicated matter. His mind may not be pure in thought, but his actions were pure. The priest walked to Akhenaten, who had been watching the scene with one hand placed on his mouth and the other resting on his hip. Meryra whispered, "My Lord, the man's deeds are pure but his mind suffers from doubt. Let us search his house and his belongings. If we do not find anything suspicious, it is my opinion that he should be set free. With your grace upon him, his mind will steady and his thoughts will evolve."

Akhenaten nodded in agreement. "Do so. Send five soldiers to search his house. We will wait here for their return. He does not live far."

Once the soldiers had departed to search his house, Mudada dared to open his eyes. He couldn't believe his luck. How to know if it was Aten who looked upon him with merciful eyes, or if it was Amun? How could he know which god had not forsaken him? He wondered if there was a difference at all. Could it be that the energy behind the names were one and the same? He prayed to both gods with all his might that the soldiers would not find the Bastet figurine.

Hadi, Otto and Arthur were watching the scene with open mouths. They knew that the old Hebrew priests had used the stones to aid in determining guilt and innocence, but it wasn't until that very moment that they fully understood that this ancient method had indeed come from Egypt. They saw how everyone was waiting in silence, hardly moving, as if in meditation. Perhaps it really was meditation, consulting the Aten and its energies to help them render justice and to prevent them from sending innocent people to prison or death.

The soldiers, who had obeyed the pharaoh's order immediately, were now arriving at Mudada's house. While four soldiers searched every niche and corner of the few rooms in the small house, the fifth soldier questioned Mudada's wife Sitre-Meraten and their first born child, Ishaq, who was struck dumb with fear. In the background, his baby brother was crying nonstop. Sitre-Meraten, who had only just come back from burying the figurine, was clinging to the shocked Ishaq while the soldiers turned everything upside down. She pushed her hands deeply inside her son's robe to hide her hands, which were still dirty. Ishaq had not been able to speak a word since his friend Khu had made such a commotion about the cat figurine and only when the soldiers arrived to arrest his father, Ishaq understood the gravity of possessing the cat figurine. Of course, his mother understood very well what had happened. As she clung to her child protectively, she swore to the soldiers that they were all great supporters of the pharaoh and the most faithful worshippers of Aten. She cried out, wailing and lamenting, but the soldiers did not respond. They were too busy searching. However, they found nothing.

Empty-handed but satisfied, they marched back to the small Aten Temple and reported to the pharaoh. Akhenaten and Meryra spoke together in silence, in private. Then, Akhenaten turned to Nefertiti and consulted with her. The queen whispered something back, but Hadi couldn't make out the words. The atmosphere was tense. Otto noticed that the other man, Her-Uben, was still present, standing in a corner with a worried expression on his face. He thought that the man had to be very brave to stay. In his place he'd have been out of there quickly. Then he saw a soldier standing behind the man, holding one of Her-uben's arms. How strange; Her-Uben had just been set free, but he was being prevented from going anywhere. What kind of a justice system was that? Otto thought.

Everybody looked up when the pharaoh walked toward the prisoner on the floor. He was holding a stone axe in his hand.

Mudada saw the axe and thought that the figurine had been found. These were surely the last seconds of his life. With highest concentration he prayed to Amun to forgive him and to look after his family.

Arthur didn't want to look and turned to Otto, who held him in his arms. "I can't believe it, I just can't watch!"

Otto could see the horror in the eyes of the man who had just been set 'free'. Perhaps this is why the soldier was holding onto his arms, to prevent him from interfering. All eyes were now on the pharaoh. With visible anxiety they watched Akhenaten approaching the man on the floor, getting so close that his feet were now only centimetres away from Mudada's head. Everyone held their breath, expecting the pharaoh to swing his axe and give poor Mudada the fatal blow to his head. Then Akhenaten spoke, surprising everyone with what he did next: he asked one of the priests to untie Mudada.

When it was done, Akhenaten spoke to him with a deep voice. His words resonated in every cell of Otto's body as Hadi translated them. "The mighty Aten has found you guilty of doubt, but innocent in deed. If you doubt me, then I command you to take the axe and use it against me. I will not defend myself. Pick it up and slay me, or leave it and go in peace for eternity."

Mudada stood up, his legs still shaking, struck dumb by the words of the pharaoh. He saw how several soldiers moved closer with raised spears ready to throw, but with a flick of his hand, Akhenaten bade them to stand down. Mudada raised his eyes, hardly daring to meet Akhenaten's gaze, unsure of the words he had just heard uttered by the pharaoh. However, the eyes he looked into were at peace, expressing wisdom and love. He saw in those eyes the greatness of the god Aten; the one who gave his life every night; the one who was reborn every morning; the one who bestowed mercy upon him and his family. He saw his pharaoh before him, who had made himself vulnerable for all to see. Mudada looked down at the axe on the floor, kicked it gently to the side with his foot and fell on his knees in front of his king.

He kneeled as low as possible, with his head in front of the pharaoh's feet and his arms spread out on the floor, in total surrender to the mercy of Akhenaten.

"Mudada, faithful servant to Aten-Ra, from this day forth, you will be called 'Menmaataten', meaning: 'Eternal is the Justice of the Aten'. You may go in peace."

Mudada, who would have to get used to his new name, Menmaataten, bowed and walked backwards, first placing the fingers of his right hand on his forehead, then to his lips and finally his chest, before leaving the sanctuary of the small Aten Temple. Without any interference from anyone, he walked out of the temple and went straight home, where he embraced his wife and sons and cried. Never again would he doubt his pharaoh, nor the god Aten, who was just, fair and indulgent. The figurine of Bastet remained buried, deep underground in their garden in the city of Akhetaten, never to be dug up again.

Meanwhile at the small Aten Temple, Her-Uben was led back to the pharaoh for a closed meeting. Everyone not directly involved in the discussion had left the sanctuary. Otto, Arthur and Hadi – unseen - were able to witness the sacred moments that followed. Moments that none of them would ever forget.

20

Tel el-Amarna, Egypt, October 3rd 2011

It had been a while since the muezzin had called everyone to
prayer and Max Müller was getting impatient. They should
have come out by now. He looked at the drinking soldiers
who were guarding the white Mercedes, so he knew that they
were still there, but where? He had searched for them
everywhere and that's what really ticked him off. He was the
best private detective in Europe in his field and he had never
lost anyone before. He was sure the man in the photos was
the man that he had followed here. His client, an Italian
businessman called Roman Corona, had confirmed his
target's identity upon receiving the photos Max had taken of
the German-speaking ferry passenger. Taking a few photos
of Otto while 'checking his mobile' had been a simple task.
"Stick to him like a wet sheet!" he had said to Max. "Be his
shadow. Don't let him out of your sight, not for a moment!"

By now, most of the tourists had already left the site and the
sun was very low on the horizon. Within half an hour it
would be dark and in the desert, darkness is very dark indeed.
Only the moon - which was just into its first quarter - and the
light of the stars would illuminate the desert. For the first
time in his successful career, Max Müller became nervous.
He had already spent half of the generous fee that Corona
had transferred to his bank account in Freiburg in advance, so
if he should fail, he no longer had the means to pay him back
and he was quite sure that Mr Corona would not give him a
break. Max took out his handkerchief and patted his forehead
to stop the sweat from running into his eyes. His sunglasses
were continuously sliding down his nose and he was getting
tired of pushing them back all the time. However, only a few
minutes later he noticed the drop in temperature due to the
setting sun and realised it was getting late. Even the soldiers
were getting impatient now. The liquor had begun to take its
toll and Ashraf, who was now getting angry, threw an empty

bottle against a distant wall. It shattered into hundreds of pieces and scattered across the sand. He turned to his colleague and began vocalising his anger, shouting, "They will not come back, I tell you they will not!"

He picked up his shotgun, walked toward the white Mercedes and smashed one of the windows with the back of the gun. He opened the door, but didn't see the key, so he tried the old trick of hot-wiring the engine by connecting the right two wires to get it started. When the engine started, he waved to Beni to get into the car. It was clear that Ashraf was more than just a little tipsy. Put off by the behaviour of his colleague, Beni took a few steps backwards.

"What are you doing, Ashraf? Are you mad?!"

"Shut up and get in. I will consider this car and whatever it contains as the rest of our payment. They can stay here and rot for all I care, I am not going to wait another minute! I'm going to my cousin in Malawi!"

Beni awkwardly climbed into the passenger seat and pointed at their own vehicle. "But what about your land rover?"

Ashraf slapped Beni's head. "You fool! Get your ass out of the car and get into the rover! Who else do you think will drive it back, huh?"

The very moment Beni had left the car and closed the door, Ashraf shot off at great speed in Hadi's confiscated white Mercedes, leaving his colleague behind in a cloud of dust and sand. While brushing off the sand from his hair, clothes and face with his hands, Beni walked to the rover, but the moment he got behind the wheel, he remembered that Ashraf had been driving before and therefore would probably also have taken the key. He checked his pockets, but found nothing but a single piece of chewing gum. He got out and allowed his irritation to take control of his emotions. After spitting on the floor and cursing his colleague, he sat down in the sand and pushed the chewing gum 'accordion wise' into his mouth. Beni sneezed twice in reaction to the heavy mint flavour and gazed anxiously into the distant, deserted ruins.

He decided he would have to hitchhike to Malawi if his clients were not going to show up before darkness fell. Little did he know that - for obvious reasons - the expedition was scheduled to come back *after* dark.

Max had watched the scene from a distance and grinned with amusement. "Another one bites the dust." he whispered to himself. However, for Max this was a lucky turn of fate. All he had to do now was make sure he was on the next ferry. He would wait for the men to cross the Nile, meet them at the ferry port and offer them transportation. Abandoned, without a car, they would surely take the bait. He blessed the cool breeze and the enchanting atmosphere of the desert at sunset and started walking the long road to the port. His dark hair was uncomfortably wet from the sweat that had collected under his white cap and his pale skin had turned to a fierce red from overexposure to the Egyptian sun. He looked at the magnificent red ball, now quickly disappearing below the horizon into the mythical realm of the dead. While humming a tune he took out his mobile phone and dialled a number.
"It's me again. Yes, I will need the car when I get back. That would be good. Danke Hugo."
The tune he sang quickly turned into a marching song and Max walked to the rhythm as if he had just won the lottery.
The Arab, however, who was still sitting in the sand next to the immobile land rover. He saw Max passing by and cursed him. And Ashraf. And those stupid tourists who had disappeared into the old ruins of Amarna.

Max hadn't been walking long when he felt the urge to look behind him. He couldn't see anything, but stopped singing his marching song as he tried to identify a sound he couldn't hear very well. It was a strange, hollow humming sound, like the distant sound of a lawnmower or an airplane. He got the strangest impression that the mysterious sound was getting closer to him, as if there was a giant bee hovering above him.

When he heard the sound once more, he brushed the air next to his ear with his hand, as if trying to swat an invisible insect. The sound was becoming clearer now. When it started, it made an odd sound like a sigh and when it stopped, there was an echo.

Then he felt something touching his skin and got goose bumps. When he suddenly felt a draft, licking his face like an invisible dog greeting his master, the hair on the back of his neck stood up straight. Then he remembered the warnings he had received when he had arrived in Amarna. "It's a ghost town," the villagers had told him. "Make sure you get out before sunset and always stick to the main road."

Max started running. The sound, however, kept up with him and appeared to be glued to his ears. Whatever was haunting him on that moment, seemed to be attached to his body. He could already see the little port with the ferry, waiting to carry the last passengers to the other shore. He began waving and shouting at the people, calling to them to wait for him. It was now almost dark and as the tarmac on the road was in a very bad shape, he stumbled at the edge of the road and fell on his face. While spitting out sand and trying to get back on his feet, he noticed that the sound had now become very loud. He could also hear words, pronounced with the rolling 'r' of the ancient Egyptian tongue. Though he could see no one, he could feel breath on his face and hear whispered words as if they were meant only for him: "Baou-Ra!"

He got to his feet and started off again as fast as he could toward the ferry dock.

Never had he believed in ghosts until today.

He had laughed at the villagers for trying to instil fear of the ghosts of Amarna in him and was sure that it was a common technique they used to ensure no one stayed behind after dark. He wondered what Baou-Ra meant and promised the ghost that he would look it up, on condition it left him alone. Immediately, the noise stopped and the draft in his face disappeared along with it.

Drenched with sweat and panting for breath, he finally reached the ferry, boarded and frantically shouted a plea to the captain, begging him to cast off immediately.

"Ten more minutes, mister. We do not want anyone to be left behind in the dark. There are ghosts in those ruins, you know?"

Max looked at the captain with a sheepish smile and caressed his moustache. "So I've heard," he said. "So I've heard…"

21

Guernsey, Channel Islands, October 3rd 2011

Izz al Din did not enjoy the sea voyage from Jersey to Guernsey and was even beginning to feel a little sea sick. In his weakened state, his poor stomach simply couldn't handle the soft sway of the ferry. A strong wind had picked up and the waves were getting bigger and bigger every minute. Knowing it would prevent vomiting, he lay down on the dirty floor of the boat. This attracted the attention of some of the other passengers, one of whom immediately sought help from the staff. However, Al Din's two strong helpers refused to let anyone come close to him. Lying prostrate on the floor did settle the nausea, but increased the throbbing headache he had suffered ever since he had come out of his coma. The steady rumble of the engine, amplified through the floor on which his head was resting, made it even worse.

"Let them help me, let them..." He muttered, just before he lost consciousness.

When he awoke, he was lying on a bed in the De Sausmarez ward at the Princess Elizabeth hospital in St. Andrew. The man with the ring was staring out of the window, keeping an eye on everyone going by. The other was slumped in a chair next to him, fast asleep. Al Din couldn't see any signs of police presence, so he immediately felt much better. Then he noticed the IV and cursed. Not again! His first impulse was to pull it out, but then he stopped, his arm frozen in mid-air. Perhaps he ought to take this opportunity to rest and regain his strength before throwing himself into a physically demanding operation. The one vital key to ensure that things continued to go smoothly for him was that his false identity, which had brought them this far, held up.

He stared at a photo on the wall. It was an unexpected decoration in the single room, which had white walls, aqua blue window shades and lavender bed sheets. The photo showed Castle Cornet with - on the foreground - a group of small sailboats, moored in the harbour of St. Peter Port.

It reminded him of his own boat, the 'Scherazade', which was currently moored at the harbour of Jaffa in Israel. The memory brought him back to happier times, when he was playing the Don Juan at jet set parties, always surrounded by the most beautiful women. His sailboat had taken him to many exotic destinations and champagne party venues all around the Mediterranean. At his spacious villa in the Jerusalem hills he even had his own harem of girlfriends, whom he had 'collected' over the years. The generosity with which he had taken care of these girls - who were usually bored tourists, lured into his web - had persuaded them stay. That and perhaps a few drops of his notorious drug cocktail every day to keep them 'loyal'. He owed this lifestyle to a hunch he'd got, many years before, on buying some inexpensive, uninhabited land from a sheik who had no idea that there was oil in the ground. The profits from the oil production had brought him much comfort, luxury and power, but he had always had an unquenchable desire for more. More money, more power, more influence...

Then, fate had brought him to Danielle. He had got wind of a laboratory in Switzerland where a new wormhole time travel technique was used to observe several important historical events in order to establish an idea of their accuracy. He had been able to infiltrate their facilities in Sion, where he had discovered the secret of the beautiful Danielle, who instantly became his new *raison d'être*. With her and her royal child on his side, he would not only be able to gain more power. He would also be able to gain access to immortality.

The door opened and the disturbing metallic jingling noise of a clunky, rolling trolley woke him up from his thoughts. A woman in a green-and-white striped uniform came in with a choice of beverages. Her cockney accent revealed that she was from South East London and immediately, Al Din produced a generous smile to compliment her lovely figure. "Sorry I'm late!" she started. "Now, what would you like to drink, sir? I have coffee, tea, or would you prefer a fruit juice?"

That sounded more like home. He was used to being served. "If you have nothing stronger, then I will have tea. Be a dear, will you please and help me sit up?"

Lars, the man sitting next to the bed, was now fully awake and scrutinised each move while the young woman attended to his employer. He whined at her like a neglected boy, still rubbing his eyes. "Hey, can we have some tea here too? I'm thirsty!"

The young woman took pity on his sleepy face and quickly walked back to her trolley. "Well, the restaurant in the Gloucester Room is closed now, so I will pour you all some tea, but then you need to leave. Visiting hours are until eight, you know."

Al Din, who knew that the pregnant Danielle had to be somewhere not too far from a hospital, suddenly turned to the girl with a logical question.

"Tell me, is this the only hospital on the island?"

"Yes sir, it is."

Al Din smiled. That was all he needed to know.

Titan, who had been staring out of the window intently, now joined them and they all waited silently for the woman to leave before they touched their tea. As soon as she was out of the room, Titan walked to the door and closed it behind her. Not long before - while Al Din was still asleep - a nurse had come in to check Al Din's vital signs and get some information for the hospital file. Lars had managed to answer a few uncomfortable questions, which seemed to satisfy her for the moment. She had left rather quickly, saying she'd be back later once the patient had woken, but the questioning had left them somewhat tense. Especially Titan couldn't wait to get out of the hospital. "What do we do now? Do we wait? Or do we leave tonight?"

"I am weak," Al Din replied, "I want to stay a few days and regain my strength. Keep an eye out for unwanted guests and when I am up to it, I'll check out, perhaps in the third night. Trust me, it'll be quieter at night."

Al Din's men turned silent; they were obviously tired from driving non-stop from Switzerland to St. Malo in France and from the ferry passage to Jersey and again to Guernsey. Also, he understood that the anxiety they had endured while he was in a coma in the prison hospital in Zürich, must have taken its toll. Aiming to keep a low profile, they had lived like hermits; secluded but ever watchful, waiting for the moment Al Din would call on them for help. He owed them his freedom, for without Lars and Titan he would not have succeeded in escaping from Zürich so easily. Their loyalty had been tried and proved.

When he had finished his tea, Lars turned to his chief to give him an update. "Sir, I've got the car parked outside. We just followed the ambulance to the hospital. They accepted the false ID I gave them, so you are now registered as a patient here at the hospital in St. Andrew. It's vital that you remember your false name in case they ask you more questions. Remember, you are Raoul Hadin, a rich businessman from Israel. If they ask you why you are on the island, you tell them that you came here to make a substantial bank deposit and that you are considering buying a house on the quieter island of Guernsey. Remember that Jersey is commonly known as a popular tax haven and consequently, the island has become particularly famous for its highly rated international offshore finance. I have already prepared an Israeli bank account in your false name, so all you have to do is transfer some money into the account - say, from one of your shell companies - to make it appear genuine."

Al Din smirked with delight when he heard the extensive details surrounding his presence on the island. "You are very clever, my friend. Give me my laptop. I will see to it immediately."

Lars walked out of the room to retrieve Al Din's briefcase from the car. Just before he left the room, Al Din shouted after him, "and take out your personal bags too while you're at it!"

Lars paused, puzzled by that last command and then walked on. The moment he had disappeared into the hallway, Al Din turned to Titan. "I want you to try and find Danielle for me. She will be in this immediate area, not too far from the hospital. Lars will stay here with me as my 'business associate'. When Lars comes back with my briefcase, I will give you some money. Act like a tourist, buy some binoculars and tell people you are an ornithologist. The moment you have an idea where she might be, you report back to me. You can take the car, Lars won't need it here."

Titan smiled, revealing a fine set of pearly white teeth. His broad chest and tall posture had earned him his nickname the first day he was hired as Al Din's personal bodyguard three years ago. The Bosnian had been the bodyguard to several powerful men before he was recommended to Al Din, who had found him to be loyal and quiet, as long as he had his money and his comforts. Lars, on the other hand, was much less quiet, but perhaps an even more valuable assistant than Titan. Lars was particularly good at cleaning up after messy jobs and since he had come from sinister circles, he always knew how to arrange everything; from transportation to false passports and from guns to high tech intelligence. If it weren't for Lars's knowledge and his high-tech gadgets, Al Din would have never discovered that Danielle was on Guernsey. Titan may be loyal, but Lars was irreplaceable.

He needed to keep Lars close to him.

The moment Lars came back with the briefcase, he handed it over to his chief, who opened it by entering a code. Titan was holding up his hand, eager to get out of the hospital. With a frown, Lars witnessed Titan being given a fat roll of notes, after which Al Din turned to Lars. "Give him the car keys."

"But..."

"You're staying here with me while Titan explores the island to find Danielle. Give him the car keys."

Reluctantly, Lars handed them over to Titan.

His car keys.

His beloved Camaro Convertible V8 SS.

"Be very, very careful, Titan and I mean, very careful. You hear me?" said Lars in a threatening voice, but Titan just chuckled while he walked out the door. With a painful face, Lars turned to Al Din. "He's so going to wreck my car!"

Al Din laughed out loud. "When he does, my dear Lars, I will get you another one and if we succeed in retrieving Danielle and returning to Jerusalem with her, I will buy you any car you want! You have my word!"

Lars walked over to the window and looked lovingly at his shining, greyish-mauve car with its convertible top and orange seats. It still had that particular pleasant smell of newness and the car was heavenly to drive. He had installed all the gadgets he had been able to collect over the past few months, including the latest navigation, which - with a particular accessory - could pick up signals from a planted bug. No other car would ever be that complete.

Not even Batman's.

"If I can have any car I want, then I want to have *my* car back *in one piece,*" Lars replied, bellowing the last words toward Titan down below. He could see the giant burning rubber on the paved parking lot as he sped out. When he spotted Titan's hand out the window - boldly extending his middle finger and obviously perfectly confident that Lars was watching him from the window above - his blood boiled. Trying to calm himself, he rubbed his face with his right hand and mumbled quietly to himself, "I so hate that man!"

Meanwhile, several miles away, a young man, having finally found a place to stay, fell face down on his bed. A minute later, Michael took out his mobile phone and checked the number his father had called from, but then he hesitated. David had told him not to come and look for him and would certainly be angry if Michael called and said, "Hi dad, guess what? I'm in St. Peter Port!" He put away his phone and turned on the TV to see what was going on in the world.

President Barack Obama 'absolutely' considers himself to be the underdog in the 2012 presidential campaign, 'given the economy' and has said that voters aren't doing better economically than they were four years ago.

Michael had no taste for politics at the best of times, so he quickly zapped to another channel, hoping to find a movie or a talk show to take his mind off the situation at hand, but when he couldn't find anything interesting, he simply turned it off. Reluctantly, he unpacked his travel bag and noticed that he had - at the last moment - thrown in a photo of himself and his father in France, standing on a rocky outcrop just outside the ruined castle of Montségur, leaning safely against a large boulder. Those were the happy days he missed and he realised that he was becoming more and more afraid that his father really was in trouble. That phone number was the only lead he had and he knew he'd eventually have to use it. He decided to send a text message instead, saying,
"Dad please call. I need you. Michael."
Knowing his father, he half-expected him to call him back immediately. However, he had forgotten that it wasn't David's phone number he was texting to; it was Mrs Peel's and at this hour, the caretaker of Rose Cottage was fast asleep in her armchair in front of her television, as usual.

22

Akhetaten, ancient Egypt, 1337 BCE

It was quiet in the temple. Everyone was staring at Her-uben, who was now blind-folded and unable to see what was going on around him. Priests, standing in two rows, surrounded him. They were all wearing a kilt. Arthur thought about the Rosicrucian and Freemason aprons and wondered if this would perhaps have been their origin. These Egyptian kilts worn by priests only, were worn with a white rope around the waist. The white rope had a particular knot at the end, pointing skyward. This knot, which was worn by the royal families of Egypt, represented the goddess Isis, but also the bearer's striving for perfection and immortality. However, worn here inside the Temple of Aten, this special knot now represented the Ankh, the ancient symbol of life, in all its meanings.

The T or Tau cross that is at the Ankh's centre, symbolises 'the Word' or 'Logos', by which the frequency of Divine Polarity came into existence, creating for the first time a division in being, divided into male and female, spirit and matter, above and below. Like a balloon blown from the mouth, the loop above the T symbolises the consequence of this vibrational frequency: Creation.

The Ankh as a whole also symbolises the Mirror of Life, which refers to the Principle of Reflection, referred to in the age old term: As above, so below - as below, so above. The world we see is a reflection of the world we cannot see from our tangible, physical perspective. Once aware of this principle, we may be able to lift the 'Veil of Isis' and push aside the obstacles preventing a clear view of the Unknown.

The priests; all sworn servants of the Ankh and Aten-Ra, now stood motionless underneath the dark night sky, channelling the Divine Light and Love of Aten to this physical plane. They were the sworn protectors of magic, a gift bestowed only upon the priestly servants of the living Aten.

The Master Initiator, the pharaoh himself, was their leader. Akhenaton was now standing before the blindfolded Her-uben, but Her-uben could not see this, so when the pharaoh started talking to him, Her-uben startled; a clear sign that he was very nervous. Akhenaton, charismatic and calm - yet clearly the master - asked the customary questions that a Master Initiator asks of a candidate who wishes to become an initiate.

Did he come to seek the knowledge?
Was he prepared to die should he betray the secret teachings of the Temple of Aten to the uninitiated?

In a soft but determined voice, Her-uben answered "Yes, my Lord, honourable Master" to each question asked. Then, someone quietly placed an obstacle in front of Her-uben that of course he could not see, as he was blindfolded. It looked like a large brick. Akhenaton asked Her-uben to walk toward him and to have faith in the Aten. Not expecting to find the obstacle placed in front of him, Her-Uben stumbled and fell into the arms of Akhenaton, who caught him and propped him upright. Her-uben could feel a rush of adrenaline as he knelt on one knee, while the pharaoh - who could feel the man trembling - held on to his arms to steady him. Then, Akhenaten began to speak again in a voice loud and clear, for all to hear.

Hadi translated as well as he could. "He who walks blindfolded without faith, will stumble and fall to his death. He who walks blindfolded, but has faith in the Aten, will be caught by the living Aten, as I, Akhenaton, Exalter of the Name of Aten, Strong Bull of Aten, have now caught you, Her-uben. Now rise, in the name of Aten!"

For the first time they could hear the proper pronunciation of the name Akhenaton, in the way it should be pronounced. Otto thought it sounded very Dutch, with the CH pronounced from the back of the throat. After publishing his book 'Crusade Against the Grail' in 1933, Otto had spoken to several readers from Holland and remembered how everyone had to laugh when he tried to correctly pronounce the Dutch word *'prachtig'* He had to practice for a long time until he could say it properly. Also, he could now hear how the last part of Akhenaten's name ended in 'on', not 'en'. 'Aton'.

Being the son of a Jewish mother, he remembered a Jewish prayer: *Schema Yisrael, Adonai Elohenu Adonai Echod* - 'Hear oh Israel, the Lord thy God is one God'. He felt that apart from the story of Moses, this prayer could have also originated in Akhenaten's time. It would make perfect sense if 'Adonai' had derived from 'Aton'. It would then simply translate to: 'Aton is the one and only God'. After all, Akhenaten had been very determined and had persevered - despite terrible repercussions - in proclaiming that Aten was the one and only God, both in his new laws as well as in the hymns and prayers to Aten. Otto smiled and whispered softly to himself, "Sol Invictus." The principal male deity has always been the invincible sun.

The sound of rattles metamorphosed into sound frequencies they could physically feel in this strange dimension they were currently forced to exist in. The frequencies were coming from a group of women priests who were walking slowly in a procession, wearing simple pleated linen dresses and rattling sistrums at a steady rhythm. The first girl in the procession was one of the princesses, Ankhesenpaaten. She was leading the solemn group of women - composed of her sisters and her mother, Nefertiti - to the altar. There, from the flame of one of three lamps that were placed in a triangular formation on the altar, she lit her own little oil lamp. Her-uben was now no longer blindfolded and had been taken to his place among the other initiates, who were still standing in two rows, facing each other. As Ankhesenpaaten walked between the two rows of initiates, holding the lamp up high before her, everyone bowed to honour the light. Hadi explained that this light symbolised the light that is within, seeing our physical body as a material 'house' for the Aten to dwell in, so we are in fact a temple ourselves; a 'Per Aten'. In Western mysticism, one would call this divine light the 'Sophia'.

Otto, who had written about this in his second book, 'Lucifer's Court', already knew that the name Lucifer was simply another name for Sophia, the child of God and that the early Christian Church fathers had abused the name, turning it into something evil. Originally, the Light bringer was a pagan goddess of fire, also known as the Barat-Anna - or Bar-Ata in Phoenician - representing the fire that is within us, the Divine Fire which gives us life and which connects us directly to God. For Rome, this - as well as the fact that a female represented this light - was enough reason to banish her to hell. Only the heretics, the 'freethinkers', still honour this goddess through Sophia. What a beautiful world it would be if only we all had the liberty to make up our own minds about the God of our hearts. Then he thought of the many brave people who had tried repeatedly to break from religious dogma centuries ago and by doing so, they had actually sowed the seeds of ancient hermetic knowledge within society, right under everyone's noses. He thought about the clever French, from whom many secret hermetic knowledge group leaders issued. Many of the noble families and powerful members of French society were deeply involved in secret brotherhoods. French membership in these hidden knowledge groups had often been the majority, especially in the 19th century. It had been from this French society that the gift was made of this goddess of fire, to the people of New York. The Statue of Liberty, *'La liberté éclairant le monde'* ('Liberty Enlightening the World') has been welcoming visitors and immigrants to America - the land of freedom - ever since.

Otto sighed contently, for he now knew that Sophia; Lucifer; the Light bringer; child of Aten; Bar Ata; the spark of life; our soul; the Holy Grail - despite its many names - has always been one and the same.

Otto snapped out of his thoughts when he felt a strange vibration coming from under his clothes. When it stopped, he quickly forgot about it as the rituals and Hadi's translations now distracted him. Watching the scene was like attending a lecture at a University. Akhenaton was the speaker whose sole intention was to teach those initiates who had come to listen and learn. Hadi wasn't able to translate it all, but apparently the lecture was about the three forms:

Aten in thought, bringing light,
Aten in word, bringing life,
Aten in deed, bringing love.

"The Sacred Love of Aten penetrates deep within us and gives life to every living creature in the land. His Love and Light animates all living things and gives Life to seeds, bulbs, nuts and all the new-born. When He rests and darkness comes over the land, He illuminates the stars and the moon, which in their turn illuminate the land at night, as proof that even in death he will keep the souls of the departed alive in His realm. For is it not through the Art of Reflection that we can see into the Unknown? The Aten Disc symbolises the Omnipotence of the High Lord - who is our Father - as well as the perfection of His Sacred Laws, by which everything is kept in proper motion. The circle is the symbol of perfection and of Aten's Omnipresence. The centre of the circle is everywhere; the circumference is, however, nowhere."

This was difficult for Arthur and Otto to comprehend. How can you see an outer line, clearly illustrating a limited space and then say that the circumference of the circle is nowhere? How can a centre of a circle, which is clearly positioned in the middle, be everywhere?

However, there was no time to contemplate. Akhenaton was unstoppable and Hadi tried to keep up, explaining as much as possible of what he heard.

Hadi heard the words 'kingdom' and 'crown' when Akhenaton talked about the circle and The Word and there was something in the way he explained it, that struck a chord in Arthur. He touched Otto's arm to get his attention.

"Remember the theme of The Lady and the Unicorn?"

Otto nodded. "I have seen several versions of it. In one, the medieval tapestry shows the garden and at its centre you see a crowned Unicorn and a Lady who holds his horn in her hand. The garden is surrounded by a round fence."

"Exactly! I have a theory. If I apply the Aten and all the things we've just learned to the Lady and the Unicorn, then I can see that God created the garden, which symbolises life on earth, but by doing so, God also created the fence, which means that everything in the material world has a limit, an ending. The Lady represents Mother Earth and the Unicorn represents the virility of the Divine Father. The scene symbolises the Sacred Marriage of spirit and matter, male and female. There are several horned gods and goddesses that represent fertility. This is also where the word 'horny' comes from. In Christianity, the Unicorn replaced the horned gods. He often wears a crown, usually around his neck. This means that God will always be the Omnipotent God; the ruler, in charge of His creation."

Otto agreed. The more he found out about ancient Egyptian religion - especially Atenism - the more he understood that Judaism and thus also Christianity may have sprouted from Atenism. At least he felt that it had been heavily influenced by its mystery school. The very school they were now secretly and invisibly attending.

Finally, Akhenaton had finished and the ritual was now coming to an end. Hadi, who was covered in sweat, was beginning to find it more and more difficult to breath. He became restless and wanted to see if he could get a closer look at the stones. So when everyone began leaving the Temple, Hadi decided to follow Meryra. Arthur and Otto, who didn't want to lose sight of Hadi again, stayed close to him. In the meantime, Meryra had already put the stones back in his little purse and because they were unable to touch anything, their only option was to follow him and find out where the priest was keeping the stones and then quickly return to the present.

Realising that their current inability to be 100% physically present in their current time destination must be due to some kind of fault in the ERFAB's programming; something Wong had been responsible for and they soon came to a consensus on their options: should Wong succeed in repairing the flaw that had brought them into the wrong dimension - or at least into the wrong layer of the right time - they would have to get back to modern times first and then try to go back to ancient Akhetaten. If, on their second try, they manage to arrive in the right dimension - being the physical layer, where they could feel and touch and interact with the tangible world - they could go straight to the stones' location; replace the Eye of Ra and press the 'home' button before they got caught. In practice, however, things are never that simple.

Meryra was striding dapperly through the courtyard and Otto and Arthur had to walk 'through' several people to keep up with him. Suddenly, Arthur also felt a strange vibration under his clothing. It was the ERFAB. The battery must be low. Slightly alarmed, he took out the device from its secret pocket inside his galabya and saw how the green light was flickering, confirming his worst fears. Picking up speed and taking longer strides - constantly reminding himself not to run toward his friends - he decided to call out to them.
"Hey guys, we have a problem!"
Hadi and Otto turned when they heard Arthur call and saw his alarmed and exasperated expression as he held up his ERFAB device. They quickly took out their devices and noticed that their batteries were also dangerously low. They would have to recharge them with exposure to a light source, but it was now fully dark outside and the only light source came from the lit oil lamps and torches, that were placed all over the Temple grounds. Hadi shrugged his shoulders, feeling somewhat helpless, but agreed that the oil lamps were the only possible solution. "We will just have to keep an eye

on Meryra and see where he goes, while we move from lamp to lamp. Come on!"

They walked as fast as they dared without running, holding the faltering devices close to the flickering light of one lamp for a moment as they passed, then moving with determination to the next. Being in a hurry, Meryra was walking straight to a different wing of the Temple of Aten and they knew that they'd soon lose sight of him. Suddenly, a sharp bleep was emitted from all three of the devices and they saw that the green light had stopped blinking on each. As had been previously decided, they immediately selected number '1', so they could press 'ok' the very moment they were ready to return to present day Egypt. This is what Alfred had instructed. They had to select option '1' as the way back, in case they failed to replace the stone. Once they arrived safely back in the present, they were to call Alfred immediately to receive new orders. They didn't know how long the batteries would hold out this time and the air was getting dangerously thin in this strange dimension, so it was indeed time to return to the present. Sadly, their mission had failed.

Although fully aware of the consequences, Hadi - who wasn't ready to give up so quickly - began to run after Meryra. Immediately, the world around him began to morph into a strange ball where time seemed to stop. He could just see Meryra entering a building when he shouted to the others. "I believe he is going to the Baou-Ra."

Otto and Arthur, who had seen how unnaturally Hadi had sped up in his attempt to run after Meryra, could only hear a high pitched voice, as if Hadi had accidently inhaled gas from a helium balloon. Otto couldn't help bursting into laughter. "What?"

Hadi stood still and allowed time to neutralise both his movement and the tone of his vocal cords. He was out of breath, panting heavily and feeling very dizzy. He took a moment to get his breath back before he could explain what he had seen.

"Meryra has gone inside the sacred library where the priests keep their religious writings and artefacts. It's called the Baou-Ra."

Otto, who was still grinning at the thought of Hadi's earlier high pitched voice, found 'Baou-Ra' to be an ever so amusing word. He repeated it, toying with the unique sounds that surprisingly energised his mouth. "The Baou-Ra? I'll have to remember that!" he said laughing. "You could scare someone with that word if you said it out loud. Baou-Ra!"

Realising that they were almost out of oxygen - which was making them feel giddy and only minutes away from fainting - Hadi made a decision. "Guys, we are running out of oxygen, we have to press the button now!"

For some reason, in being transported from their modern date of departure to this strange intangible dimension, oxygen had also accompanied them. It was as if they had travelled in an air bubble. The oxygen that had been transported with them when they had entered this dimension had slowly been transformed into carbon dioxide, exhaled with each breath. Hadi looked sternly at everyone, demanding absolute attention. This was a terrifying moment. Perhaps they were to be trapped in this dimension forever. The ERFAB had been wrongly programmed once, what if the calculations were wrong again? He didn't dare think of what could happen, but they had no other choice than to try.

"Are we all ready? Pressing 'ok' in 3 seconds!"

While Hadi was counting down, Otto slowly turned to Arthur and at the very moment they all pressed 'ok', he impetuously shouted close to his ear:

"Baou-Ra!"

23

Sion, Switzerland, October 3rd 2011

Alfred was in a lot of pain. The insidious, steadily growing tumour was doing its damage and he was clearly running out of time. He was still hoping that his field team would succeed and bring him the Eye of Ra, his beloved Urim, from Akhetaten. He had already taken the Thummim out of the ring and the shining black stone was now housed in a beautiful, silver box, silently awaiting reunion with its partner. Anxiously he was looking at the clock. If the mission had been successful, they would be here at the laboratory in a few minutes' time. If not, Alfred would get a call on his mobile phone, which should also be soon. He had tried to reach Georg, but Georg's mobile was switched to his answering machine again, making Alfred even more nervous. The last time this had happened, Georg had been in big trouble. However, he didn't have to worry long as that very moment, Georg's car came to a screeching halt in front of the house that hid the entrance to the base. By the time he arrived at Alfred's glass office in the lab, Georg was gasping, struggling with each laboured breath. As much as he hated to admit it, he knew he was still weak from the drug. When he reached Alfred, he was shocked to see his pale face. It was clear to him that Alfred was suffering and that he couldn't hide his agony very well any longer. Understanding the misfortune of each other's situation, a mere nod was exchanged. Georg calmly asked the inevitable question.

"Are they here yet?"

Alfred shook his head and rubbed his unshaven face with his right hand. "No, Georg. I have a strange feeling that they didn't make it. A profound feeling of loss went through me a moment ago and that's not a good sign. I feel as if they have been ripped out of their very existence and are no longer part of our universe. If this is so, I will have the surgery done right away. I no longer wish to wait."

Alfred cringed as he succumbed to another attack of sharp pain and Georg stood by, feeling helpless and powerless. Though he was torn in two over the wisdom of silence and sharing a problem, Georg decided not to confront his employer with his suspicions about Otto. He decided to merely keep an eye on the German and make sure he stayed within the lines. That is, if he came back.

Meanwhile, Wong was staring at the glass office from the lab. He felt insecure, nervous and guilty. Wong had waited too long to tell his chief about the flaw and consequently, Alfred hadn't been able to reach the field team in time to inform them that the mobile ERFAB devices had been improperly programmed. In fact, Wong had no idea where he had sent them and whether they would ever make it back to the present in one piece. He felt responsible for his employer's pain, believing the bad news he had shared that afternoon had made it worse.

Time seemed to pass ever so slowly, as it always does when one is waiting.

They should have arrived by now.

When the clock on the wall clicked to 19.01 hours, they knew for certain that the mission had failed. The mobile ERFABs had all been programmed to have them returned to the present at 19.00 hours. Alfred took out his mobile phone and gazed at it in perplexed anticipation. Minutes went by and still the phone did not ring. The waiting was paralysing. What else could have gone wrong? What if they did make it back to the present, but discovered that their phones had been stolen. That was after all a realistic possibility. In that case they'd have to call from another phone and this might take time. Alfred was a positivist and refused to give up hope, but he knew that he had to make a decision soon about leaving for the hospital. He decided to wait until 19.30 hours and then have Georg set everything up. Alfred noticed how Wong was trying to make himself invisible down in the lab. The already short man had slumped even lower in front of his computer and had now started to softly bang his head on the desk. Wong would never forgive himself if his mistake had taken the lives of three people who had trusted him.

Feeling sympathy for the professor, Alfred decided to talk to him. "Don't torture yourself, Wong. I take full responsibility. They knew the risks when they signed up for the job. Your predecessor wasn't completely faultless either, but somehow things always worked out. Keep faith, young man, keep faith."

Before he left, Alfred tapped him on the shoulder and whispered, "… but fix that flaw, okay?"

Alfred returned to his glass office, sat in a chair, made himself comfortable and started to meditate. It was the only way for him to overcome his pain and to use his ability to send out positive thoughts to the mission and his upcoming risky surgery. He knew that everything is energy and knew that if everyone knew how powerful thoughts really are, no one would ever think anything bad again.

Georg walked out the office and selected the phone number of the surgeon who would take on Alfred's operation next week. It only rang twice before the surgeon answered; he knew the number of the caller well enough by now.

Georg immediately came to the point. "Doctor Waldheim, I wonder if we could reschedule and speed things up. Yes. It's got worse. Yes, we will. Thank you so much, doctor!"

Georg hung up and returned to Alfred to share the news.

"If we go to the hospital tonight, he can operate tomorrow morning at 08.00 hours. If that's what you would like, then it's best if we get going. You can still answer your phone all night. I will come with you."

Alfred nodded. "I've prepared a bag, but it's not here, it's at the house. We will pick it up on our way to the hospital. Wong will stay here just in case. I'm sure he'll be alright in the lab on his own, but make sure the location is sealed until one of us returns."

Immediately, Georg went out to prepare the base for his absence. He had only been gone for ten minutes, but when he returned, Alfred had fallen on the floor of the glass office and was struggling with the excruciating pain. Wong was bending over him. "He just collapsed, Mr Hauser!"

Georg began to lose calm and tried to make him sit upright. "What can I do? Call for an ambulance?" asked Wong, wanting to help. Alfred knew that he had no choice. Higher powers were now at work. He had to let go of the urge to control everything; something he had always found extremely difficult. Accepting his fate, Alfred gave Georg a quick nod and raised his hand, so that Georg could help him up. His voice sounded hoarse. "Yes, Georg. That would be best; do what you have to do."

An hour later, Alfred was lying comfortably in a private room at the hospital in Sion. An IV was feeding him a small dose of morphine to take away most of his pain. On one side of his bed, a nurse was taking blood samples. On the other side was Georg, sending short text messages to Hadi and Otto on Alfred's phone before he was forced to turn it off, hoping there would soon be a reply. He felt badly about the entire situation, it's as if some kind of a curse had been placed on the entire mission; Izz al Din, who had broken out of the hospital ward at the prison in Zurich; Alfred's medical condition and then, their failed mission to Akhetaten.

However, being close to men like Alfred and Alfred's father had also taught him something valuable. He had learned how to protect yourself from negative influences by creating an imaginary bubble of light around yourself and your loved ones and filling the bubble with love. So while they were waiting for the surgeon, whom he had called again to request moving the operation even further forward, he decided to put the safety bubble visualisation technique into practice.

He closed his eyes and visualised himself, Alfred, Danielle, David Wong, Hadi, Arthur and even Otto inside a light sphere. Then he added the two stones to the sphere and put them into Alfred's hands. He tried to hold this image and feed it with love until suddenly, something remarkable happened. In his mind's eye the white stone in Alfred's right hand began to shine more brightly than he could bear. He quickly snapped out of the visualisation and opened his eyes, only to see Alfred looking at him with a proud face and a broad smile. "You did it! You did it! I am so proud of you, Georg!" A tear escaped Alfred's eye. Georg had never shown any interest in mysticism before, so Alfred was pleasantly surprised. Too sick to meditate properly, the entire mission and his own wellbeing - as well as that of his beloved friends - was now in the hands of a higher power and the powers of others; others like Georg.

Alfred had trained Otto to visualise and polarise; turning negativity into positivity. He also knew that Georg too was capable of powerful visualisation, but only if he believed in his own power. Apparently, now at last, he did believe in his own power. It's as if only in times of great trouble, people find out what they are really capable of.

Georg knew by the look on his face that Alfred, a seer, had seen something and he wondered if he had seen the same.

"Did you see what I'd visualised?"

"Yes, Georg, I did. The stone was shining so brightly that even you lit up completely, my friend. If only my father were here to witness it! He had always said you had it in you! You are powerful, my friend and I will teach you more if you are ready."

Georg, who had been so filled with anxiety and worry until now, couldn't help feeling uplifted. If anything, meditation takes away negative emotions and enables positive emotions to replace them. It also allows positive events to take place.

That very moment, as if the universe was arranging the entire scene, a good-humoured surgeon enthusiastically walked in. The expression on his face was similar to that of a famous TV personality, who had been asked to surprise the owner of a winning lottery ticket. The Austrian born Mikael Waldheim had already met Alfred several times in the past few weeks. He was a cheerful man and one of the most skilled surgeons in Europe. Nevertheless he was aware of the risks and had discussed them with Alfred at each meeting, but he also knew that he had to try, for this time, there was no Plan B.

"Gruß Gott meine Herrn! Good news! I have called in a colleague from Bern to replace me tonight and take over my shift. He is already on his way and will arrive by helicopter in about 30 minutes. So! I can give you my full attention now, my friend! I am waiting for one more call and then we can cut that bastard out. After you have filled in these forms, you will be taken to the surgery block. We will do some more quick tests before you get the anaesthesia. When did you last have food?"

I had a cup of tea at lunch. I skipped the sandwiches because I was in too much pain, so I haven't had anything since early this morning and even that wasn't much."

"Brilliant. Now listen carefully. I know you have arranged everything just in case I don't succeed, but I need you to focus on me being successful and that you will be back here before midnight, alive and well. Do we have a deal?"

Georg couldn't help but smile over his optimism. It definitely seemed to do Alfred good.

"Mikael, I have all the confidence in the world that you will succeed, my friend! Now Georg, help me sit upright, I have some forms to fill in and sign."

Georg paced up and down the hallway later that evening while Alfred was in surgery. He had been drinking enough coffee to keep him awake for a week. However, he was anxious to check Alfred's mobile phone. Maybe by now he would have a text message back from either Otto or Hadi. So he went downstairs where he could turn his phone on again. Still, he didn't want to be too far away from Alfred while he was fighting for his life. He was getting hungry, so he forced himself to have a snack to keep himself from fainting. It was now 21.30 hours and he hadn't eaten anything since the omelette at the mansion.

Again he checked Alfred's phone.

No new text messages.

He decided to call Wong to see if there was any news at the base, but just before he dialled the number, Alfred's phone rang. Georg looked at the number. Unknown. Should he take it? Maybe he should... "Yes? Who is this?"

"Fred, is that you?"

Georg immediately knew that it was Otto. He was the only one who called Alfred 'Fred'.

"Otto, It's Georg!" he shouted with relief and joy. "Where are you! What happened?"

"Long story my friend, but we are fine. We didn't get the stone though, but we now know where it is. Where's Fred?"

"He's in surgery. His tumour; it grew too fast. They have to take it out now."

There was a silence on the other side of the line. Then, Georg could hear Otto explaining the situation to the others with a soft voice.

"I so hope he makes it!" said Otto, "So, what do we do now? Our car with our mobile phones and all the files had disappeared by the time we got back, so we're now getting a ride back to Cairo from our new friend Max. It's his mobile phone I'm calling from. So, Alfred had said something about Plan B?"

Georg was alarmed. "Oh no! Those files were important! Plan B was hidden in one of the files. Did you read the contents of all of them?"

"No, we didn't have time to read everything. As I said, it's a long story!"

Georg closed his eyes. What would Alfred do now?

"Listen, Otto, can you give me Hadi for a moment?"

The line cracked and there was some commotion on the other end of the line.

"Hadi here. I will take care of them, Mr Hauser, do not worry. As soon as we have my car back and the files, I will contact you. We will go to..."

Suddenly, the line was disconnected.

The last thing Georg could hear was a muffled scream.

24

Aswan-Cairo Road, Egypt, October 3ʳᵈ 2011

Max Müller wasn't born yesterday. He hadn't become one of the best detectives in all of Europe by being haphazard or predictable. Quite the opposite; he had mastered the art of complex planning that appeared to be quite simple. So on this occasion he decided to play it very cool. He was just a naïve and good humoured tourist who 'coincidentally' happened to have a car when his target, Otto Rahn, needed to be taken to Cairo along with his two friends. Like hungry fish, unaware of the hook that awaited them, they had taken the bait.

It had been easy to win Rahn's trust. As German compatriots do when in a foreign land, they had already created a bond on the ferry to Amarna earlier that afternoon. So when they met again, the whole group seemed happy to see him again. Max couldn't believe his luck when he saw them approaching in the distance, yelling while running, hoping to catch the ferry. He found that the white skinned Otto and his equally pale British friend looked ridiculous in their white galabyas.

The ferryman, who wasn't big on punctuality, had waited patiently until they were all aboard, hoping to get an extra dollar for his kindness, but when he found out they didn't have any money at all, he became angry and wanted to throw them off his ferry. Max had taken advantage of the situation, presenting himself as the saviour of the day, not only paying for their passage on the ferry, but also offering them a lift to Cairo. However, the Egyptian among them had insisted on stopping in Malawi to collect a package first. Reluctantly, Max had given in, as he didn't want to look suspicious and betray his eagerness to get Otto to Cairo without delay.

Private Detective Max Müller didn't know much about Roman Corona, the man who had hired him to find Rahn. He only knew that he was being paid to stalk him, lure him to a certain address in Cairo and keep him there, if necessary by force. The fee that Corona had paid him was unusually handsome. After this job, Max wouldn't have to work again for the rest of his life. So, obviously, Max was very determined to give Corona what he wanted. Müller had previously worked for clients in Germany, Holland and France, but he had also been to India once, on a particularly challenging assignment. Compared to India, driving through Egypt was a piece of cake. Though driving was comparatively favourable, this particular job required a lot more than just observing, stalking, photographing and reporting; this time he had what he boldly liked to call 'live prey' sitting in the backseat of his car. Since he couldn't afford taking the risk of being hit on the head while driving, his assistant, Hugo, was now behind the wheel, while he himself checked the rear-view mirror on a regular basis to keep an eye on his prize. However, his prize was now behaving very suspiciously in the backseat of his silver-grey Nissan X-trail.

Otto, while playing along as if he and Max were new best friends, didn't in fact trust him at all. He had been forced to stalk people himself when he joined the SS in the mid-1930s and, as a trained spy, he had quickly recognised Müller's game. While they were getting into the car, he had exchanged looks with a worried looking Arthur, who had also found the entire situation too good to be true and when two people are as close as they were, all you need is eye contact to get a message across.

Otto had noticed that Max was frequently watching them in the rear-view mirror. What did Max want from them? Maybe he knew about the ERFAB devices and wanted to steal them? Otto just knew something was amiss and that they had to get away from Max as soon as possible, but they hadn't been able to communicate their feelings to Hadi, who was now on the phone with Georg. Before their adventure had even started, Alfred had given orders for Hadi to be followed in the event that Plan A failed and now he was about to reveal information about Plan B while on the phone with Georg. So before Hadi could betray too much in front of Max, Otto quickly muzzled Hadi, after which he pressed the key to end the call. In a smooth move he shuffled Max's phone across his lap and handed it over to Arthur. Quietly, he whispered in his ear, "Please delete the number we just dialled"

Arthur nodded and exchanged an anxious look with Hadi, who was still reeling from the shock, trying to understand Otto's sudden, uncharacteristic move. Otto bent over to him and whispered as quietly as he could, "I don't trust Max."

Hadi nodded, now fully realising why Otto had reacted this way.

Max, who was sitting in the front seat, behaved as if he hadn't noticed the sudden silence in the back of the car, but he wasn't stupid. He realised that soon he would have to take more forceful action to protect his prize.

They were now driving into the town of Malawi and Hadi was eager to get to the money he had hidden on the way to Amarna. He was happy that he had cleverly hidden the money at the very last minute. Still playing along, good-humouredly Max ordered Hugo to drive into the mentioned side street to park the car.

Then, Arthur spotted it.

Hadi's white Mercedes was parked just outside one of the houses in another street, a little further up the road, though only the back of the car was visible. It didn't look as though Max recognised the vehicle, so after elbowing his side-passengers, Arthur put his index finger to his lips and quietly pointed into the direction of Hadi's car. Otto and Hadi could barely suppress their relief and happiness. Not mentioning the fact that he had just found his stolen car to Max, Hadi left the car and disappeared into a different street, so he could reach the Mercedes from the other side.

However, as he tried to break into his car without being seen, Hadi was in for a nasty surprise. The drunken Ashraf - who had stolen Hadi's car earlier that evening - had damaged the car while attempting to park it. Hadi was furious when he saw that not only one of the windows was shattered, but also his front right headlight was smashed. On these roads at night, driving with just one headlight was very dangerous.

After taking in the damage, Hadi ran off to collect the bundle of money from its hiding place before returning to his car. He smiled when he looked inside the car. In his intoxicated state, Ashraf had even left the key in the ignition. He signalled with his back lights to Arthur and Otto, who were now getting out of Max's car, pretending they needed to stretch their legs and get some air. Though Max was suspicious, he couldn't do anything without blowing his cover completely. For now, he had to let them wonder off into the street, but he followed them carefully with his eyes, nonchalantly stretching his own legs not far behind them. Then suddenly he spotted the white Mercedes, which was now slowly reversing toward Otto and Arthur. With horror he watched as they ran off and jumped into the white Mercedes. "Verdammt!" he cursed. Max ran back to his car and jumped in, but a large truck filled to the top with bananas was now blocking the way, allowing Hadi a head start. Hadi hit the gas and sped off toward the main road to Cairo.

"Buckle up, gentlemen! This is going to be a bumpy ride!"

Hadi raced through the town and out of it, into the darkness. The moment he was on the main road, he turned off his lights. He now wished that his car were black; a white car would always be a little more visible than a black one under a clear, moonlit sky.

While driving through Minya, Hadi made an exception and turned on the one working headlight to make sure he didn't drive into a donkey or run over a dog. As theirs was not the only car on the road, he couldn't see if Max's Nissan X-trail was one of the cars behind him. Also, the headlights of the car directly behind him blinded him when he looked into the rear-view mirror and he couldn't identify the car model, but while driving through one of the towns - with the streets lit up by the city lights - he thought he could just make out the silver grey car in the distance, 4 cars behind him. Not taking any risk, he decided to take an alternative route north by overtaking a truck at great speed and then making a last minute right turn over the bridge and into the town centre. Otto and Arthur were holding onto the front seats as they were speeding southward alongside the *cornische* with all the luxury hotels. Without warning, Hadi took another sharp turn right. They passed the Saladin Masjid Mosque and its two beautiful towers and then drove over the Kobri Al Ehsasi bridge, crossing the railroad and the river to return to the left bank of the Nile.

Now they should be driving *behind* Max.

The moment he realised what Hadi had done, Otto started to laugh out loud. "That's brilliant! You are smarter than you look, my dear Egyptian friend!"

"Thank you, Mr Adler, but you must also realise that we can still be recognised by our one headlight, so from now on, we must drive without headlights."

The moment he thought it safe enough, Hadi pulled over, so Otto and Arthur could change into their regular clothes again. "I will match the speed of the rest of the traffic and try not to attract too much attention." said Hadi, "You must try and get some sleep, I will wake you up when we reach Cairo."

The moment they were back on the main road to Cairo, Hadi turned on his radio to keep himself awake. Otto looked over at Arthur, who wore a look of resignation, tinged with the dark sort of humour one feels when the bleakness of a situation becomes almost laughable; on his lap were the files he had been waiting to browse through, eager to find the missing information, but he couldn't see a thing. They were driving without headlights and couldn't risk revealing their presence in the velvet blackness by turning on the ceiling light either. Dejectedly, he shrugged his shoulders and pushed the files back into the briefcase. "Well, we can't read any of the files in the dark, so we might as well get some rest."

Since they now had all their belongings back, Otto was able to get back to Georg on his own mobile phone. It had been an hour since their last conversation on Max's phone and he

183

hoped he hadn't alarmed poor Georg too much by disconnecting in the middle of the conversation. "Georg?"

"Otto! What the hell happened? I thought you'd been attacked! I am organising a rescue mission as we speak! Where are you?"

"Long story again, my friend, so I will give you the nutshell version. We're fine; we've got the car back and also our personal belongings and all the files, but there's something important I need you to do for me, though. Will you get me everything you can find on a certain Max Müller from Freiburg, Germany. He's interfering with our mission."

"Max Müller, from Freiburg? I'm on it."

"How's Fred doing?"

"They're still working on him. No one can tell me anything yet. It's a waiting game. Let's keep him in our prayers."

Otto nodded. "Let me know the moment you have some news!"

As soon as he'd hung up, Georg cancelled the rescue mission and immediately started to investigate Max Müller. Within minutes he found out that Müller was a private detective and Georg became very worried. He thought of the ERFAB devices; top secret technology that interested parties would certainly love to get their hands on. He thought about Wong's seemingly harmless trips into the mountains around Sion and how easy it had been for Al Din to kidnap him at the airport. He was getting more and more certain now. SBS-Sion had a leak.

Meanwhile, both Otto and Arthur - having decided they simply had to take advantage of the road time to get some rest - squirmed and stretched, trying in vain to find a comfortable enough position in the back seat of the car to sleep. They had no other choice than to believe that Hadi had the situation in hand and would successfully get them back to Cairo safely, while driving with no headlights, being blind on a dark road.

25

Sion, Switzerland, October 4th 2011

Alfred was floating around the hospital room and estimated that he was hovering about two meters above the floor. He felt as if the scene beneath him should be shocking to him, while he was in fact perfectly calm. He could see his body lying on the operating table, blood seeping out of the opening in his abdomen. The surgeon and several assistants were working fast, trying to get the defibrillator in position. He could see that the lifeline had gone blank, showing lack of any heartbeat. Slowly, the hollow sounds of the flat-line beep and the shouts of the now panicking staff began to echo and fade, until he couldn't hear anything anymore. Even the images of the hospital room had melted into a foggy blur. A rainbow coloured hot wind sucked him into a void and suddenly he found himself surrounded by deceased loved ones; his parents, his little sister who had died when she was only four years old, even his beloved pets who had passed away many years before him, were there.

There was no question about it; he had died.

Somehow he knew that his mind was now in complete charge of his next step and that he could go anywhere and 'any-when' he pleased by the simple power of his will and thought. He chose not to stay long with his beloved family, friends and pets, but instead decided to explore the many realms of the heavens as soon as possible, in case he was pulled back. Here too were dimensions that could answer so many questions and he knew that it was simply a question of focusing on someone or something and asking permission to be taken to it.

However, he hadn't counted on what happened next.

An unknown entity approached him. Alfred couldn't make out whether it was a man or a woman, as he couldn't see the face properly, but from what he saw, the entity was clearly a higher being, evolved to a certain level and most probably in charge of guiding souls such as himself through the realms that seemed to exist in-between the worlds. Alfred allowed the entity to lead him to another dimension, where he was shown something that he knew he needed to see, although he didn't know yet what that would be.

He could make out a garden, filled with vegetables, flowers and fruit trees. Behind a group of cypress trees was a large, white building with just one floor. The roof was made of orange clay tiles. Beyond the house was a valley with a winding, glistering river, stretching all the way to a low mountain range with rugged edges. At first, there seemed to be no one at the house, but then a group of people came out to welcome him. They were all dressed in white robes and he recognised them from the way they greeted him, with their arms crossed in front of their chests and their gentle bow of the head. These were the Essenes, the chosen ones, the *Theraputae* of old. Their communication with Alfred wasn't verbal, but telepathic. They spoke as one, in unison, as if of the same mind. "Greetings, Councillor of the Holy Light. Do not fear us, we have come to heal you."

Alfred was puzzled when he heard them call him that. So many times he had wanted to ask his father about his ancestors; their quests and adventures and about the origin of their name, Zinkler, but his father had died before he could ask what his father expected of him in his own life. He had felt lost, like a new group leader who was staring into the expectant eyes of his people, not knowing what to do, not knowing what to say.

When Alfred turned to ask the entity what was expected of him, it had already disappeared. Suddenly, Alfred felt that one of the Essenes had taken his hand and it startled him. The Essene spoke with his mouth closed, but he could hear the voice in his head clearly. "Come. There is not much time."

In what seemed to be slow motion, they moved to a pasture, but when he looked at the horizon, the view had already changed. He felt he was watching a theatre show, seeing one backdrop replacing another. He could see an ancient seaport and noticed two large ships with massive sails, dropping anchor just outside the harbour. He immediately recognised the red Templar cross on their white sails. Then he saw a sloop filled with boxes approaching the pier. When the sloop was properly tied to the pier, most of the goods were taken to the hidden entrance of a fortress that stood towering over the harbour. Among the goods was a small box, covered in a red scarf. As soon as the cargo was inside the fortress, the door was bolted and two knights took place on either side of the door, their hands on the hilts of their swords, legs slightly apart, to secure the entrance.

Suddenly - as if time was something one could fast forward by mere thought - night fell over the harbour and the sea. The otherwise bright colours in the harbour scene had faded into shades of grey and even the water of the sea seemed to have fallen asleep along with the town. All sounds had dimmed and Alfred thought he couldn't possibly make out any more in the blackness of the night and the heavy silence.

Then, something unexpected happened.

A bright star fell from the sky and at first, Alfred thought it would fall into the sea. It fell instead to the roof of a tiny chapel on a rock, not far from the lighthouse tower, where it landed as if it were a seagull. The star was shining so brightly, that Alfred covered his eyes to protect them.

The Essene smiled. "You do not have to protect your eyes anymore, Alfred. Look at it. Allow the light into your eyes. It won't blind you. If anything, it will enable you to see."

Alfred obeyed, blinking his eyes until he could look into the light more comfortably. The light penetrated deep within Alfred's mind, turning the world outside in, instead of inside out and now, all of his mind became illuminated. For a second he knew everything; he just couldn't store it and in that moment of complete understanding, Alfred exploded into sweet laughter.

Suddenly, everything returned to its natural state again and he instantly forgot what he had seen and learnt, but he did gain something from the experience. He knew that everything would be all right in the end if he could only remember the one vital thing; the location of what he had witnessed. He quickly opened his eyes and looked around, still with an amazing feeling of happiness and contentment. To his surprise, he was still in the Essene village, surrounded by smiling people who were now pointing their fingers into the same direction and when he looked, he saw a man approaching. It was his father, wearing an apron and looking still in his prime; not the old man Alfred had seen on his deathbed.

"Father?" he said, melancholy.

Zinkler Senior smiled. "I know this is not what you expected - or maybe it is - but I need you to be still and listen to me carefully. I only have one chance to share this with you, now that it still may have a purpose."

In the meantime, on the background, the Essenes started to intonate the word 'Kay'. Confused but also curious, Alfred was just about to speak again, when his father put his index finger to his lips.

"I said be still and listen! Throughout the ages, bold men and women have risked their lives to protect and transmit vital, ancient knowledge; handed down to us from forgotten civilisations. In face of the attempt to centralise power to ensure control and domination of the people and of all life on earth, this knowledge can one day prevent the total destruction of mankind and all life on planet earth. In their honour and for the sake of free will and life on earth we must continue to do just that. We must, with all our energy, retrace the old steps, rediscover the ancient knowledge and protect and preserve it and above all, we must share it with the world. Secret brotherhoods were necessary to preserve this information, because for the mere possession of it, any man or woman would have been burned alive at the stake, to say the very least! Now the time has come to reveal the knowledge to all, for many people on the planet are in dire need. No more hidden secrets! It must be available to whoever is ready to study these teachings, be them a child or a scientist. Scientists must understand that they need to open their eyes and study metaphysics as thoroughly as they are currently studying physics. A battery doesn't work when it has only the negative polarity. It also needs the positive polarity to empower a device. They must use the Art of Reflexion and learn transmission to discover what is hidden behind the Isis Veil to better understand the wholeness of the Universe, how it works and how it is interdependent. It is now time to understand all of the faces and sounds of God. Oh, how man mocks the other in his attempt to fathom the secrets of ancient civilisations. What disgraceful behaviour there is between men! Every day, scientists throw out the baby with the bathwater, stubbornly rejecting someone's theory the moment they find even the tiniest flaw in the other person's research. Ego steps in, the moment someone steps into the spot light. Insecurity and fear are emotions felt by any man whose otherwise possibly plausible theory or hypothesis should be made available to the public to assess. Oh how judgmental man has become! How arrogant man has become! Arrogance and ego will one day be the downfall of man!"

Like a weak TV channel that flickers, the image of Alfred's father flickered for a moment before it was restored. "No one has the right to manipulate the truth and no one owns history! Since the library of Alexandria was burned, we have been left to guess our own history and to decipher what parts of what we have been told have a grain of truth in it and what doesn't. We can only attempt to come to terms with our own conclusions and to respect those who do the same. The truth is; there are no rules, but there *are* Cosmic laws. These laws require working with the heart; overcoming negative emotions, transforming them into positive emotions and always letting love be your guide and your message and conducting yourself in accordance with your message of love. You can only do this properly if you accept and love yourself. So, son; you are your own judge, your own Ma'at and measure. Would you want to be with yourself if you were another person? Do you love yourself?"

Alfred was taken aback by this question. There was much to take in, but he never expected to be standing here, facing his father and hearing him say this. Did he love himself? Would he want to be with himself if he were someone else? The answer came to him faster than he thought it would. Yes, he did love himself. Yes, if he were someone else, he would want to be with himself, but perhaps today was the first day he'd ever felt this way about himself.

His father didn't need to wait for his son to formulate the answer. He could see it in his eyes.

Slowly, Alfred's father started to fade away.

"Father, wait! I have so many questions!"

However, it was too late. He had disappeared.

In the meantime, the Essenes were still intonating their therapeutic sound, making him feel sleepy. He allowed himself to lie in the grass and for a moment he thought he was back on Earth. He could smell the grass, feel it tickle his nose and cheek and when his gaze rested on the horizon, he could see a strange looking tree at an odd angle. It reminded him of the Kabala tree, but then he looked closer and realised that it *was* the Kabala tree, alive and massive. He saw three spheres at the top; *Kether, Chokmah* and *Binah,* which he knew represented the crown, wisdom and understanding.

The second three spheres were *Chesed, Geburah* and *Tiphareth,* which represented mercy, strength and beauty.

The third three spheres were called *Netzach, Hod* and *Yesod,* representing success, splendour and foundation.

And at the very bottom, one sphere united them all: Malkuth; representing kingdom. These are the states of 'becoming', describing the nature of Creation.

The tree just stood there; rooted, steadfast, proud in its silence, humble in its service and content in its existence. Alfred gazed at it as if it was the most beautiful thing he had ever seen, but then his eye caught something that seemed to be slowly falling off the tree. First he thought it was a seed or a bird's feather, but then he saw it more clearly.

Twirling down to the ground as if it was dancing on the wind like a Dervish, a piece of paper was falling. For some reason he knew the information inscribed on it would reveal the *Verbum Dismissum,* the 'Lost Word' to its reader. Alfred, ever curious, willed himself to the horizon where the tree stood and once at the foot of the tree, he sat up and without hesitating, caught the piece of paper just as it reached the ground. He tried to read the inscription on it, but suddenly felt as if he were sucked into the earth. He lost the piece of paper in the non-existent wind and fell through the earth into a deep, dark pit.

The nothingness was overwhelming; there was no sound, no smell, no sight, no touch, nothing. There was not even the sound of his own scream. He was confused; one moment he was about to read an divine message - the next he was in total darkness. Then, he began to perceive a sound. It was an ever increasing, but steady sound, that seemed to come from his left.

Beep, beep, beep...

In the distance he heard a hollow voice he thought he recognised. Then he opened his eyes. "Georg!"

His Number One; his right hand, was sitting next to him, holding Alfred's cold hands in his own to warm them up. Georg was visibly tired but relieved to see his employer and friend still breathing.

"You almost died last night." he said with a soft voice.

Alfred chuckled. "I know. I had an errand to run."

The two men smiled at each other and somehow, Georg knew what Alfred was referring to. Alfred was special; surely he would have taken advantage of his temporary death. Georg had learned that everything happens for a reason. Naturally, he had been frightened to his core when Alfred had clinically died the night before. The surgeon had been successful in getting everything out. There had been one large tumour and two smaller ones.

Then, Alfred's blood pressure had dropped dramatically during a sudden haemorrhage and as an effect, his heart had stopped beating, but instead of jumpstarting Alfred's heart immediately, the surgeon had his body temperature brought down even lower while he finished the exploratory work. This was done to ensure there were no more traces of the tumour or any other signs of cancer left in the surrounding area. Then he had started the wound closing process. Dr Waldheim knew he had to act fast, but he could work without a heartbeat, so there was no blood pumping through his patient's veins and wounds. He knew that by keeping Alfred very cold, he'd have a maximum of four minutes to close the wounds properly - enabling his body to take the blow of the defibrillator - and it had worked. Alfred had immediately responded to the first blow of the defibrillator and seemed to have slept quite comfortably through the night, stabilising his vital signs while he remained in a deep, healing sleep; one that had been secretly enhanced by the Essenes from the other side of the veil. When Alfred woke up and realised that he had pulled through, he only had one remaining question to ask Georg. "Is Plan B active?"

Georg's eyes widened at his chief's determination.

"Yes, sir. They've arrived in Cairo and they are all okay. Although they didn't acquire the stone, they have seen it and know where it is kept. In any case, they have proven your theory that the Urim and Thummim indeed originated in Egypt. They even witnessed how Meryra used the stones for divination at court; for judgment. Just like in the old days of the Hebrews."

Alfred was happy and jealous at the same time. He would have given an arm and a leg to have been able to witness that. Although this information was most satisfying to Alfred, the memory of his journey into the otherworld that night was priceless to him. He closed his eyes and concentrated with all his might, trying to remember every little detail he had seen and heard. Georg, who noticed that Alfred was still very sleepy, thought he'd better leave him in peace and get some breakfast, but as he was standing in the doorway, he suddenly remembered something, so he turned around to Alfred and cleared his throat. "Sir, I am intrigued by an unusual painting in your salon at the house. It's the Dalí. I'm curious to know what the painting means to you?"

Alfred opened his eyes and turned their bright blue light on Georg. "Ah! 'The Chemist of Ampurdan in Search of Absolutely Nothing!' I bought it, my dearest Georg, because it reminded me of my grandfather, who looked more or less the same as the man in Dalí's painting. You know, when he was still alive and I was a very young man, I used to enjoy some precious hours in his company, listening to his stories, or just chatting. In short, he allowed me the delightful moments of wasting time. Wasting time is a luxury that heirs to important positions - or people who have to live up to high expectations - cherish immensely. Of course, my father always wanted me to do something useful, something I could learn from and if he did catch me doing nothing, he'd find something for me to do. So, whenever my grandfather and I were enjoying ourselves, doing absolutely nothing but chatting and he heard my father coming through the hallway, he'd say, "Here comes God. Quick, look busy!" and then we'd pretend to have lost something on the floor."

Alfred sighed and remembered the words his father had told him during his temporary journey into the nether realm,

"We must, with all our energy, retrace the old steps, rediscover the ancient knowledge and protect and preserve it and above all, we must share it with the world." he recited softly to the room in general, before sinking into a deep sleep. Georg smiled affectionately and quietly left the hospital room. The weight of SBS-Sion was now on his shoulders.

26

Guernsey, Channel Islands, October 4th 2011

The weather was sunny and warm on the island and a myriad of small sailboats darted about on the open water. The delightful coves, idyllic sea views and lush countryside, together with the sound of the powerful waves crashing against the rocks and the pungent scent of the salty air had made this part of Guernsey popular with tourists for generations. Stunning views from cliff-top paths had always been appealing to even the most timid of hikers, offering one breath-taking view after another. The large number of holiday accommodation in the area had convinced Titan to first check out the coastline around Icart Bay, south of St. Andrew. If Danielle was hiding somewhere, it would not be in a hotel. It would be somewhere more private; something like a cottage.

The tooting of a 1920s car horn from his pocket demanded attention and he hurriedly answered his mobile phone. When he saw that it was Lars calling him, he said in a condescending tone, "Lars! No worries, your car is still in one piece!"

"It better be, Titan! Listen, I did the search you asked for and I now have a list of all the cottages in southern Guernsey that are for rent. I checked each and every one of them to see which were rented out and guess what? One of the links that Google came up with didn't work. When I checked, it said that the page for the cottage had recently been taken offline."

Titan grinned broadly. "Which one is it?"

"Rose Cottage, not far from St. Andrew. I will text you the address."

Within a minute, Titan had received the full address of Rose Cottage on his mobile phone.

Meanwhile, Danielle and David were enjoying each other's company and getting more relaxed with the restrictions of their secluded life. Georg had just texted David on his mobile that Alfred's operation had gone well, which they were both very relieved to hear. All seemed to be quiet and the beautiful weather had drawn them outside into the garden. Danielle had made herself comfortable in a lounge chair and was enjoying the warm rays of the sun on her skin. Her loose-fitting, cotton dress allowed her to free her legs and while she gently rubbed her belly, she noticed the somewhat sheepish smile on David's face as he watched her simply being happy and peaceful. They didn't need to say anything. In fact, they hadn't spoken much since that first kiss. It seemed to be sufficient to just exchange looks and smiles once in a while to know exactly what the other person was thinking or feeling.

Danielle was doing exactly what the doctor had ordered. She was resting and reading a lot, mainly light, feel-good novels with happy endings. For her it was also a time to process all her emotions, memories and traumas of the past Summer and she was now coming to a point where she could give it all a proper place in her mind. At first, Danielle had felt lonely, unable to share her secret with anyone and she deeply missed the father of her child, but ever since she had arrived on the island, a calmness had come over her, as if the energy of that particular spot in the world - one where great ocean currents meet and ancient seafarers found refuge - allowed her to lock into the footprint of her soul. She felt strongly that she was exactly where she was meant to be and had finally found acceptance in her situation. The loneliness she had felt until coming to the island had been completely erased by David's presence and by the love he demonstrated to her, which she reciprocated. At first it had frightened her, but she realised how strong she had become the very moment she had decided to kiss him. It had been an experiment, to see if she really felt anything for this man. So when her underbelly reacted, she knew.

To David it had been a complete surprise as he hadn't expected Danielle to love him back at all. He had also surprised himself that he had the courage to flirt with her.

After all, she was Alfred's adopted daughter. David was responsible for her safety and had sworn to Alfred that he would guard her with his life. If Alfred had known he was flirting with her, he would undoubtedly be very angry with him, but David didn't know how wrong he was. Alfred had secretly wanted them to team up - both professionally and privately - but had never made those feelings clear to them, simply because Alfred didn't want to force his idea upon them.

You simply cannot force love.

Now that Danielle had responded positively to David's advances, they were both much more relaxed around each other, though the forces of attraction were increasingly tugging at their bodies and at that moment, David decided to give in to his urge and walked over to her. After joining her on the lounge chair he simply had to touch her legs, her hair and her face. She was so beautiful. When her bright, blue eyes looked deeply into his hazelnut brown eyes, he could do nothing but let magnetism take over. As if no force on earth could keep them apart, their lips met. With great care he caressed her full breasts and was very happy to see Danielle undoing his shirt buttons.

Suddenly there was a strange sound in the distance. Startled at first, David looked up, but when he didn't see anything, he relaxed.

"Probably one of the agents. They are constantly walking up and down around the perimeter of the house. Maybe we should go inside where we can have a bit more privacy."

Grinning like guilty teenagers, they sought the safe seclusion of Danielle's bedroom and for half an hour they forgot the world. They forgot where they were and why they were there. Their world had become as small as their entangled bodies. Nothing else existed.

It became noon. Still wet from their shared shower, Danielle kissed him and suggested enthusiastically, "Let's have lunch on the beach! I will wear a hat and sunglasses and we will melt into the crowd. It's only a few minutes away! We'll be back within an hour. Oh darling, please, let's do it!"

Blinded by his love for her and this new relationship with the woman he worshipped, he gave in to the foolish whim of the happy Danielle, whom he couldn't possibly refuse anything anymore. Trying to convince himself that the decision was a safe one, David explained, "Alright, but only this once! It's already October and even here, the weather will change at some point, so we'd be foolish not to take advantage of it. We'll be stuck in here long enough once the winter sets in. I'll have one of the agents follow us, while the other one will stay here to keep an eye on the cottage."

Fifteen minutes later their car stopped at the car park of the Fermain Beach Café. Danielle was right; it was indeed busy, but they succeeded in finding a table for two, right behind a large plant, tucked away in a far corner. It was perfect. Still, David kept an eye on every person there, just to be sure he was aware of any sudden changes in atmosphere. He noticed that Barry, the personal protection agent they had taken with them, had strategically posted himself behind the 'Pepper Pot'; one of the 18th century loopholed towers that had been built to defend the island from attacks from the French during the Napoleonic wars. From the loopholes, artillery could cover every possible approach and protect the coastline. It would be a good place to hide in, he reasoned. Just in case.

David couldn't believe how unusually sunny and warm it was for this time of year and tried to convince himself that he was merely on a holiday outing with his lady friend, rather than taking forbidden chances by leaving their hide-out. With great contentment, he watched Danielle carefully cleaning each of her long fingers with the miniature lemon water soaked cloth after finishing her succulent and ever so satisfying seafood plate. He could pinch himself and still not believe it. While ordering another alcohol-free beer, David felt as if he was the luckiest man on earth, having not the slightest warning that his luck would soon change.

Michael had woken up late that morning from the sound of screeching seagulls, coming from the half-open window. It took him a moment to fully remember where he was and why he was there. He had arrived at the hotel the evening before, soon after darkness had fallen, so when he opened the curtains in the full light of the morning, he was astounded by the most picturesque of views. His room looked out over a lovely old town, a beautifully kept harbour, a medieval castle and beyond it, the blue sea. He couldn't help but smile. It felt like a holiday and while stretching his arms, he filled his lungs with the salty sea air. Then, the smell of sausages, bacon, eggs and toast penetrated his nostrils, so he decided to take a quick shower, have a good breakfast and then continue his search for his father. He checked his mobile. No reply. How odd. Normally his father would always reply within a few hours' time.

When he arrived in the small breakfast room with its well-padded carpet and old fashioned furniture, he saw that he was alone. Someone was already cleaning up the used cups and dishes from other, deserted tables and when he looked at the breakfast bar, he was alarmed to see that there was hardly anything left. He decided to have a seat by the window, overlooking St. Peter Port and hoped he wasn't too late.

The young girl attending the dining room forced a smile and politely explained the situation. "I am so sorry sir, but we stop serving breakfast at 10 am and it is now 20 past 10. However, if you could wait here for a moment please, I'll see what I can do. I'll check with the kitchen staff."

Michael nodded sheepishly and couldn't help looking admiringly at her shapely ankles as she left the room. She caught his look out of the corner of her eye. It didn't take long before she was back with a clean plate, cup and saucer and a small basket of assorted, warm breads, butter and marmalade. Proud of her ability to negotiate food out of the kitchen past the official breakfast time, she coquettishly winked at him as she placed it all on his table.

"Now, what would you prefer, tea or coffee?"

Over breakfast, Michael slowly built up the courage to simply call the number that David had previously called from. It was his only hope of ever finding his father. As small as the island seemed on the map; in reality it was quite big. Michael looked at the town below, knowing it was just one of the many towns and villages on the island and he just didn't know where to start. After he checked out of the hotel - not knowing where he would be staying the following night - he reached for his phone and opened his call log. He selected 'call this number' and took a deep breath. Here goes nothing. Michael was relieved to hear that it rang, so the line still existed, but when nobody answered, he disconnected. He'd simply have to try again later. With no idea where to go to now, he decided to follow his nose and headed toward the harbour. There is always a strange magnetism that attracts people to the sea. All over the world, shorelines are overpopulated with towns, cities, resorts and tourist attractions, all stubbornly resisting the dangers that large bodies of water can create the moment the weather turns bad. Like moths attracted to a flame that ultimately burns them, people are attracted to the coast. Although the sea can take life and be very dangerous, there are aspects of it that can also be put to advantage. The 13th century castle Cornet, built on a rocky outcrop in the harbour of St Peter Port, can only be reached at low tide, just like the old smugglers' caves on the far-flung, lesser-populated edges of the island.

Michael constantly asked himself the same question. If he were his father, where would he go? He decided to visit the castle and take a chance on his luck, knowing David wouldn't be able to resist visiting medieval buildings, but by the time the noonday gun was shot from the castle grounds, he hadn't seen anyone who even remotely looked like David, so he decided to send another text message, this time sounding even more desperate, hoping that his father would now finally respond to it.

'Am in trouble. Call me. Michael.'

Michael wished he had a car, so he could move around a lot quicker. When he passed an available taxi, he reluctantly took out David's gold card, an emergency credit card, given to him by his father, who had made him swear he would only to use it in emergencies. Was this not an emergency?

Michael smiled, opened the back door of the blue Peugeot and handed over the precious card to the driver, who immediately gave it back.

"Cash only, my friend!"

With a sour face, Michael stepped out of the car again and set off to find an ATM to withdraw cash. The driver, however, had smelled money when he saw the gold card and seemed to change his mind. "Oy! You! Come 'ere!"

Michael turned and saw the man waving at him. Feeling hopeful, he returned to the car.

"So tell me lad, how long do you need a car for?"

"A few days, perhaps. I am searching for my father. He's somewhere on the island and I've got to find him."

"Is that a genuine gold card you have there, son? I mean, will it draw you cash money?"

"Yes, of course! So, if you could point me in the direction of an ATM, please?"

"Get in. I'd be crazy to let go of an opportunity like this, but it won't be cheap! I hope you know what you're doing."

"How much would it cost per day, not driving all the time of course, but hiring you for let's say, eight hours a day. Could we make a deal?"

"Well, I'd do it for 500 quid."

Michael quickly stepped out of the car. That taxi driver was crazy!

"Oy! Get back 'ere! Okay, 200 quid, but not a penny less!"

Michael stood still and smiled before he turned around to face the driver and reached out to shake the man's hand.

"I'm Michael Camford."

"Stuart, your very own private cabby. Nice to meet you, son. Now, where do you want to start lookin'?"

The widow Mrs Peel walked into the kitchen. She had just returned from her daily shopping and was about to put the kettle on to make some lunch, when she heard a tune coming from the dining room. It was her mobile phone, which she had left on the table. She didn't know why she always forgot to take it with her. Thinking it was a message from her son, she quickly read the text and was alarmed at what it said. Someone called Michael was in trouble and asked to be called. It was probably one of her son's friends. Then an alarming thought struck her like lightning. Perhaps her son was also in trouble! Immediately she decided to call her son, who answered the phone on the second ring.

"Mum, are you alright? You sound upset!"

Mrs Peel explained that she had received a message from someone called Michael and that he was in trouble. However, her son didn't know anybody called Michael in his immediate circle, but then he thought of another possibility. "Has anyone else used your phone off late, mum? Have you lent it to anyone?"

Mrs Peel suddenly remembered that she had indeed lent it to David a few days before, so he could call his son. Immediately the penny dropped. Michael must be David's son. His son's in trouble!

Without saying goodbye she disconnected, took the key from the table near the front door and started the short walk to Rose Cottage at a brisk pace. However, David wasn't there when she arrived. Instead, she noticed that one of the mysterious men in black that she had seen before, was lying on the ground in a strange position. The other one was nowhere to be seen. When she came closer, she noticed to her horror that his throat had been cut. There was blood everywhere and his lifeless eyes were staring up at the sun without blinking.

Mrs Peel didn't have the time to scream. In the blink of an eye a tall man jumped out from behind her.

Then, everything went dark.

27

Cairo, Egypt, October 4th 2011

"Yes, yes, yes!!" Otto tried to hug the Sphinx and the pyramids from where he stood at the living room window at the Pyramids View Inn B&B. "Georg, I owe you this one!"
With a giant smile on his face he turned to Arthur, who was busy rearranging his luggage in the bedroom.
"If only we had time to visit!" he exclaimed.
"I'm with you on that, Otto, but Georg wants us to stay put for a bit. Ever since we told him about Max, we seem to be on red alert. Now knowing that Max is some kind of private detective and that he might be planning to steal our devices, it would be a mistake to show our faces in public at such a popular tourist attraction, but I couldn't agree with you more, Otto. This location is to die for!"
A short melody from a Debussy piece played on Otto's mobile phone. It was a text message from Georg, saying that Alfred had made it through his operation and that he was recovering well. Although both were relieved to hear this, Otto realised how much he had worried about Alfred in his subconscious mind. He could feel tears pricking his eyes and he quickly rubbed them with his fingers; to have Arthur discover his deep fears and true emotions was the last thing he wanted. Keeping a brave face, he had managed to hide his almost constant anxiety from Arthur so far. If anything should ever happen to Alfred, Otto would have left SBS-Sion to look for another home base. Not leaving anything to chance, he had already set something up, just in case. That was something he hadn't shared with Arthur yet, as it was his very own, back door exit; *his* plan B.
There was a soft knocking on the door, which startled him back into the present. "Pssst, it's me, Hadi, let me in!"
In two long strides to cross the room, Otto was at the door. He unlocked it and let their Egyptian guide in. Carrying a heavy tray filled with breakfast goodies, Hadi headed for the tiny glass table with quick, small steps.

Otto hastily removed the ashtray from the table to make room for the tray, but while he was holding the ashtray in his hands, he looked at it longingly, with a reluctant disappointed expression, not unlike a child who had just opened an empty chocolate box. In moments of great joy - or great stress - his desire for a cigarette increased. Arthur, who had been attracted to the sight and smells of the delicious looking breakfast, noticed Otto's overly theatrical expressions of agony and couldn't help making a sarcastic crack.

"Oh Otto, I know it sucks, but sometimes you just have to, you know, suck it up."

With curled lips, Otto pulled up a chair for him and remarked under his breath, "When I find your vice, I will rub it in so hard!"

Hadi, who was slowly beginning to feel as if he was their mother instead of their guide, poured them each a cup of tea. "Now, girls, if I may have your undivided attention? I presume you have also received the text message from Mr Hauser that Mr Zinkler has made it through his operation. He also texted me to abandon plan A and move to Plan B without delay. Unable to return safely to the time of Akhenaten, we must now follow the lead of the famous archaeologist Flinders Petrie, who - in his research and diggings - had succeeded in retracing some of the old trade routes and discovering the location of several ancient Biblical sites in Egypt, Israel and other ancient seaports throughout the Mediterranean. Files on these subjects and details of Petrie's work are already in your possession. If you find an interesting location, we must contact Mr Hauser, who will then discuss it with Mr Zinkler. If and when Mr Zinkler gives us a green light, we will move to that location and continue our search for the Eye of Ra."

Arthur was deeply disappointed.

"So, we won't be going back to Akhetaten?"

"No. Until Wong succeeds in repairing the flaw, sending us back would be too dangerous. For now we must simply follow the footsteps of those who fled Jerusalem in 597 BCE.

You must carefully study the potential bearers of the Temple relics and what location those candidates may have taken them to. I guess you will both have to prove your worth today and come up with potential locations and make a choice before nightfall. In the meantime, I will keep an eye on the surrounding area and make some arrangements to find us a safer, more private way of travel."

Otto and Arthur both nodded, but remained silent. They all had mixed feelings about Plan B. Part of them was sad that they couldn't go back to ancient Egypt, but they were also relieved. It had been a crazy and dangerous mission, that could have gone very wrong. Otto also remembered exactly how he had felt the very moment they were 'sucked' back into the present, regretting to have said 'Baou-Ra!' as loud as he did. He felt as if his lungs had almost collapsed in reaction to the pressure of travelling through the wormhole while shouting the words. Even the dead had probably heard him, he thought.

After breakfast, Hadi left the apartment, leaving behind an envious Otto and Arthur, who had itchy feet and would have loved to explore the Giza plateau. Reluctantly they took out the unread files, spreading them out onto the table and the sofa, so they had a clear view of all the topics. This way it was easier to spot a connection that could perhaps lead them to a location.

With a deep sigh, Otto sat down and browsed through Flinders Petrie's discoveries while Arthur started reading one of Petrie's books: 'The Status of the Jews in Egypt'. He found it interesting to read how Petrie concluded that time and time again, the Jews went 'back' to Egypt at times of great upheaval. About 40 kilometres north of Memphis, a new Jerusalem had been built during the Greek repression. At that time, the old Jerusalem was no longer the religious home of the Jews. At the same time, the influence of the Buddhist way of life - brought to Egypt by Buddhist missionaries from India around 300 BCE - was, according to Petrie, the spark that had ignited the birth of the Essenes, whom the Greeks called the *Therapeutae*. Arthur felt that going back to the source had given him a completely new perspective to things. Everything seemed to have originated in Egypt.

Otto brought back the glass ashtray and put it on top of a pile of print-outs of Flinders Petrie's work, to stop the draft from blowing away the sheets. He elbowed Arthur and mumbled, "Petrie dish."

Arthur chuckled at Otto's pun. "Very funny. If it could only automatically cultivate some answers eh?"

Suddenly, through the bottom of the glass ashtray, an interesting detail caught Arthur's eye. He pulled the sheet out from under the ashtray and leaned forward, poring over the text.

"Listen to this: At the time of the fall of Jerusalem, the prophet Jeremiah was persuaded to accompany a group of Jews to Egypt; to Tahpanhes, to be exact. If he carried some of the relics, perhaps he brought them to Tahpanhes? Petrie discovered the site in 1886 and found out that Tahpanhes was the ancient city of Daphnae, now called Tell Defenneh. According to this article, Jeremiah even went to Memphis! Wow, Otto, it is quite possible that the Eye of Ra made it back to Egypt after all!"

Otto ran his hand through his short, dark brown hair and sighed. "It's still a needle in a haystack, Art. Realistically speaking, that stone can be anywhere around the Mediterranean." Interested to read the article nevertheless, Otto took the page from him and as he did, Arthur saw something written on the back.

Antiques and Desert Glass – Dr R. Soongh –
[saharagems.com / soonghssouvenirs.com]

"Hey look, I think we have a possible link here, Otto. We should check him out. Do you know what desert glass is?" Suddenly, Otto had an epiphany and became very excited.

"That's it! I know of an old book, written in Arabic, in which the author mentions the find of rare pieces of strange glass rocks and shards in Egypt, which he called *peridot*. Do you remember the impactites I talked about, when we were discussing the mission, just before we left Sion? Desert glass was created in the Sahara many millions of years ago, when a meteorite entered the earth's atmosphere. Its impact caused such intense heat, that the sand beneath it turned into glass. Because this particular glass is impossible for mankind to replicate, these glass rocks have become precious collectable items. The ancient Egyptians used them in jewellery and if I am not mistaken, one of these glass nuggets was used to adorn Tutankhamen's necklace. It may not be very far-fetched to presume that perhaps the original Urim was also made of this very same desert glass!"

Arthur, who shared Otto's excitement, raced toward the laptop and began an online search. Within seconds he had found a photo of Tutankhamen's famous necklace and in that necklace there it was, for all to see, a yellowish-green inlayed desert glass scarab.

"Here it is! You are right! It says that this glass scarab on Tut's necklace is made of Lybian desert glass. This type of glass can also be whiter or more transparent and can you guess what the ancient Egyptians called it? 'The Rock of God'! And their sun god was, of course, Ra!"

Eagerly they continued surfing the net. On another webpage they could read how one of the twelve stones of Aaron's breastplate could have also been a peridot.

"Otto, do you remember if the Urim we saw was completely white, off-white or greenish?"

Otto shook his head and pursed his lips, thinking.

"No, it was so dark when we were in the Aten Temple, that I never really got to see the stones properly. Although it looked bright and shiny from where I was standing, it could still be either semi-transparent, off-white, yellowish-white or greenish-white. You know, I think we should call Georg and ask him if we can call Mr Soongh to make an appointment. If he deals in desert glass and antiques, he may be our most promising link right now."

"I agree!" replied Arthur, without looking away from the laptop. "Bingo! I just found Soongh's website. It says here that his shop is in Memphis! Well, as we now know, Jeremiah went to Memphis, most likely bringing several relics from Jerusalem. This is definitely worth checking out!"

While Otto took out his mobile phone to call Georg, Hadi had already made the biggest mistake of his life. He had gone to a garage to see about fixing the broken headlight and window of his Mercedes and at that, private detective Max Müller couldn't believe his luck. Covering every possibility that might lead him back to his prize, Max had checked most of the garages in Cairo that morning, asking for a white Mercedes with a broken headlight. He had at last got a result in Giza. Max kindly asked the owner of the garage to discretely detain Hadi at the garage as long as possible and the moment he approached the garage, he was just in time to watch the white Mercedes leave.

All he had to do now, was follow.

Hadi, who hadn't expected Max to find him so quickly, had stopped at a local café to get a coffee and he was just about to call a friend to call in a favour, when from the corner of his eye he saw Max coming through the door. Hadi dropped his mobile and froze on the spot as Max walked straight toward him. He didn't know what to do; whether to smile, or to run. By fleeing from Max the night before, Hadi, Otto and Arthur had clearly demonstrated that they had seen through his cover, so Max didn't bother putting on a friendly smile this time. Instead, he grabbed Hadi by the arm, threw a few coins on the bar to pay for his coffee and took the now panicking Egyptian guide outside. "We need to talk, my fat little friend. I want you to take me to your German friend, but first we will have a friendly chit chat. What is he after? What is his mission?"

Sweat was pouring over Hadi's face as Max twisted his arm behind his back. If Max put just a little bit more pressure on his arm, his shoulder would surely dislocate. The German detective was at least a head taller than he was, so Hadi knew it would not be wise to fight him. The only thing Hadi could do now, was stall for time. "What business do you have with Otto? If you tell me, perhaps I can help."

To Hadi's great relief, Max let go of his arm and looked straight into his dark brown eyes. "I know that your friend, Otto Adler, is really Otto Rahn, the mysterious Nazi relic hunter who worked for Himmler before the Second World War. I happen to be working for a man who has an interest in him. So, you either bring me to Otto and I will take him off your hands, or I will use your family as leverage. You wouldn't want anything to happen to them, would you?"

Completely taken aback by Max's ruthless threat, Hadi could not respond. He knew he had no choice but to give the man what he wanted. Though he wanted to remain loyal to Alfred, he was afraid that Max had indeed found his family, so he decided to give in. "Okay, you win, but I need to go back inside and retrieve my mobile phone. I need it to set things up for you."

Max, who didn't trust the Egyptian, walked right behind him when they re-entered the café. As they were walking through the door - and unseen by Max - Hadi rolled his eyes at the owner behind the bar, who immediately knew that it meant trouble. Slowly he reached for the indispensable item that experienced bartenders always kept close at hand and while Hadi approached the bar and bent over to pick up his mobile phone from the floor, the barman lashed out with a club and knocked Max out cold. Hadi, feeling Max's heavy body collapsing partly on him, gasped, looked at the barman with gratitude, sputtered thanks and raced back to the apartment as if the devil was chasing him.

On arrival he banged frantically on the door until it was opened by a worried looking Otto, who was just about to call Georg.

"Hadi? What's going on? What's happened?"

Shouting partly in Egyptian and partly in English and waving his arms in wild panic, Hadi appeared to be trying to attack him. Finally, Hadi managed a coherent sentence. "Who did you talk to? Did you tell anyone who you really are? Think man, think!"

Arthur looked at Otto with an alarmed face. He knew for sure that he hadn't told anyone and he'd be surprised if anyone else had revealed Otto's true identity. Besides, who would be aware of it? So, it could only have been Otto himself. Arthur had only to look into Otto's eyes to see that he was indeed the guilty party. Feeling awkward, Otto looked quickly from Arthur to the floor. With his hands in his pockets, he sauntered toward the window and looked out onto the Giza Plateau. Staring in a state of melancholy abandonment at the pyramids and the Sphinx - which were now scorching in the midday sun - he tried to explain his motive in a soft voice.

"In June, when my mission for SBS-Sion in France was over, Fred decided not to send me back to 1939, so he gave me a new name, a passport, a handsome bank account, my freedom and my independence. However, after some time, he wanted me to come back to Sion to send me on a new mission; this time to Egypt. Although I feel deeply indebted to Alfred and knowing I owe him my life, freedom is something that is very important to me and I had already made other plans. So the next day, after Alfred had called me back to Sion, I took off on my own, new adventure, following an old dream. I had always dreamed of sailing the Mediterranean on my own, retracing the journey of the Golden Fleece and the Odyssey of Odysseus and to ultimately write a new book on my findings. Not knowing where to start in a world without friends or family, I reached out to the only one I could possibly think of; Roman Corona. He was indeed where I hoped he would be; at his family palazzo in Rome, Italy. In 1937, I had been a friend of his late grandfather and I had spent many delightful hours browsing through the old books in his library in search of forgotten history. I used the same pretence as before to get inside; expressing my interest in his library and my desire to study some of the books there. So when I arrived at the palazzo and was shown to the library, it felt like a homecoming to me. The impressive Italian palazzo with its old, crackled paintings, 18th century furniture and high ornate ceilings hadn't changed at all. Inside, the house looked as if time had stood still!"

Otto looked away and saw the reflection of his face in a mirror on the wall. Realising that his own time had stood still for over 70 years, Otto couldn't help finding it a comical coincidence to refer to the unchanged palazzo, as if no time had passed there either. Looking sheepishly at his own, unchanged face, he blinked a few times to break his digression and returned to the story.

"Anyway, Roman Corona and I got along well and at the end of my first day of research, he asked me to stay at the palazzo instead of going back to my hotel. That night I told him of my dream and ended up buying his old clipper; a small sailing boat with a two-man crew, that I rechristened 'Laurin'. It was moored at the harbour of Paphos, on the island of Cyprus, where Corona had another villa. As I continued my research over the following weeks, I also began organising my Mediterranean voyage, but my mind seemed to be constantly wondering off. I couldn't help thinking about Fred, about this new secret mission to Egypt and of course, I often thought of you."

He took Arthur's face in his hands, looked deeply into his eyes and then gently kissed his forehead.

"So, although I had spent a lot of time and energy in planning, organising and preparing my first sea voyage, I changed my mind; I contacted Fred and the rest of the team and asked to meet up at St. Peter's Square on the very day I was actually meant to fly to Cyprus."

Otto shook his shoulders and looked at Hadi. "Of course, when I brought Arthur to the palazzo that night, instead of flying off to Cyprus, I owed Corona an explanation. So once

Arthur had gone to his room for the night, I stayed with Corona, who had no difficulty in persuading me to have more than a few glasses of Amaretto with him."

Otto held his head in his hands and mumbled "Ow, I shouldn't have done that!" He looked up again and continued. "I soon felt comfortable enough to tell him who I really was, that I had been a close friend of his grandfather's and that I might be going on a mission to Egypt first, before starting my sailing adventure. I thought I could trust him, but how I was mistaken! He immediately was fascinated with the little I'd told him and wanted to know more about what I would be doing in Egypt. He started asking me all sorts of questions; about relics, but also about Himmler and Hitler. So I broke off all contact with him and went back to Switzerland, but this time with Arthur at my side. Really, I never thought he would ever find me."

Arthur, who understood much more now, walked over to him, gently rubbed his back and said cheerfully, "So, we have a boat?!"

28

Guernsey, Channel Islands, October 4th 2011

It was already two o'clock when David and Danielle decided to head back to Rose Cottage. Black crows scattered from the gravel parking lot as the car came to a crackling halt. Still in a holiday mood, David courteously opened the car door for Danielle, who noticed that something was wrong the moment she stood next to the car. Not only was it completely quiet, she also didn't see the other SBS agent anywhere, who surely would have checked on any car driving up to the cottage. She took off her sunglasses and spotted irregularities in the foliage of the rose garden in front of the house. There were spaces between some of the flowers and plants that hadn't been there that morning, as if something or someone was lying on the ground, pushing aside some of the rose bushes. David noticed her standing stock still and followed her gaze. He held up one arm and whispered, "Wait here!"

Barry, the second SBS agent, who had returned with them from the beach café, immediately walked over to Danielle to take David's place. Alarmed, he slowly brought his hand to his Glock, which he carried in a holster across his chest.

Danielle could feel her own heartbeat in her chest and throat. "What's wrong, David?" she shouted, no longer able to contain herself. David got up from his kneeling position and looked pale. For a second he had frozen to the spot when he had spotted his dead agent nearly decapitated. Whoever had cut his throat was strong, ruthless and an enemy to be feared. That enemy had now clearly found them.

"Don't come any closer, you mustn't see this. Stay with the car, I will check the house."

His voice was hoarse from the shock. Now it was down to David and only one other agent to protect Danielle. As their cover was obviously blown, he could feel the pressure and anxiety paralysing his system. Not knowing how many people he was up against, he thought he'd better take extreme care when checking the house.

David also carried a concealed Glock, hidden on his lower back underneath his jacket. Hardly making a sound, he took out the lethal weapon and entered the living room of the cottage. One of the floorboards squeaked and millions of dust particles seemed to exist only inside the bright beam of sunlight that penetrated the room through the half-open door. The rest of the house was dark and David's eyes had to adjust, but when he saw that nothing had been moved or been taken out of place, he decided to check out the kitchen, his bedroom and the main bathroom. There was no one there. However, when he entered Danielle's bedroom, he could see that it had been thoroughly searched. To his horror, David also spotted wet bloodstains on the carpet. Danielle had an en-suite bathroom, which was now locked from the outside. He saw the key in the lock. With great care, he slowly turned the key with his handkerchief and opened the door. He jumped at the sight, which almost made him vomit. Covering his open mouth with the back of his hand, he desperately tried not to make a sound. Lying on her back in the empty bathtub was poor Mrs Peel; her clothes and hair drenched in her own blood.

In his panic, David raced out of the cottage and searched the back garden to make sure the murderer was no longer there. Seeing him in this state of fear and despair, Danielle knew that something was very, very wrong. She disobeyed David's order to stay put and entered the cottage, followed by a protesting but still protective Barry, who was frantically looking in all directions as they entered, his loaded Glock stretched out in front of him and his other arm in front of Danielle. Ignoring him, she broke through, sped to her bedroom and saw that the photo of herself and Gabby, which she had kept on the night table, had disappeared.

Danielle's heart sank.

By that detail, she knew for sure that Izz al Din had found her.

When David returned to the car and saw that neither Danielle nor Barry were there, he lost all control.

Shouting Danielle's name, he didn't realise that Barry - who heard the call from inside the house - thought it was Al Din calling her. Barry, who had just found Mrs Peel's body in the tub, knew they had to move fast and pulled Danielle out of the room. "Come on, we need to leave, quickly!"

He flanked her on their way out, protecting her with his body just as David re-entered the cottage through the kitchen door. Barry saw the silhouette of a man entering the house through the kitchen door and with the adrenaline running rampant in him, he thought it was Al Din. Without wasting a valuable second, he pulled the trigger and fired a shot. Danielle screamed when she saw her loved one fall to the floor. "Daviiiid!!"

She ran toward him and the entire world in her mind's eye suddenly came to a complete standstill. As if she was under water, sounds and visions became blurred and muffled. She no longer cared about Al Din or herself. At that moment, the only thing in the world she cared about was David. She bent over him and was relieved to see he opened his eyes. While trying to reach up to her face with his hand, he groaned and whispered, "Sweet Danielle, my god...dess..."

Then, David's arm dropped and his head lolled to one side.

Danielle cried out to the agent, who couldn't believe what he had just done and was paralysed on the spot, still holding the weapon in front of him. Danielle was beyond panic and yelled at him. "Don't just stand there, get some help!!"

Immediately, Barry dialled 112, knowing that they had no choice but to call in help from outside. How could this have happened? This was exactly the kind of chaotic situation he had been professionally trained for, but already he found himself failing SBS-Sion terribly. Barry also had an emergency number to contact Georg, so immediately after he had called for an ambulance, he speed dialled Georg to explain the situation. While he was waiting for Georg to pick up his phone, he examined David's condition.

It looked more serious than it was.

When he saw the wound, he noticed that the bullet had gone straight through his side and when he estimated the blood loss, he believed that it had probably missed vital organs and important blood vessels. The force of impact, however, would have knocked anyone out. David was nevertheless bleeding and Barry decided to give the phone to Danielle. He took off his shirt, tore it into strips and started to bind the bleeding wound as tightly as he dared.

"Don't worry, Danielle, he'll live. I'm so sorry! I didn't see that it was David. If Georg answers the phone, you tell him what happened, okay?"

Danielle wiped her face - that was streaming with tears - with her sleeve and nodded. Caressing David's face with her fingers, she waited patiently for Georg to answer the phone. It took such a long time, that she half-expected to get his voicemail anytime now and had begun to mentally formulate the message she would leave, to explain the situation, but then suddenly, there was a click. Hearing Georg's voice restored her hope. "Barry, what's up?"

"Georg? It's Danielle. Al Din's been here, one of the guards is dead and the other one has accidently shot David. We need help!"

Georg was completely shocked. "Oh God! How is he?"

"Barry says he'll live, but we had to call 112. What do we do now?"

"Let me speak to Barry."

Danielle gave the phone to Barry, who had done a good job binding David's wounds to stop most of the bleeding. With blood-stained hands he carefully took the phone from her and couldn't help bowing his head when he spoke to Georg.

"I'm so sorry, sir, I thought he was Al Din and having Danielle right behind me I panicked and fired before identifying him. The housekeeper has been killed too. She must have walked in on them"

"Don't torture yourself, Barry, these are very dangerous people. If they've killed your partner and also the housekeeper, they are very serious. Take just Danielle. Go to the new safe house address as quickly as you can. I will send in a new team and they will meet you there. Leave David behind, but make sure he is carrying his mobile phone in his pocket. Take all the equipment and erase all traces. Now go!" Barry started to work as fast as he could, taking down all the surveillance equipment and bringing it all to the car. He could hear the ambulance in the distance while he was wiping off those traces that could unnecessarily complicate the police investigation. He drove off quickly with Danielle - who had found it difficult to leave David behind - and they had only just turned the corner when the ambulance arrived. Danielle was afraid that David would be seen as a suspect, but part of her also trusted Alfred's influence. Surely, he would not let anything bad happen to David.

As they were driving off toward the new secret location, Titan followed them intently through his binoculars. When he was sure that they were heading for St. Peter Port, he jumped back into the car and checked the navigation system. One dot was blinking faithfully on the radar. Titan whistled a tune and seized his mobile phone. With his thumbnail he selected a number, all the while keeping an eye on the narrow country lane as he increased speed. A light brown cloud of dust billowed behind the car.

"Found her, chief! She wasn't at the cottage when I got there, but I found a photo of her on the night table, so I know she was there. I planted a bug in her beauty case and checked the tracking navigator in Lars' car and guess what? It works! It looks like they are leaving the island. Do you want me to follow?"

Titan nodded when he heard the answer and made a sad face. "Yes, chief. I'm on my way."

A blue Peugeot was slowly driving through the countryside heading toward the south coast, when it almost crashed into a speeding Camaro Convertible V8 SS that had just turned onto the main road from a small country lane without looking. Stuart had to hit the brakes so hard that Michael's travel bag flew through the car and hit the windscreen. Stuart wasn't amused. "Bloody hell! What was that?"

"I don't know, but I have a bad feeling about this. I hope this has nothing to do with my dad."

Michael, who hadn't told Stuart anything yet, knew that his father was on a mission and that Guernsey wasn't the kind of island that saw a lot of crime. In his mind he was making a connection between the fast moving, very expensive looking car and David. Unconsciously, he squeezed his hands.

A little later, when they turned a corner, they almost crashed into an ambulance moving at break-neck speed in the opposite direction, cutting the corner to keep the van stable.

Michael felt a sting in his stomach. "Stop the car!"

Stuart stared hard at Michael. "Why?"

"I said, stop the car! We have to follow that ambulance. It's a gut feeling. Just trust me will you?"

Stuart slowly stopped the car by the side of the road and began manoeuvring into a complete turn about to start the pursuit.

"Will you hurry up, please?" exclaimed Michael nervously.

Stuart became a little irritated. "There's just one hospital on the island! I'll get you there alright, so don't start jumping all over me, son!"

Michael apologised. He so wanted to tell him everything, but also felt the need to keep silent. He didn't know Stuart well enough to trust him, but the man kept on looking at Michael and he knew he had to tell him at least something.

"Okay, here's the story. My dad's missing and I'm afraid that someone is after something he is protecting. My gut feeling says he's in that ambulance and that that car we almost crashed into is the person who's harmed him."

Stuart was silent for a minute. He had to take a moment to process all this. In his line of work he drove tourists and businessmen; locals who wanted to be taken home after a party; elderly women going shopping and the odd guru, but never did he feel as if he was being sucked into a crime movie. "So, is your dad a good guy or a bad guy?"

Michael looked at him and smiled.

"No worries, he's a good guy…"

It didn't take long before they drove into the parking lot of the Princess Elizabeth Hospital in St. Andrew. The ambulance had already arrived and Michael rushed out of the car to see if it was indeed his father who was being carried out on the stretcher, but when he saw an unconscious elderly lady with a serious looking head wound, he had mixed feelings of relief and disappointment. Michael was just about to walk back to Stuart when he saw how a second person was being carefully taken out of the ambulance. The man's side was oozing blood through the sheets that covered him.

"Dad!"

David, who had been well attended to in the short drive in the ambulance, had regained consciousness and couldn't believe his eyes when he saw his son bending over him.

"Michael! What on earth are you doing here! You must get off the island! Now!"

Michael backed off, shocked by his father's pale complexion and alarmed reaction to his presence. What on earth had happened? Michael had to watch his father being taken into the hospital's emergency entrance and didn't know what to do next. He couldn't just leave; he had come all this way and had never expected to find his father so quickly, but now that he had, he knew he couldn't obey him, he couldn't just desert him. Whatever trouble he was in, Michael wanted to help him, protect him and take care of him.

Before he went inside, Michael took out his wallet and gave Stuart 35 Pounds, knowing that it more than covered the fare up to that point. While he grabbed his travel bag, Michael looked at his driver one last time. "Thank you, Stuart, for everything."

Stuart gave him his business card. "Sure son, go look after your father and if you ever need me again, you call me!"

"Thanks, mate!" Michael slapped the roof of the blue Peugeot as a signal that he had taken everything out and watched Stuart driving off with his hand out of the car window, waving a last salute. Nothing in the world was now more important to Michael than his father and he intended to sit in the waiting room until he could visit him and talk to him properly. They say that blood is thicker than water; that the bond between father and son can be so strong that oceans can't keep them apart. For Michael, his life felt less important than that of his father and he wasn't afraid. However, Michael didn't understand that David, who was already angry with himself for having failed to protect Danielle, couldn't possibly deal with having to protect his child as well. Michael had no idea what kind of people they were up against and for David, the unexpected presence of his son was more of a burden than a blessing. Still, David knew his son wouldn't leave, so he wasn't surprised when Michael walked through the door. He smiled at him and gently patted the side of the bed to invite Michael to sit down.

"Well, the bullet went straight through my side and miraculously didn't sever anything vital, not even broken a rib! They've stitched me up, but the bandage is awfully tight though. They've told me I need to stay for at least a week to let it heal and enable me to get mobile without rupturing the wounds. Of course I can't, so I'm going to need your help to get me out of here as soon as possible."

"Sure dad, you can count on me. We're a team, right?"

David nodded and their fists boxed in ritual commitment. They didn't know that only a few rooms away, an impatient patient was making plans to leave the hospital that very night.

29

Sion, Switzerland, October 4th 2011

The usually cool, calm and collected Georg, who had always been able to handle everything so well for Alfred, was now beyond panic. After a tense meeting with the surgeon, who had decided to put Alfred into an artificially induced sleep for a few days to enable him to heal better and quicker, Georg realised that he was, regrettably, on his own. He understood how fragile Alfred really was and that a small rise in blood pressure could cause haemorrhaging, so Georg had no choice but to leave him in the good hands of the medical staff. Since he could - for the time being - no longer consult Alfred on important matters, Georg decided to return to the base. However, nothing could have prepared him for the chaos about to break loose at his meeting with professor Wong in the lab later that morning.

First of all, 'Mission Safe House 1' had been compromised and David had been shot. Georg had been on the phone non-stop to activate 'Mission Safe House 2', placing everyone in their new position. Alfred always had a plan B and Georg knew that the moment Plan B was to be activated, Plan C needed to be created. Therefore, Georg had to set up a third, new safe house location in case the second one also failed to protect Danielle, who was now guarded by just one agent; Barry Price.

Next, Georg had to have David retrieved, who was now publically exposed in the hospital on Guernsey. Any moment now, the police would undoubtedly arrive and interrogate David about the terrible events that had taken place at Rose Cottage. Being the victim of a gunshot wound wouldn't immunise David from becoming a suspect and Georg was worried that David would end up being arrested. If that wasn't enough; what was he to do if the press showed up? Georg realised that he had no choice but to get David out of there quickly.

It was time to call in some favours.

Kneeling on the floor of the glass office in the lab, Georg now looked at a highly confidential item that was stored in the safe underneath Alfred's desk. He hesitated for a moment, knowing that he was only allowed to touch it - let alone open it - in an emergency. Even then, he'd only be allowed to open it once everything else had failed.

Unfortunately, this was such a moment.

With extreme care and respect, Georg entered the secret password and opened Alfred's brown leather briefcase, containing his personal and top-secret documents. Before going into surgery, Alfred had given Georg the password to the briefcase in case something went wrong. The briefcase contained all his personal information; his carte blanche details; his private address book; a copy of his will and much more. Several items were hidden inside envelopes and sealed with an old-fashioned, red wax seal. Pressed into the seal was Alfred's coat of arms; three Moorish heads beneath a triangle, at the centre of which was the All-seeing Eye. Rays of light were shooting from the triangle. Georg immediately recognised it as The Eye of Ra. The three Moorish heads were from the coat of arms of Hugues de Payens, the first grandmaster of the Knights Templar, who was, according to Alfred, his several times great grandfather. The seal was flanked by a simple, stylised fleur-de-lis. Georg remembered how Alfred had told him the story of the origin of the fleur-de-lis - which had come from Egypt - symbolising the Godflame, the Holy Light that lives within the material world of the mother goddess. The Godflame was symbolised by the golden iris or 'lis'; the *Iris pseudacorus,* because of its colour and form. This symbol - sometimes depicted abstractly and sometimes in a more elegant manner - had not only been taken to Israel and used as a mystical symbol during the time of King Solomon; it had also found its way onto the banner of the Catholic Clovis; King of the Franks, after which the fleur-de-lis became the Christian symbol for Mother Mary. In the 10th century, cities whose Patron Saint was Mother Mary began to include the fleur-de-lis in their coats of arms.

In 1147, King Louis VII of France adopted it as a *symbole de la dignité royal capétienne* and showed the golden lily on an azure blue background. From that moment onward it would become the symbol of royalty and divine protection. In 1611, John Guillim published his *A Display of Heraldrie* in London, in which he also mentioned the coat of arms with the fleur-de-lis. He described it as 'three toads erect, saltant', after which the French were often called 'toads' or 'frogs'. It had made Georg laugh out loud, telling Alfred that he should write a book: 'The Fleur-de-lis; from Godflame to Toad'. Georg had never seen Alfred laugh so hard.

Although he had been surprised to see the fleur-de-lis as part of Alfred's coat of arms, he had come to learn that Alfred Zinkler was a man of great secrets. Alfred was the silent one, the servant and boasting about his bloodline or family history would never have occurred to him. Even those who were very close to him would only know tiny fragments of his real identity. Georg knew only that when Alfred needed help, even kings came to the rescue.

Georg carefully took out an address book and a book of codes and resisted checking out everything else. He was very curious about Alfred's background, but what he really needed right now were the names and addresses of people he had to contact to secure their mission. The codebook would give him access to hidden information on Alfred's laptop, as well as an emergency bank account, from which new missions could be funded. With melancholy eyes he stared at the opened suitcase, where a large, wax-sealed, blazon stamped envelope caught his eye. On the envelope, the words 'Post Mortem' were written in a black, gothic style fond. Georg knew that that particular envelope was to be opened only after Alfred had passed away. Georg prayed it would never come to that. His eyes grew large when he browsed through the address book. Alfred knew all these people? Personally? He paused and stared without blinking at the one particular name he had never expected to see in that book. He thanked God for not having to call that number. Yet...

It took him a few hours before he had made the necessary calls to set everything up to retrieve David. The moment agent Barry phoned in from the island of Sark, confirming that they had safely arrived, he couldn't help taking a deep breath and as he blew out the air through his mouth, he released with it the strenuous tension of the last few days. Wong, who hadn't dared disturb him until now, saw that moment as a good opportunity and approached Georg slowly, cautiously raising his right hand like a schoolboy with a question. "Sir, I have some good news."

Georg turned and was pleased to see Wong's happy face.

"Oh Wong, you're a sight for sore eyes! I would certainly appreciate some good news. Do sit down!"

Wong entered the glass office and parked himself in one of the comfortable leather office chairs. He couldn't help but smile, as his confidence in his own work had finally returned. "I have new uploads ready for the field team in Egypt. After the upload, their devices will be reprogrammed with the correct co-ordinates. I have added some new options, one of which may come in handy if they should ever find themselves in a situation where they have to split up."

Wong paused, grinning from ear to ear; his folded hands wrapped around his left knee. Georg, who was now very curious, knew that Wong was intentionally trying his patience. "Well, what are you waiting for? Tell me!"

"I have repaired the flaw and they can now safely return to ancient Akhetaten. If they press 'home', they will return directly to the base in Sion in real time. When they arrive back from ancient Egypt, it will still be the same time they left, only losing 10 seconds. Returning just after their departure is a safety precaution to make sure they won't bump into themselves on their return. If they select '1', they will equally return to the present, also in real time, but they will still be in the same location they departed from. To be able to use option '2', they first have to insert the device into the supplied adapter to pre-program any date and co-ordinate they might need, that will contribute to their mission."

"To get back from that particular past, they also simply select '1', or, when their mission is accomplished, 'home'. I have created a manual, so they will know how to use the adapter and how to activate the various destination options."

Georg was pleased. "That sounds fantastic!"

"That's not all though. Should they become separated, Otto and Arthur would simply have to select '3' to be reunited with Hadi, as both their devices have been programmed to lock onto Hadi's device. It doesn't matter if they are in the past or the present, or anywhere in the world, option 3 will get them to wherever Hadi is."

"You are a miracle worker, Wong! How can they download the new data and options?"

"It's simple. All you have to do is contact Otto or Hadi and ask them to activate the yellow button on their devices. For safety reasons, the mobile ERFAB devices have been programmed to not send out any signal until someone uses it, for example, when a number is selected. However, there is a yellow button, which, when pressed, sends out a short signal to the mainframe ERFAB computer here. I will then see their signal here at the lab and make sure the data and new options are safely uploaded to their devices. I will also send the adapter and the manual to their coordinates through our main ERFAB here at the lab."

"Is it ready?"

"Yes, sir, it is."

"Then I will call Otto and tell him to stand by for the download."

On his way out, Georg grasped the professor's arm and gripped it firmly for a few seconds. "No flaws this time, okay?" he said, while looking hard at the professor. Wong jumped at Georg's sudden move and quickly shook his head. "No, sir. No flaws, sir." He could understand why Georg was worried though; last time Wong's ignorance had come close to killing the field team.

Wong forced himself to smile at Georg.

"I am quite sure this time!"

Georg nodded and turned to make a call to Otto on his mobile, excited to tell him the good news. Little did he know that his excitement would soon turn into a whole new nightmare. Otto's phone rang 5 times, 10 times and after the tenth ring, Georg's stomach started to churn. This didn't feel good. Had Otto lost his phone? Or, had he bolted again?

Georg left a message before he dialled again.

"Pick up the damn phone, Otto!"

Still, there was no answer. After he had left another message, Georg decided to call Hadi, but when even Hadi didn't answer his phone, it became clear to Georg that his worries were far from over.

30

Cairo, Egypt, October 4th 2011

There was a strong wind coming from the desert and the sand rustled against the window, which was now shut. Hadi was sitting on the sofa with his head in his hands. When Alfred had hired him for his knowledge about the Amarna period and his ability to understand ancient Egyptian, he didn't think he would ever be putting his family in danger. He himself had understood the risks of time travelling, as Alfred had always been quite transparent about that. He was happy to accept the fact that his safety would never be guaranteed, but because he had been curious to discover what Akhetaten looked like in the old days of the famous heretic pharaoh and his beautiful queen, he had enthusiastically signed both the contract and the attached damage waiver. Hadi knew that the mission was secret and that he was responsible for Otto and Arthur from the moment they arrived in Egypt, but this whole assignment proved to be much tougher than he had expected.

Hadi had taken them to ancient Akhetaten and he had brought them back safely, so he had done everything that Alfred had asked for. Hadi had even succeeded in protecting them from the likes of Ashraf and his sidekick, Beni, but now, all of a sudden, this mysterious private detective pops up from nowhere and starts making serious threats and that had not been in the job description. Hadi's family was his life. He had parents, grandparents, brothers, sisters, nephews and nieces, whom he all loved dearly and although he did not have a wife or children himself, it was through his loved ones that Private Detective Max Müller had found the only way that Hadi could ever be bribed.

The choice had been easy. Blood is always thicker.

Still, he promised God that if they could get away from Max on time, he would honour his contract with Alfred and being a Coptic Christian, Hadi was very serious indeed when it came to promises to God.

After learning about Hadi's painful encounter with Max at the café, Otto - who had been a spy for a short time in the mid-1930s and knew how it all worked - wondered if Max's driver could have followed Hadi all the way back to their accommodation. He cautiously walked toward the window and looked into the street. There wasn't much to be seen from there, but he didn't want to expose himself by walking onto the balcony for a better look. He'd be a sitting duck.

Mist! If only I could see the entire street from here.

"I don't feel safe here anymore." said Otto without turning. "When you were away, we discovered a possible link to the stone and I was just about to phone someone called Dr Soongh; a dealer in antiques and desert glass, who may be our first link to finding the Eye of Ra. I think it would be to our best interest to meet him, but that also means we need to leave the apartment at some point."

Otto turned and looked at Hadi with serious eyes.

"Are you sure you weren't followed by anyone?"

"I just drove very fast, so you will understand that both my eyes were needed on the road in front of me, but I'm telling you, Max was out cold when I left the café."

"I'm not talking about Max, I'm talking about his driver."

Hadi rubbed his eyes and groaned. Why hadn't he thought of that.

All the while, Arthur had been very silent, thinking about all the possibilities they'd have, if only they were able to use Otto's boat as a base. The very place where they might have privacy was on the open waters of the Mediterranean.

The only problem was, how to get there.

Otto, still standing with his hands thrust deep into his pockets, turned to look at him and observed how his boyfriend was obviously deep in thought. His lips were firmly glued to his knuckles. Otto had always loved Arthur's cleverness, the depth of his knowledge and his ability to see logical connections where others could only see chaos. He looked at his dark curls and azure eyes - eyes that he could drown in. Eyes he actually did drown in, several times a day.

Their relationship was still so fragile and innocent; Arthur was not yet ready for real intimacy and consequently, their young love affair had already suffered some tense moments. Otto understood that he himself was fifteen years older and experienced. His attraction to the young man was much more passionate in comparison to the more gentle Arthur, who did not yet want to go beyond the usual cuddles and kisses. It had disappointed Otto, but deep inside he understood that Arthur just needed some more time.

Otto walked over and kneeled in front of him. With the eyes of a friend, a lover, a father, a brother and a soul mate all at the same time, he looked at him and said with a soft, gentle voice, "My darling boy, you remind me of Rodin's 'Thinker'."

Arthur awoke from his thoughts saw Otto in front of him, so full of love and admiration. He couldn't help touching his cheek and returned the smile. Then he spotted the shocked face of Hadi, who - up until that moment - had had no idea that Otto and Arthur were more than just friends and colleagues. Arthur quickly got up and shared his thoughts about using Otto's boat as a base, should their quest for the stone take them out of Egypt and into the Mediterranean. Hadi nodded in agreement.

"That is actually a great plan. We must, of course, discuss this with Georg. However, first things first. We need to visit Dr Soongh, which indeed means that we have to leave the premises. We must find a way to get Max and his driver off our backs. Any ideas?"

Arthur blurted out in an attempt to be funny, "We can dress as women!" but spotting Hadi's worried look, Arthur quickly cleared his throat and resumed a serious demeanour. It amused Otto. In spite of his introverted character, which was mainly moulded by traumatic life experiences, Otto still loved to laugh. Seeing that youthful sense of humour in Arthur, who was always able to cheer him up somehow, gave him much joy. Arthur made him feel younger, more carefree, but interestingly enough, also less naïve.

Feeling responsible for Arthur, who trusted him completely, Otto would never take Arthur for granted and had actually become even more considerate than ever before. Otto understood what the young man had given up just to be with him. He also respected the fact that Arthur had never asked him questions about his past, even though he knew how curious he must be about his life in Nazi Germany, about his work for the SS and what it was that seemed to eat his soul. The whole package that was Arthur Griffin had made Otto feel comfortable with him from day one. With Arthur he felt strong; relaxed and, perhaps more importantly; happy.

As they couldn't possibly use the white Mercedes anymore now, Arthur suggested they hire another car, preferably something big that they could hide behind the moment they left the building. As if he had had an epiphany, Hadi took out his mobile phone and called a number from his phone log. Although Otto and Arthur couldn't follow the conversation, which was in Arabic, it was obvious from the tone of Hadi's voice that he knew the person he was speaking to very well and by the time he got off the phone, he seemed to be in a better mood. "Okay guys; we have a car! A friend of mine, who still owes me a favour, has a large SUV and he has offered to take us to where ever we need to go, provided it is today, as from tomorrow onward he is no longer available. So, I think we should make an appointment with Dr Soongh without delay. Where is the note with the telephone number?"

Otto had left it on the table so he pointed at the stack of print-outs, not realising that they belonged to a secret file that was only meant to be seen by him and Arthur, but Hadi didn't seem to be interested in the text; only in the phone number and the address and Otto blew out his cheeks, releasing his tension. He felt so stupid. Alfred had said not to trust anyone.

It took two hours before Dr Soongh finally answered his phone. He agreed to see them at four o'clock that afternoon, so without wasting any more precious time, Hadi called his friend back with instructions to pick them up as soon as possible. Otto regretted having to leave this accommodation, as he couldn't get enough of the view, but he knew that this address was now no longer safe.

In the next hour they packed all their luggage and got themselves ready for departure, leaving the apartment as they had found it. Carefully, Otto wiped off the fingerprints just in case, making it clear to everyone that they could no longer touch anything, unless they were wearing their cotton gloves. Suddenly, the sound of a car horn made Hadi's hair stand up. Mumbling curses in Arabic, he saw how a chocolate brown SUV was parking in front of the door of the apartment. Not having been able to share the details of their rather delicate situation with his friend, Hadi was afraid that he would accidently blow their cover.

Otto left the room walking backwards, holding onto as much luggage as possible and trying to memorise the pyramid view he had fallen in love with. Suddenly he dropped everything; seized his mobile phone; took a photo and smiled contently when he saw how beautifully the photo had turned out. He had found taking photos with a telephone amusing, as he so well remembered how he used to set up a camera in the 1930s, then having to use a dark room to develop his own photos. Modern technique was just so much more practical. Rushing to join the rest in the hallway downstairs, Otto nearly fell off the steps and twisted his ankle, narrowly missing a sprain. He limped toward the SUV, trying not to attract too much attention.

Arthur had already squeezed himself and his luggage into the backseat of the almost new Ford Expedition, which smelled of cigarette smoke, sweat and cheap perfume. "Cool." he said while looking around in the car, "Tinted windows and everything. We should be okay I guess!"

Otto, who joined him on the backseat, nodded with a painful face while he rubbed his ankle. Arthur noticed.

"You alright, Otto?"

"Yeah, yeah, I just almost broke my ankle back there. I missed a step on the stairs."

Hadi climbed into the front seat and immediately shushed his friend Jazir, who was just about to greet him with the customary, rather noisy embrace, which would surely attract too much attention. While hearing Hadi's short explanation, Jazir's broad smile turned into a serious frown. He understood that they were on the run, so with increasing speed he headed toward the south, nervously checking his rear mirror every five seconds.

Dr Soongh's bizarre antiques shop was in Memphis, about half an hour south of modern day Cairo. It was located on the eastern side of the touristic road that leads the curious visitor to the famous step pyramid of Saqqara and the Memphis museum. As Memphis and Saqqara are popular destinations for a day excursion from Cairo, it was an excellent location for an antiques shop. Visitors could find it easily when they wandered around the neighbourhood in search of a restaurant or a café, but that didn't mean that Soongh would keep his shop open at lunch time. He was far too in love with food and relaxation and wouldn't receive his potential clients any sooner than at four o'clock. So when the team arrived half an hour earlier than the agreed time, they decided to visit the famous step pyramid to kill some time. Hadi and his friend Jazir had been keeping a sharp eye out on their surroundings, but when they didn't see anything suspicious, Hadi felt it was safe to get out of the car and stroll around the site, something that obviously made Otto and Arthur very happy.

Saqqara is a very special place; it is unique in the world. The huge pyramid complex is part of a vast necropolis that belonged to the ancient royal city of Memphis, which had been a capital city for thousands of years - going back to the first dynasties of Egypt. As they had expected to see a lonely pyramid in the desert, they were surprised to see that the structure wasn't by any means the only one there. Within the 37 acre large pyramid complex, a number of functional and non-functional buildings were slowly eroding in the desert sand. The architecture of the sleek, stylish buildings that belonged to the *Hed Seb Court,* vaguely reminded Otto of the Art Deco style that was popular in Germany in his time. These 'dummy' buildings were probably only built to serve a purpose in the pharaoh's afterlife. Remembering the ancient Egyptian philosophy; 'as above, so below' and 'as below, so above', Otto guessed that the fake doors, for example, were there to allow the ghost of the pharaoh to come in or go out at leisure. As well as the bigger buildings, there were the remains of shrines, chapels, facades, walls, terraces, large statues, columns and pavilions and that was counting only what was visible above ground. Underneath the pyramid lies a maze of tunnels and chambers, most probably built to frighten off tomb robbers. Nevertheless, the tomb was robbed extensively throughout the millennia and all that remains of the old pharaoh today is his mummified foot.

Otto had never imagined that there were so many pyramids in Egypt. He had always believed that there were just the three main ones at Giza, with a few smaller ones dotted around them. Unable to hide his emotions, he started to recite a fragment from Goethe's 'Faust',

"Whatever is the lot of humankind
I want to taste within my deepest self.
I want to seize the highest and the lowest,
to load its woe and bliss upon my breast,
and thus expand my single self titanically
and in the end go down with all the rest."

Arthur smiled at Otto, enjoying his friend's enthusiasm. He had read enough about ancient Egypt over the past few years to be able to explain some of the pyramid's history and decided to share it. "Speaking of titanic; this particular pyramid is actually considered the first ever massive manmade structure. It is the tomb of pharaoh Horus

Netjerykhet, better known as Djoser. According to most scholars, the tomb was designed by the enigmatic architect Imhotep, who himself became worshipped as a god of healing and architecture after his death. As of the 20th century, the entire funerary complex has been painstakingly excavated and restored by the French architect and Egyptologist Jean-Philippe Lauer, who spent 75 years of his life at Saqqara. When he was still working on the site at the age of 90, the Egyptian workers thought he had been 'forgotten by God'."

Otto smirked cynically. "Forgotten by God? Hilarious!"

Protecting their eyes from the sandy wind, they walked toward the mortuary temple, which was located to the north side of the pyramid. When Otto became confused, expecting the mortuary temple to be at the east to greet the sun, Arthur explained that at the time of Djoser, the religious cult was stellar, not solar.

When they arrived at the so called 'Temple T', the beautifully carved Djed Pillars on the lintels immediately caught Otto's eye, reminding him of the Sion Universal Temple logo. This 'SUT' logo also contains a Djed Pillar, coincidently in the letter 'T'. 'Fred's pride and joy', Otto thought fondly and while they were walking toward the southern temple, he couldn't help wondering how his friend was doing in recovery. Subconsciously his hand touched his mobile as they arrived at the ruined building.

Arthur suddenly pointed at the top of the wall. "Hey! Check out those cobras!"

A line of large, stone cobras topped the wall of the temple. The cobra was a symbol of royal protection and at the time of Djoser it also symbolised the north. Otto, who very much disliked snakes, looked away. Snakes gave him the shivers, even in stone. "I killed a snake once, you know? On one of my walks in the mountains in France. It was just about to attack me."

Arthur smiled and put his arm around him.

"Yeah, I know. You wrote that in one of your books."

The wind was now so strong that they had to protect their faces from the sharp sand, which was violently striking every bit of exposed skin. It felt like an attack of pins and needles. Their sight hindered by the sand, they gazed with difficulty at the old stones that made up the giant pyramid. For almost 5000 years, Pharaoh Djoser's last resting place, which was constructed in the Old Kingdom's third dynasty, has bravely resisted countless sand storms, but one day, the old king's tomb will undoubtedly be weathered to its core.

Holding his hands around his mouth, Hadi shouted at Otto and Arthur to return to the car. It was time to drive into Memphis.

With its strategic harbour on the Nile River, the ancient city of Memphis had served as an important centre for trade, religion and commerce for almost two thousand years, until the new Greek port of Alexandria took over in the 4th century BCE. The site of Memphis-Saqqara is therefore one of the highlights of any visit to Egypt, but the modern town is much bigger than the old capital, which is now in ruins and part of a protected archaeological site and open air museum. In Alfred's files - that Otto and Arthur had carefully studied - they had not only discovered that the prophet Jeremiah may have taken the Eye of Ra, the Urim, to Memphis in the 6th century BCE; they also discovered that Flinders Petrie - the same archaeologist who had found the Thummim; the black stone in Alfred's ring - had lead several excavations in Memphis. Therefore they were hopeful that somehow, the Eye of Ra had indeed been found and that - like its black sister stone - it hadn't been recognised for what it was, simply because it had been discovered alone, without its pair. There was a tiny chance that it could still be in the area; perhaps in an old antiques shop, that also stocked desert glass. Dr Soongh's shop was an unnumbered house in a street not far from the Memphis Museum. The front of the shop, which had been painted in a variety of colours, showed all sorts of stylistic illustrations, among which figured a lotus flower, an Ankh symbol and several Arabic sentences. Above the entrance it said, in plain English:

Dr R. Soongh, Antiques, Desert Glass, Egyptian artefacts and souvenirs

'Who needs a house number!' Arthur thought with amusement. The door was closed, but when they knocked, a short, obese man with Chinese features hastily unlocked the door. Four locks were opened with four different, small keys, before he turned the main key that was still in the door. Another padlock was unlocked before he took off the door chain, which was apparently the final safety precaution. This man was clearly very afraid of burglary. On the door was a small sign that said: 'closed', but Soongh didn't bother to turn it around. Another sign said: 'Wir sprechen Deutch'.
While elbowing Arthur, Otto smirked in an unidentifiable emotional response, "Naja, schau dich das mal an..."
Dr Soongh introduced himself to Hadi first and then hesitated a moment before he shook the hands of Otto and Arthur, all the while giving them an untrusting look. Then suddenly, in a fraction of a second, his serious face realigned into a forced, exaggerated smile. "Gentlemen, if you would follow me?" he said, in a strange, high voice. Otto and Arthur looked at one another with raised eyebrows. Bending himself into a bow with some difficulty, Soongh showed them in and quickly locked the door behind them. Hadi recognised this as normal, as shopkeepers like Soongh could never trust a visitor or leave the front door unlocked, even when present. Theft and murder over golden jewellery or historical artefacts in private collections were not uncommon in the orient. One could never be too careful.
"May I ask the gentlemen to empty their pockets and leave everything on this table, please? Slowly."
Hadi nodded to Arthur and Otto to do as he had said and started by emptying his own pockets. Soongh noticed how Hadi and Otto exchanged looks before they simultaneously

put their Glocks onto the table, hesitating to give up their weapons. As soon as all the items were exposed, including the mobile ERFAB devices and mobile phones, Soongh took a large, white scarf and threw it over the table, so no one could get to it quickly. As soon as he had done this, the same greasy smile reappeared on his face, as if someone had turned on a switch.

"It's for my own safety. I'm sure you understand." he said.

Arthur wondered how the man could still see when he smiled, as those horizontal lines between the folds of his fat cheeks almost completely hid his eyes. However, the eyes they *could* see, didn't match with his smile at all.

It made them all feel uncomfortable.

While keeping a careful eye on his potential clients, Soongh took them to the back of the house. Every doorway had a curtain that he firmly closed behind him. When they entered the dark, jam-packed back room - a square room without windows, lit only by a single light bulb - Otto folded his arms and looked around. Displayed on numerous shelves were many numbered, dusty boxes of unknown content. All kinds of gemstones of amazing colours, fragments of ancient pottery, beautiful blue faience items, crumbling parchments, antique idols of gods and goddesses, shabtis - the funerary figurines once given to the dead to assist in the passage to the afterlife - and papyrus drawings of scenes from famous tombs, crowded the shelves. Tucked away in a corner stood a huge, stuffed cobra that frightened the living daylights out of Otto, who jumped at perceiving the giant rearing cobra and at that, his right hand hit a jar, filled to the top with little blue scarab beetles. He only just caught it in time. Otto closed his eyes for a moment and waited for his heartbeat to settle. As he put the jar back on the little side table, he decided to come straight to the point. "So, tell me Mr Soongh, do you have any desert glass items?"

"I do, mainly from the Sahara desert. What exactly are you looking for?"

Otto scratched his chin, thought for a moment and replied,

"Whitish stones or shards that have been carved into beads, or stones that look like beads, or round stones that may have at one time been inlaid into an object, like a headpiece of a staff or a wadjet eye."

Soongh rubbed his face and seemed to be in deep thought. Suddenly he raised his index finger and without saying anything, he walked over to a cabinet, pulled out a thick catalogue and started to leaf through it. It didn't take long before he found what he was looking for.

"This is a list of carved stones that have been created from desert glass. The items are numbered and the numbers refer to photographs. Let me know when you see something that interests you and I will get it for you."

Otto took the catalogue and from the corner of his eye he noticed that Hadi was sidling toward the doorway. Without looking up at him, he said in a monotone voice,

"Going anywhere, Hadi?"

The Egyptian guide turned around, giving him an offended look. "No, of course not, I just thought I heard my mobile phone ring."

Arthur could second that. Even though they were on the other side of the house, he recognised the classic ringtone version of a Wagner piece that was undoubtedly Otto's mobile phone. A moment later, Hadi's mobile phone rang again with its 'Aïcha' ringtone. It was probably Georg, but Hadi couldn't pick up now. They were prevented from taking calls as long as they were inside Soongh's shop.

They now felt the pressure to get down to business quickly and so they returned to studying the catalogue.

They would call Georg back later.

However, to everyone's disappointment, there was not one item that could possibly be the Eye of Ra. They realised with heavy hearts that the only way to get hold of the stone - this minuscule needle in a gigantic haystack - was to go back to the source. They had to go back to Akhetaten.

31

Guernsey, Channel Islands, October 4th 2011

It was getting late. The sun had already set, transforming the sky into an energetic palette of autumnal colours - a soft orangey shade of red with delicate touches of yellow. A luminous horizon in the west could still be seen, though dark was falling. The family and friends of the patients at the Elizabeth hospital were reminded that visitor times were over and the hallways were filling up with people who were on their way out. Michael, however, didn't move a muscle. With tightly folded arms he stood at the window with a melancholy stare, focusing on the rapidly vanishing colours just above the western horizon. Things were going to change now and he didn't know where to put his feelings. Should he be angry with his father's shooter, or be thankful that it had gone this way? After overhearing his father's phone call with his superior, he felt a bit of both.

David had just received a phone call from Georg. They were going to replace him and bring him back to Sion to recover from his wound. Being forced to leave Danielle in the hands of another made him sad and angry at himself. Why did he have to get himself shot! At the same time he also realised that he couldn't change the past and he couldn't possibly look after Danielle in his current condition either. However, there was at least one development that cheered him up. David had permission to bring Michael to Sion.

Georg had worked out all the logistics. He had arranged for a helicopter to take David from the hospital on Guernsey to London and a private jet to take him from London to Sion. Two SBS agents, who had been sent their way late that afternoon, would take over the entire operation. Then, Georg had had a long phone conversation with the chief of the Guernsey police. Naturally, as David was the main suspect for the murder of the agent and the attempted murder of Mrs Peel at the cottage, they had been reluctant to believe him at first, but the moment Georg had given them a short explanation along with Alfred's secret identity codes, they guaranteed their full co-operation. Finally, also the hospital was briefed on the situation, so everything had gone smoothly from that point forward. However, Georg had not counted on David being so stubborn. David had refused to leave Danielle and it took Georg great effort to make him realise that returning to Sion was not optional. It was an order. However, when David raised the question of Michael as his leverage, Georg understood that he would only gain David's full cooperation if he agreed to have him bring his son to Sion.

David looked at his son while he put his mobile phone down on the bedside table. "Well, I've got some good news and some bad news. The bad news is, I've just received orders to go back to Switzerland. The good news is, I have permission to bring you with me. I believe that Danielle will be in good hands - all SBS agents are much better trained than I will ever be - but still, I don't know what would give me more stress; protecting Danielle myself, or having another person do the job. At least from our base in Sion, I will be able to keep myself up-to-date. Hey and you'll be able to see where I work! Isn't that cool, huh?"

Michael nodded. He was excited. Ever since last summer's adventures, he had been longing for more. The knowledge that in a few hours' time he would actually be on his way to one of the most secret bases in the world, certainly made his heart beat a little faster. He also realised that he had to find a way back to London before the weekend, to get back to studying. Knowing that worrying never solves anything, he decided to follow the flow of things without resistance, as this always had a way of working out. So he decided to listen to his gut feeling and focus on the adventure that lay ahead. However, things rarely go according to plan.

It was ten o'clock in the evening when the stretcher came. Carefully minding the wound, the nurses moved David from his bed to the stretcher. The new SBS agents introduced themselves with their ID cards, which David immediately recognised by the SUT logo and specific number code. Agents Jack Hayes and Manfred Tänner were dressed in the customary black clothes, short hair and mirroring sunglasses. Michael found it all a little bit over the top. How can you travel incognito in that outfit? Then he thought that maybe these guys weren't trying to be incognito. Maybe they were dressed like this specifically to make a statement.

The police officer who had previously stood at the door, guarding David's room, accompanied the little group to the exit. They moved very fast and Michael found it hard to keep up without running. Suddenly, one of the agents received a message in his earpiece. With one abrupt move of his hand, the group came to an immediate halt. Apparently, the chief of police was on his way to the hospital to ask David some final questions about the events at Rose Cottage before he was allowed to leave. Being only a few minutes from the hospital, they were to stay put and wait for him at the spot. They had not the slightest inkling that they were only a few meters away from the room where Izz al Din and his two accomplices were waiting for the right time to silently leave the hospital that same night.

Titan moved to the door and while ensuring nobody was observing him, he took a quick peek around the corner to see what was going on. The moment he spotted the police officer, his heart skipped a beat. If the police were here, it may have something to do with his actions at Rose Cottage. Carefully eavesdropping on the conversation with the chief of police, who had just arrived, he quickly understood that it had everything to do with it. However, Titan had never seen the man on the stretcher before. He had, of course, killed only one agent and hadn't found anyone else at the cottage, until the unfortunate woman came by. She had simply been in the wrong place at the wrong time and had seen too much. Titan hadn't yet told his boss about the 'extra corpse'. What he didn't know was that Mrs Peel had survived the hard blow to the head. She had looked unquestionably dead when he had thrown her into Danielle's bathtub.

At the same time, Al Din was getting curious.

"What the hell is going on, Titan? They aren't looking for you by any chance, are they? I gave you strict orders. You were to find Danielle, not get yourself into trouble. Who was the man on the stretcher that just came by with the police officer and the official looking men in black?"

Titan didn't say a word. He was too busy listening in on the conversation in the hallway between David and the chief of police: "So I understand that you were shot by a colleague? Was your colleague also the one who slashed your other man's throat?"

"No of course not!" David said with an irritated undertone. "It was an accident. He thought I was the killer."

"And are you?"

"Good grief man, are you even thinking straight? Why would I kill my colleague, who is on my side helping me protect a woman in a safe house? I thought my employer had told you everything you need to know about my mission. So if you don't mind, I'd very much like to leave now."

"But I do mind, Mr Camford!" he said resolutely. "So far we haven't been able to reach your colleague, who has mysteriously disappeared from the island. What's more, we haven't found any trace of a third party and if you're gone, the only one left for us to question is that poor woman who was found in your bathtub. She's one strong lady, Mr Camford. The surgeon was able to repair the damage to her skull and give her a blood transfusion. He told me that he is expecting her to recover completely and that it shouldn't be long before she wakes up and that's when we will be there; to question her. What if she confirms that you were her attacker? As far as I know, the moment that helicopter takes off, you become an untouchable."

After hearing the chief's rant, agent Hayes decided to intercede.

"Excuse me, but Mr Camford already is an untouchable. From the moment you received the call from Mr Hauser, he became one and if you do not co-operate, I will be forced to call him and ask him for new orders."

The chief raised both his hands to emphasise his words.

"No, no, you go ahead, take him. I just need to find the killer, that's all and I am not convinced that this man is innocent. You guys really know how to obstruct an investigation and..."

"I didn't kill anyone! Okay?" David shouted. "Now stop wasting your time and find the Arab who did!"

David had lost his patience and had raised his voice loud enough for Al Din and his comrades to hear everything he said.

The chief frowned. "Arab? Alright Mr Camford, we will look out for a man with an Arabian appearance. It seems we have no choice but to let you go."

David rubbed his face with both hands, as if this - though just for a moment - could make the world go away. Ready to continue the transfer, agent Hayes tipped his forehead in farewell, which was immediately copied by agent Tänner. Within a minute, the now silent group arrived at the helicopter, which had landed on the heliport on the lawn just outside the hospital. The engine was still running and they had to stoop to protect themselves from the wind caused by the dangerously fast-moving rotor blades.

Then, Michael saw it.

There was a large red stain on the white blanket that covered his father. "Dad! You're bleeding!" he exclaimed. The nurses, who were pushing the stretcher, immediately stopped to take a look at the wound. When David saw his wound, he suddenly became much more aware of it and instantly became dizzy, feeling the pain even more than before.

"Just get me out of here, please..."

However, in his heart he knew that leaving wouldn't be possible now. He had to be returned to the operating room and have the wound treated before he could travel.

Knowing that that would take at least another half hour, the helicopter pilot turned the engine off and while the rotor blades were slowly coming to a halt, David felt as if he was trapped on the island. As if he would never make it out alive. He turned his head to his son and tried to put on a brave face. "Michael, listen to me. If anything should happen to me, I want you to take the first flight out back to London, you understand? It's too dangerous here."

Michael shook his head.

"No dad! I will not leave you alone!"

David reached out to touch his arm, but where he was going, Michael couldn't follow. David was rushed into the operating room, while Michael had to stay in the waiting room along with the others. The doors closed mercilessly - as if to confirm the separation - and Michael reluctantly sat down in the brutally hard chair, covering his face with his hands. *Think positive thoughts. Positive thoughts...*

Titan had followed them from a distance and when the group had unexpectedly reappeared on their way to the operating room, he had to run and hide behind a corner, so he wouldn't be noticed. Having followed them to the waiting room, he now carefully peeked around the corner to take a closer look at the men in black. Izz al Din hadn't yet briefed him on the SBS-Sion organisation, so he had no idea who he was dealing with, but it certainly looked impressive. With wide eyes he studied the agents, who were still in the presence of the police officer, the chief of police and his assistant. It seemed as if they outranked even the local chief of police, who was now studying their ID cards. He noted the dominant body language of the men in black, indicating their feelings of superiority to the apparently lower ranking behaviour of the chief.

Who were they?

Titan quietly sneaked back into Al Din's room to report what he had seen. As expected, he saw Lars behind his laptop, typing away, but he was surprised to see the empty bed.

Al Din was standing at the sink, dressed in his suit and brushing his teeth. When Titan entered, Lars stared at him with a disgusted look. "Did you *have* to kill that man, Titan? And, really, that poor woman!"

"Since when did you become a girl, Lars?" snapped Titan.

Al Din, who had just wiped his mouth on the towel, turned around and slapped the back of Titan's head. In an impulse, Titan swirled around in a fraction of a second, all ready to punch, but then his fist froze in mid-air. Al Din was staring deeply into his eyes, eyes that betrayed sadness as well as domination. "You touch me and I will have you hung, drawn and quartered. You should not have killed or injured anyone. My orders were to find Danielle. You were not given permission to injure anyone."

"Then what about that guy we kidnapped at the airport in Sion? You gave him a lethal injection!"

"No I didn't! I only told him that to make him betray Danielle's location and to buy time so we could copy his mobile phone for Lars to use a beacon. The injection was a heavy dose, yes, but never lethal! Your lust for violence has jeopardised our entire mission!"

Completely confused, Titan lowered his arms and sat down dejectedly on the bed.

Al Din sighed and sat down beside him. "I know your background, Titan. I know that the population of your village was almost entirely massacred by a roaming group of looters and that you already had your own rifle when you were 8 years old. I know how hard you trained to become invincible and fearless, qualities that make you a first class bodyguard. Anyone who looks at you and sees this *gigantor,* with those ruthless and emotionless eyes, would be wise enough to stay away, but I never expected you to use unnecessary violence. I sent you out to play the ornithologist, watching birds, while trying to find Danielle's location. I did not send you out to become a killer."

Titan sat up straight and faced his employer with raised eyebrows, anxious to explain his actions.

"Then may I tell you what happened? Or have you judged me already?" said Titan defensively.

Al Din's wide eyes stared hard at Titan. "Pray, tell!"

"Well, I had found the cottage, which had been taken off the website and saw how it was guarded by a man in black, the same type as the two men who are here looking after the guy on the stretcher. I didn't hurt him, by the way - apparently his colleague shot him. However, the other guy at the cottage must have heard an alarm go off - I probably tripped a wire or something - because as if he could see through a wall, he suddenly came running out in my direction and chased me around the house and the gardens. He was carrying a large knife and a pistol - probably a Glock - and I felt threatened. So I had to be smart. The moment he thought he lost me, I appeared right behind him and was able to slit his throat with his own knife before he could utter a sound."

"I sneaked into the house, wearing gloves and found that photo of Danielle, posing with some other woman. Then I heard a woman approach the cottage and it was as if she was talking to someone, but soon I realised that she was just talking to herself. Of course, when she saw the body in the garden, she had seen too much. I was not going to let myself be caught, so I sneaked up behind her and hit her on the head with a thick piece of slate. When I thought she was dead, I took her inside and threw her into the bathtub. The moment I had planted the bug in Danielle's beauty case, I heard a car approaching, so I ran back to the car and took off, but sure, go ahead, judge me! I didn't ask to be noticed by that stupid guard, I simply underestimated their security system. I never asked for that woman to show up, but when she saw too much, I had no choice but to knock her out."

Al Din shook his head. "Tragic, simply tragic. Remind me to teach you how to take someone out without slitting a throat. Now, get yourself back there and let me know what you find out. Don't get caught and please don't kill anyone!"

Titan looked at Lars - who had followed the conversation discretely - and left the room without saying another word.

Al Din sighed. He was upset about the situation. "Lars, would you be able to get into the hospital's main computer and enter my dossier? It's time to leave, so it would be good if you could add to the list that the doctor has released me. Then there won't be any questions when we pass the reception desk."

Lars immediately started typing on his laptop. "I'm sure I can hack their computer, piece of cake, but will you please promise me that I won't have to allow anyone else drive my car from now on?"

Al Din nodded in approval and smiled with amused understanding. "I promise, my dear Lars, I promise."

It was in the wee hours of the morning when David and Michael finally arrived at Alfred's manor house in Sion, Switzerland. It had been a complicated wound to treat, but when he had finally been released and the helicopter had taken off, the feeling of relief that had come over him was so immense that he could actually feel it physically.

Georg had chosen the manor house over the Sion base, because David would be much better off in a comfortable bed, surrounded by a proper staff to take care of his every need. After all, the main thing he needed was rest.

Michael had been given the room next to him. Although he had stayed in luxurious hotels before, he had never been a guest in a stately home. Since he had always had to do everything for himself, the ever watchful - and sometimes even hovering - staff had made him feel a bit uncomfortable at first, but he quickly warmed to the idea of being served a late snack and a hot chocolate in his room. While sipping his coco, he felt like a king reclining into the many pillows on his queen-size bed. He summed up the present situation:

He had found his father; they were no longer in danger; David's wound would certainly heal soon enough and they were both staying in the most wonderful accommodation.

All was well again in Michael's world.

For now.

32

Memphis, Egypt, October 4th 2011

The sounds of the howling sand storm gave the dark room at the back of Soongh's shop an eerie atmosphere. The light bulb on the ceiling now started to swing slowly and the shadows of some very strange objects moved around like lurking demons, coming out to play. Although he still managed to smile, Soongh was now nervously squeezing his hands. His clients - who had looked very promising at first - didn't seem to find what they were looking for and desperate to make a sale, he wanted to see if he could sell them something else. He was just about to show them something special in his collection, when Otto clicked his heels like a soldier. "Right. Let's go! This place is giving me the creeps." Striding straight through the house to reach the front shop, with Arthur and Hadi following closely, he was keen to leave that scary back room and eager to recover their personal belongings, which were still waiting for them, unguarded, under the scarf on the table. Soongh surprised everyone by his speed; he suddenly raced passed them to reach the front of the shop before they did, heading for the little table. With one swift move, he took the scarf and swept the items into it. Looking more like a sack now, he handed over the scarf - including the items - to Hadi. Soongh was clearly paranoid. "I am so sorry to see you go so soon, my friends! I still have many items that might be of interest to you. Are you sure you would not like to look around and stay a little longer?"

Hadi shook his head. "I'm afraid not, Mr Soongh, but thank you for your time and patience."

Hadi took the sack and the moment Soongh had finally and reluctantly unlocked the door, the team left the antiques shop. Arthur turned around one more time, feeling as if they had missed something, but when they were all back in the car, Jazir had some bad news and he quickly forgot about it.

"Guys, I hate to be a spoil sport, but we are being watched. Do you see the land rover at the corner of the street? He's been standing there for the last 20 minutes now and no one has come out. If I am not mistaken, there are three people in the rover. Do you know who they are?"

Hadi froze. "Shit, it's Ashraf and his sidekick. How the hell did they find us so soon!"

Jazir knew that his car was fast and would easily be able to outrun an army rover, so he decided to take a chance.

"Buckle up, guys!"

Like an Arabian horse stabled too long, the car took off with screeching tires and passed the army car like a whirlwind. It took a few seconds before Ashraf could turn the car around and follow them, but as soon as they were on the main road, the distance between the two cars became shorter and shorter. "That rover goes fast, my friend!" Jazir said with great concern. "His engine must have been tuned-up."

Suddenly, Hadi had an idea and turned toward Otto.

"Give me my mobile phone, quickly!"

Otto opened the sack and found Hadi's phone. He also handed him his Glock, after which he put his own piece safely away. He hated guns. It brought back the worst nightmare of his life and he hoped fiercely that he'd never have to use a gun ever again.

Hadi checked his phone log and immediately saw a missed call. It was indeed Georg who had tried to reach them while they were in Soongh's shop. Without consulting with Otto first, Hadi called Georg back immediately. Otto felt annoyed by that, as he had planned to be the first to call Georg himself and ask after Alfred, hoping deeply that there had been no complications to his condition. "Ask him how Fred's holding up," he said to Hadi, leaning forward from the backseat. Hadi held his hand up as a signal to Otto to be quiet, as the connection wasn't very good; he heard a noise which reminded him of a helicopter and when Georg picked up the phone, the noise was still there, but at least they could hear each other well enough to have a conversation. Georg was in panic, "Jesus, Hadi, where the hell are you? Where's Otto? Why didn't you pick up the phone when I called?"

"Long story, Mr Hauser. Details will follow later, but first things first. Our mission has been compromised. We still have people on our tail and we need to go somewhere safe. We haven't found the stone yet, but we're hoping to get back to Akhetaten as soon as your professor can send us the new data, preferably without a flaw this time."

"Alright, Hadi, I will talk to Wong about it. In the meantime, I do have good news for you. We have the new data ready for immediate upload. The new version will also give you more mobility. Now listen carefully; I need you all to press the yellow button on your ERFAB devices, so Wong can see your signals and upload the new data. Call me back when you are ready."

"Yes, sir. I will call you back a.s.a.p.."

Hadi hung up and Otto suddenly got very angry with Hadi. "Why didn't you ask him about Fred? I want to know how he is doing!"

While Otto was sulking, his eye fell on the unfolded scarf on his lap and he noticed there were only three devices left; his mobile phone, Hadi's mobile ERFAB and his own.

Where was Arthur's?

"Have you already taken your ERFAB, Arthur?" Otto asked with slight panic.

Arthurs eyes grew big. "No. Isn't it there?"

"No it isn't. We must have left it at Wong's! Hadi! We need to get back to Wong's shop! Now!"

"No, Otto, we can't." said Hadi, while looking at the rear-view mirror. "We have to get away from Ashraf and Beni and I have a good idea who that third person is. I bet you it's Max Müller."

Otto turned around to take a good look at the land rover, which was now close enough for him to recognise its passengers. "Yes, you're right. It *is* Max! Ach, Scheisse! What do we do now? This is a serious problem!"

Without hesitation, Otto called Georg, who had been waiting for the signal.

"Otto! Why haven't you pressed the button yet?"

"Georg, listen: We have lost Arthur's ERFAB and cannot possibly escape our pursuers. I won't go anywhere without knowing Arthur is safe, so until you solve this problem, I will stay with Arthur."

Georg moaned and there was a short pause, which Otto immediately took advantage of. "Is Fred okay?"

"Yes, yes, he's fine. Now, give me a minute to talk this through with Wong and I will call you back as soon as possible, okay?"

"Okay Georg. Thanks!"

Otto hung up and looked at his friend. Arthur was covering his face with his hands. It looked as if the time travelling adventure had ended there for him and he was close to tears. Though Jazir was driving like a madman through Memphis, they all felt as if this whole adventure had now come to a screeching halt. Little did they know that the adventure had only just begun.

When Hadi called Georg back, the solution Wong had come up with sounded like the craziest plan ever. They were to drive to the nearest garage, have the car - including all of them as well as their luggage - weighed on the vehicle scales, measure up the car carefully and prepare themselves to be transported to a deserted part of Cyprus; car and all. They had to round up the weight, just to make sure nothing of the car would stay behind in the garage. Jazir, who wasn't too sure of the plan, as it also involved himself and his car, called a friend who owned a garage in southern Cairo. He knew for sure they could measure the weight of the car there. All they had to do now was shake off their pursuers to buy some time. So, with only one hand on the wheel, Jazir continued the dangerous race through Memphis and Otto was beginning to feel nauseous. They hadn't been drinking enough water and he had been lightheaded since their visit to the Saqqara necropolis. His eyes searched the car for a water bottle and spotted one on the shelf behind him. While seizing the bottle, he saw that the rover was now only two cars behind them.

"Hadi, if we can't outrun them, maybe we need to think of another plan. What about hiding?"

"No, Mr Adler," said Hadi with a nervous voice, "the car is too big to hide. We need to keep on pushing ourselves as fast as possible through the traffic until they are out of sight."

That moment, the wind died down, as if someone had turned off a giant fan. Sitting in the backseat, Arthur decided not to pay any attention to Jazir's risky driving method and his mind wondered off to Cyprus and Otto's boat. He had no idea what the boat looked like, or how big it was, but Otto had told him that there were two sailors on board. Would that be enough? However, *he* didn't know how to sail and knowing for sure that Otto didn't know how to sail, he wondered if Hadi did.

"Hadi, do you know how to sail? I mean, Otto and I don't."

Hadi turned to Arthur and smiled mysteriously. "Actually, yes I do. When I was a little boy, my father took me on his felucca on the Nile and taught me how to sail. Falling in love with the water and the winds, I decided to go to a nautical school in Alexandria to become a sailing captain. After receiving my certificate, I built up my own shipping company there, with one big and two small sailing boats, until a client swindled me. I had to sell everything, including my beloved boat to pay the bills I was left with. I left Alexandria and went back to my family in Cairo, where I befriended a Coptic Christian monk, who saw my pain and frustration. Within a week I entered a Coptic monastery where I stayed for two years. There I found a new passion: The Amarna mysteries. I learned to speak the old language, studied the hieroglyphs, the history and the culture of the 18th Dynasty and became a tour guide. Saving up a bit of money, I was able to buy the white Mercedes, so I could do the tours on my own, but my heart still yearns for the sea. So to answer your question, Mr Griffin, yes, I know how to sail."

He winked at Arthur and turned back to face the road ahead. It looked as if they were heading into a traffic jam. Being used to busy traffic, Jazir carefully drove onto the pavement and passed a truck blocking the road, fuming dirty diesel exhaust into the busy street. He closed the windows and smiled. "I think this is going to work! We're almost at the garage, so prepare yourselves to work swiftly. We need to know the circumference of the car, so Hadi, if you look into the glove compartment, you will find the car manual. In it you will find the measurements and dimensions of the car."

Hadi opened the compartment in front of him and saw a thick manual which was well leafed through. It didn't take Arthur long to come up with the needed figure. Now all they needed was the total weight, hoping that the scales would work properly and indicate the correct number.

A few minutes later, Jazir drove into the garage and they smelled the greasy, pungent odour of oil and gasoline. After a quick greeting, Jazir explained that they were in a hurry and needed to get themselves onto the scales as quickly as possible. Carefully, Jazir drove onto the scales and watched the digital counter becoming active. Hadi, who had a clear view of the counter from the front seat, quickly wrote down the weight on a piece of paper along with the circumference and other measurements of the car and then read them out loud and clearly to Georg and Wong. A few moments later, Hadi and Otto were ordered to press the yellow button, so Wong could download the data into their devices and send them the adapter and its manual. As soon as this was done, the adapter and manual magically appeared in mid-air inside the car, after which it fell on Hadi's lap. Jazir, who had watched it through his rear mirror, couldn't believe his eyes and stared hard at Hadi, who put his finger to his lips. "Top secret."

"I wish Georg could send me another ERFAB this way too!" Arthur remarked, hoping to inspire Otto and Hadi to ask Georg if that were possible, but he knew that Wong had only built 3 devices.

So far so good, but now came the tricky bit: to find a spot - preferably out of sight - where they could execute the transport sequence.

The disappearance of an entire car would surely attract unwanted attention. Still bedazzled by the strange adventure he had now been caught up in, Jazir carefully drove out of the garage. When he knew for sure that there was no car in sight, he took a risk and drove into the street. At the first alley they came across, he turned and parked the car in a shady spot. However, Jazir had become extremely nervous and suddenly announced that he would not be going with them to Cyprus. "I'm sorry gentlemen, but I have too many things going on in my life already. You are welcome to take the car, though. Only, how do I know that I will get it back safely?" he added with a worried frown.

Hadi patted his shoulder. "You don't, but I will assure you one thing. If we can't get it back to you, you will get twice the money this car is worth for everything you have done for us. I guarantee it."

Jazir reluctantly got out of his car. Knowing from experience that Hadi's word was as good as gold, he gathered his belongings and took his leave.

The moment Jazir had rounded the corner, Hadi slid across the seat and got behind the wheel. Otto picked up the phone and composed the number to Georg, who answered immediately.

"We're all ready, Georg." said Otto with determination. He turned around one more time to check if they were indeed completely alone and unseen and he had only just said that all was clear, when the Army rover came to a screeching halt at the end of the street. While holding his breath, he watched it turning toward them, advancing at great speed.

Anxiously, he shouted into the phone: "Georg, now!!"

A trembling noise of low thunder sounded when the air closed-in around the vanished car and by the time Ashraf, Beni and Max arrived at the spot, all they could see was a large, smoking pothole in the tarmac.

33

Cyprus, October 4th 2011

A male yellowhammer bird was chirping his song half way up a pine tree, not knowing that it had been spotted by an Englishman with binoculars. The birdwatcher carefully took out his camera, trying to not make a sound. Finally he was able to prove that there were indeed yellowhammers on the island after the summer. He had just taken two dozen photos when the bird suddenly flew off along with all the other birds in that immediate area. While admiring his photos - in particular the sharp and colourful close-ups he had just taken - he took a deep breath of clean mountain air and smiled contently. The soft breeze that came from the south had a spicy scent, mixing the dry forest air with the more humid, salty sea air. The Troodos Mountains on Cyprus were very peaceful and very quiet.

Usually.

Suddenly, a chocolate brown SUV appeared from out of nowhere in a clearing, only two meters behind the ornithologist, causing the air to tremor and emitting a strange, indescribable metal-rubbing-metal noise that lasted only a second. The Englishman jumped the moment he heard the sound behind him and then slowly turned around to see what it was. A Ford Expedition was standing at a strange angle on top of a piece of old tarmac.

"Oy! You there!" exclaimed the ornithologist with one arm in the air. "What are you doing, sneaking up on me like that with your electric soundless engine, scaring the living daylights out of me!"

Arthur couldn't help laughing. Not only had they outsmarted their pursuers and survived the teleportation, they also seemed to have been teleported to an otherwise uninhabited, tranquil part of Cyprus, right next to the only person around. They were lucky that the man simply assumed their car had a quiet, electric engine. Arthur's laughter was contagious and even Hadi smirked when he got out of the car, until they noticed the plaque of Egyptian tarmac underneath it, which admittedly was a bit awkward and might be difficult to explain. However, the fragment had been pushed into the sandy soil rather than onto it and undoubtedly, nature would surely absorb it soon enough. Hadi immediately understood how this had happened. Being too afraid to participate in the teleportation, Jazir had backed out at the last moment, but as they had already given Georg the total weight of the car including Jazir, the ERFAB in Sion most probably had compensated for Jazir's lack of human weight by absorbing the piece of tarmac.

Fortunately, the ornithologist didn't notice the tarmac, probably presuming it was just a dark rock in the sand, but he did notice the Egyptian license plate. Curious and in an effort to break the ice, he walked toward them.

"Did you come off one of the cruise ships? We were planning on taking a cruise to Israel and Egypt next week, my wife and I. May I ask when you will be going back?"

Hadi, thinking it would be a good idea to play along and be the tourist, shook his hand.

"Good day sir, I'm sorry to have frightened you. We're on a journey through the Mediterranean, so we won't be going back to Egypt for weeks, but I certainly recommend a visit to my homeland."

Arthur and Otto also shook his hand. With that, their relationship now seemed as firm as their manly handshakes.

"Pleasure to meet you all. I will certainly book that cruise then. My wife's more the cultural enthusiast, while I prefer shooting birds. With my camera, of course!" he chuckled. "Actually, I'd just spotted a very rare yellowhammer bird, so I'm quite satisfied with my day!" With great pride he showed them the close-ups of the little yellow bird.

"Well, I'd better be heading back to Ayia Napa, or I won't be back before dark and then the Mrs will get upset." he added with his fat, Cockney accent. Arthur knew for sure the man was a Londoner, like himself and for a few seconds he felt homesick.

He resisted the urge to grab Otto's hand, desperate for some alone time with him.

After saying their goodbyes, they watched the man disappear into the trees and as soon as he had gone, they began their attempt to get the car onto the road. However, getting the car off the fragment, into the soft, sandy soil and onto the road - which was about 50 meters away from their landing point - could be a problem, so they decided to use the tarmac as a jumping board. A few broken branches and some flat stones on the first part of the track were able to stop the wheels from spinning themselves into the sand. Fortunately, the car being an SUV, the job was easier than they had expected and within a few minutes they found themselves on the dusty road.

"Do you have any idea where we are?" said Otto to Hadi, while he grabbed his phone to call Georg.

"One moment Mr Adler, I will activate the GPS."

"When will you start calling me Otto, Hadi? Seriously."

"Never, Mr Adler. We're colleagues on a secret mission, not school children on an outing."

"So your first name is not Hadi?"

"Yes, it is. My last name is not important."

Otto shook his head and was just about to add a funny remark when Georg picked up. "Otto! Thank God! How did it go?"

"Not too bad, Georg. Not too bad, but Hadi's friend had a change of heart and decided not to join us after all. He found it too risky, so Hadi promised him twice the value of his car in case we should fail to bring it back safe and sound. Then we took off - car and all - without him. So, as you can imagine, future archaeologists may one day be puzzled how a piece of weight-compensating Egyptian tarmac ended up in the middle of nowhere on the island of Cyprus. Apart from that, we're all fine. How's Fred?"

"Mr Zinkler is doing well, Otto. He's being kept in an artificial sleep, so that his body can heal quicker. He won't have to eat and drink this way either, as everything is piped in through the IV. The surgeon is pleased and it looks as if he's in no pain. All vital signs are stable."

"Thank God for that!" Otto said with relief. "When are they going to wake him up?"

"That will be decided by the surgeon, but as far as I know, they plan to keep him into this state for at least five days. I will keep you informed. So, do you know how to get to your boat, Otto?"

"Yes, I have all the details with me, including the mobile phone number of one of the sailors; the one who will be Hadi's first mate. Will you call him, or shall I?"

"I don't see any reason why you shouldn't call him, as you are the owner of the boat now. We can only hope that the previous owner, Roman Corona, won't think of using it as a trap. So whatever you do; please, be very, very careful."

"Aye, aye, Sir!" Otto replied while automatically saluting in the brainwashed 'Heil Hitler' manner. At seeing that, Arthur breathed in sharply and slowly shook his head, after which Otto gave him a sheepish smile. He shrugged his shoulders and whispered, "It's an old habit. Sorry..."

The line started to crackle and Otto, who was afraid of losing his connection, wanted to wrap things up with Georg quickly. This was not a good time to be disconnected.

"Georg? I will call one of the sailors now, hoping we can sail tonight. The weather looks good enough. The clipper also has an engine, so we can leave the harbour quickly and raise the sails later."

"Okay Otto, that sounds like a good plan. Move as fast as you can until you are in the open sea and try and get some rest tonight, but tomorrow I would like you to continue your mission to find the Eye of Ra and start preparing for a new expedition to ancient Akhetaten. In the meantime, Wong is working on a new ERFAB device for Arthur, but that will take a few days. On your first expedition you may have to travel alone with Hadi."

Otto looked at Arthur. He knew they wouldn't be gone long, just 10 seconds in current time, but he still disliked the thought of leaving him behind while he himself would be on a dangerous mission, a mission from which he might not even return.

"I understand, Georg, but I'd prefer to take him along, as you may understand."

Georg remembered how he had felt when Alfred had taken off in the helicopter, flying from Sion to Zürich without him. He remembered being a bit anxious while alone at the airport, waiting impatiently for Alfred to return. He remembered how he had ignored the strange stomach cramps, which was really his sub-conscience telling him that he was in danger. He also vividly remembered the intense shock he had felt, the moment he was kidnapped by Izz al Din. He had felt alone, abandoned, vulnerable and afraid for his life and thus - from his own experience - Georg could easily understand why Otto didn't want to leave Arthur alone and for the first time, Georg felt sympathy for Otto.

"I hear you, Otto. We'll make sure that Arthur is in total safety when you return to Akhetaten."

That moment, the GPS revealed their location; they were only a few kilometres outside the small town of Omodos and from there, they could easily get to Paphos harbour where Otto's boat was moored. Hadi was translating the GPS information, which was still in Arabic. "It wants us to go through Omodos and directly south to the A6. Then we will be on the main road to Paphos. The whole drive should take us about 50 minutes."

"Don't forget to drive on the left side of the road, Hadi!" Arthur added, remembering that Cyprus had been part of the British Crown for several decades, long enough to leave its mark on the island, such as left-hand traffic, which would be considered the *right* side to all the inhabitants.

Otto, who was now sitting in the front seat, could hear his stomach rumbling. "I sure hope they have something to eat in that town. I'm starving."

Arthur, who was sitting in the middle of the back seat, agreed heartily.

"Yes please, Hadi, can we stop at Omodos? Ever since we teleported I feel a bit funny."

As Hadi started driving, he blurted out, "Who am I? Your mother? Okay, okay, we'll stop at Omodos!"

Arthur and Otto smiled a grin of complicity to each other with the joyful feeling of victory and allowed themselves to relax. The adventure had indeed become a bit of an energy vampire by now and even Hadi, whose task, he felt, was much underestimated by Otto and Arthur, was now getting tired. He welcomed the break as much - or perhaps even more - as the others did.

Omodos was a pretty village amidst the vineyards with whitewashed houses and orange rooftops, where local wine growers had set up their wine-tasting shops. As Cyprus is an island shared by both the Turks and the Greeks, the typical Cypriots who live in the Troodos Mountains are happy to stay away from both camps. The architecture in the mountains is very different from that of the coastal strip, as is the attitude of the people, who are very friendly and inviting. Before they knew it, they were sampling wines and honey and a variety of olive oils trickled over freshly baked bread. They found themselves chatting away with the locals as they feasted on the typical Mediterranean fare. Sitting underneath the sycamore trees and looking out over the picturesque cobbled street was for the small group of explorers a moment they could momentarily forget that they were on a dangerous mission. An hour later; packed with provisions for their sea voyage, they walked back to the car. Otto, who hadn't drunk much alcohol for years, could feel the wine starting to affect his legs and vision and he tried very hard not to sway. Suddenly, his mind made a connection between this moment and that particular evening at the palazzo in Rome, when he had had far too much of the Amaretto that Roman Corona had offered him and he was struck by an idea.

While getting into the car, he carefully dialled the number of one of the sailors, Andrei Kyriakou, Hadi's first mate.

He told him that he was on his way to Paphos, hoping they could depart that same night, but then he added something clever, "Oh and Andrei? Mr Corona said you didn't have to call him anymore. Everything is okay."

For a moment it was silent on the other side of the line, but then Andrei responded, "Right, sir. I will see you later then."

This time, Hadi looked at Otto with wide eyes and smirked with complicity. He thought it to be a very smart move and hoped that it would indeed keep Andrei from informing Corona that they had arrived. With a bit of luck, they could now disappear from the radar completely and get on with their mission.

However, things wouldn't go as smoothly as they had hoped.

They enjoyed the scenic drive across the beautiful, hilly landscape of southern Cyprus and regretted the fact that they didn't have the time to visit the island properly. Being strategically close to both the Near East and Egypt, Cyprus had been inhabited since as far back as 12.000 years ago. Over the ages, many towns and harbours had been inhabited by both peaceful civilisations and war mongering civilisation super powers, among them the Phoenicians, Greeks, Persians, Egyptians, Assyrians and Israeli-Judean peoples, some of whom had come to harvest the island's copper rich soil. In times of conflict, the island had also become a safe haven for refugees. In early Christianity, for example, towns like Paphos were popular places where many early Christians went to escape from the ruthless Roman persecution in Judea, although the apostle Paul had been arrested while preaching publicly in Paphos. The Romans had sentenced him to the infamous 39 lashes and the pillar to which St. Paul had been tied to endure his torture, still stands among the ruins of the old Roman forum. Lazarus, who - according to the Bible - was raised from the dead by Jesus himself, had been the first bishop of the Cyprian port of Larnaca, where he was buried - as the story goes - for the second time.

After having been occupied by the Byzantines and Arabs, the island was used as a jumping board for the Crusades in the late 12th century and when Jerusalem itself fell to the Saracens, Cyprus even became the new Kingdom of Jerusalem. After the reign of the Lusignan dynasty, the island consequently fell into the hands of the Venetians and Ottomans. In 1878, Cyprus was placed under British control and in 1960 it finally became independent. However, the Greek and Turkish Cypriots are still fighting over the island and although a border was drawn to separate the two peoples, the island is still disputed by both parties. This doesn't seem to halt or even slow tourism, which is mainly carried out in the coastal towns. Surprisingly, many tourists who come to the island for a holiday on the beach are rarely interested in the rich history and ancient sites - places that the team of explorers would have loved to explore. Unfortunately for them, there simply wasn't enough time.

Otto's clipper was the first boat to attract the team's attention as they arrived at the harbour. Even with the sails down, the beautiful, white vessel with the two big masts and five black sails was the most beautiful boat in the bay. Otto felt proud to be its owner and couldn't help grinning from ear to ear.
He elbowed Arthur, who stood gaping at it.
"Oh Otto, did you know it was this big?" said Arthur softly.
"Yes, of course I did. I was shown photos and some film footage. You can understand why I fell in love with her. This would have been my means of transportation, to follow the myths of the Golden Fleece and the story of the Odyssey of Odysseus across the Mediterranean. Of course, my entire bank account - which Fred had so generously opened for me in July - has gone into the purchase of this boat. So, apart from owning this boat, I am completely flat broke."
Arthur smiled sourly. What's new? Otto had always lived his life from one day to the next, because tomorrow might never come. He elbowed him back. "I love the name."

"Laurin? Haha, yes, the Teutonic King of the Elves. I thought with having a boat like that and using it to discover the backgrounds of all sorts of myths and legends, it might as well be named after a mythical king."

"Well, maybe when this mission is over, we can go on your very own quest." Arthur added. However, Otto shrugged his shoulders and stared at his shoes while making a sad face.

"It costs a fortune just to pay for the fuel and the harbour fees, not to mention the salaries of the two sailors. I'd have to ask Fred to get me a steady job instead of a freelance one. So, unless I come up with a successful end to this mission to get the promised bonus, I probably will end up having to sell it before we can go anywhere."

Arthur became irritated. "Mr Zinkler promised you a bonus? You never told me that!"

There was so much that Otto still kept from him, that it sometimes scared him. He knew that Otto could be very introverted at times, but as his friend and partner, he expected him to be more open to him on matters that concerned both of them. It proved once more that their relationship, which was supposed to be built as much on trust as on love, was not as close as he would like, but then Otto turned to him as if he could feel Arthur's upset heart. "My darling boy, I kept it from you because if we fail, you'd be so disappointed. However, if we do succeed, it would have been a sweet surprise. I withhold nothing that is important to you or in your interest to know."

He kissed Arthur's brow and smiled at him. He realised that while he may be many things to Arthur, his young friend was also many things to him. Most importantly, Arthur was his best mate, without whom he would have felt bitterly lonely. Arthur was his guide, without whom he would be lost in a modern world of new techniques, ways of travel, communication and media. He was the reason Otto had to keep up a brave face and conquer his fears, his nightmares and his addictions. He needed him and he wanted him to be happy, without any worry. So when Arthur returned his smile, everything in Otto's world was alright.

Despite the bad news that they couldn't sail until the next morning, they decided to get on board, settle in and get some rest. The small sloop - one of the two rescue boats that were attached to the ship - was just big enough to carry them and their luggage to the ship. Hadi made one last call to Georg, informing him that they had arrived at the ship and that they were going to sail tomorrow at dawn. Hadi also explained that there was a car in the safe-parking area of Paphos that needed to be returned to a certain address in Cairo, along with an extra envelope of promised cash.

Georg was pleased. So far, so good.

While Hadi, Otto and Arthur were checking into their cabins and making themselves at home, Andrei stepped out to make a call from his mobile phone. He looked behind him to make sure that he was alone and then turned to dial a number. Otto's instructions over the phone had confused him and he wanted to make sure.

"Mr Corona? It's Andrei Kyriakou. You asked me to contact you the moment Mr Adler shows up? Well, he is here now with two others. So, am I still getting my fee? Great, many thanks! Yes, sir, I will text message you our destinations. No, thank *you*, sir."

34

Sark, Channel Islands, October 5th 2011

The baby inside Danielle's belly was kicking the moment they got off the ferry, which had taken them to the smaller island of Sark the morning after that terrible day. She hadn't slept much that night, even though she was kept hidden and guarded by three men. The 45 minute sea journey had been pleasant and she had enjoyed watching the antics of the cute puffins who were flying high above the black rocks off the coast. For a brief moment, it had taken her mind off David.

As there were no cars permitted to circulate on the island, Georg had arranged for them to be picked up by the traditional means of transport, a horse-and-carriage. The idyllic island was like a fairy-tale, affectionately preserved as if time had stood still. The dramatic cliffs around the harbour formed an impressive gateway to the soft, romantic countryside with its lush green forests and wide fields. The road that led to the harbour was so steep, that the resourceful locals had rigged up a tractor to a 10-seater carriage to haul it up the steep hill. The tractor with carriage sat waiting just on the other side of the tunnel to take the ferry passengers to the top of the hill and into the only town on the island; The Village. As this would have been too rough a ride for Danielle, a private 'Victoria' carriage had been rented for her. She was helped into the small, comfortable 3-seater carriage by David's replacement, special agent Jack Hayes, who was to accompany her to their new accommodation. Another privately hired carriage, carrying agent Barry, the new second agent called Manfred and the rest of the luggage, closely followed them.

Danielle did not like Jack. She was put off by his closely-shaven face, stiff, painfully introverted manners and unimaginatively cropped, dark hair. She longed for David to be at her side and no other could ever take his place. Danielle eyed Jack, scrutinising each gesture as he gave orders to the driver of the horse-drawn taxi - speaking with an affected, elitist tone - insisting that the hood was properly raised. Though she understood that he was merely performing his job focusing on her own privacy and safety, she couldn't help thinking about what he might know about her; how much he had been told at his briefing. Still, the last thing she wanted was to start a conversation by asking him questions, so she kept quiet.

Danielle let her mind wander off as they drove through the country lanes, in and out of the tree-filtered sunlight. In her mind's eye she could see her baby girl already, wearing a little red dress and a white vest, running across the lawn in a place where everyone was reunited and happy. She visualised it strongly, as Alfred had taught her. "The power of visualisation is stronger than we think." he had said. "Open up the doors to the future and picture yourself walking into the world and life you have in mind for yourself. Visualise the room or the garden, the situation or the conversation. Visualise it so clearly and fully that you can even feel the breeze upon your face, its caress upon your skin and smell the scent of your surroundings and loved ones."

She closed her eyes and visualised her baby girl, running around in her red dress, laughing and giggling. She did this exercise time and time again, whenever she had a moment, hoping that one day this vision would come true. On a certain moment, a grey feather swirled into the carriage and fell onto her lap. A dove had taken flight from a branch above them as they passed. She could still hear the flapping sound of his wings and the muffled rhythm made her smile. Danielle knew this was a good omen. Oshu, the father of her baby, once told her that when you find a feather on your path, angels are watching over you, but when the feather drops from heaven, the Father is watching over you.

It gave her goosebumps.

Oshu had been such a soft and gentle man, yet strong and incredibly wise. She missed him so. Feeling the sorrow welling up inside of her, pricking her eyes, she quickly returned to the happy vision of her baby, who was, again, kicking. Her hands touched her belly to feel the kicks and she now let her tears flow freely. She felt as if the baby was sharing her thoughts and was running around giggling in her mother's visualisation.

Jack noticed that Danielle was crying and smiling at the same time and wondered what this enigmatic woman had gone through. At the same time he couldn't help noticing her stunning beauty and incredible eyes and he had to stop himself from staring at her, afraid that she would notice. It would only make her feel even more uncomfortable.

SBS-Sion had hired Jack Hayes for his outstanding record and experience with MI6, the British Intelligence service. He had never heard of the Swiss organisation before the day he was interviewed and was wondering how they had managed to persuade his commanding officer to put him on this particular job. He only knew what he was allowed to know and he wasn't too keen on the fact that it didn't include satisfactory answers to his why's and how's. His assistant, Manfred Tänner, who had come directly from the base at Sion, Switzerland, didn't seem to know much either, only that there were three men trying to kidnap Danielle and that her safety was their top priority.

Jack had repeatedly checked every corner, every angle and every person he saw during their journey to the new safe house location, but so far, he hadn't seen anyone with Arabian features or anyone who looked in any way suspicious. Al Din probably didn't even know they were on the isle of Sark. As he only knew the address of the safe house, Jack had no idea what it would look like. Georg had told him that he would recognise the place by its majesty and invisibility. How that would be possible, he did not know. It had made him anxious and curious at the same time, but when they arrived, he couldn't believe his eyes.

The grand castle-like manor house called *La Seigneurie* stood proudly in a tranquil garden which was partly open to the public. They would never have chosen something this accessible for Danielle, thought Jack, but he quickly learned it wasn't the castle that would be their safe house; it was the secret bunker from World War II, located at the back of the castle's private gardens underneath a folly. Compared to Rose Cottage, the accommodation itself was a lot less romantic, but at least it was safe. No one knew of its existence except the Seigneur of Sark, who had agreed to let them stay in the bunker for a short time. It was of small proportions and dark, lit only by two light bulbs hanging naked from the ceiling, but the owner had tried to make it as comfortable as possible. It had everything they needed to hide out for a few days. Danielle was given the most comfortable bed, which had been placed behind a green, velvet curtain, so that she could at least have some privacy. Exhausted, she immediately walked over to it and lay down, drawing the curtain to create at least a feeling of privacy; being momentarily detached from the overly complicated world. Within the minute she was fast asleep.

Jack sat down at the small, wooden table. He had just finished briefing Georg on their current situation and his orders were to set a trap and capture Al Din to get him off their backs. Danielle could then be safely moved back to Sion. Georg, however, hadn't told him that Alfred had already foreseen Al Din's escape from the Zürich prison in a vision, which was the reason Danielle had been sent to a safe house in the first place. At the time, Alfred hadn't known when or how that was supposed to happen, but he had never expected it to happen so soon. Unwilling to risk the wellbeing of Danielle's unborn baby, Alfred was against using the ERFAB to retrieve her, unless there would be a life-threatening situation and he absolutely had no other choice. So Georg had ordered agent Hayes to come up with a plan. Jack carefully unfolded a map of the Seigneurie and sighed. He now had to study the grounds thoroughly and find a way to lure Al Din into a trap. He wondered if Al Din even knew they were on Sark, but couldn't afford to take the risk of assuming he didn't. As the next ferry wasn't scheduled to arrive until 2:45 pm, there was still time to set things up.

Meanwhile, agent Barry - wearing jeans and a colourful shirt in an effort to imitate a tourist - had been sent out on a bicycle to become familiar with the layout of the island. A brochure that he had studied on the ferry related a bit of Sark's history. An ancient people called the Veneti, a seafaring Celtic tribe from the French mainland, had inhabited Sark before the Romans conquered it. In the Middle Ages it had become a safe haven for both Christian monks and pirates. In 1565, Queen Elizabeth I ordered Helier de Carteret, Seigneur of St. Ouen in Jersey, to keep the island free of pirates and have it occupied by at least 40 of her Majesty's subjects. Following the queen's orders, de Carteret brought 40 families, mainly from St. Ouen, to the island and was appointed first Seigneur of Sark.

As a royal fief and part of the Bailiwick of Guernsey, the small island has its own laws and parliament and even its very own UN country code. Sark stands out from the rest of the Western world, characterised by its slow-moving daily life, disturbed only at the holidays by a handful of daytrip tourists. By choosing to remain free of artificial lights outside the private residences, Sark was also the first island in the world to become a member of the Dark Sky Community. Barry, however, was particularly interested in the southern tip of the island called 'Little Sark', which is separated from the main island by a small isthmus called 'la Coupée'. It is so isolated, that the inhabitants still speak Sercquiais, the native Norman dialect. As the isthmus land bridge is quite narrow and high and therefore easy to control, 'Little Sark' would be an ideal trap. Barry's eyes lit up when he plan formed in his mind.

The Camaro Convertible V8 SS was not granted passage on the ferry and Lars was still cursing when they moored at the little harbour of Sark. "I can't believe I had to leave my car again! Besides, the tracking system is an inbuilt system, so without the car we will not be able to use it to track down Danielle."

"Then we will find her by using our eyes, ears and minds!" Al Din added, raising his voice. His patience was now beginning to dwindle. Weak as he was, he didn't like the prospect of walking either, but the island wasn't big. Sark measured a tiny 5.44 square kilometres, so it seemed that finding Danielle shouldn't be too difficult. However, one thing was certain; one of them had to remain at the harbour to ensure she didn't leave the island again. Al Din didn't trust Titan to work on his own anymore, so instead he decided to leave Lars at the harbour, who now angrily kicked a rock. "Perfect. Just perfect... and what am I going to eat? Where am I going to sleep? How am I g..."

Lars' luggage was propelled unexpectedly into his face, knocking him backwards onto the hard, rocky ground. The green-brown, army-like bag was quickly followed by a plastic bag, which Titan threw mercilessly into Lars' unprotected lap.

"There're still some Snickers in there and a couple of cans of cola, but I wouldn't open one right now if I were you." taunted Titan, grinning from ear to ear. These were the leftovers of his own little mission the day before; a mission that had resulted in the death of the agent and the widow Mrs Peel's head injury.

Al Din slapped the back of Titan's head again. "Stop that nonsense, the both of you! We must be quick or we will miss our transportation up that hill and I for one do not want to climb it myself!"

Irritated, he walked toward the tunnel. The 10-seater carriage, which was attached to the diesel-fuming tractor, was just about to leave. Titan brought the rest of the luggage and while following Al Din through the tunnel, he turned around one last time and couldn't resist smiling victoriously at his colleague, who was left behind in possibly the most uncomfortable spot on the island. The harbour was nothing more than an L-shaped stone pier and if he wanted to keep an eye on the tunnel, he wouldn't be able to position himself on the more comfortable, sandy beach.

Lars spat on the ground and resisted his urge to respond. He couldn't possibly hate Titan more than he already did.

The two men were so different from one another. Titan was born in a war-stricken land. He'd seen his neighbours shot, his school friends marched away from school, never to return. He'd listened to his sister's screaming as she was dragged away, raped and returned a shell of the caring, confident, loving big sister she had been. He was as detached from love and emotion as humanly possible. Lars, on the other hand, was the over indulged son of a modest, Scandinavian father and a domineering, American mother. He had always been fond of the latest gadgets, inventions, apps and even more importantly; hot cars and his family had always helped him procure them. He had found out long ago that a normal job would not pay him enough to allow him to buy everything he desired, so he had decided to find a job in the world of crime. The only downsides were the risk of betrayal, the risk of being caught or getting involved in violent situations and he didn't know which was worse. He hated Titan for his cruel nature and lust for violence and he knew Titan probably hated him back for that. Nobody wants to be confronted by his own madness, or weakness.

Back at the Seigneurie, Danielle was still asleep and agent Barry had just returned to tell Jack about Little Sark. Jack rubbed his eyes and leaned back, recognising the possibility of using this remote part of the island as a trap for Al Din.

"Jolly good!" he said to Barry with a crooked grin. "Now all we have to do is find him and lure him to Little Sark. Barry, I want you to cycle back to The Village, play the tourist and then call me on our safe line when you spot him. Manfred and I will stay here and guard the bunker."

Barry nodded, checked his watch and left immediately, knowing that the ferry must have just moored and he only had a few minutes left to reach The Village in time before the new visitors arrived. He sped down the Rue de Rade, only slowing down when he reached the crossing.

The carriage with the passengers from the harbour had just gone past and was now coming to a halt at the beginning of the village. Slowly he cycled past it while whistling a joyful song. When he spotted the pale Al Din climbing off the carriage, assisted by a mean looking hulk of a man, he was struck with a jolt, making it hard for him to keep to the tune. Although Barry had been trained for such situations, seeing the men who had killed his colleague caused his stomach to turn with adrenaline. The other thing that worried him was the fact that there were just two of them.

Jack had specifically mentioned *three* men.

He decided to park the bike and enter the small post office to quietly contact Jack for further orders. Stepping into the little post office, Barry positioned himself strategically behind a postcard rack, so he wouldn't lose sight of them. With a soft voice he reported to Jack, simply saying, "They're here…"

Jack was surprised that Al Din had found their new destination so quickly.

"Blast! We were so careful! I will search our luggage to see if we are carrying some kind of tracking device. They must have planted a bug while they were at Rose Cottage. Keep an eye on them while I come up with a plan to lure them to Little Sark. I will get back to you a.s.a.p.."

"Yes, sir."

Barry ended the call and jumped when he saw Al Din and his hulk walking straight toward the post office; straight toward *him*. He quickly put away his phone and started to browse through the postcards. While doing this, Barry could overhear their conversation when they entered.

"… so a church, a pub or a post office are good places to start. A priest, a bartender and a post office clerk usually know everything that is going on in a small village. They may have seen her arrive, or pass through the street. Now, Titan; watch and learn."

Al Din courteously walked over to the woman behind the desk and gave her his most charming smile. He had found that being a handsome man has its advantages when it came to addressing women and even though he was looking somewhat poorly, the woman indeed returned his warm smile. "May I help you sir?"

"Yes, you may, my dear madam, I am looking for my sister. We seemed to have missed each other at the ferry, so I had to take the next one. However, I appear to have no signal on this island, so I am unable to reach her with my phone. Perhaps you have seen her? She is a blonde, pregnant woman, accompanied by several men."

Al Din had used his most dignified Oxford accent, which he had picked up when he studied at the renowned University many years ago. It gave him a most civilised impression, adding favourably to his good looks and sugar sweet charm. The woman thought deeply, but couldn't recall seeing her. Danielle and her agents had turned north at the crossing and had never come near the village.

She pursed her lips and shook her head. "I'm afraid not, sir, but you are welcome to try our landline."

Al Din turned down the offer politely and raised his hands. "It will not do any good, my dear, because if I have no signal, she won't have a signal either. We share the same mobile telephone company, you see?"

"Then I wish you good luck in finding her soon."

"I thank you for your kind help."

Gracefully he took his leave and walked back out. Titan followed him and put his finger into his throat, symbolically throwing up over his boss's sweet-talking.

"I saw that, Titan! But you must remember that kindness goes a lot further than smashing people's brains in or slitting someone's throat!"

"Whatever you say, chief, but what do we do now?"

"That is obvious. We hire a horse-drawn taxi and explore the island in search of anything susceptible to house Danielle. Lars would have already booked one by now..." Al Din added with a disappointed undertone.

The moment Al Din and Titan started walking away toward the taxi stand through The Avenue, the main street of The

Village, Barry quickly contacted Jack. The small shops with their big windows and low roofs were set side by side in the sandy main street, displaying all kinds of local produce and island souvenirs. Colourful plants and flowers in terra cotta pots were placed on windowsills and along the roadside, creating romantic charm and Titan stood out like a hammer in a sorbet. Barry had witnessed Al Din's softness and Titan's rudeness. At first sight of Al Din, Barry had already wondered how such an elegantly dressed man, with that kind of posture and gait and such a light weight, could have slit his colleague's throat. So after hearing the men's conversation, Barry knew for sure that it had indeed been the hulk.

"Jack? It's Barry again. They're off patrolling the island in a small private carriage."

"Good. I will send Manfred out on horseback, wearing our black SBS-Sion outfit. That will certainly attract their attention. Manfred will try to lure them to Little Sark and then you must block the road at La Coupée together with the local constable. Go now, find him, use your ID card, prep him and ask him to call for back-up."

"Yes sir, I'm on it."

The island constable, however, was nothing more than a local resident who had volunteered for the job and Jack realised that Barry's ID might not be recognised and not carry the weight it did everywhere else. Still, if the constable would cooperate in the name of a crime and contact the Guernsey police for assistance, the officers would need time to get to Sark from Guernsey. Barry also knew that the hulk was an opponent not to be underestimated and for the next hour at least, they'd be completely on their own. He braced himself. This wasn't going to be easy.

35

Paphos Bay, Cyprus, October 5th 2011

The first pinkish morning light was coming through the cabin porthole and Otto could now make out the details of the small cabin they were sleeping in. A tiny shower room was cleverly placed in a niche in the corner, while the space underneath the high bed was a wardrobe. The whole cabin had a fine lacquered, cherry wood finish and a built-in TV-DVD combination. Otto remembered the documentary on Akhenaten Alfred had wanted them to see before their departure and wondered if the DVD might be hidden somewhere among the files. Forever on the lookout for more insight on the ancient ways and daily life at Akhetaten, he softly slid out of bed to look through the folder. Arthur groaned and rolled over, clearly not yet ready to wake up properly. Otto quietly slid into his trousers and opened the briefcase in which all the files were kept. Not able to see things clearly, he turned on the light above the small table and started to sort and look through the various files. Otto knew that they had not read everything yet. They had read the main files when they were in Egypt, but now he discovered that there were also other files with several print-outs in a separate part of the briefcase. With great curiosity he opened up the first file entitled 'Yuya' and started reading.

'Yuya was most probably not a native Egyptian, but a Hebrew from Retjenu [the old Egyptian name for Canaan or Syria], who had arrived in Egypt at a young age and had managed to climb up to a very high position at the royal court, including that of the 'King's Lieutenant' and 'Master of the Horse'. For some reason, he had also become one of the most important prophets in Upper Egypt. He had fathered a beautiful daughter and two sons. Yuya's daughter Tiye married pharaoh Amenhotep III and became the mother of Akhenaten. Yuya's first born son was Aanen, who would not only become the Chancellor of Lower Egypt under

Amenhotep III, he also became the Second Prophet of Amun, Sem-priest of Heliopolis and was given the title 'Divine Father'. Tiye's second son was Ay, who in his later life became Tutankhamen's successor. Discovering the importance of Yuya and of his children within the royal bloodline of Egypt's 18th Dynasty has proved to be of great interest to scholars, as it might explain why there are Hebrew influences within the Egyptian belief system of the 18th Dynasty. While listening to the stories of his grandfather Yuya, the young Akhenaten might have heard stories about a Hebrew god called Jahweh - 'He who is One' - which had probably inspired him to dedicate so much energy to converting his people to monotheism when he became pharaoh of Egypt.

Several scholars believe that there is a relationship between the Biblical Joseph of Egypt and Yuya. As many books in the Biblical Old Testament had only been written during or after the Babylonian Exile [6th century BCE], cold hard facts to certify the story of Joseph, the Exodus and the backgrounds of Biblical people like Aaron, Moses and Joseph, are yet to be discovered. It is believed that the stories are, however, based on actual historical events and real people - who may have been renamed in later times - conveniently adding kinship and hereditary rights to the story for political and/or religious reasons. However, it cannot be neglected that the titles worn by Joseph are similar to those of Yuya, including the rare title of 'Father of God', which refers to the fact that he was the father-in-law of Amenhotep III, the divine pharaoh of Egypt.'

Otto rubbed his eyes, still feeling a little bit tired after the short night, but the subject fascinated him and he quickly turned the page to read on.

'Joseph of Egypt was the much loved 11th son of Jacob of Canaan, who was also called Israel. Jacob loved his son Joseph more than the others, so he gave him a multi-coloured coat to honour him. His brothers became so envious that one day when they were out into the fields, they sold Joseph to Egyptian slave traders. After dipping Joseph's beautiful coat into the blood of a slaughtered animal, they went home and told their father Jacob that a wild animal had killed Joseph. Jacob was so upset about this news, that he wished he were dead. The brothers, who were alarmed to see their father so heartbroken, sincerely regretted their deed before the day was over. Alas! There was no other option open to them than to stick to their lie.'

'In the meantime, Joseph had been taken to Egypt and sold to Potifar, the captain of the palace guard. When Joseph did not want to give in to the seductions of Potifar's wife, she accused him of rape and he was thrown in prison. There, he discovered that he had the gift of interpreting dreams. The news quickly reached the pharaoh himself, who was suffering from nightmares, which he himself could not explain. Joseph explained that there would be seven years of abundance, followed by seven years of famine. That same day, the pharaoh bestowed upon Joseph the title 'revealer of secrets' and made him overlord of Egypt, in charge of filling the storehouses in preparation for the famine. From that moment on, Joseph became a famous prophet and - as was customary in the Near-East and Egypt - he was given a special, silver divination cup. Filled with water, its sacred reflection speaks to the seer, who interprets what he sees and reveals secrets hidden from the world.'

Otto paused and grinned.

Mirror, mirror...

'After the seven years of abundance had passed, there came indeed a famine over the entire region, including Canaan. Joseph's brothers then travelled to Egypt to ask the pharaoh if his family could come and live in the Egyptian province of Goshen, where food was not yet scarce. Not recognising their own brother - as Joseph was wearing a wig and his eyes were lined with kohl in the well-known Egyptian manner - Joseph decided to teach his brothers a lesson.

He ordered a servant to hide Joseph's silver divination cup in the luggage of his beloved younger brother Benjamin, who was the second son of Rachel, Jacob's second wife and therefore his only full brother. When the cup was 'discovered', Joseph acted as if he were angry and ordered Benjamin to stay behind. Unable to change Joseph's mind - and still not recognising him - the brothers were distraught and begged Joseph to let Benjamin go and to take Judah, another brother, instead, for it would surely kill their father if he lost Benjamin too. Unable to hide his emotions any longer, he finally revealed that he was their brother Joseph, whom they had sold into slavery many years earlier. He forgave his brothers and they were permitted to fetch their father Jacob and live peacefully in the land of Goshen in Lower Egypt. That is how the Hebrews came into Egypt and how one of them, the prophet Joseph, came to be such an important nobleman in the Egyptian royal house.'

'When Jacob arrived with the rest of the family, counting ca. 70 people in total and bringing all their livestock, Jacob was overjoyed to see that his beloved Joseph was still alive. He even lived long enough to see Joseph's own sons, Ephraim and Manasse. Jacob blessed them both, promising them the biggest part of his [Israel's] lands and giving them more rights than Joseph's brothers. Naturally, the brothers were now once again living in the shadow of Jacob's love for Joseph and their heirs would later try to claim back the lands and all the rights that Jacob had given to Joseph and his children, leading to many tribal disputes and the redirection of history.'

Otto chuckled and whispered quietly to himself, "What's new..." He checked on Arthur, who had even started to snore softly. He watched him for a moment, not sure if he wanted to wake him just yet. On the next page he saw a photo of a beautiful necklace that he had already seen before. It was Tutankhamen's famous breastplate with the desert glass scarab in the centre. Then, suddenly, his eye fell on a detail he hadn't noticed before. The winged scarab was holding in his claws a lotus flower and a fleur-de-lis. A fleur-de-lis! Quickly, he turned the page and read on.

'This is, however, not the only link between the Hebrew people and Egypt. Jacob, the father of the original 12 tribes of Israel, may himself have been the grandson of an Egyptian pharaoh. As southern Canaan [Djahi] had been part of Egypt for centuries, both the Hebrew and Egyptian culture show many signs of cross-pollination. Circumcision, for example, was already known in ancient Egypt in the Sixth Dynasty [2345–2181 BCE], predating Abraham. This suggests that Abraham had probably seen it in Egypt before imposing the practice to his own people. According to several scholars, Abraham's wife Sarai - an old name meaning 'princess' - was taken by the pharaoh to be his wife, because she had told him that Abraham was her brother. One must consider the possibility that Abraham's son Isaac may in fact have been the son of this particular pharaoh, which could indicate that Isaac's son Jacob already had family ties with the Egyptian royals through his grandfather. This would explain why, at a time of famine, Jacob had sent his sons to the pharaoh of Egypt for help. This theory may also explain why Joseph was able to make such a rapid climb in rank and perhaps even how the fleur-de-lis had made its way into ancient Egypt. If indeed Egyptian royal blood was mixed with the blood of the Hebrews, it is understandable that this specific family, the heirs of Joseph/Yuya and thus Abraham, saw themselves as the 'chosen people'. Joseph's ancestors, the children of Abraham known as the 'Ibrim' or Hebrews, had already been wandering the Near-East for centuries, looking for their 'promised land'. A promised land that Akhenaten had thought to have finally found at the sacred location of his beloved city, Akhetaten.'

For the first time in his life, Otto felt a peace he could not describe. In the 1930s he had been torn between his Jewish mother - whom he had loved dearly - and his anti-Jewish employers. He hadn't known where to put his feelings, or what to think. His confused reaction had caused a fall-out with his family, although he had also had regular fall-outs with the head of the SS, Heinrich Himmler. For some reason, Himmler had always let him get away with it. Perhaps he had been too fond of Otto to have him punished for his insolence, but at this very moment, the knowledge of having Jewish blood coursing through his veins enabled him to feel more deeply connected to his mission. He felt a certain bond to Akhenaten, whom he esteemed a very brave man. Changing a religion which was already thousands of years old and deeply rooted in the people's culture, must have been a huge shock to the Egyptians. What that 'heretic' pharaoh had started, 3400 years ago, was technically the cradle of the three most popular religions on the planet today: Judaism, Christianity and Islam. Although these three religions seem to differ on several subjects, they all have one thing in common - the belief in one God. Unfortunately, monotheism soon mercilessly exiled God's bride, the Mother Goddess and gave way to a patriarchal belief system, resulting in the discrimination of women and a disrespectful treatment of our planet, Mother Earth.

Otto realised that, in many ways, religion has always played a dominant role in the ever present lust for world domination, making us forget what it is really all about. After his traumatic experience in pre-war Germany, Otto himself had become more of an Atheist, only holding on to a tiny straw of hope that there is a higher source behind our earthly existence. Though he had come from a Lutheran background, he had disliked Christianity and any other religion that purported a certain 'truth', while having indeed become greedy and violent. The moment a religion becomes too exoteric, displaying material wealth, it can no longer function properly. When people no longer find themselves comfortable within a religion, it is usually because it no longer preaches love and kindness, two key assets to a genuine Christ-like way of life that are not bound to a religion, but emanate from the *Sacre Coeur,* the Sacred Heart that is within the heart, the dwelling place of the Divine Light, the Godflame, or fleur-de-lis.

A thump behind him startled Otto. He had been reading and pondering in such deep concentration, that he hadn't noticed that Arthur had woken up until he had jumped out of bed.
"Hey, what are you reading?" Arthur asked inquisitively.
"It's about Akhenaten's grandfather, Yuya. Fred thinks he might have been the Biblical Joseph of Egypt, son of Jacob. It makes sense. You should read it."
Otto gently planted a kiss on Arthur's neck and took a clean shirt and trousers from the wardrobe. With curiosity, Arthur started leafing through the file on Yuya, but couldn't resist slapping Otto's butt when he passed him on his way to the tiny shower room. "You've put on more weight." he said approvingly. Otto had been underweight when he and Otto met and Arthur was glad that his health was improving. He had gone through the proverbial 'needle's eye'.

Otto loudly hummed Wagner's 'Ride of the Valkyries' in the shower. This was going to be a good day. Soon they would be sailing across the deep blue sea and what could be more delightful than studying the rest of Alfred's files while cruising the Mediterranean on his very own ship? Otto started to hum even louder and attracted a seemingly irritated Hadi to their cabin.
Arthur opened the door. "Who killed the cat?" Hadi said with a shocked face in an attempt to be funny.
Arthur laughed and let Hadi into the cabin. "He's in such a good mood today! What time are we sailing?"
Hadi looked at his watch. "In about an hour. So I was thinking, maybe we could have breakfast together, contact Georg and talk over our plans. I need a direction to sail in, a destination, as I assume we are not just going to go around in circles."

"Sounds good. I'll let him know when he gets out of the shower. We'll be over as soon as we're ready."

Hadi nodded and left.

When Hadi's mobile phone rang, he thought it was Georg, so he immediately answered without looking at the display. "Good morning!"

The voice of an emotional woman sounded on the other side of the line and Hadi immediately recognised the distressed voice of his sister. His stomach cramped.

"Hadi, it's me, there is a man here asking about you and he…" The line cracked.

"Mira! Mira! Are you still there?"

"Hello Hadi, Max here. So glad to have found your lovely family. I believe we had a deal. First you give me Otto, then you will get your family back. No one gets hurt and we will all be happy. So, where are you?"

Hadi was as pale as a ghost. How on earth had Max found his family? He had no choice but to play along for now. Maybe he could buy some time.

"If you hurt my family, I promise you, you will not leave Cairo alive. Do you hear me?"

"Come now, my dear man, it's a big city. You don't even know where I would be, but since you want to threaten me, maybe it is time for me to threaten you."

Max turned to Mira and produced a knife. The sight of the knife alone made Mira scream out loudly.

"Don't you dare hurt my sister! Ok, OK!!! I'm on a boat in the Mediterranean and cannot just come over to you. I don't see how I can be of any use to you!"

"Then I will kill your sister. Your mother will be next. Think hard, Hadi. I am serious."

Hadi broke into a sweat and walked from one side of the boat to the other, trying to think of a means to keep Max busy. Suddenly he thought of the ERFAB device that Arthur had left at Soongh's shop. He hesitated, but when he heard his sister scream again, he decided to reveal it to Max. Hadi felt he had no choice but to give him what he wanted.

The moment Max hung up, Hadi's legs began to tremble. Never before had he been in a situation like this, but then he thought that even if Max had the ERFAB device, he'd still not be able to do much with it. Despite the fear for his family, Hadi staretd to smile as an idea crept into his mind. There was possibly a way to get rid of Max once and for all.

36

Sion, Switzerland, October 5th 2011

Michael woke up late that morning. Not yet fully conscious, he slowly opened his eyes and was startled to see a Templar knight on a horse in a mountainous landscape, boldly brandishing a sword. When he realised that it was only an elaborate tapestry, he chuckled quietly at his dismay. He hadn't really studied the beautiful furnishings in the room yet, as they had arrived so late the night before. It was a luxurious room, with dark, wooden wall panelling, a wooden beamed ceiling, an elegant four-poster bed and an en-suite bathroom. Heavy, ruby red, velvet curtains partly covered the lead paned glass windows. He could only hear the sound of the wind, caressing the trees and the songs of autumn birds and while getting out of bed, he recognised the song of a red robin and smiled. There had been lots of those in France, too. He didn't bother getting dressed and while only wearing the dark blue bathrobe that he had found in the bathroom, he briskly walked toward his father's room, which was next door. However, when he entered the hallway, he noticed that the door to David's room was already open. Upon entering the room, he saw that two uniformed nurses were focused on tending to David's wound. Then he spotted the IV and the bag of blood, hanging ominously beside the bed. What alarmed him most was the look on his father's face. Alarmed at the scene and seeing that his father was obviously in great pain, he blurted out, "Dad?"

David opened his eyes and tried to produce a smile.

"Michael, come on in, it's okay."

Without waiting a second longer, Michael anxiously strode across the room, understanding the seriousness of his father's condition. Yesterday had been traumatic for David. The shot had not been fatal, but his body hadn't recovered. The transfer from Guernsey by helicopter and airplane to Sion had drained him, more than anyone could have anticipated. Throughout the night he had had another bout of heavy bleeding and the loss of blood had almost stopped his heart. Had David been alone, he would have died, but Georg had been wise enough to take precautions against any risks and had ensured that David was well attended to by a highly capable medical team. Exhausted, Michael had slept right through the commotion and he wondered to himself if they would have woken him if his father's situation had become critical. David noticed the worried look on his son's face and started, "Have I ever told you how proud I am of you?"

Michael put his finger to his father's lips with gentle reassurance to quiet him. "Don't talk, dad. Just get well, okay? Save your energy. Please, just get well!"

David turned and looked toward the window. "Don't worry, son. I have a mission to finish and I most certainly want to be at your graduation."

David had wanted to add, "and there is a woman waiting for me" but he stopped himself just in time. It would hurt Michael too much. The nurses, who had just finished rebinding the wound, left the room to give them some privacy and as soon as the door closed behind them, David took Michael's arm and gently pulled him close. "Georg is looking after me well and I'm grateful to be here in the main building, surrounded by Alfred's personnel and the medical team. The room has been turned into a hospital room; look how I'm wired up - I'm even getting a blood transfusion. They said it's the fastest way to get my strength back. The nurses are keeping a close eye on my vital signs, so you don't have to worry, Michael. I couldn't be in a safer place right now. Trust me."

Michael agreed. Here, his father was receiving full attention and individual care, which is rarely possible in a busy, understaffed public hospital.

"Do you live here? I mean, is this your room?" Michael asked inquisitively.

"No, but look out the window. Do you see the gatehouse over there? That's where I live."

"Wow, wicked! It's massive!"

"Yep, it is, but I am not the only one living there. I share it with the staff who look after the grounds and the gardens," and with a mischievous smile, David added, "and the horses."

Michael suddenly remembered that his own horse - which had previously been stabled at the B&B in southern France - had also been transported to Sion the previous month - along with David's possessions - and he bristled with excitement.

"Is Beau here?" he asked, holding his breath.

David nodded. "Why don't you take him for a ride this afternoon? I will probably sleep most of the time anyway."

"I can? Really?"

"I don't see why not. Just be careful. No broken limbs this time!"

"I swear dad, this is so cool. but I better get some lunch first. I'm starving. I'll come and visit you again before I go out for the ride!"

Michael hugged his father carefully and went back to his room to get dressed. He knew that rest was the best cure for his father now and if it weren't for his horse, he felt he would become very bored indeed.

Meanwhile at the lab, Georg was finishing his cold coffee and made a sour face. His stomach was rumbling. He'd been on the phone in Alfred's glass office since the first light of day and now he had also missed his lunch. Not being able to talk to Alfred, as he was still in an artificial sleep at the clinic, Georg himself had to choose a destination for the Laurin, which was now on its way to the Greek island of Crete. He had acted on a hunch, since he knew Crete had many deserted beaches on its south coast and would therefore be a great jumping platform for the new mission to Akhenaten.

At the same time, from a distance, he was trying to handle the situation on Sark, where Danielle was hiding out in a bunker, secretly tucked away on the private grounds of the Seigneurie. Agent Jack Hayes had just called to discuss their latest plan that meant luring Al Din to Little Sark and keeping him trapped there until the Guernsey police arrived. To get the job done properly, Jack needed a horse for agent Manfred Tänner, so Georg was back on the phone again, this time with the owner of the Seigneurie. The Seigneur was willing to lend them one of his dark bay horses, if Georg could guarantee that his horse would never be in any danger. Ignoring his gnawing stomach cramps, Georg had no choice but to give his personal guarantee, although he knew deep inside that he wasn't entirely sure he could back up his promise.

Sark, Channel Islands, October 5th 2011
The leaves of the trees had begun to change colour and driving through the country lanes of the calm and picturesque island of Sark was simply idyllic. Even Titan - whose inner thoughts were normally dedicated to things that bothered him, giving him an excuse to abreact, to release his inner anger - felt calm for a moment. He thought about Lars, who had to stay behind at the rocky harbour pier at Creux harbour and couldn't help grinning. He found him to be such a sissy - always with his nose into technical stuff; trying to kiss up to his chief; being 'in love' with his car... though he had to admit, that was a fine car. Al Din was sitting next to him in the horse-drawn carriage, his face no longer pale but with a slight rose tint, a sign that he was beginning to get his strength back. Titan looked up to Al Din. He had been around long enough to know that he was a very wealthy and powerful man in the eastern Mediterranean. He knew Al Din lived in a spacious villa in the hills just outside Jerusalem, but Titan had no idea why his chief wanted Danielle so very badly. Al Din had never disclosed more information than he thought was necessary, not even to Lars. So far he had spent a fortune to obtain this woman. Not only had he followed Lars' plan to open up a bank account in Jersey under his false name, he had also arranged a helicopter to stand by at Jersey Airport to fetch them. On top of it all, Al Din had even

arranged a private jet - now standing by at a small airport in western France - to fly them from France to Israel as soon as they arrived by helicopter from Jersey. It was an expensive operation. So, what was so special about this Danielle? She was beautiful to be sure, as were many women. She was also pregnant. What could possibly interest a man like Al Din, who could possess almost any woman in the world, to this point, to obtain this woman? Titan could no longer suppress his curiosity and decided to ask.

"So, why does this woman mean so much to you?"

Al Din stared hard at him, as if he was surprised that he' would ask such a question. Especially because the cabby, who sat in front of them, would be able to overhear everything they said. Al Din spoke in a soft voice, making signs to alert Titan not to speak too loudly.

"Titan, there are things in this life that are above average, goals that can only be reached when you jump higher than you could ever imagine jumping. Danielle is such a goal. Not just because she is the most beautiful woman I have ever seen, but also because of her unborn baby."

"Yours?" Titan whispered, astonished.

"No, Titan. All you need to know is that I need her by my side and that I want to raise that child as my own. The child is very special."

"Why? Who is the father? Is he someone important or powerful? A millionaire? Is it about a ransom? I thought you were rich enough by any standards!"

Al Din couldn't help laughing out loud, thinking Titan still had the mind of an eight year old.

"No Titan, this is not about money. This is about influence.., but enough said. It is none of your business."

Al Din waved his hand, making it clear that the conversation was over. He looked around him and became irritated and impatient.

"At this moment we're just going around in circles and so far we have only seen islanders and tourists. Don't just sit there, give me the map!"

Titan handed over the tiny map of the island and Al Din studied it. With his expert eye for grandeur, he spotted the Seigneurie in the northern part of the island.

"What's that?" he asked Titan, while pointing at it.

"It's where the lord of the island lives. Maybe he is hiding them."

Al Din smiled. That would be an obvious place for Georg to hide Danielle. He looked around and realised they were going in the wrong direction; they had to go back to The Village and turn north, so he tapped the cabby's shoulder and said in a kind, well-mannered tone, "My dear man, could you be so kind as to drive us to the Seigneurie?"

The driver, a man in his late twenties with medium long, dark hair, nodded and turned the horse and carriage around. As it is forbidden to drive fast on the island, they drove back to The Village at a slow pace. Titan yawned, "and here we are, breaking speed records again."

Meanwhile at The Seigneurie, agent Manfred Tänner had just mounted a dark bay horse called Elliot.

"So remember," said Jack - who had just got off the phone with Georg - "The Seigneur wants the horse back sound. No galloping on the paving stones and no jumping farm walls, which often have barbed wire at the foot of them. Be careful of the tourists on bicycles who often don't realise horses have a mind of their own"

"Yes, sir! I will take no such risks, of course! I will only lure them to Little Sark, occupy the isthmus to block the way and wait until Barry arrives with the island police."

"Good luck!" Jack said, while gently slapping horse's rump. As he walked back to the bunker, he momentarily glanced over his shoulder to see agent Tänner trotting off in well-schooled form. With agents Barry and Manfred now away on their dangerous mission to capture Al Din, he was left alone to safeguard Danielle. He knew that inside the bunker, he'd have no control whatsoever over what might take place outside, so to be able to keep an eye on the grounds, he had no choice but to take a strategic position somewhere on the grounds of the Seigneurie. Jack had expected Danielle's hesitant reaction when he broke the news to her. Being all alone in that dark place, not knowing what was going on above ground and not being able to contact him, would have been nerve-racking for anyone. At the same time, it was of vital importance that neither of them emit a phone signal unless they absolutely had no other choice.

After having studied the grounds of the Seigneurie thoroughly, Jack knew exactly where he wanted to set up his guard post: at the top of the 19th century Le Pelley church tower, just outside the formal, walled Seigneurie gardens. From there he'd have a fantastic view. When he reached the top of the tower, he opened a light-grey hard case and started to assemble the pieces of a M24 sniper rifle. He then used the telescopic sight of the sniper gun to browse the grounds. Hidden behind one of the triangle shaped walls that stood at the top of the square tower, he peeked through the round hole at the centre of each triangle. Though the triangle with the hole may symbolise the all-seeing eye, he knew that he could never look in all the cardinal directions at the same time and became nervous. It was only a matter of time before someone showed up.

Now that she knew she was on her own, Danielle did not dare to go back to sleep. If only she could phone Georg and ask after David, as she was very worried about him. His wound had looked quite serious, despite his brave show of courage and in her fear, her mind raced uncontrollably. What if they hadn't told her the truth and David was really critically wounded? She couldn't help feeling guilty; David was in pain, suffering, perhaps dead or dying and all because of her. They were all prepared to give up their lives for her and for her baby. Perhaps if she could talk to Al Din, he would listen to reason. She felt that since this whole mess was about her, she was the only one who could put a stop to all the hurting. Determined to follow up on her impulse plan, she walked toward the door of the bunker and tried to open it, but it was locked and the key was not inside the lock. A jolt went through her like an electric shock. Jack had locked her inside! How could he? A cold chill crept up her body and she folded her arms in an attempt to warm herself up. It was damp and cold in the bunker and realising she had no other choice than to stay there and wait, she finally decided to curl up underneath a plaid in the corner of her bed. Though she was alone, she closed the curtain to reduce her world to a womb-like environment. All she wanted was to get it all over with, so she could get back to Sion. While rocking herself gently, she prayed softly to the father of her child for help.

After a short ride, Manfred had reached The Village just in time to see the carriage carrying Al Din and his giant assistant driving down the main street. Dressed in his black SBS-Sion uniform he casually approached the carriage close enough for them to see him, but he was careful not to look at them. Manfred needed them to think that he hadn't seen them, so they would follow him.

Taking the road west to the junction, he suppressed the urge to turn around to see if they were following, but when he arrived at the junction, he turned left toward Little Sark and could see from the corner of his eye that they were indeed following not far behind him. His heart was racing. His thoughts now went to agent Barry, who, if all was going according to plan, was attempting to persuade the local law enforcement to contact the Guernsey police for assistance. If Barry should fail to get the necessary police support, they'd be completely on their own. Unconsciously, his hand went to his Glock, although he knew that using it was only allowed if everything else should fail.

The moment he rode across La Coupée, the isthmus separating Little Sark from its big brother, he saw how narrow it was and how high. He could see the waves crashing onto the boulders at the foot of the sheer sides of the rocky cliff, far beneath him. Even Elliot - the sturdy, calm gelding he had borrowed for this quest - was getting nervous. Knowing that horses always pick up the rider's emotions, Manfred quickly pulled himself together and concentrated on the horizon ahead and the moment he arrived at the other side, he searched for a place to hide behind. Spotting a possibility, he galloped toward the La Sablonnerie hotel - a series of attached, white cottages with grey roofs and lovely rose gardens - and waited on the other side of the hotel, hiding behind the buildings. As soon as the carriage with Al Din and Titan had passed, he raced back to the isthmus and remained there, blocking the road. So far, so good. Any minute now, Manfred should be here with police back-up.

Al Din, who realised what had just happened, became furious. "It's a trap! Turn the carriage around! Yalla!"

The cabby became worried at the sudden change of behaviour in his passenger, but he had no time to protest. Titan's large fist knocked him out cold before he could say a word and after kicking him off the seat, Titan took over the reins and speeded toward the isthmus.

Not only Manfred saw the fast approaching carriage, Elliot too spotted it and neighed nervously while bouncing from one side to the other, paying no heed to Manfred's shushing and requests to settle down and the very moment that the carriage sped up to the isthmus, Manfred could no longer hold Elliot. The horse turned and bolted back toward The Village. Trying to not fall off, he clung to the saddle, hunching over Elliot's neck. Then he heard the whiz of bullets flying past his ears and knew that while riding in one straight line, both he and Elliot would be easy targets. Manfred cursed.

He managed to veer Elliot off the road and into the fields where the carriage could not follow. For now he was able to outrun them, but the plan had failed miserably.

37

The Mediterranean, October 5th 2011

Otto was crying silently. He was overcome with emotion as he witnessed the hoisting of the Laurin's black sails for the very first time. The Laurin had now set course for Crete and was heading to the open waters of the deep blue Mediterranean Sea. He was so proud; his dream had come true. Arthur, who shared Otto's emotions, gently put his arm around Otto's waist and pulled him close.

"There you go, buddy. Off on a new adventure, on your own boat. How cool is that, eh?"

The lump in his throat caused a tremor in his voice when he replied, "Phantasmal."

Hadi - now completely aware of their relationship - observed the two men and shook his head. However, he had other things on his mind right now. Max Müller had kidnapped his sister and had threatened to hurt her if he didn't cooperate. He'd had a brainwave when he thought of telling Max about the lost ERFAB device, hoping to use it against him the moment an opportunity arose. He had explained to Max that he had only to select '3' on the device to be instantly teleported to Hadi's coordinates and wondered if this idea was really as clever as he initially thought it to be. He had said it to buy some time, so he could think of a good plan to get Max off their backs. Naturally, he hadn't dared to share this unfortunate development with any of the others, let alone Georg. He had created this mess, therefore he felt that he was solely responsible for clearing it up.

Following Georg's orders, Hadi - being the captain of the Laurin - had obediently set course for Crete and they were now helped forward by a by favourable wind. Before heading into open waters, they first had to round the point of Paphos Bay and Otto - who was watching the island disappear into the vibrating distance - suddenly spotted something white on the southern coast and became excited.

"Art, can you see the large, white rock, just off the shoreline? It's Aphrodite's Rock: *Petra tou Romiou.* According to the myth, this is where the goddess rose from the foaming waves. The Italian Renaissance painter Sandro Botticelli painted the scene in which the goddess Venus, the Roman version of Aphrodite, arrived from the sea while standing on a large scallop shell. The painting was commissioned by the powerful Medici family, by Lorenzo di Pierfrancesco de Medici to be exact and was based on an older, now lost work by the Roman painter Apelles."

Arthur was a little envious of Otto's incredible knowledge. The man seemed to be capable of absorbing everything he heard or read, so he replied, teasingly, "So, was Aphrodite born on the rock, or on the shell?"

Otto saw the sarcasm in Arthur's sparkling eyes, but it was charmingly alleviated by his naughty smile. It amused him.

"You can make fun of it all you like. In the realm of myth and legend, artists get full poetic license. In Roman mythology, Venus rises from the sea while standing on a scallop shell."

"Why a scallop shell?"

"The scallop shell is a symbol of the vulva, so in Botticelli's painting it was directly hinting at the Birth of Venus. Showing her not as a baby, but as a mature woman - which could be confusing - Botticelli had her standing on the shell to emphasise the birth. Of course when you look at it symbolically, the scene goes much deeper. It refers to the knowledge of the natural world, into which mankind has been born. Throughout the ages, a scallop shell was looked upon as a Grail-like symbol of the Divine Feminine and the knowledge of the Hermetic Teachings, hinting at the Golden Ratio and nature's mathematical constant: Pi."

"That particular shell reminds me of the St. James shell that was given to the pilgrims who had been to Santiago de Compostela in Spain." Arthur remarked.

"Correct! Before the tomb of St. James was found in Galicia, Spain, there was a Hermetic Pythagorean school there, studying mysticism, astrology, physics and metaphysics. At night they would sit in the field to share the knowledge of the stars and the phases of the moon. That is why the place is called Compostela; 'field of the stars'. Those who had joined one or more of the classes, received a scallop shell as a token of their participation. Obviously, this habit was copied by those who first started the pilgrimage to Santiago de Compostela in the 9th century CE."

Arthur still couldn't believe how much his boyfriend knew.

"You should have been a teacher!" he exclaimed.

Otto smiled and gazed at the horizon.

"I was, my dear boy. I was."

Arthur just stared at him, at his man of many mysteries. He recalled what Otto had just told him and thought of the baptism scene in the Magdalen church in Rennes-le-Chateau, a small village in southern France, known for its unsolved mysteries. Could the scene in which John the Baptist baptises Jesus with a scallop shell be hinting at the possibility that perhaps this particular baptism was more a question of hermetic teaching? Had John shared his knowledge with Jesus the moment they were reunited? Arthur smiled. It was all starting to sound very logical to him.

Aphrodite's Rock was now almost out of sight and Arthur suddenly thought of something Otto had said previously.

"What did you call that rock again? Petra something?"

"Petra tou Romiou. Rock of the Greek."

"Greek is Romiou in Greek? That is odd."

"You're very sharp, Art. You know, Greece has had many names. First of all, Ellas or Ellenas, named after the mythological patriarch Hellen. When the Romans first invaded Greece, the Romans called them Graeci, but later, when all of Greece including Cyprus became absorbed by the Roman Empire, they were sometimes referred to as the Rhomioi, or Romanised citizens. I must admit it's very confusing."

Suddenly, the ship began to dance under their feet and they quickly grasped the sturdy railing. They watched in awe as the boat surged into deeper waters and across the troughs of the deeper waves. As the waves grew higher, the troughs between them appeared deeper, creating intimidating walls of water. Abruptly, as the bow cut through a large wave, the spray of the salty seawater showered the deck. Strong gusts of wind tested the sails and everyone noticed that the clipper was gaining speed rapidly. They had reached the sea current. Hadi kept a close eye on the main sails, which were taking the toughest beatings and Andrei went below deck to check the weather report again. Being an experienced sailor, he knew the weather can change rapidly on the Med and that strong gusts of wind often betray changes in pressure.

"We're being pushed hard," Hadi shouted at Otto. "We may have to reef the sails if the wind gets too strong."

Otto looked up and noticed that the laminated sails were indeed withstanding quite a bit of stress and admitted,

"Yes, it would be cruel to have damage so early on in our voyage. Do what you must."

In the meantime, Arthur had become a little grey around the nose. "I don't feel very well, I'm going back to our cabin."

Otto, who had been on a ship before, could understand very well how his friend must be feeling and encouraged him to lay on the bed for a while. Caring deeply for Arthur and at the same time not wanting him to lose his last meal anywhere near his expensive leather shoes, Otto decided to accompany him to the lower deck to make sure he was alright. Trying to take Arthur's mind off his plight by making casual conversation, Otto continued,

"Did you know that the fraction that is often used to approximate Pi is 22/7?"

Suddenly, Arthur broke loose from Otto's grip, ran back up the steps and flung himself against the railing - but even after he had vomited, he continued to feel very nauseous.

"I'm just going to stay here Otto, you go and do your thing. Okay?"

Otto felt so helpless, but then he thought of something.

"Actually, I may be able to help you get over your seasickness. Come, give me your hands."

Arthur obeyed and watched with curiosity as Otto pressed certain spots on his wrists. He had to admit that it made him feel a little bit better. "It's acupressure. Fred taught me this a while ago."

Arthur shook his head. "You just never seize to amaze me, Otto."

Andrei, who had heard the commotion, threw a water bottle toward Arthur and asked Hadi to join him in the cockpit. With an alarmed expression and a sobering tone of voice he broke the news to them.

They were heading into a severe storm.

Hadi saw the twirl on the meteorological report, approaching from the north. "That is bad news. While sailing westward, we also need to mind the *Meltemi,* coming in from the north. I suggest that once we are closer to Crete, we reef the sails the moment the wind gets too strong. Also, about our landing party on Crete; it'll be dangerous to moor when the weather is that bad. There are too many cliffs. As soon as we are in Crete's lee and sheltered from the Meltemi, we must take advantage of the westward flowing current and go straight for Malta as fast as we can, using the engine if necessary. Then maybe, just maybe, we can outrun the storm."

Andrei pursed his lips. "We have sufficient supplies and fuel to last us about three days, but Malta is still very far. If all goes well, we will just make it before running out of food supplies."

"I know, but turning back is not an option. We will chart a course for Malta."

Hadi resolutely walked out of the cockpit, realising they would now be at sea for three full days. Was it really a question of chance that their mission to ancient Akhetaten was again delayed? He would have to break the news to Georg. In the meantime he could only hope that Max wouldn't do anything stupid with Arthur's ERFAB.

Memphis, Egypt, October 5th 2011

Soongh was overjoyed when he saw a potential customer waiting outside his shop and hastily unlocked the multiple locks on the door. Pulling his pliable cheeks into his well-rehearsed smile, he humbly invited the man in and studied him. It was another Westerner, probably a German, he thought. "Welcome, sir. Ich spräche Deutsch and English."

Max could hear that his German was pronounced very badly and to avoid the labour of trying to understand it, he felt it better to stick with English, which seemed to be more familiar to the shopkeeper. As Hadi had told him that the ERFAB device looked like a normal mobile phone, he decided to come straight to the point.

"Yesterday you had a visit. There were three men - friends of mine - and one of them has forgotten his phone. I have been sent to pick it up."

Soongh was disappointed, realising that this man had no intention to buy anything. Although he did remember Otto, Arthur and Hadi, he had not noticed if they had accidently left something behind. He waddled over to the little table and checked again, even the floor, but neither of them could find anything that looked like a mobile phone.

Max scratched his head. Hadi had said that the device *had* to be there. If it really wasn't there, it would be a huge setback. He took a quick look around the shop and stared at the strange items, the souvenirs and other curiosities. "How unfortunate, but can you tell me why they were here, what they were looking for?" he queried.

Soongh anxiously rubbed his hands together and tried to recall exactly which item they had been after.

"It was a small, round, desert glass stone, the lighter shade of yellow, I believe, but sadly they didn't find it. Shall I take you to my collection?"

Max was getting curious. Though Mr Corona hadn't shared the fact that Otto Rahn was a relic hunter - going after the Holy Grail itself in the 1930s - this information was all over the Internet and he had discovered that detail on his own.

Max quickly did the math and understood that they must have come to Soongh's shop to find a certain relic. It had to be a relic that was connected to Amarna, or they wouldn't have gone there in the first place. If this relic had anything to do with pharaoh Akhenaten, then he could understand Mr Corona's interest in Otto, for Roman Corona was not only following in his ancestors' footsteps by collecting ancient books, he was also a fanatic collector of ancient relics and reliquaries. Maybe this wasn't about Otto at all. Maybe Corona was after something of much greater value.

"Yes, please. Go ahead, good man, let me see what you showed them."

While the two men walked off toward the dusty, dark room at the back of Soongh's house, Arthur's mobile ERFAB device - that had previously fallen to the ground and had accidently been kicked into a corner under a cabinet - had now started to vibrate nervously.

38

Sark, Channel Islands, October 5th 2011

The main street of The Village was almost deserted. Most of the visitors who had come to Sark that day were exploring the delights of the island and there were only a few people in the town itself. All was calm. Barry, however, was getting more and more uptight. He couldn't believe the stubbornness of the local constable, who refused to cooperate. The man clearly had no idea who he was dealing with, nor what they were up against. Barry tried one more time, "I'm telling you, sir, these people are armed and dangerous. I need more than just two officers; I need assistance from the Guernsey police to find them and bring them in."

"Armed and dangerous? Here, on Sark? You gotta be kidding mate. Do you really think that plastic ID card gives you the right to order me around? Oh hang on a tick, it's a candid camera trick, isn't it? Where's the camera?"

Constable Jones turned around, trying to spot any signs of a camera hidden somewhere out of sight. Barry rubbed his face and sighed. He had a growing feeling that his attempt to get police back-up wasn't going to work. "Alright, let's try this again; there is a dangerous criminal on the loose on the island. He has two aides and he's planning to kidnap a woman we are protecting, who is here on the island in a safe house. My orders are to bring him in with the help of the local police and since there are only three of us at the moment, I feel that we should ask for assistance. If we call the Guernsey police now, they can be here in fifteen minutes, but we do need to hurry up. The woman in question could be in danger already. My colleague is out there right now, hoping to trap them on Little Sark, but at this very moment he is out there all alone, so I suggest that we call Guernsey and then head out to Little Sark immediately to assist him."

The constable shook his head. "No mate, you are pulling my leg. There is no criminal here on the island and I am not going to call the bloody Guernsey police. Now am I making myself clear?"

Barry gave up and decided to go to La Coupée on his own, but just as he was cycling out of the main street, he spotted Manfred galloping through the fields toward The Village. He stopped and ran his hands through his hair. Obviously, something had gone very wrong at the isthmus.

Titan had no choice but to stay on the road. Although the horse that was pulling the carriage was in full gallop, he knew Barry could easily outrun them. The carriage was slowing them down.

"Chief, if you want me to catch him, I have to take the horse and disconnect the carriage. Go hide somewhere and as soon as I catch him, I will call you."

Al Din wasn't sure if that was such a good idea, but Titan didn't wait for an answer. He jumped on the back of the horse, disconnected the carriage and raced off into the direction of The Village. Al Din came to a screeching standstill when the now horseless carriage tilted over forward and scraped the road. He could only just stop himself from tumbling out. "You're insane!" he shouted after Titan, "Come back here!" but the giant didn't even turn around. Titan only had one goal: to find Manfred and make him talk. He would pick up his chief later.

Al Din climbed out of the carriage, took his bag and started to walk toward a large, stately country house that had been turned into the Stocks Hotel. He felt his pockets and smiled. His false identity papers and generosity will surely persuade the reception to give him a comfortable room and some privacy. After all, he had no choice but to wait for Titan's call and hope that he wouldn't do anything stupid, like slitting Manfred's throat.

Meanwhile, Titan dug his heels into the horse's sides, urging it to go even faster. As Manfred's horse had left a clear trail in the grass, he knew he had to be closing in on him.

He bent over and took out his Magnum, ready for confrontation. Danielle had to be somewhere and he was determined to find her. The island life was so quiet and its inhabitants so meek, that he had no fear of being caught. He thought of Al Din's helicopter and knew that if he could strike quickly and get back to his chief on time, they could all be out of there soon enough.

Barry dropped his bike and grabbed the reigns of Manfred's horse. "What happened?"

"I couldn't hold them on my own," Manfred replied, still panting. "Where the hell were you?"

"Blast! Well, we're on our own then. The constable won't take me seriously and even thinks I'm making it all up. I was just on my way to join you."

That moment, Barry spotted another rider in the distance.

"We have company. Look!"

Manfred turned and saw Titan galloping toward them at great speed.

"Come on, perhaps this will persuade the constable."

They both raced toward the police station and ducked inside to take cover. Manfred had to release the horse, hoping he would make his way home on his own. When constable Jones saw them enter the station, he stood up in an angry response. "What the hell do you think you are d..."

The sound of gunshots made them all jump behind the desk. The front window had shattered and Manfred heard his horse whinny and gallop off into the distance.

Hopefully, Elliot hadn't been hit by a bullet.

As they couldn't go outside to confront Titan, they overturned the constable's desk as a barrier. Hiding behind it, both Manfred and Barry could defend their position with their Glocks, but only until they ran out of bullets. Barry took out his mobile phone to call Jack. The situation had suddenly got serious. However, one positive thing had come from the worrisome situation they were in: Constable Jones was now finally on the phone, calling Guernsey for back up.

In the meantime, at the beautiful country house hotel, Al Din was making himself comfortable. As if this was all part of the plan, he lay down on the bed and called Lars.

"How are you holding up, son?"

Lars had wondered when his chief would call. He was getting tired of sitting at the pier.

"Never mind me, chief, have you found Danielle yet?"

"No, but Titan is busy distracting her aides, so I need you to do something for me. Get a ride to The Seigneurie and play the tourist. If you see anything suspicious, call me and I will tell you exactly what to do."

Lars was excited. Finally he had been given a mission.

"I'm on it, chief!"

Lars put his cap on, grabbed his bag and walked toward the tunnel. However, the moment he came through the exit of the tunnel, he couldn't believe his eyes. All he had seen so far was the rocky part of the island at Creux harbour and he had no idea that such natural beauty and green vistas were on the other side of the tunnel. Not knowing when or if he would be able to get a ride to The Seigneurie, he strode up the path that led to the top of the hill and chuckled. While Titan was busy 'distracting', he was being sent on the actual mission. His chief must have a lot of faith in him, but it could also mean that he might have to use his gun; kidnapping someone hardly ever happens without the use of some kind of violence. The thought was rather sobering, as he knew that avoiding violence whenever possible was the best way to remain discreet. He had held people at gunpoint before, at a gas station robbery or a mini market robbery, but he had never actually shot anyone or seriously hurt anyone physically and deep inside, he hoped he wouldn't have to.

He was already halfway to The Village when a carriage passed. He tried to hitch a ride by sticking his thumb out and was surprised that the cabby actually stopped.

"Where are you going to?" the cabby asked.

"Something called The Seigneurie, can you take me there?"

"Sure, that'll be three Pounds please."

Lars produced a five Euro note and apologised for not having any British Pounds, but the cabby had no problem taking the note instead. The cabby flicked his whip into the air and they were quickly on their way. To avoid conversation, Lars plugged in his earphones and played the music from the American rock band 'The Grateful Dead' at maximum volume. He chuckled to himself. Somehow he found the provocative music combined with the idyllic landscape very amusing.

Jack, who was still positioned at the top of the church tower, jumped when he heard his phone go off. It was agent Barry.

"Sir, we have a situation. Our plan has failed and we are now trapped at the police station. One of Al Din's assistants, the hulk, is outside shooting at us. I don't know if Al Din is with him. I thought you said there were three of them? So far we have only seen two."

Jack cursed. "Did you call for back-up?"

"Yes, sir. The constable has just made the call."

"Good. Now, buy some time and if you see a possibility, neutralise the hulk. The third guy has to be somewhere on the island. If only I knew what he looked like!"

He hung up and immediately called Georg to explain the situation. "So, none of us have seen the third person yet and I have a gut feeling he's on his way here. I need you to tell me what he looks like, so I can take him out before he finds the bunker. Do you remember enough to describe him?"

Georg thought deeply. When he was in the car with Al Din in Sion, the tall man was driving, while the other man was in the passenger seat. It was coming back to him now; the man in the passenger seat had been wearing a cap and sunglasses.

"Jack, the third guy is wearing a dark blue cap."

"Thank you, sir!"

On arrival at The Seigneurie, the first thing Lars did was check out the area that wasn't part of the public gardens. What would *he* do if he had to secure these grounds?

Lars looked around and was immediately drawn to the church and its characteristic tower with the four triangles at the top. There was a round opening at the centre of each triangle, called an *oeil-de-boeuf*. He walked to the back of the church and when he looked up again, he thought he saw something move behind one of the triangles. Immediately he ducked away and took shelter behind one of the surrounding trees. He took out his Magnum; now he knew for sure that he was in the right place. If there was a lookout post on that tower, Danielle must be somewhere close by. He scouted the surroundings from where he was standing and saw a strange folly in the distance. As the tiny, donjon shaped building was situated on the private grounds of the manor house, he had to climb a wrought iron fence to get to the folly and hoped that he hadn't triggered any security systems in doing so. Once he was over the fence, he stood still for a few seconds to make absolutely sure that no alarm was ringing. When all remained silent, he sneaked toward the folly and tried the door.

It was locked.

While cursing silently, he took out the tools he always kept with him to break into houses. Suddenly, he heard a helicopter flying overhead, but as it was set against the bright sky he could only see the silhouette and was unable to make out if it was private or military. He worked even faster, trying one tool after the other to get the lock to render. If it was indeed Al Din's helicopter, then he had to get Danielle out as quickly as possible.

Inside the bunker, Danielle froze when she heard the scratching of metal inside the lock of the door.

"Jack?" she asked softly. "Jack is that you?"

No response. Danielle didn't like that at all and crawled back behind the curtain, hiding under the bed's coverlet. Her heart was beating fast. She grabbed her mobile and called Jack.

"There's someone at the door."

Jack immediately aimed his rifle at the door of the folly and felt a jolt in his stomach when he spotted the man with the blue cap, trying to break in.

Lars was getting tired of the fussing and fired his Magnum at the bunker lock, which sprang open immediately. Danielle screamed as she saw the unknown man coming for her.

"Jack! Help me!" she screamed through her mobile.

Then suddenly, another shot was fired. Hit in the back, Lars fell down the stairs and groaned in agony. With focused resolve, attempting to overpower his pain, he stared at Danielle and tried to get up. She watched as Lars shuffled toward her on his hands and knees, still holding his Magnum in one hand and obviously suffering, but she was too horrified to feel any sympathy for him. As she had already reached the furthest end of the small bunker, she knew there was nowhere else to go.

Back in The Village, Barry and Manfred didn't have to wait long before the Guernsey police arrived. Within fifteen minutes after constable Jones had made his call, a helicopter with six armed police officers had arrived, which was now parked on a field just outside the town.

Titan, who had run out of ammunition, had tried to bolt upon seeing the helicopter landing, but was quickly overtaken by the officers. Face down, knees in his back and his arm bent behind his back to breaking point, he realised he didn't stand a chance. Using Titan's mobile, the Guernsey officers were able to find Al Din's phone signal, pointing toward a certain spot on the island and as soon as they had located his exact coordinates, the helicopter lifted off again, this time with Barry, Manfred and four agents on board, to arrest him at the country house hotel.

Al Din, who had expected a call from either Titan or Lars, was taken completely by surprise. Knowing he was too weak to flee, he wisely surrendered without a fight.

When the officers returned with Al Din, Manfred spotted Elliot in the field below. The horse looked unharmed and they were relieved to see two local inhabitants walking him back to The Seigneurie.

While still in the helicopter, Barry tried to contact Jack, but got no answer. Now seriously worried and tired of the ever grinning Al Din in front of him, he turned to constable Jones. "We have to go to The Seigneurie; Jack's in trouble."
"The Seigneurie?" queried Jones.
"Yes. It's a long story, but we need to be fast. It's a matter of life and death. We don't have a minute to lose!"

While Titan and Al Din were being locked into Europe's smallest prison - guarded by constable Jones and two police officers from Guernsey - the others took off again in the helicopter and as soon as they were hovering over the domain of the lord of Sark, Barry and Manfred stared at the grounds and spotted Jack, running toward the bunker.
They also noticed that the door was open.
"Put us down, right here, right now!" Barry shouted. Immediately they landed and both Barry and Manfred ran out, followed by the other officers. They knew it would be a matter of minutes, seconds even. Hopefully they wouldn't be too late.

Danielle pushed away Lars' groping hand. He felt himself growing weaker and getting dizzy and knew that this was not a good sign. His chief was obsessed with this woman. If he had to die trying to bring her in, he wanted at least to see her, touch her, to be able to understand why.
Suddenly, his gun dropped from his grasp and he collapsed on the floor next to Danielle's bed, clinging to the side. Feeling somewhat safer, Danielle looked him in the eyes and behind the pain she also saw intelligence, loyalty and sense of wonder. She saw that this young man had been used by Al Din to track her and did not believe that he would have done anything to harm her. So when Lars - who was clearly suffering from Jack's shot - reached out with his hand, she took it and whispered, "Poor man, what has he done to you?"
Both heard the helicopter approaching and Danielle looked at the door. "It's over now. You will soon get some help."

Sion, Switzerland, October 6th 2011

David woke up and noticed he was no longer in as much pain. He had slept a lot and had only briefly talked with Michael after he had returned from his ride with Beauséant. The white horse with black spots had clearly missed him and the few hours of trotting through the woods and galloping around the fields at Sion had been a wonderful outing for both Michael and the horse. David was happy for Michael, but he was worried about Danielle. Georg was almost always at the base and there was no mobile phone in sight. Still wired up, David was also totally dependent on the nurses, even when he had to visit the bathroom. That, he had to admit, was exceedingly humbling and very annoying.

Still being somewhat sleepy, David was startled when someone suddenly touched his arm, as he had half-expected to be alone. Turning, he looked straight into the beautiful blue eyes of Danielle.

"Hello my darling." she said softly.

"Danielle! How did you get here?"

"I arrived last night. Al Din's been caught, so I've been brought home. I'm home, David!"

At the base, Wong was working non-stop on Arthur's new ERFAB device, which would replace the one that had been lost. His head was spinning; the lack of sleep and irregular meals were now clearly having an effect on him. He seized another Mars bar and walked over to the canteen for a fresh coffee. When he returned, he placed the coffee on his working desk, next to his beloved bonsai tree, which looked terribly neglected. Wong noticed it and thought he'd give it a nice spray of source water. He walked off and returned with a sprayer, filled with pure Valais mineral water.

Just as he was about to spray the bonsai, he bumped the bottom of the sprayer against his coffee mug, which consequently toppled over and emptied its contents onto the half-finished ERFAB device.

Wong had observed it all in slow-motion.

Still in shock, he returned to his chair and slowly started to bang his head on the desk. He would never be able to finish another one on time now. The team's next mission to ancient Akhenaten was now seriously jeopardised, for Otto would never leave Arthur behind.

Wong was certain that Mr Zinkler will be terribly disappointed in him, just like his father had always been. In a sudden rage, he took his bonsai and threw it as far away as possible, smashing its terracotta pot as it came down. He immediately regretted his violence and ran toward his treasured miniature tree, which he had cherished and trimmed for so many years. Carefully he lifted the tree and removed the shards from its roots. Then he raced toward the canteen and demanded an oven dish. Everyone watched as he replanted his beloved tree in an orange-brown, clay oven dish and watered it with the sprayer's source water. He trimmed back two small, broken branches with a pair of scissors and then took a few steps back.

Everyone applauded Wong - who had hardly recovered from the initial shock - and tears were rolling over his cheeks when Georg entered the canteen to see what had happened. Wong turned to Georg and said, "What do you want first, the good news or the bad news?"

Georg stooped and replied, "The bad news, Wong. What happened?"

"I've damaged the ERFAB device, sir, I am very sorry, but the good news is, I was able to save my bonsai!"

39

Sion, Switzerland, October 8th 2011

Morning often brings a feeling of promise and on this bright, sunny day, Alfred was not only incredibly grateful to be alive; he was especially appreciative that he had got the morning off to a good start with a complete briefing from Georg. He also knew he had to take care of himself and focus on eating properly again. Just the previous day, the doctor had allowed him to swallow some liquefied food, to see if his stomach could handle it and thankfully, so far he had no discomfort; a positive sign that he body was regaining its strength and tolerance. Although he still needed a lot of rest, he seemed to be recovering well.

"I will be allowed to sit up today," he said to Georg with an awkward smile, "which I am sure will be stressful, but I can't wait to go home. I am honestly quite looking forward to joining David in my own hospital 'ward'. How's the good man doing anyway?"

"David's making a quick recovery. He's strong and now that Danielle is back, well, you know, love heals all things."

Alfred grinned and unconsciously his mind went to Otto.

"So, our field team has landed at Malta?"

"Yes, they're setting up a base on a deserted beach. They have gone through all your files now and are much better prepared than last time, so somehow, whatever happened, has happened for a reason."

"It always does. The Universe works in mysterious ways, but it's sad to hear that Otto refuses to be transported directly to Sion base in the event that he finds the stone."

"He won't leave Arthur alone on the island, but if they succeed, I can always send your private jet to Malta to fetch them."

"Yes, that is true."

Georg was still worried about Alfred's trust in Otto. What if the German did have another agenda? Seeing the otherwise so strong and powerful Alfred now so weak and vulnerable in his bed, Georg was afraid that Otto would take advantage of the situation and betray him. Georg loved Alfred like a brother and he'd be terribly upset if he were hurt.

"Why must you trust Otto so much? What if he bolts again and this time with your precious stone?"

"Oh, he won't." Alfred said resolutely. "And I will tell you why I trust him with all my heart. When I teleported Otto from his era to ours to help me find the forgotten tomb in southern France, I had brought him from 1939 to 2011. While filling him in on the missing 72 years, I had an awkward conversation with him about his employers. Obviously, we ended up discussing highly sensitive subjects concerning the holocaust, which was mostly carried out between 1939 and 1945. He refused to believe much of what I told him, because he had been brainwashed with false information and propaganda by the Nazis. Therefore I made it my job to deprogram him back to reality. I showed him not only hours and hours of archived material for him to see with his own eyes, I also showed him two movies; 'The Boy with the Striped Pyjamas' and 'The Pianist', which more or less wrapped up what I was trying to explain to him. When he came out of my private theatre, he was terribly upset and cried while trembling all over. "I have been abused!" he shouted, "They lied! They lied to me! They took advantage of me!" Of course, I understood what Otto meant."

Alfred shifted to find a more comfortable position and continued, "After all, Otto's research had indeed been abused and his legacy polluted by the actions of those who had abused him. Strangely enough, the day after, Otto confided in me. He looked as if he had not slept. He touched my arm and said, "There is something you need to know about me, Fred. One night, when I was doing my guard duties at the Buchenwald concentration camp, I shot someone who was fleeing over the fence. I thought he was a dangerous criminal, but later I found out that his only crime was having been born a Jew. I am a Jew too, through my mother! From that moment onward I had no idea what I was doing there and I just wanted to get out as quickly as possible. Afterwards, I had asked Himmler about it, wondering what had been written in my report and he had confirmed it all. Himmler had responded ever so calmly, as if I had only slapped someone's face; "Du hast eine Juden erschossen, es steht fest." I had shot a Jew. It was a fact. It was all in the report, black on white." After he had said that, Otto just stood there, gazing at the wall as if he had just seen a ghost."

Trying to maintain his composure, Alfred continued,

"Then suddenly, Otto embraced me and started to cry like I've never seen him cry, saying, "Fred, they have turned me into a murderer!" Georg, his spirit was tortured over it. His heart is not the heart of a killer."

Georg had listened to Alfred with wide eyes. He understood immediately that this was the sin Otto couldn't live with; the sin that was eating his soul.

Alfred continued with tears in his eyes, "Do not think poorly of Otto, Georg. He is a good man, he's just a victim of a very traumatic period in our history. It's not just him - there are many others who have suffered similar fates in all kinds of wars and this still goes on. Of course Otto will have his own agenda, of course he is seeking freedom, I can't blame him for that, but if you truly love someone and you want that person to trust you and love you back, then you have to let him go."

Alfred closed his eyes and allowed the tears to flow.

"… and he always comes back."

Malta, October 8th 2011

Arthur was standing in front of Hadi and Otto with his arms folded. "So, if I close my eyes and I count to ten, you will be back again?"

"That's it! That's right my friend." Otto replied, "hopefully in one piece and with the stone. Fingers crossed!"

"Good luck, go get that stone!"

Arthur took a deep breath, not sure if he could handle the stress.

If anything should go wrong, this would be the last time he'd see Otto.

"Close your eyes, Art. I'll be back before you know it."

The moment Arthur closed his eyes, Otto and Hadi pressed the button on their ERFAB devices, which would transport them to ancient Akhetaten. He started counting to ten and opened his eyes again when he heard an eerie sound in front of him. Otto and Hadi had indeed reappeared 10 seconds later. While Hadi was sitting on his knees, covering his head, Otto was stretched out on the floor and appeared to be unconscious. Both of them were bleeding from multiple wounds. Arthur was aghast. What on earth had happened?

Akhetaten, ancient Egypt, 1337 BCE

On arrival in the ancient Egyptian city of Akhetaten, Otto and Hadi looked down to see if they could see their shadows.

"Oh, thank goodness," said Hadi, while touching the sand on the floor, "we're in the right dimension, but where are we?"

They looked around and saw that they were in a forest, planted solely with banana trees. Otto closed his eyes. "Oh no, we're in the jungle. Wong must have it all wrong again!"

However, when they spotted some people in the distance, they saw clearly by the way they looked and the way they were dressed, that Otto and Hadi were in the right place after all. By observing their environment, they also noticed the remaining traces of a sand storm. Men and women wearing galabyas were tending to the plants and cleaning out the irrigation system. There was a path not far from them, so they quickly put away their mobile ERFEB devices and walked toward the farmers.

"Remember what I told you." Hadi whispered, "Keep quiet, let me do all the talking. They are used to strangers here, but you, my dear man, will still be the centre of attention with your white skin and blue eyes."

Otto zipped his lips. "No worries, I'll keep my mouth shut."

They were surprised to find everyone so friendly. As soon as the farmers - who were tending to the banana farm - spotted

Otto and Hadi, they were welcomed with open arms and brought into town as if they were long lost friends. Immediately they were offered food and drink and while they were eating, Hadi finally found the courage to share with them the reason they had come to Akhetaten; to become students at the pharaoh's mystery school.

Everyone fell silent.

An elderly man lifted his hand and waved it at them in a disapproving manner. "That is a big secret, my friend. How do you know about the school?"

"Oh, well, you know how it goes, the word is spreading fast. Do you know how we can join?"

The man shook his head in an awkward way and they were not sure whether it was a yes or a no. It was uncommitted.

"You must go to the priests. They will know."

Hadi touched his heart and thanked him for his advice and Otto copied it, mispronouncing the word for 'thank you' and making everyone laugh out loud. He studied his thumbs and smiled. What's new...

After this, the atmosphere was back to normal again and Otto and Hadi finished their meals with gratitude before departing toward the Aten temple.

"They were actually very friendly, don't you think?" said Otto with a wide smile of relief.

Hadi nodded. "Yes, but we must tread carefully. Obviously the mystery school is still a big secret and its secrets may be guarded well. At least we have one advantage now; we can recognise Meryra, but also Her-uben, who has already joined them. If we can talk to him, we may be able to get an introduction."

"Hadi, you never cease to surprise me. What a clever plan! But remember, Her-uben was caught snooping around the temple and arrested before he was initiated. What if the same happens to us?"

Hadi smiled. "Trust me, I have studied the Amarna period well. Your chief has chosen me for a reason."

Otto studied his travel companion and pursed his lips while slowly nodding his head. "Hmmm, I had actually figured that out already, Hadi."

They enjoyed walking through the busy, but now also quite dusty town of Akhetaten and Otto couldn't help touching everything. This time they could smell all the scents; the freshly baked bread, the smoke coming off of the many fires and ovens, even the cattle, as well as their dung. This real dimension enabled them to also see the ancient town of Akhetaten 'unveiled', without the haze of the bubble they had been in last time, which had been the side effect of Wong's miscalculation. They noticed how most people were skinny, as if they were underfed.

Although they were happy to see their own shadows, Otto in particular felt how the hot sun was beginning to burn his white skin. Remembering what they were actually there for, he checked his purse underneath his robe and felt the stone that was inside it. It had to match the Eye of Ra or he wouldn't be able to switch them. The priest would surely notice the difference.

Getting into the temple took no effort at all, as it was a public place in which everyone was allowed to enter to worship Aten. People with short brooms were sweeping out the sand that had been blown into every corner, nook and cranny. When Hadi inquired after Her-uben, a priest called Panehsy approached them. He asked Otto and Hadi to wait in one of the niches that provided some welcome shade in the otherwise roofless temple. They watched the priests use the many small altars to offer bread and fruit to the sun god Aten before the people were allowed to consume it.

"This is customary, explained Hadi, "it allows the KA energy to enter the food. All food must be impregnated with the god's life giving rays, or all the food you eat is dead, unable to give life. Look around you; all of nature is worshipping the sun. Plants reach toward the sky, the branches of the trees grow upward as if they are in silent prayer and flowers turn their heads to face the sun, so that its life-bringing rays can touch their seeds and pollen. If all of nature worships the sun, the Aten, then who are we to deny Him?"

Otto had a somewhat quizzical expression. "You sound like a converted Atenist, my friend, but I see what you mean."

They did not have to wait long before Her-uben arrived and recognised him immediately, although he, of course, had not been able to see them the last time they were in the temple.

Her-uben was curious. "What can I do for you, my friends?" Hadi immediately invited him to sit with them.

"We would like to become initiates, like you."

Her-uben was aghast. "But how do you know I am an adept? That is a closely held secret!"

Hadi touched his lips with his index finger and assured him that his secret was safe. "All we want is to become students of the pharaoh's mystery school."

Her-uben was silent for a long moment, but then spoke resolutely, "Alright, follow me. I can only bring you to Meryra, who may have some time for you now. Come, follow me."

The three men walked deeper into the temple, where it was less busy. At the far end, Her-uben asked Otto and Hadi to wait, while he himself went into one of the houses where the most important priests lived. When he came back out, Meryra was with him. Otto and Hadi felt honoured to actually meet the second high priest after High Priest Akhenaten. This was the man whom Alfred thought was Aaron.

"Peace be upon you, my friends. Her-uben has told me you would like to become initiates. I am surprised that so many people can find us. The news must travel fast, but before I can take this up with the pharaoh, I need to talk to you in private and ask you a few questions. Let us go inside, so we can be alone."

Hadi touched his heart and bowed in gratitude for the priest's time. Again, Otto copied the gests.

As soon as they were inside, they could see that the tiny room hardly had any comfort. There was a low bed on the floor as well as several large cushions and a beautiful earthenware decanter with a very long neck, which looked dangerously fragile. Meryra allowed them to sit down and offered them some water, but both Otto and Hadi knew that they couldn't drink anything, unless it had sufficient alcohol in it. Having had plenty of food and wine only a short while ago, they politely refused. Meryra sat down and closed his eyes, as if he was trying to meditate, but the conversation that followed, almost made Hadi forget their mission.

"The Mystery School is not just a school that teaches knowledge; it is a school that teaches life and the Alchemy of Life. Before we can burst into flower like a rose, we must grow from seed for many years and produce leafs and branches first. Only when we are strong - with enough experience and understanding - we will be able to produce the buds, which then turn into flowers with the aid of Aten."

Meryra looked at them with a most sincere expression.

"Are you strong enough? This is not a study you enter lightly. It is the start of a new life and a new way of life."

Hadi, who had dreamed of this ever since he had studied the Amarna period and the Egyptian Mystery School teachings, nodded without even looking at Otto, who had no idea of what had just been said. Hadi was so wrapped into the uniqueness of that moment, that he had forgotten to translate Meryra's words. However, being afraid to interrupt the conversation - which seemed to be going according to Hadi's satisfaction - Otto decided not to ask.

"You have come to Akhetaten on a very special day." Meryra explained with some degree of caution. "The sandstorm has mercilessly blown out the eternal holy flame of the Aten lamp. Therefore, the pharaoh and the queen, accompanied by the royal family, will be arriving here shortly to re-ignite the holy flame above the main altar. To honour this flame - this holy union - we will celebrate this like we would a holy day, starting at sunset, which will last for 24 hours. The opening of the Eye of Ra will be a special event and you are welcome to witness it."

Hadi almost couldn't suppress his enthusiasm and he bowed his head in sincere gratitude. "We would be most honoured."

In the next hour, Hadi and Otto tried to make themselves useful by helping to clean the temple, which was much appreciated.

"To be of service is the duty of all people, from farmer to pharaoh," Hadi explained. "No one should do nothing when others are at work around you. However, it also serves another purpose. This way we will be seen as part of the 'crew' and it should protect us from being escorted out of the temple when the pharaoh arrives."

"The only thing that bothers me is the fact that I cannot boast about this!" Otto complained. He always loved to impress people by recounting his adventures. Being a witness to an important historical event that has been lost in time would have been a mighty tale to tell, but he understood all too well that this mission was secret.

When the pharaoh and his family arrived - once more surrounded and followed by the chariots and foot soldiers of the police - everything was ready for the ritual. Meryra was waiting at the altar and everyone became quiet in anticipation. This time, Meryra was wearing a larger hat, also white and the same beautifully pleated, white linen skirt he had worn last time. Nefertiti was dressed in the same way too, although this time, her white dress bared much more skin. The royal daughters were also wearing beautiful white dresses. They noticed immediately that Akhenaten - who looked very impressive in his thick, double wig of black, beaded hair - was not wearing his false beard. Neither was he wearing the high blue crown. Instead he was wearing a beautiful blue and gold striped headscarf and a breastplate that looked a lot like the one that had been found in Tutankhamen's tomb. The sun's rays were now straight above him at a certain angle. Then, seemingly from out of nowhere, Akhenaten produced a black staff with a rounded top that immediately drew Otto's attention. He elbowed Hadi and pointed at it. "Look! It's the stone. Do you see it? It's inside the rod's top piece."

Hadi became anxious and put his hand on his forehead. "Blast! How on earth are we going to get to it now!"

"I don't know. We will wait and see where the pharaoh takes it. Like last time, we will have to try and follow him."

"That will not be so easy, he is never left alone. It's going to be close to impossible to pull this off!"

The pharaoh had already started to speak and Hadi stopped to concentrate on what he was saying.

"Oh Aten, great Father who is in the Heavens, hear me, your son, Neferkheperura, Sole-one-of-Ra, whom you have taught your ways and your mightiness. You are the All and the All that is in the All. I implore you to open your Eye and give us your Light so that all of your children may witness your eternal presence here on earth in this Holy Place."

Then followed a series of spells, which Hadi could not translate. He did understand that it was the spell for the deity to enter the lamp, which was placed on the altar. The lamp, which was filled with the finest olive oil, had a small cotton wick. Akhenaten raised the staff and held it so that the stone, the Eye of Ra - at right angles to the sun - filtered the sun in a concentrated beam toward the wick. The wick began to smoke and an instant later, the wick caught fire and the lamp was lit.

It was true. The stone had indeed been used as a lens, just like Alfred had expected. The holy light was symbolised as an eternal flame; a flame that wasn't supposed to go out. As the people of Akhetaten had found the fact that the sand storm had blown out the flame a bad omen, the pharaoh could only hope that restoring the fire to the lamp would also restore the faith of the people.

Because Otto had come from a mixed Jewish and Lutheran background, he knew that in the Lutheran church, the ever-burning sanctuary light represented the presence of God. He also thought of the *ner tamid;* the sacred eternal light that burned in every synagogue and remembered reading about the Roman goddess Vesta, in whose temple burned an eternal fire, painstakingly guarded by the Vestal Virgins who were its sacred keepers. This eternal flame, featured in so many religions, could perhaps have originated right here, in Akhetaten, during a ritual much like this one and though it was hot, Otto's skin was covered in goose bumps with the insight on the magnitude of this moment.

Again the pharaoh spoke words Hadi could not translate and finally, the ritual ended. It was clear that everyone was in awe of what had just happened. Most of the witnesses to this unique ritual prayed silently at the foot of the lamp on the altar before they left. Hadi was so caught up in this historic moment, that Otto had to help him snap out of it by tugging him toward Meryra, who was now holding the staff of Aten-Ra. "It's now or never, Hadi!"

Walking against the stream of people - who were now walking toward the entrance, following the royal family - they spotted Meryra walking to the far end of the temple, probably to take the stone out of the staff and reunite it with its black sister. Otto and Hadi knew that they could disappear quickly by using their devices, so they called on their deepest courage that could only be equalled by the world-weary with nothing left to lose.

Meryra noticed the two men - who had previously been so anxious to join the mystery school and whom he had invited so generously to the unique ritual - approaching him with great haste. He wondered what they wanted of him now and why they would be so bold as to follow him to this sacred part of the temple, interrupting him in his holy duties, putting away the holy staff and the holy Eye of Ra. It was not only very rude, it was also a violation of trust.

Quickly, Meryra took the white stone out of the headpiece, closed his hand tightly around it and placed his fist behind his back. "You are overstepping your privileges!" he said angrily.

Hadi, who felt terrible about having to be so persuasive, had thought up a clever plan and put up both his hands in an attempt to calm the priest.

"We come in peace, my friend, but we have an urgent matter to discuss with you. There are people who want to steal the stone. You need to hide it in a safe place."

Otto smiled. That was a fantastic plan. He looked at Hadi and had to admit that Alfred had indeed made the right choice in picking Hadi as their guide. Meryra seemed to fall for it. Ever since the sand storm had blown out the holy light of Aten, everyone had felt as if something bad was going to happen and Meryra believed Hadi.

However, the very moment that Meryra moved his fist forward and opened it to show them the stone, Otto snatched it from his hand and made a run for it, leaving Hadi no choice but to run after him.

Meryra cried out for help. "Stop them! Don't let them escape!"

While running, Otto took out the fake stone and dropped it in such a way that Meryra saw it fall. Both of them knew they could never escape and while running, they took out their devices, ready to press '1'.

After Meryra had picked up the fake stone, he immediately saw that it wasn't the real Eye of Ra. This stone was much brighter, although it did have the required round, 1,5 mm shallow indentation that enabled it to become a lens. Alfred had thought of everything, knowing that the Urim, apart from being a divination stone, also had to be able to produce a ray of light to set something on fire. Meryra stopped and turned back, confident that the thieves would be caught any minute now, but he couldn't help wondering why those two men would want to replace the stone with another, similar one.

Otto and Hadi were now heading into the crowd and the police, who surrounded the royal family in an attempt to protect them. However, it wasn't the police they needed to worry about. Several people were now shouting, "Thieves! Desecrators of the holy temple! Kill them!"

Two men grabbed them and threw them onto the rocky ground. Quickly, Otto and Hadi took out their devices in an attempt to escape their fate, but a sharp stone hit Hadi in the face and the impact caused him to drop his device. A larger stone hit Otto's back the moment he covered his head. In fearful anticipation they gazed at the crowd, now forming a circle around them. Slowly, people began to pick up more stones and sharp rocks from the ground. The royal family had stopped to see what was going on. When Akhenaten saw that the two men were about to be stoned, he raised his arms and protested, but General Ay, who was afraid for the safety of the royal family, interfered. Ay was adamant; it was never wise to interfere when a crowd was angry. As if the pharaoh had no input, the general turned the chariots around and the royal family was escorted back to the palace in full trot. It seemed that Otto and Hadi would not be able to escape their fate.

Still hiding his head underneath his arms, Otto turned to Hadi, "Press the button!"

"Do you have the stone?"

"Yes! Press the bloody button!"

A shower of stones now came down on poor Otto and Hadi, who found it almost impossible to press '1' while they were being mercilessly stoned by the angry people of Akhetaten. To be able to press the button, they'd have to use their hands and at that moment, their heads would be unprotected and vulnerable. They took a deep breath, simultaneously reached for their devices and pressed '1'.

Malta, October 8th 2011

When Arthur was faced with the two men covered in blood, he was terribly shocked. While Hadi was trying to get up, moaning and groaning, Otto was still on the ground.

He didn't move.

"Otto! Are you okay? Talk to me, buddy!"

However, Otto did not react.

Hadi turned toward him and they now noticed the wound on Otto's head. It had clearly been hit by a stone at the exact moment they had pressed '1'. The stone had even come with him. It was lying next to his head, covered in blood.

Using a handkerchief, Arthur wiped the blood from Otto's face and slowly, Otto opened his eyes. Arthur, who was overjoyed that Otto had come round, couldn't help making an ironic remark. "I said, 'go get that stone,' not 'go get stoned!'"

Otto smiled broadly and his locked with Hadi's.

"Thank God! We made it!"

A moment later, Hadi, who was pressing a paper tissue against the bleeding wound on his cheek, explained to Georg what had happened. Alfred, who sat next to Georg, grabbed the phone straight out of Georg's hand the very moment he heard that Otto had been hurt.

"Hadi, is it serious? He's breathing isn't he?"

Hadi, who recognised Alfred's voice, immediately stood upright in an automatic response. "Yes sir, he has just taken a nasty blow to the head, but he's awake."

"Do you think he can travel?"

"No sir, he really can't fly in this condition. The wound looks serious, it probably should have stitches and he should rest. I believe he would be best off in his cabin on the Laurin. We do have the stone, though. What are your orders, sir?"

Alfred sighed and thought for a moment. He remembered the vision he had had while he was having his near-death experience and wondered if the port that he saw, with the Templar ships and the chapel on the rock, was a clue to a destination. In his mind's eye he saw a chapel on a rock, which then became illuminated with a bright light. Then he remembered a document he had seen earlier that year. A document that was part of the Tomar Templar files he had studied for the previous mission. In it was a list of sacred items and relics that had been brought to a certain port in the western Mediterranean.

In a sudden epiphany, he remembered the name of the port. At the end of the 12th century, the Headquarters of the Knights Templar were situated in the ancient Castrum of Caucoliberis; present day Collioure.

"I want you to set course for the harbour of Collioure, in southern France." said Alfred resolutely. "For some reason, I feel that the stone has to go there. Hopefully, by the time you arrive, Otto will be able to travel by plane. I will arrange for the transportation from there. Keep the stone safe, don't let anyone see it."

Hadi nodded. "Aye, sir!"

All stared at the Eye of Ra. Otto had shown so much courage that Hadi almost felt humble. He hoped with all his might that Max wouldn't find the ERFAB device and that they would be able to complete the mission successfully.

For all their sakes.

40

Collioure, France, October 12th 2011

Powerful waves thrashed persistently against the Laurin as it approached the bay where the Pyrenees plunge into the Mediterranean. The ancient port, where many treasures, relics and saints had come ashore, leaned casually against the sloping black volcanic cliffs of the bay. Otto, Arthur and Hadi had become pleasantly accustomed to the salty scent of the sea, the cries of the seagulls, the sometimes forceful gales and the rocking of the waves. The sky was blue and clear, as the strong wind had blown all the clouds away. The black sails were filled and taut, pushing the clipper ever forward and the team would arrive at the harbour of Collioure earlier than they had anticipated.

The two crew members, who had been operating the boat since they had left Cyprus, lowered the sails as they approached the harbour entrance and dropped the anchor where it was still deep. Because the clipper was too big to dock at a small berth, it was carrying a lifeboat on each side of the ship, one of which would be used to take the passengers to the pier. Otto, whose head injury had healed well enough, stretched and turned to Arthur, who was standing behind him on the deck. "I am looking forward to being on solid ground again and to having a real coffee!"

"Absolutely! And I have some good news for you. Hadi just asked me to tell you that he will stay with the boat until our transportation arrives, so we can go ashore earlier. We don't have to stay on the ship until two o'clock."

Otto looked at Arthur with welcome surprise. "Oh hey, that's awfully nice of him. Someone does need to stay behind to keep an eye on the ship and to be honest, I am happy it's Hadi. I still don't trust Andrei. He's been on his phone a lot. He was the first to leave the ship when we were on the island of Mallorca to get supplies and I have no idea what he'd been up to. He came back very late that night, do you remember?

By the way, I noticed that even Hadi has been inseparable from his phone this morning. He looks a little uptight."
Arthur shook his shoulders and didn't think too much of it. "They're probably just talking to their families, keeping them posted. Are you coming? I'm going to get my bag."

Collioure was the last stop for the Laurin before she would be taken to her winter dock and over the past hours, Otto had been busy writing his report for Alfred. Their mission had been completed and they were now preparing to return to the base in Sion. To ensure a safe journey, Alfred had sent his private jet to Perpignan to transport them, their luggage and the Eye of Ra to Switzerland. The van, which would collect them from the harbour, would be there at 14.00 hours, so they still had some time to kill.

Otto's suspicions, however, proved to be well founded. Hadi was indeed uptight and once he had seen Arthur go down to his cabin, he took advantage of the situation and tried to lure Otto away from the ship, preferably without the stone. With a broad smile, he walked up to Otto. "Hey, I was thinking, as I am staying here anyway and you only need to be at the pier at 14.00 hours, why don't you just leave the luggage here for now, get off the boat, have a coffee, visit the castle, have a nice lunch and then come back to the ship to get the luggage. What do you say?"

Despite the gnawing feeling that he should be cautious, Otto's eagerness to get ashore ruled his decision.

"Sounds good, my friend. I will tell Arthur."

Hadi was relieved; it was all going according to plan. He had to be alone on the ship for the next few hours. Earlier that morning, private detective Max Müller had sent him an urgent text message, which had given him a terrible shock, saying, 'Max here, I have the device. You are being watched from the cliffs. Give a signal the moment you are alone. Then I will teleport myself to you. Cooperate, for your family's sake.' So the moment the sloop took off toward the dock, Hadi scrutinised the view of the cliffs above the town.

He could see a red sports car, parked at one of the viewpoints and waved in its direction as a signal to Roman Corona that he could go ahead and call Max. Upon spotting the pre-arranged signal, Corona drove like a madman toward the town centre and parked the car boldly on the side of the pavement. Excitedly, Corona took out his mobile phone and speed-dialled a number.

"Max, where are you? Do you have the device ready?"

"I'm in the Memphis Museum, Mr Corona and yes I am holding the device right now, but you have no idea what I had to go through to get it! Do you know who had it all along? The antiques dealer, Soongh! The price he asked was extortion! As far as he's concerned, he's been paid him what he was trying to extort, but in reality I only gave him 10% of his asking price in real notes, the rest is fake paper money. Hahahaha!"

Corona, who was running down to the docking pier and really didn't have any time to chat, was irritated at Max's eternal self-worship. Grinding his teeth, he snapped loudly, "I don't care! Do you have the device ready?"

"Yes of course! I have already selected number '3', which will take me directly to Hadi."

"Then press it, you fool! Now!!"

Max leaned over the railing that separated the visitors from the famous museum piece below and watched the caretaker meticulously dusting the gigantic horizontal statue of the old pharaoh Ramses II, which was too damaged to stand upright. He swallowed nervously, as this was the first time he would be time travelling. He had no idea what it would feel like. His finger trembled and he had just found the courage to press the button, when someone tapped on his shoulder. Taken by surprise, he turned and looked into the angry eyes of Mr Soongh, whose fast approaching fist boxed him backwards over the railing and onto the floor, landing him next to the giant statue with a dusty thump. The ERFAB device fell onto the pharaoh's chest and slid off to rest in his majesty's armpit.

The shock of the fall, however, had activated the signal and just when the irritated caretaker wanted to flick the device off with his duster, the entire colossus of Ramses was transported to the Laurin, which immediately exploded from the pressure. The weight of the statue took down the entire clipper and within seconds it had sunk to the bottom.

A moment later, coughing and gasping for air, the shocked caretaker in his white galabya surfaced next to the statue. Behind him, his duster popped up, accompanied by a large air bubble. He suppressed the urge to grab it and tried to keep himself above the surface of the water by paddling wildly like a frenzied dog to stay afloat. Now, almost entangled in his long robe, which was floating around him like a giant white jellyfish, he desperately searched for something to hold on to. However, he saw that he was not too far from the beach. Feeling the surge of a tidal wave, he allowed the force of it to carry him to the shore. Trying not to bump into the floating furniture the mini tsunami had swept off the boulevard, he safely reached the beach the moment the tidal wave retreated around him. Completely shocked and bewildered, he gazed at his new environment with open mouth and witnessed how the great King Ramses stared back at him with a granite smile. Aghast and dismayed, but thankful to be alive on dry land, the diligent caretaker finally broke down and cried.

Meanwhile on the boulevard, Corona had been struck dumb by the entire scene. He realised very well what had happened and cursed Max for being so stupid. Having now lost his desired relic, the only thing left for him to do was to follow Otto and Arthur, who were now walking away from the boulevard. In minutes, helicopters from Collioure's naval base had swooped in to check out the harbour from the air. Also the police had just arrived and both villagers and visitors were now gathering on the boulevard with curiosity to see what had happened. It was, needless to say, a remarkably strange sight that no one could really fathom - the gigantic pharaoh starkly staring back at them as if he had just taken command of the area, looking very much like an Egyptian version of the ancient Colossus of Rhodes.

Corona noticed Otto and his friend, walking away from the scene and saw that Otto was on his mobile phone. He wondered who he was talking to; who Otto was working for. Careful not to be seen, he approached them from behind a windscreen and could now overhear the conversation.

"Fred, the Laurin just exploded! Yes, the Eye of Ra was on board, but also Hadi, all our research, your secret files and just about everything we possess. A leak? A leak? The whole damn boat is kissing the harbour floor!"

Arthur touched Otto's arm and persuaded him to move on, but then, as they turned around, they now saw the Colossus of Memphis sticking out of the water in the harbour. Otto was just about to get back to Alfred when he spotted Corona, who was looking straight at them, standing only a few meters away. Corona smiled sourly, "So we meet again."

Otto pointed in dismay at the gigantic statue of the pharaoh.

"Did you do that?"

"No, I didn't. That was Max. He had found your device, which you conveniently left in Memphis and he was just about to teleport himself on board, take the stone and disappear, when suddenly, this monstrosity arrived instead."

Corona, who was more than just a little bit irritated, waved at the statue with uncontrolled drama, befitting to a native of Rome. Letting his emotions take over, he made matters even worse when he pulled his gun from his pocket.

Arthur walked backwards , holding up his hands. "You gotta be kidding, not here, not among all these people!"

However, Corona was serious. He grabbed Otto's arm, turned him around and pressed the cold metal into his back.

"Come on, move." With a maniacal tone of disdain mixed with pleasure, he added, "There's no way am I letting you out of my sight ever again, Mr Rahn."

Like cattle, Corona drove them toward his car, which was situated close to the parking lot on the side of the road.

If it hadn't been for the explosion of the clipper, the police would surely have had the car removed by now. Knowing that Otto couldn't drive, Corona threw the keys toward Arthur, while he himself jumped onto the backseat. He carefully held the two men at gunpoint, so that neither of them would risk doing anything silly.

Corona looked around feverishly and decided to take advantage of the commotion. "Drive! Go left!"

Arthur started the engine of the red Maserati GranCabrio Sport and despite the tricky situation they were in, he thoroughly enjoyed hearing the roaring sound and feeling the heavy vibration of the engine. Respectfully, he drove onto the road. While looking to his right, he winked an eye at Otto, who immediately understood his silent language and braced himself. Suddenly, Arthur went into reverse as fast as he could and crashed violently into the public toilet building. Corona, who was sitting in the back, had taken the full brunt of the blow and was now unconscious. Losing no time, they both leapt out of the car and raced off toward the castle grounds. While jumping up the castle steps, Arthur couldn't resist looking at the car. "Damn, that hurt!"

Otto touched his friend's arm. "Are you hurt?"

"No, but it was painful to crash that amazing car!!"

Otto chuckled as he looked over his shoulder, but then, suddenly, his face went pale.

Corona was no longer in the car.

Sion, Switzerland, October 12th 2011

Alfred refused to panic. Panicking never solves anything, it just eats away precious energy and prevents thinking straight. He knew that this was the day when the Laurin would reach the harbour of Collioure and he had expected Otto to call, but never had he expected something like this to happen.

Who would want to blow up Otto's boat?

Georg had briefed him on Max Müller, the private detective. Hadi had explained to him that Max was working for Roman Corona, someone Otto had confided to a few months ago.

He knew that Max was pursuing Otto, but had hoped that Hadi had shaken him off the moment they were teleported to Cyprus. However, now it seemed like Max and Corona had the winning hand.

Turning on the TV in his hospital room to follow the news station reports, Alfred couldn't believe his eyes when he saw the gigantic statue of Ramses II, sticking out of Collioure harbour. The colossus was being filmed from both the port boulevard and from a helicopter. He rubbed his face and groaned at the thought of it all. Then he called Georg to exchange thoughts.

"So, my guess is, that the third ERFAB device has been found and someone obviously wanted to be teleported to Hadi when everything went wrong. There must be a way to use the ERFAB to undo this situation?"

The phone went silent for a moment, but then suddenly, an excited Wong came to the phone. "I have the perfect solution. No worries, sir, I'm on it. I will solve this!"

Alfred smiled sourly, knowing that Wong was a brilliant scientist, but that his low self-esteem and flighty personality had already contributed to some serious and disappointing failures. He hoped with all his heart that Wong had indeed found a way to repair these last 30 minutes. Not only would it restitute Hadi's life and secure the Eye of Ra, it would also be incredibly good for Wong's lagging self-esteem.

It was now or never.

"Do your magic, Wong."

Collioure, France, October 12th 2011- 30 minutes earlier

Hadi looked at the cliffs above the town and could see a red sports car parked on one of the viewpoints. He waved at it as a pre-arranged signal to Roman Corona that he could go ahead and call Max. On spotting the signal, Corona drove like a madman toward the town centre and parked the car boldly on the side of the pavement. Excitedly he took out his mobile phone and speed-dialled a number.

"Max, where are you? Do you have the device ready? Max!"

However, it was not Max's voice on the other end of the phone.

"You must be Roman Corona," said Georg. "What business do you have with Mr Adler?"

Corona was aghast. "Where's Max?"

"Max is here, safely transported to our headquarters the moment he activated the device. He won't be able to do your dirty job for you now, though, but I have asked you a question. What business do you have with Mr Adler?"

Corona disconnected and stared at the Laurin with a pale face. They were on to him! Who *were* they? Realising that the desired stone was still on board, he simply needed another way of getting to it. Then, from the corner of his eye, he noticed that Otto and Arthur were having a coffee on one of the terraces on the boulevard. Corona walked over to them; he'd simply have to carry this out without Max.

Otto was just about to call Alfred when a text message came in. He showed it to Arthur. "It's a message from Georg. It says, 'Corona is near, keep him busy, the police are on their way. We also have Max.' Wow! How did that happen?"

Arthur looked around and felt a violent surge in his stomach when he spotted Corona. "There he is!"

"Just keep calm; let me do the talking." said Otto softly.

Corona slowed his pace the moment he saw he'd been spotted. He smiled, "Why, what a coincidence to see you here! This is such a beautiful place, isn't it? I see you have come with your new boat! Do you like her?"

"Roman, my man! Good to see you! How have you been? Sit down, have a coffee!"

Corona was surprised to find Otto being so friendly and immediately became suspicious. How much did they know? Would he play along? Maybe he had no choice. He had to get to the stone somehow.

"No coffee for me, thank you, but I will have a seat. So how does she sail? May I come on board?"

Otto shook his head. "No, Roman. Sorry, not today."

The entire atmosphere changed when Otto's face became stern. Corona disliked his piercing look and began to feel uncomfortable. Turning to Arthur in an attempt to break the sudden icy barrier, he started, "So you two are still together then?"

Arthur looked at Otto, who's expression had softened a bit. Not waiting for Arthur to answer, Otto boldly said, "Back off, Corona, he's way out of your league."

Arthur was surprised. Otto had never hinted that Roman was also gay.

The police approached and Otto casually pointed at the Laurin, drawing Corona's attention to it, so he wouldn't see the team closing in on him. "She is a beauty, isn't she? She sails like a queen. We were even able to outrun a storm."

One of the officers was now at the table. "That red sports car, does it belong to any of you?" he demanded.

Otto immediately pointed at Corona, who didn't understand the situation.

"I'm afraid you will have to come with me, please, sir."

The moment Corona got up from his seat, the other officer turned him around and cuffed him. Corona was aghast. "Hey, what's going on? So I parked my car in an awkward spot. Give me a fucking fine and let me go!"

However, the police officers didn't respond and took him away. The moment Corona was out of hearing range, Otto phoned Georg to brief him on the situation.

Georg was pleased. "Good to hear that went well. I will see you in a few hours' time at the manor house in Sion. Oh and don't forget to bring the stone, will you?"

Sion, Switzerland, October 22nd 2011

The celebration at Sion was the first get-together in quite some time with Alfred present in the dining hall. His appearance had changed dramatically since he had lost so much weight and he was still on a ruthless diet, but thankfully he was still alive and healing well. The festive occasion at the manor house that evening was not only in celebration of Alfred's home coming, but also to toast to the successful mission and Danielle's safe return.

It was getting late, but everyone was still at desert, laughing and feeling grateful that they had all made it through the horrible past weeks. Even Michael was still at his father's side, seriously considering taking Alfred's offer to study in Sion rather than in London. David now occupied an important position at Danielle's side and was therefore directly under Alfred in the role of protecting Danielle and her baby. Michael - being David's son - was therefore now looked upon as an important member of the SBS-Sion family. David's wound had healed well, although it was still a bit painful at times.

Alfred gazed with appreciation at each person seated around the table. He was so proud of Georg, who had successfully taken over all operations while he was at the clinic. The two men had grown even closer over the past 10 days.

Alfred's eyes went from Georg to Hadi, without whom the entire mission to ancient Akhetaten would not have been possible. Wong was sitting proudly at Alfred's left hand, feeling more confident than ever before. If it hadn't been for him, Hadi would not have been there today. Clever Wong had come up with the idea of writing a letter to himself and Georg after the explosion of the Laurin, explaining what had happened. It had enabled him to change future events. He had simply sent the letter by ERFAB, going back in time just one hour. The letter had landed on his own desk in front of his nose. After reading the letter, Wong knew exactly what was going to happen if he didn't intervene and had immediately informed Georg. All he had to do was to find the signal of the lost ERFAB device in order to transport its user to the lab, so the moment Max had activated the device in Memphis, Wong received the signal and had him teleported to Sion immediately.

The complex plan had worked flawlessly.

Alfred was also proud of Arthur, who had been a great assistant to Otto. However, Alfred couldn't help being a little envious of the young man, who was clearly much loved by Otto. Discovering these feelings, Alfred became annoyed with himself; realising his own desire to be closer to Otto than he already was, should not engender jealousy of Arthur. Still, he was pleased to see them both happy and had offered both Otto and Arthur permanent places on the Sion team. Alfred had high hopes that this time, Otto would stay. On the other hand, he knew that Otto was born with itchy feet and that he would leave Sion as soon as he felt he could and then, Alfred would miss him dearly.

On Alfred's right hand sat the beautiful Danielle, who had been through so much. Fortunately, both she and her unborn baby were in good form and Al Din was now no longer a threat.

Alfred was pleased.

He stood up and ticked his water glass with a knife. "Alright everyone, I have an important announcement to make."

Everyone went quiet, not sure whether to feel excited or alarmed.

"Over the past weeks we have all gone through a difficult time, but we have all made it. Although some of us are still somewhat weak, overwhelmed or simply exhausted - and I must admit I am all of these - our missions have been successful. The bad guys have been caught and locked up and I have survived tricky surgery that has - as you can see - knocked the wind out of me. However, I also have some news to share."

Alfred shuffled a mobile phone across the table toward Arthur, who immediately recognised it as his own mobile. Alfred understood that Arthur must be anxious to check his messages, to see if his parents had responded yet, so he gave Arthur a quick nod, encouraging him to go ahead and do it privately. Arthur's eyes grew big when he read his mother's message, saying that they loved him back and that they would like to talk soon. Otto, who had leaned over, also read the message and gently boxed Arthur's shoulder.

"You see? All they needed was some time."

Next, Alfred produced a small silver box that everybody expected to contain the two stones, the Urim and Thummim, now again reunited. However, when he opened it, it contained *three* stones; the Eye of Ra or the Urim, the Eye of Horus or the Thummim and a third stone.

Otto's jaw dropped when he recognised it. "But… that's the fake stone I left behind for Meryra to find! How on earth did you get this?"

Alfred laughed out loud. "Well, Otto, while you were at sea, healing from your head wound, Georg and I had a bit of an adventure of our own, isn't that right, Georg?"

Georg, who had been the usual quiet one at the table all evening, couldn't help looking a little bit mischievous and even produced a smile. Alfred continued with a joyous tone, "A short time back I had a vision of Collioure, which reminded me of an old and dusty Templar file from Tomar that I had browsed through earlier this year. I found out that on a certain date and time, a Templar ship had arrived, carrying several relics and sacred items from Malta and Cyprus. Among the objects in the cargo was a monstrance, holding a miraculous host. Inlaid in this monstrance, which had come from Cyprus, there was a very bright stone. It was a holy stone from Jerusalem. In 597 BCE, King Nebuchadnezzar II of Babylon had laid siege to the city and many relics, holy items and scrolls were consequently carried to safety in secret, to protect them from falling into enemy hands. The Thummim, as I have already explained, was taken to Shur, where it was dug up many centuries later by the archaeologist Flinders Petrie. The Urim was taken to Cyprus, where, many years later, a local artisan used it to ornate this holy monstrance. The Knights Templar, who had discovered the monstrance, brought it to Collioure, where it rested for three days and three nights in a particular room inside the fort before it was taken elsewhere. Georg thought it would be worth going there to see if he could find it. So, when we were certain of the date and we had the exact coordinates, Wong transported Georg to that particular location inside the fort where the monstrance was kept. Tell them what happened, Georg!"

Alfred, who was still very weak, was grateful to be able to sit down again and allowed Georg to finish the story.

"Well, when I was teleported inside the fort, I knew I only had 15 minutes to find it before Wong was going to teleport me back, so I took out my pocket lamp and started searching. The room was filled with many other items and I tried to avoid knocking anything over. Most items were covered with a cloth or stacked in wooden boxes, so I had to be very careful not to make a sound as I explored. However, I was in luck. I found the monstrance hidden beneath a beautiful red scarf. I grabbed it quickly and firmly and waited for Wong to transport me back. It worked! I couldn't believe how easy it had been! But here's the best part: the moment we took the stone out of the monstrance, we immediately saw that it was indeed the fake Eye of Ra!"

Alfred chuckled, "It was the most amazing experience to see how an item I had created here in the 21st century, had actually made it through history and had ended up becoming part of the Templar treasure. In my vision, the Eye of Ra illuminated the chapel in Collioure, so it had become a beacon to me. I am grateful that I've learned to pay attention to my visions."

Alfred paused and stared hard at Otto. "So, now we have a dilemma. Which one is the true Urim? The piece of desert glass, used by Akhenaten and Meryra, or my creation, which was actually taken to the Holy Land by Aaron and used by the Hebrew Priests?"

Everyone was silent, until the sheer ironic hilarity of the moment finally struck them and made them all laugh.

It was Arthur who came up with the most perfect solution: "Let them choose for themselves. Throw the stones! The two that end up closest together will be the true pair."

Alfred applauded Arthur's clever suggestion and he seized the stones, but suddenly, he hesitated. Who was he to throw those holy stones like this, on impulse?

He was following a most ancient and sacred tradition. Alfred closed his eyes for a moment to ask permission and to ask for the wisdom to throw them correctly, but that moment turned into minutes. Alfred drifted off to a distant realm and found himself lying underneath the Kabala tree again. The piece of paper, on which the Forgotten Word had been written, was still spiralling down, until it fell on his nose. Unable to move his arms, he tried to read it and he could almost see what was written on it, until suddenly, he heard a voice.

"Alfred? Alfred!"

He woke up from his short meditation and saw that he was still sitting with the stones in his hand at the round table in the dining room of his manor house. Realising the importance and sacredness of that moment, all eyes were now fixed upon him. Everyone was silent, so when Alfred spoke, everyone listened.

"These are sacred stones. A spell or prayer must be pronounced for them to be properly activated. Prayer unifies and perfects the sacred throne of Isis, of Auset, of Mother Earth, the Holy Queen, through the mystery of Oneness, so that the Divine and Holy King may sit upon it. The one who prays is reunited with the Holy Light and is adorned by the many crowns of the Holy King. All the power of ire and forces of severity are uprooted and the domination of evil upon the worlds ceases. Only in this state of Oneness and Purity can one throw these holy stones."

Alfred looked deeply at his audience, one by one, urging them to listen even more closely.

"Life on earth is a means to a goal. Like a raindrop is drawn to the earth by gravity, all living beings are drawn to the physical world. In that sense we are all fallen angels. From the moment you were born, you have been given choices and challenges that shape your life and your character, leading to soul growth. This process of soul shaping can be compared to the polishing of a diamond, allowing light to shine through its many facets. This process is known as 'the Great Work', turning lead into gold, negative into positive and death into eternal life. When you are a constructive person; generous, kind, forgiving, loving and creative, you are working according to God's laws. If you work with your heart and you follow the path of love, you are in essence not only a good Christian, but you are also, for example, a good Muslim, a good Buddhist and a good Jew, because this law applies to everyone, also if you are a free-thinker or an atheist. For whether you realise it or not, if you work with your heart, you are working alongside the divine plan of the Universe and you will be judged not by others, but by the state of your own heart and by your own conduct. This has been so from the beginning of time, before religions were created and it will be so until the end of time."

Alfred closed his eyes, felt the stones in his hand and then released them from bondage as he threw them like dice onto the table. The outcome was obvious. Everyone smiled and repeated after him when he said, "So mote it be!"

~Epilogue~

Occitania, February 2015

"Debbie! Don't go too close to the river, sweetheart!"

A young girl, now 3 years old, was chasing a black cat, that clearly didn't want to be caught. Deborah Parker Zinkler cried out with laughter when the cat ran toward her and bowled her over, after which it disappeared behind the stupas. Danielle quickly picked her up and set her back onto her bare feet. She had turned into a beautiful doll child, with long, black hair, blue eyes and white skin. Quite a Snow White, she thought.

Danielle had given birth to her baby girl on January 23rd 2012. However, the Birth chart she had received from Ashtara, a wise woman who understood the language of the planets, had saddened her; Deborah would not have an easy life. For now, her darling girl was happy, safe at a Buddhist Temple, tucked away deep in the Pyrenees, away from the world, but soon she would receive training to enable her to take her place in society. Life would change for her and Danielle knew she might not be able to protect Deborah from the vicissitudes of life much longer. However, thanks to Ashtara, she was able to see some of the challenges coming. It helped her think about ways in which she could assist her child in developing inner peace, harmony and balance, equipping her with strength of spirit, self-confidence and perhaps even wisdom, to better face such challenges.

The Buddhist Lama noticed Danielle's sadness and decided to engage a conversation with her.

"I can feel your sadness, dear Dani, but do not let it take away your joy. Your child is special; she is a bearer of light. Remember, a torch is not needed in a room filled with light. Torchbearers are needed in dark places. Bearers of light would not be equipped with empathy, understanding or wisdom if they have only ever known a carefree life. They do not know happiness and fulfilment until they can lift people up and help heal their wounds. They are incapable of turning a blind eye to the horrors of life, because they need to attend to them. Deborah will not like her destiny. She will go through trials and tribulations, through sadness, feelings of isolation, depression and fear and until she is ready to truly understand suffering, she will experience those pains herself. Your job is not to make her perfect, Dani. Your job is to be a mother to her, to be there for her. To console her, to comfort her and to reassure her that the world is her oyster when she ventures out of her immediate environment. Yours are the eyes she will see life through in these formative years. Her interpretation of it will be yours, first. You may not be able to save her from grief and pain, but your job as a mother is to teach hew how to find joy and to always be there for her when she needs you."

Danielle nodded. She knew this was true, but she loved her baby so much. How painful it is for a mother to allow her child to go out into the world, to risk the dangers, to follow her own individual path to a destiny that most surely will take away her innocence forever. This child would not lead a common life and Danielle longed so much for her little girl to have a typical family with the typical connection and sense of belonging that a typical family life offered. Nevertheless, Danielle was grateful for these past few, virtually carefree years. Nobody would ever take away these happiest moments of her life: the moment Debbie was born, the moment she spoke her first words and took her first steps on her own. The most magical moment was when Deborah had called Danielle 'mama' for the very first time, though she found it interesting that it had come second to the word 'ima', which is Aramaic for 'mama'.

There had been many magical moments in these past few years and it had become obvious to everyone that her daughter was indeed special. Deborah could still see energy as clearly as she saw the tangible people. She would point at people with particularly bright light with a big smile. She had no fear of the unknown and welcomed all new experiences, even when that new experience had come in the form of drinking from a cup as well as from her mother's breast, or from the taste of homemade table foods.

Although Debbie was too young to understand the concept of a genetic father - her own, biological father - Danielle had shown her a photograph she had taken of Oshu while they were on their second expedition to ancient Judea. Danielle had told Debbie that he was her 'daddy'. Danielle had often thought of Oshu. How he would have loved her, doted on her and how he would have taught her. Even though the girl grew up without her genetic father, she did have a stepfather and a grandfather, who both loved her more than anything in the world. David and Alfred visited every month to discuss both business and pleasure and each time, David would stay at least a week in order to spend time with his beloved Danielle and what he considered their child, whom he loved and wanted to protect as if she were his own.

While David adored her and lavished her with caring, carrying, attention and loving interaction over his entire stay, Alfred was almost always a silent observer, blessing every second he could be near the child. When Deborah came to him, he always welcomed the interaction with gratitude, but he allowed David to play the majority of the role of a father figure. He knew that Deborah would one day take over SBS-Sion and inherit not only all of Alfred's assets, but also the tasks that came with it as well as the responsibility and in the years that lead up to that moment, Alfred wanted to participate, teaching Deborah how to make a difference; how to help bring constructive change to the world; end the domination model and make it a better and safer place for the inhabitants; how to bring enlightenment to the people; how to bring them consciousness of their own sovereignty and ignite the spark that would one day force the leaders of the world to follow the people's march to peace and global co-operation for a safer and more stable future for our beloved planet.

Alfred was a wise man and Danielle would never forget the stories he shared with her; how the Essenes and the Jewish refugees had tried to turn Occitania into the new promised land in the first century CE; how he had followed the trail of the Ark of the Covenant from Ethiopia to Occitania, where it might still be today; how these same Knights Templar had also tried to create a Templar State, a new Holy Land, right there, in that same special corner of southern France. The day the world was supposed to face its biggest trial, December 21st, 2012, he had told Danielle, "There is a prophecy. When the end of the world is near, the original Ark of the Covenant will be placed in a new temple in a new Jerusalem, to prepare for Christ's second coming. Whatever is meant in that prophecy, I believe this is that time."

However, since that moment, nothing had happened and not much had changed. The destinies of the people of the planet were still in the grips of the leaders whose fortunes depend on keeping the world in war mode. The vast majority of the planet's population was focused on what is portrayed in the media as being important; wealth and happiness through material gain, relegating spiritual growth to a pastime. Many children were still being raised to believe that material wealth should be their priority; their life's goal. Most children were still not encouraged to make choices according the joy that a given activity gives them, or to develop their own unique skills according to their own particular talent. Meditation - the silencing of the mind - still wasn't part of the public education programs, despite Alfred's suggestion to the highest of circles that it should be, for including meditation in education curriculums would contribute to more peaceful, less aggressive behaviour in schools. According to Alfred, nothing had changed and it was the reason why Danielle had kept her precious jewel, Deborah, from the world.

The world simply wasn't ready yet.

Danielle watched her little girl, running around in her little red dress with her fluffy white cardigan and couldn't help smiling, but then, suddenly, Debbie stopped. She looked toward the gate and stared hard at something. Danielle followed her eyes, but she couldn't make out what or who the little girl was looking at. Danielle wasn't expecting anyone; Alfred and David had visited only a few weeks ago. Maybe Debbie had just seen a squirrel, she thought, but Debbie continued to walk slowly in the direction of the gate and before Danielle could stop her, she ran as fast as her little legs could carry her toward the far end of the garden, where there was another, smaller entrance. With wide open arms she ran toward a now suddenly visible target, calling out in her high-pitched voice, which betrayed her emotion and happiness at the same time, "Daddy!"

At first, Danielle couldn't believe her eyes. She thought she saw Oshu coming through the door in his white galabya, but when she came closer, she could see that it wasn't Oshu.

It was David, dressed in white.

It was what Alfred would have wanted. "No black clothes on my funeral", he had said, "I want to be buried in white. All must be white."

David's sad face alarmed Danielle. He took her hands and said in the most gentle of voices, "Oh darling, I have come to bring you the most terrible news."

Danielle could feel her legs tremble. "Alfred?"

"I'm afraid so. I didn't want to tell you on the phone."

Danielle sank to the ground and cried with deep grief, for she loved Alfred like she would have loved a father. Deborah looked at her mother with big eyes, which were now filling up with tears. She was too young to understand what was going on, but she could feel her mother's pain. Danielle pulled her close and felt she needed to explain why her mama was so sad. "Grandpa has gone to heaven, sweetheart, he is now our guardian angel."

Suddenly, Danielle realised that David must have also come to take them back to Sion, as Danielle was now officially in charge of SBS-Sion, Alfred's estates, his holdings and all his duties. Danielle was Alfred's sole heir.

"When is the funeral?" she asked with a broken voice.

"Sunday week, so we have about a week to organise everything. Otto has said he'd stay and help. Obviously he and Georg are both distraught. Otto has broken down completely, but I'm glad that Arthur is such a loyal friend to him and that Otto and Georg have finally teamed up. These are trying times and we need stability. It won't be difficult to organise the funeral though, as Alfred wanted it to be private and modest, like the man himself has always been, but it will be hard to keep everyone away. Also, he wanted everything to be in white, to honour the divine light and the Sophia within us all."

Danielle nodded. "What was the cause of his death?"

"The tumour came back with a vengeance and it just spread like wildfire. Nevertheless, Alfred was completely ready and accepted his fate, as if he knew. He probably did. Alfred always talked about you and Debbie, but he didn't want you to know he was ill. He wanted you to remember him the way he was when we visited you last month, which was only days before the return of the tumour was discovered."

They slowly walked back to Danielle's accommodation. It was time to pack. "How are we going back to Sion?"

"The private jet is parked at Perpignan airport, so you will go back the same route you came."

Danielle allowed her tears to flow, knowing that holding back her pain would only bottle up her emotions and she would need all her strength in this most difficult week that lay ahead. She had spent happy years here at the Buddhist centre in Occitania, away from the world and today this period had ended. In her mind, she hugged Alfred and remembered his wise words; "New beginnings are usually disguised as painful endings."

When tea was brought to the table outside the main buildings and Danielle had calmed down a bit, David gave her a package and took her hand. "Alfred wanted you to have this." Danielle unwrapped the brown package with shaking hands. All the while, Deborah was holding onto her mother's colourful, fluffy trousers, looking up, thinking it was a present.

When she opened the silver box that was inside, Danielle saw two stones, one black and the other white and a note which said:

'My dearest daughter Danielle,
Please give this box, containing the Urim and Thummim, to Deborah on her 12th Birthday. By then, she will know the significance of these stones; the Eye of Horus and the Eye of Ra and she will know how to use them.
Guard them well and remember: Beauséant!
Be fair! Walk straight! Be just! Preserve the knowledge!
All my love, Alfred.'

Danielle put her trembling hand to her mouth. Tears were flowing uncontrollably. Then, suddenly, David handed over another, smaller package, also from Alfred. She unwrapped it carefully, as if she wanted to save the paper the item was wrapped in. "It's my diary!" Danielle cried out. She had totally forgotten it. Alfred had kept it for a while to study the contents - a detailed report of her visits to the ancient Near East, but then he had put it away in a safe and over time the diary had been forgotten.

As if she was browsing through an antique book, she carefully leafed through it and smelled it; the scent of the herbs and leafs she had collected and kept in-between the pages and the sweet scent of the wood on the cover.

She didn't notice that while she was doing this, a piece of parchment fell out and floated to the ground. Deborah quickly grabbed it and showed it to her mother. Danielle first thought it was just a tree leaf her daughter had picked up from the ground and she had to look twice before she saw it wasn't. "What is it, darling?"

Deborah pointed at the diary and Danielle understood it must have fallen out from behind the cover, which was coming lose. The parchment was small, but she could make out the writing clearly.

Her knowledge of the Greek language was still sufficiently fluent to read the text. David noticed she was smiling and wondered who the author was. "Danielle?"

She looked at it, still in a state of disbelief. "She must have put this in the cover of my diary when we were on the ship." she said, without looking up.

"Who?" queried David.

"Mary Magdalene."

David frowned. "What does it say?"

"I will translate it for you."

To Myriam Dani, my soul sister
Where you come from and to where you go, I know not,
but my beloved spoke of you as the mother
of a prophetess, who will become a great seer
and a true servant of the Merkabah,
protected throughout her life by a Seraphim.
That is why I am carrying your child in my heart,
knowing you will carry mine in yours.
Until we meet again. May you find deep peace.
Your sister, Marianne

Danielle looked at her little girl and smiled proudly at her, savouring the Magdalen's blessing.

"Deborah, my beautiful darling, my little prophetess!"

Acknowledgements

This book would not have been possible without the research and/or assistance of the following people:

Robert Bauval, Graham Hancock, Tim Wallace-Murphy, Charlotte Yonge, Ms Baiden, Peter van Deursen, Ashtara Tara, Marwa Kabeel, Jenny Chor, Hussein Abdo, Roland Brunner (eaglehelicopters.ch), visitguernsey.com, David Rohl, Andrew Gough, Christian Jacq, Patrick de Koscis, Thomas Stalder (saharagems.com), Terence DuQuesne, the Rosicrucian Order AMORC*, the Templar Organisation OSMTH** and others who have asked to remain nameless. You know who you are.

Last but not least I would like to thank my muses for their inspiration and insight. It was an honour to be your 'hands'.

The Rosicrucian Order AMORC is a community of Seekers who study and practice the metaphysical laws governing the universe. More: www.rosicrucian.org

**The OSMTH is an active and modern ecumenical Confraternal Order that seeks to address the very real needs of today's world. Such work is often carried out in partnership with and for the benefit of other faiths, creeds and ethnic backgrounds.*
Their mission consists of humanitarian aid, human rights, interfaith dialogue, peace-building and sustainable development. More: www.osmth.org

Also from this author:

WHITE LIE

THE QUEST FOR THE HOLIEST RELIC

Thriller

JEANNE D'AOÛT

www.jeannedaout.com

Jeanne D'Août is a writer, historical researcher, tour guide and producer. For 40 years she has been researching the hidden history of mankind and its religious and cultural path. Ever since she was a child, she has enjoyed discovering hidden mysteries, while visiting many countries including Italy, Greece, Cyprus, Turkey, Israel and Egypt. The biggest mystery, however, was discovered when she moved from the country of her birth (The Netherlands) to a region known as Occitania (southern France). As a tour guide she was able to explore the area and its many secrets to her heart's content and in 2008 she decided to start writing a thriller book to share her findings. Her first book, "White Lie", was first published in 2011.

Jeanne had discovered that some of her ancestors had actually come from Occitania and while investigating, she found a family seal with a dove, sitting on a branch, while holding a laurel twig in its beak. Apparently, the family had fled the region during a period of violent religious conflicts; a holocaust, better known as the Cathar Crusade. The family moved to the north into Flanders and translated the name Août into the local dialect. To honour her ancestors, Jeanne decided to use a nom de plume based on her ancestral name.

Otto Wilhelm Rahn, author of 'Crusade Against the Grail' and 'Lucifer's Court', was born in Michelstadt, Germany in 1904. Being a researcher of myth and legend he was interested in the origins of European religion. He fell in love with Occitania and the Cathars of the Middle Ages. As a member of the SS he worked for Himmler as a relic hunter and researcher of Arian origins. However, he was terribly shocked when he discovered the violence of Hitler's Germany. In the Spring of 1939, his body was found, frozen in the snow in the mountains near Söll, Austria. He had taken his own life.

Tutankhamen's breast plate with desert glass scarab,
fleur-de-lis (left claw) and lotus flower (right claw)
18th Dynasty Egypt

The famous bust of Nefertiti at the Neues Museum, Berlin

Akhenaten, 18th Dynasty Pharaoh of Egypt
(14th century BCE)

One of the steles found at Amarna, Egypt

Made in the USA
Lexington, KY
14 March 2015